ROSE OF ANZIO - REMEMBRANCE

A WWII Epic Love Story

ALEXA KANG

ACKNOWLEDGMENTS

Rose of Anzio began as a personal challenge for me, but over the course of last year, I discovered that writing a full-length novel (four novels, in fact) is a group project. Words alone cannot express my gratitude to everyone who had encouraged me and helped me bring this series to its completion. I am still amazed at the time and efforts of those who volunteered to help me make this story stronger and better.

Thanks to Anneth White, who first encouraged me to write this story and continuing to inspire me by following it faithfully throughout. Thank you to Pamela Ann Savoy, who gave me great feedback on story ideas and development along the way, and took time out of her super busy schedule to proofread my work as I wrote. My utmost gratitude to Mylius Fox, author of the thriller novel *Bandit,* who reached out to teach me the ropes of self-publishing, and gave me valuable advice and support throughout the process. Also, a very special thank you to Ms. CandyTerry, who gave me a huge amount of moral support, as well as the first platform for me to introduce this story.

My heartfelt thank you to both Kristen Tate, my editor, whose suggestions and insights helped me improve my story significantly. A special thank you to military historian Geoff Byers, for his tremendous help and advice on how to create and construct my battle scenes throughout the entire series, so I could keep the story as realistic as possible, and also to Aaron Sikes, my battle scenes editor, for making sure my war story stays grounded. Thanks to Stephen Reid, for making sure

Tessa speaks proper British English. Thanks also to my proofreaders T.J. Moore and Patrick Cunningham, for making my story a truly polished piece of work.

Last but not least, thanks to my husband, Dan, for his unending amount of patience and support.

For Anneth White,
for her steadfast faith in me and this story.

*"Two things fill the mind with ever-increasing wonder and awe...
the starry heavens above and the moral law within me."*

— INSCRIPTION ON TOMBSTONE OF
IMMANUEL KANT

CONTENTS

ROSE OF ANZIO - REMEMBRANCE

Part One

ROME

Part One
Part One

CHAPTER ONE

KLAUS! The elusive German army commander had gotten away again.

With no hope of pursuing him, Anthony led his troops back into the heart of Cisterna after the medics took the injured Captain Harding away. From the fields beyond, more American tanks were rolling in. A tempest of explosions shrouded the city as the tanks detonated German landmines beneath the ground. The mines disabled several Shermans and mortar vehicles as they tried to pass through, but those that escaped continued to forge their way in, firing volleys toward their enemy to clear the way for the Third Division forces still to come.

Anthony and his men ran toward the Palazzo Caetani to take their positions. The American forces closest to them were locked in a fierce gun fight at this bombed-out, two-story palace built on the ancient fortress of the Frangipane. All around him, phosphorous smoke blew and mortar fire burned, clouding his vision and choking his breath. When the explosions of mines and cannons subsided, the arriving American infantry troops emerged from behind the smog.

A battle between the two sides ensued.

Joining the Third Division from behind a mound of rubble, Anthony fired round after round. His memories of what happened from one moment to the next were as hazy as the concrete dust falling from the shattered building walls. His mind held one single thought—to survive. Keep firing so they could all survive.

How he did survive, he would never know. When the fighting ended, he lumbered along the sidewalks to gather his troops. Abandoned weapons and helmets lay strewn all around. Next to collapsed buildings, blown-up tanks and armored vehicles burned. Tired, he tripped over a corpse while watching the dying flames. A foul stench of decay swept up into his nose. He took a reflexive step back from the body, which had bloated under the boiling sun. A swarm of flies hovered over the deceased's eyes, mouth, and wounds. At the sight, Anthony gagged and stepped further away. In front of him, more corpses lay littered throughout what remained of the streets.

While Anthony took stock of the devastation around him, groups of captured German POWs marched along with their hands clasped above their heads. The enemy had surrendered. The Third Division had broken through Cisterna. At last, this unbreakable German stronghold had fallen.

Good news continued to come in the following days. Down south, the Allied troops at Monte Cassino had broken through the Gustav line. They were on their way to join up with the forces on the Anzio front. After months of bitter struggles and stalemates, the Germans' main line of resistance was destroyed. The Battle of Anzio had come to an end.

Along with his regiment, Anthony and his troops continued onward north. They swept through villages and towns, while the German resistance fell. At Valmontone, where the Germans made a last attempt to resist and failed, Anthony could finally tell his company what everyone wanted to hear. They were going to Rome.

Rome. As he rode with his division toward the capital of Italy, Anthony thought of everything that had happened since he had first set foot on Anzio Beach. He wished Wesley could have been alive to share in this moment of triumph. And for once, he wished Wesley could have heard Axis Sally's voice hailing from the radio. "The Blue and White Devils have won this time," the treacherous woman announced. "Today, it looks like, as long as there is blue and white paint, there will always be a Third Division."

Anthony glanced at the blue and white stripes of their division insignia on his uniform. The Blue and White Devils. Wesley would have liked that.

In the evening after their shifts at the 33rd Field Hospital had ended, a group of doctors, nurses, and medical corpsmen gathered around a small campfire to relax before they turned in for the night. Sitting on the ground with them, Tessa hugged her legs and watched the sparks flicker into the air. Someone was passing around the bottles of wine that the Germans had left behind in an abandoned military outpost. As everyone's inhibitions loosened, a young doctor, Brent Doyle, started to tell jokes. He had joined the 33rd only a month ago. With little to do for entertainment, his jokes had become the staff's daily diversion since he arrived.

While everyone laughed, Tessa listened to the tree branches crackle in the fire. Only a month ago, this casual gathering would have been unimaginable. Back on Anzio Beach, they could not build a fire out in the open at night. Even if the army command had not imposed a blackout, they would not have made any light that would have drawn the attention of the German planes.

Now that the Allies had broken out of Anzio, their situation had turned. Their victory buoyed the spirits of the entire hospital staff. The enemy air raids still came, but German aerial attacks were now sporadic and rare. With the Allied units and hospitals on the move, the Luftwaffe could not locate their targets in the dark. Besides, they had heard that the Germans were running out of planes and ammunition. After months of misery, Tessa could now feel hope.

We'll see each other again in Rome. Anthony had said when they last saw each other.

Without realizing it, Tessa reached for the rose pendant around her neck. The pendant was no longer a trivial present she had received on her sixteenth birthday. It had become a reminder of the love that had grown between her and Anthony during their time in Anzio.

A member of the army band brought out his accordion to perform, and Ellie led the group in singing "When the Lights Go On Again." The radio played this song often. They all knew the lyrics, which embodied their hopes for the day when everyone could return home to their lives and be free.

When they finished, Brent Doyle followed up by telling more of his jokes. "Two tomatoes were walking down the street," he said, gesticulating wildly with his hands. "They decided to cross the road. On the way over, one of the tomatoes got squished by a car. The other yelled, 'Come on, ketchup!'"

The punchline sent everybody rolling in laughter. Tessa wasn't sure if they in fact thought the joke was funny, or if they were simply laughing because they were drunk from the wine. She stared ahead beyond the group. Dr. Haley was exiting the makeshift mess hall with his dinner rations. She glanced at Ellie, who was laughing at Dr. Doyle's jokes along with everyone else. Quietly, Tessa got up and slipped away to speak to Dr. Haley.

Coming toward the mess hall, Fran Milton was planning to pick up her rations when she found Aaron Haley standing outside, watching their staff singing and laughing around the campfire. He didn't even notice her coming. After all this time, he still didn't recognize the sound of her footsteps.

"You're not seriously thinking about joining them, are you, Doctor?" she asked.

Surprised by her presence, Aaron turned around. "Good evening, Captain."

"I came to pick up my dinner. Would you like to join me?"

He hesitated and glanced at the group. She followed his gaze, not at all curious about the staff's off-hour activities until she saw Ellie. The sight of Ellie Swanson sparked her irritation. "I should remind you, Colonel. It is inappropriate for an officer of your rank and position to mingle with the staff members."

"Yes, Captain. You've reminded me of that many times, and you know how I feel about that. The army ranking rules are for soldiers. Here, for us, they're formalities. If you ask me, the day we can return to work at civilian hospitals without these rules can't come soon enough."

Fran held her tongue. Aaron Haley rarely spoke in such an annoyed manner. She looked over at the group again. Brent Doyle, the new doctor, was saying something to Ellie and making her laugh. Without thinking, Fran said, "It's nice that Dr. Doyle and Lieutenant Swanson are seeing each other." She didn't know how the lie slipped out. For a moment, she regretted letting her emotions get the better of her. Her impulse had superseded her good sense.

"Dr. Doyle…" Aaron frowned. "He's seeing Ellie? You mean they're dating?"

Fran paused. She did not mean to make things up. Yet, the wounded look on Aaron's face emboldened her. Before she knew it, more lies escaped her mouth. "Lieutenant Swanson has been very upset since her friend Sarah Brinkman died. It's a good thing Dr. Doyle came along. He's helped her cope with that."

Aaron's eyes turned to Doyle. Doyle had everyone's attention now, and he was making them all laugh. Ellie, too, seemed as wowed by him as anyone. "Dr. Doyle has a good sense of humor," Fran continued. "I can see why Lieutenant Swanson is so taken with him."

Disappointment washed over Aaron's face. Fran couldn't help feeling a sense of satisfaction. Now he, too, knew what it felt like to be in her place. She wasn't even sorry about her lies anymore. Come to think of it, if Brent Doyle and Ellie became an item, what would be so bad about that? Doyle was a respectable man. A doctor. Ellie Swanson didn't need Aaron. Ellie Swanson was young. She would do fine without Aaron. There would be plenty of young men like Brent Doyle out there for her.

Anyhow, the way Fran saw it, she was only doing what was fair. She had already lived half her life. She had dedicated years to nursing and medicine. She worked harder than anyone, and no one ever thanked her. Didn't she deserve to get what she wanted for once, after everything she had done and given?

Ellie Swanson could not be seriously interested in Aaron anyway. Not with the way she was laughing her heart out over Brent Doyle's jokes. If she truly cared for Aaron, she would not be so easily impressed by another man.

Fickle girl. Aaron would do much better without Ellie Swanson, and Fran knew exactly what she had to do to make things right.

"They look good together, Doyle and Swanson. Don't you think?" she asked Aaron.

Aaron didn't answer. He stood dejected, his hopes dashed. For the first time since he had turned down all her gifts, Fran felt justice was served. "I'll be off now, Doctor. You have a good night."

"Good night, Captain," Aaron said. His voice was so low, she could hardly hear him.

Good. It was time to put an end to his infatuation with Ellie Swanson once and for all.

After Fran left, Aaron started his way back to his tent, but Tessa approached him. "Dr. Haley."

"Tessa." He forced himself to smile, despite feeling discouraged and glum. "Good evening."

"You haven't had dinner yet?" Tessa glanced at his box of rations. "Why don't you join us?"

Aaron looked over at Ellie. She was talking to Brent Doyle and seemed to be enjoying herself. "Thank you for asking," he said to Tessa, "but I'm calling it a night."

"Are you sure? Ellie would like it if you joined us."

"Yes. I'm sure. I need to sleep and rest after I eat. I've got a lot of work tomorrow." Then, only half-joking, he said, "I'm too old. I don't have the energy to keep up with you all."

She seemed puzzled at his remark, but didn't press the issue. "Good night then, Doctor."

"Good night."

Tessa walked away. Aaron turned from the group and left to return to his quarters. Behind him, Fran stood by the kitchen. Unbeknownst to him, she had noticed Tessa approaching him and decided to stay to see what Tessa wanted. She did not like what she had heard. Not at all. She did not like Tessa Graham trying to bring Aaron and Ellie Swanson together. From now on, she would have to keep a closer eye on Tessa. She could not allow Tessa Graham to interfere with her plans.

As she watched Tessa rejoin Ellie and Brent Doyle, it became clear to Fran what she had to do. She had to find some way to bring Brent Doyle and Ellie Swanson together. Maybe give them more chances to work with each other. If Ellie became interested in Doyle, all this nonsense would go away, and Aaron would finally see how fickle and unreliable the affection of a pretty girl like Ellie was.

Satisfied with herself, Fran picked up her rations from the kitchen and returned to her tent. At last, order was restored. Everything was back in her control.

CHAPTER TWO

IN THE EARLY morning at 0800 hours, Anthony entered Rome with the American troops and convoys moving into the newly occupied zones. Thousands of locals had lined up on the streets, cheering and waving American flags. They held their fingers up in a "V" sign for victory as the army vehicles and marching soldiers weaved slowly through the crowd.

"Lieutenant!" Jonesy, their company's first sergeant, walked up to Anthony's jeep. With a wide grin, he tossed a copy of the *Stars and Stripes* onto Anthony's lap. The headline "WE'RE IN ROME" splashed across the front page. Following their victory in Cisterna on May 23, 1944, the Fifth Army had continued to gain ground at rapid speed. They pursued the Germans all the way up north along Highway 7 to the mountain region of Colli Laziali. On the morning of June 4, the entire Fifth Army had swept into Rome and captured Italy's capital city.

Anthony smiled at the headline and looked up. An Italian girl ran up to Jonesy, threw her arms around his neck, and gave him a big wet kiss. Jonesy stumbled back and nearly fell, but he quickly recovered and grabbed the girl to kiss her back. Anthony's driver blew a loud whistle before they drove off.

The convoys passed the Palazzo Venezia, where Mussolini had made his infamous speeches. Il Duce and his speeches were no more. When Anthony saw the "X" mark over the graffiti of the swastika above Mussolini's name on the building's front wall, he felt more certain than ever that everything they had done in the last six months was justified. After all the fierce battles and all the miseries they had endured, and all the casualties and deaths, they had prevailed. Rome was liberated.

The army vehicles took the officers to Piazza Navona, where the ancient Romans once held their athletic contests and chariot races. Anthony left his driver, grabbed his rucksack, and got out of his jeep. Nearby, a group of small children greeted him and the arriving troops with signs reading "*Benvenuti*" and "Welcome." A little girl about nine years old ran up to him and gave him a bouquet. "Hello, American soldier. What is your name?"

"Hello." He accepted her flowers. "I'm Anthony. What is your name?"

"My name is Sonia. Sonia Montello. My family would like to invite you to quarter with us while you're here."

"Is that right?" That sounded like a fabulous idea to him.

"Yes. My uncle is a priest, and all the members of his church who can speak English are volunteering to host Allied officers."

"I'm delighted that you asked," he said. "Thank you."

"Come with me." She surprised him by taking his hand. He didn't have much experience interacting with little girls. Her hand felt small, and she held his with so much trust. Touched, he tightened his hand around hers.

"Can I tell you something?" Sonia asked.

"Of course!"

"I saw you riding up, and I wanted to invite you right away.

You look like my brother Renardo. He was part of the Italian Resistance."

"A member of the Resistance? He must be a very brave man. Where is he? Is he home?"

"No." She lowered her face. "He was killed last year."

Anthony's heart dropped. "I'm so sorry to hear that."

"Mmm. But my other brother is here." She led him to two teenagers waiting by a lamp post. The younger one, a girl, looked about fourteen. She had the same curly hair as Sonia but had thinner cheeks. The boy looked about sixteen. He had the kind of pleasant smile that instantly put people at ease.

"*Ciao*." The boy held out his hand. "I'm Paolo."

"*Ciao*." Anthony shook his hand. "I'm Anthony. Anthony Ardley. Thank you for inviting me to stay at your home."

"I'm Sophia," the teenage girl introduced herself.

"Sophia. That's a beautiful name. My mother's name is Sophia."

Pleased, Sophia gave him a big smile. "Welcome to Rome."

"Come with us," Paolo said. "We'll take you to meet our parents."

"Our Mama is planning a special supper for tonight," Sophia said to Anthony. "Would you like to join us?"

Would he ever! "Absolutely!" A home-cooked meal sounded divine.

Paolo laughed and started singing. His sisters joined him, and they sang all the way home. The Italian lyrics were lost on Anthony, but to him, there was no better reward for all his efforts in this war than the singing voices of these children.

When Signora Montello saw her children return with Anthony, she gave him a big hug before they were even introduced. Signor Montello, too, immediately came out to greet him.

"Welcome! Welcome to our home!" He gave Anthony a hearty handshake and invited him inside.

On entering, Anthony was surprised to see the large group of people who had gathered in the living room. Every member of the Montello family, it seemed, had come to meet the American soldier who the children would invite home. He could not tell at first who was who despite their introductions. When they talked, they talked over each other all at once. But their warm hospitality more than made up for the state of confusion they had thrown him in. Signora Montello ordered Paolo to draw Anthony a bath, and Sonia took his laundry. Signor Montello had a different agenda altogether. He opened a bottle of wine and poured Anthony a glass filled to the brim.

The family passed the glasses of wine, from Signor Montello to his sister, Fabia and her husband Vito, and Vito's sister Mia and brother Sergio, plus Signor Mauricio, Signor Montello's best friend. Unable to follow their fast-paced conversation, all Anthony could make out was that Signor Montello was a professor at the Sapienza University of Rome.

While everyone talked, Anthony noticed a boy sitting quietly by himself. The boy was taller than Sonia, but thinner. His eyes lacked the spirit of the other Montello children.

"Hello," Anthony introduced himself. "What is your name?"

The boy stared at Anthony with large, frightened eyes.

"*Sono Anthony*," he tried again with the limited Italian he knew. "*Come ti chiami?*"

The boy only looked at him.

"He can't hear you," Sonia said and joined them. "He's my cousin Rocco. He's deaf. He was ill when he was a baby. When he recovered, he lost his hearing."

"How old is he?" Anthony asked.

"He's thirteen."

Thirteen? The boy looked small for his age. Anthony gave

him a friendly smile and patted his shoulder, but the boy flinched.

"He's afraid of you," Sonia said.

"Why?"

"Because you're a soldier. The German soldiers were here before you came. They forced us to put them up at our house. They were terrible to him because he can't hear. One of them used to throw stones at him."

Dismayed, Anthony frowned. For all the atrocities he had seen in this war, the idea of someone hurting a frail, deaf boy was still difficult to take.

"Anthony." Paolo came down the stairs. "Your bath is ready."

Anthony got up. A bath sounded like heaven. Before he left the room, he smiled at Rocco again, but the boy shrank into his seat.

After washing up, Anthony changed into a clean uniform and returned to the living room. Rocco was still sitting by himself. Anthony went up to him again. This time, he brought with him a bag of butter cup candy as a gift. At first, the boy was afraid to take them. Anthony took out a piece and nudged it into his hand. Warily, the boy unwrapped it and put it into his mouth. Then, tasting the sweetness, he gave Anthony a timid smile. He chewed the candy as if it was the best thing he had ever eaten in the world. When he finished, he took the bag from Antony and ate another one.

Watching Rocco, Anthony thought back to his own childhood. He had lived a life of peace and comfort growing up. He never wanted for anything. His parents had seen to that. All the adults he had known were kind and generous. He never had to witness the ugliness and cruelty that Rocco had seen. If the Allies hadn't come, Rocco would still be living in fear under the torment of the Germans. When Anthony thought of this, he had no more doubt about his own role in the war. He would not hesitate to fight if children like Rocco could live a normal life and be able to enjoy their childhood the way they should.

The doorbell rang. Another member of the Montello family had come to join them. This person wore a distinct black robe with a white clerical collar. Anthony guessed he must be Sonia's uncle who was the priest.

"Anthony." Paolo brought the man over. "This is my uncle Lorenzo, Papa's older brother. He's the priest of the Santa Lucia Parish."

"Pleased to meet you, Father." Anthony shook his hand.

The priest nodded. "You must pardon me. I speak very little English."

"No. You must pardon me. I speak hardly any Italian except to say *mangiare*."

Overhearing them, Signora Montello entered, "Then you're in luck." She wiped her hands on her apron. "Supper's ready."

By the time dinner began, several bottles of wine had been served, and the family had become even more animated as they took their places around the dining table. "How did your family get the wine?" Anthony asked Paolo. The Italians hadn't had enough food for a very long time because of the war.

"I'm not supposed to tell you," Paolo said, "but Papa paid a lot of money he had hidden away. He bought the wine from the black market as soon as the Germans left. He couldn't wait to celebrate with an American soldier."

Sonia took Anthony's hand again and led him to a seat next to her at the table. They stood behind their chairs and waited for Signor Montello, who entered the room last. Before taking his seat, Signor Montello came over and stood next to Anthony.

"Anthony, my dear friend." He raised his glass. "On behalf of everyone in my family, thank you. Thank you for bringing us victory. Thank you for coming to Rome. We are happy to have you here. Because of you and your fellow soldiers, we are free today. We salute you and the American army, for your courage, for your sacrifices, and for saving our people."

Everyone applauded. Although Anthony felt he himself hadn't done enough to take credit for the efforts of the entire U.S. Army, he raised his glass out of courtesy and accepted the toast.

"And now, I want to give you this." Signor Montello handed him a small pistol. A Beretta. "This belonged to my late son, Renardo. He carried this with him the entire time he fought with the Resistance."

"No." Anthony tried to give it back. "Signor, I can't accept this. You have to keep your son's memory."

Signor Montello insisted. "Renardo fought for freedom. You're continuing his fight. He would want you to have this." He closed both of his hands around Anthony's. "Keep it. Remember him. Remember what he died for. Remember what you fight for."

The man's words were so earnest. Beneath his words, Anthony could hear his pain in losing a son. It was impossible to refuse the poor father's wishes.

"Thank you." Anthony took the gun.

Signor Montello broke into a huge smile and swung his arm around Anthony's shoulders. "Another toast," said the family patriarch. "To our friend, Anthony. No. Not friend. Family. You are now part of our family. *Cincin.*" Everyone clinked their glasses. Anthony thought his moment in the spotlight was over. But as soon as he sat down, Signora Montello, Fabia, and Mia all came over and hugged him. They showered kisses on his head and his face.

Yes. Definitely a hero's welcome. His own family would have a ball when they heard about this.

After Father Lorenzo said grace in Italian, dinner began. A light green salad, followed by a pasta dish with brown sauce, which Anthony couldn't identify but found mouthwatering all the same. It was a simple meal, but he knew it was a feast. After being at war for years, food in this country was scarce. People in many parts of Italy were starving. The Montellos must have pooled their rations for this meal—if they had rations—or paid a lot of money to get the food. Tomorrow, he would have to speak to his company's cook and see how they could provide some food for this family.

"Anthony." Sonia tugged his sleeve. "Can I ask you for something?"

"Yes, Sonia. Anything."

"Since Renardo is not here anymore, would you be my big brother?"

Anthony lowered his fork. "Of course. I'd be honored to be your big brother."

Sonia got out of her seat and gave him a big hug. Anthony now felt he was truly a part of this family.

When dinner was over, the family retreated to the living room to continue their conversation. Anthony, however, had something else on his mind.

"Father Lorenzo." He caught the priest before they left the dining room. "May I have a word with you?"

Father Lorenzo smiled at him, ready to offer whatever solace or grace the American soldier needed.

CHAPTER THREE

By the time the medical convoy drove into Rome, Tessa was seeing a city that was vastly different from the one she remembered.

Years ago, she had come with her father when he wanted to see Rome as part of his preparation for the role of Brutus in his upcoming performance of Shakespeare's *Julius Caesar*. Unlike the Rome they had visited, the ancient city today was filled with Allied soldiers everywhere on the streets. She wondered if this scene was similar to Caesar's triumphant arrival in Rome.

"Will you all look at that!" Gracie pointed at the Coliseum. "I never dreamt I would see anything like this."

Ellie and Tessa exchanged a smile. "It's amazing," Ellie said. "I've never seen anything like this either."

"I'm definitely looking forward to taking a breather." Gracie leaned out to snap another picture with her camera. "I hope we'll have plenty of time to do some sight-seeing. I want to take a lot of photos to send to my friends back home. I can't wait to show them what Rome is like." She retreated back into the vehicle. "Ellie, do you think Captain Milton will give us the rest of the day off? I mean, we just arrived."

"I'm not sure," Ellie said. "We'll probably have to help set up the hospital. The patients could be arriving soon."

"Ugh," Gracie moaned. "I hope we'll at least have a few hours off. I need to look for Jesse and let him know I'm here." Her face lit up when she mentioned his name. "I hope he and I can spend more time together while we're here. Tessa, do you know when you'll be meeting up with Lieutenant Ardley?"

Without answering, Tessa smiled and looked out to the street. Although she wouldn't say it out loud like Gracie, she couldn't wait to see Anthony. Dr. Haley had already told her she could have a three-day pass whenever she wanted while they were in Rome. She intended to take full advantage of it.

They came to an old hospital building which would serve as the 33rd's base. The nurses climbed out of the truck, ready to unload their belongings and to stake out a spot in the hospital quarters to sleep at night. Before they went inside, Brent Doyle approached them with his rucksack over his shoulder. "Hi ladies, need some help? Captain Milton asked me to give you all a hand moving in."

Unsure, Tessa, Ellie, and Gracie looked at each other. Milton didn't normally concern herself with anything but work. She wasn't one who cared whether or not the nurses needed help setting up their personal quarters.

"Thank you, Dr. Doyle," Ellie said. "We're fine. We've done this many times before. Actually, we should be the ones to ask if you need help. You're new to the hospital."

"You got a point there," Doyle said. "What do we do now?"

"We go inside and find our sleeping quarters. I reckon we'll be receiving instructions soon if we have any work to do."

They took their bags and walked toward the building. Doyle followed. "What happens after we settle in?"

"I want the rest of the day off," Gracie said. "I want to explore this city."

"Me too," Doyle said. "In fact, Lieutenant Swanson, Captain Milton said she will give you a day's pass. She said you've been working harder than anyone these last few months. She thought you could use a break. She said I should ask you if you would like to do some sightseeing with me."

The three nurses looked at each other again. Noticing their doubtful expressions, Doyle asked, "Did I say something wrong?"

"No, Dr. Doyle," Ellie said. "Not at all. It's just strange that Captain Milton would suggest for any of us to go sightseeing."

"Why?"

"Because," Tessa said, "Captain Milton usually just wants everyone to work. She never cares about anything else."

"She's a slave driver," Gracie said.

"Really?" Doyle asked. "I don't get that feeling from her. She's been very nice to me." They arrived at the building entrance, and he pushed the door open for them. "Regardless, if we do have the rest of the day off, how about we all tour the city together?"

"That would be lovely, Dr. Doyle!" Gracie said. "But wait, I want to find Jesse first."

Inside, they separated from Doyle and found the nurses' quarters on the second floor. A group of nurses had already laid down their cots to stake out their sleeping area. Tessa, Ellie, and Gracie decided to join them. Afterward, Ellie went to look for Captain Milton to see if she had any orders for them.

In a small room that was once an office on the third floor of the hospital building, Fran picked up a file and checked to see how many patients would be transported to Rome to be under her care. Their medical convoy had arrived only a few hours ago, but she was ready. Her typewriter had been set up. Her files had all been brought to her and neatly stacked on her desk for her review. She knew how to be efficient. It never took her long to set herself up and be ready. All she needed for herself was her cot, which she had unrolled on the floor on the right side of the room. Her mess kit and her toiletries, a simple hair brush and a hand-held mirror, lay on top of a wooden cabinet by the window on the left. Everything was simple and practical.

Except for the wooden heart. She took the defective wooden heart ornament that Aaron Haley had carved for a soldier a few months ago from her belongings and placed it on her desk. The soldier had wanted to send a Valentine's Day gift for his fiancée. Aaron had offered to carve a wooden heart for him. He chipped the first heart by accident and made the soldier another one. Later on, Fran had asked if she could have the heart that was chipped, and he said yes.

While she was deciding how to best display the wooden heart, Ellie knocked.

"Come in," Fran said.

"Captain."

"Yes, Lieutenant."

Ellie entered the room. "Captain, I came to ask if you have any plans for us today. If not, Tessa, Gracie, and I would like your permission to take the rest of the day off to explore the city."

Fran returned to her desk. These young nurses. There was so much work to be done, yet all they could think of was play. They couldn't resist excitement and remember their duties as their priorities. Who did they think would be around to set up the hospital and get everything prepared for the patients to arrive?

But of course, Ellie Swanson could use a day off. Fran had special plans for Ellie.

"You can have the rest of the day." Fran adjusted her

glasses. "In fact, why don't you take tomorrow off too. I'll grant you a day's pass for tomorrow."

Surprised her request was granted, Ellie started to say thank you, but Fran continued. "I'm afraid Lieutenant Graham and Lieutenant Hall will have to stay. Colonel Callahan is on his way here. I may need help if we are given any new assignments." Fran smiled. No need for those two to get in the way of Ellie Swanson and Brent Doyle either.

The excitement on Ellie's face disappeared. "In that case, I'll stay too."

"No. Take your time off, Lieutenant. You need to rest. That's an order." Fran opened a file. "And since you have time, could you please see if Dr. Doyle wants to join you?"

"Dr. Doyle?" Ellie asked.

"Yes." Fran softened her voice. "He's new to the hospital. I want him to feel welcomed. I would appreciate your help to get him acquainted."

Although reluctant, Ellie didn't dare to object. "Yes, ma'am."

"Didn't he ask you to accompany him sight-seeing while we're here? I already told him I planned to give you time off. He was very relieved you would be available. He's still adjusting to our new environment here. You wouldn't want a new colleague to feel unwelcome, would you?"

"No, ma'am."

"Good. That'll be all." Fran returned to the file she was reading. "You're dismissed."

"Yes, ma'am." Ellie turned to leave the room. On her way out, she noticed a wood-carved heart ornament on the desk.

"It's very pretty, isn't it?" Fran picked it up to show her.

"Yes, it is. It looks like the wood carvings Dr. Haley makes."

"Of course it does. He made this too. It's a Valentine's Day gift." She put the wooden heart down.

Ellie's face turned pale. She stared at the ornament, unaware that Fran was observing her reaction.

"You may go, Lieutenant," Fran said.

"Yes, ma'am." Looking confused, Ellie left the room.

After she left, Fran picked up the wooden heart again and stroked it with her thumb. She could not deny it. It pleased her to see the hurt and confused look on Ellie's face. It was okay. The hurt would help the girl get over her little infatuation with Aaron, and the sooner she got over Aaron, the better it would be for everyone.

Anyhow, Fran thought, she wasn't lying about the ornament. The wooden heart was indeed a Valentine's Day gift. It was the soldier's Valentine's Day gift to his fiancée back home.

She put the wooden heart back on top of her desk. Really. She was doing Ellie Swanson a favor. Brent Doyle was right for her, even if Ellie herself couldn't see it yet. If the girl must endure a little temporary disappointment, so be it. Her disappointment would pass. It wouldn't matter in the long run. What mattered was that everything would be set right. Everyone would get what they deserved.

Toward evening, Tessa sat alone on the steps in front of an abandoned church across from the hospital. It was time for dinner, but she didn't feel hungry. She only came outside to get a break from boredom and pass the time. Old grouchy Milton had decided to keep her and Gracie on site, despite having nothing for them to do. Almost everyone not under Milton's direct supervision had gone out, either to prowl the streets or to visit the local bars. Others who were too exhausted after their long journey to Rome had turned in for an early night of sleep.

She took a piece of bread out of her bag, tore off a small

piece, and threw it onto the ground. A pigeon swooped down and pecked at it. More pigeons followed. She tore more pieces and tossed them at the birds.

A shadow approached her. "Welcome to Rome."

She looked up. Before her, Jesse stood with his hands casually tucked in his pockets, his handsome face basking in the early evening sun. His radiant smile almost as dazzling as the golden sunlight shining behind him.

"Jesse!" She was so glad to see him.

He sat down on the steps beside her. "Why are you sitting here by yourself?"

"Milton wouldn't let me leave. She made me and Gracie remain on the premises." Another pigeon flew down. She swung her arm forward to throw a piece of bread at it. "Are you looking for Gracie?"

"I'll find her later. Actually, I came to see you." He took a sealed envelope from his pocket and handed it to her. "Ardley wanted to give you this."

Excited, she took the envelope. She wanted to open it right away, but didn't because she wanted to read it in private. "Thank you."

"How do you want to thank me?" He sidled up to her. "Want to come dancing with me one night? We can plan a night out like we did back in Naples."

"If Milton will let me off." She laughed. She had her three-day pass, but she didn't mention it. Anthony might have plans for them already.

"She has to let you off some time. She can't keep you trapped here."

More pigeons swarmed in front of them, cooing loudly, demanding food. Tessa broke the rest of the bread into halves and gave some to Jesse. In silence, they fed pieces of bread to the pigeons. When the bread was all gone, he stretched out his legs, showing no intention of leaving.

"Don't you have anywhere to go?" Tessa asked. "The whole army is out celebrating. Don't tell me you have no plans for the evening."

"I don't," he said. He almost sounded shy. "I like sitting here with you. It's peaceful."

Across the street, Gracie ran toward them. "Jesse!"

His smile disappeared at the sight of her. Nonetheless, he stood up to greet her. She ran up to him and threw her arms around him. "You found me!"

"Hi Gracie," he said, sounding less than enthusiastic. He took her shoulders and lightly pushed her away.

"I'm so happy you're here. That old hag Milton wouldn't let me leave, so I wasn't able to come look for you."

"That's all right."

"But I'm free now. She finally let me off for the evening. I don't even know why she kept me here in the first place. The staff already set everything up, and our patients haven't even arrived yet." She took his hand. "Let's go. I've got so much to tell you. We'll go to the bar down the street. Everyone's there." She turned to Tessa. "Tessa, do you want to come too? Milton said she doesn't need us anymore."

"No," Tessa said. What she wanted was to read the message that Anthony had sent her. "You two go ahead."

"Okay! We'll see you later." Gracie pulled Jesse along. Helpless, he looked at Tessa, his eyes begging for her to rescue him. Tessa only smiled. With mischievous delight, she watched him suffer the consequence of a mess of his own making.

After they left, Tessa opened Anthony's note. Reading the short message inside, her heart swelled with sweetness.

"Meet me in front of the Trevi Fountain day after tomorrow. 1800 hr. Can't wait to see you. — A.A."

Part Two

THE ETERNAL CITY

Part Two

CHAPTER FOUR

"Meet me in front of the Trevi Fountain."

TESSA FOLDED Anthony's note into her pocket and looked at the landmark where Anthony had chosen for them to meet. The magnificence of the Baroque masterpiece took her breath away. Legend had it, a young girl had once guided a group of thirsty Roman soldiers to a source of pure water at a spring not far from the spot where the fountain now stood. Afterward, the Emperor Augustus had ordered the construction of an aqueduct that channeled the water from the spring into Rome. The fountain was built as a tribute to that legend.

At the top of the fountain, the sculpture of the Roman sea god Neptune towered mightily above the sea in his shell-shaped chariot. Below him, a scene depicted by statues unfolded, telling the story of his son Triton taming the wild seahorses. The fountain's images were glorious. The entire structure was a symbol of triumph. No doubt, Anthony meant for them to remember their reunion with a picture of victory.

Tessa took a step closer. She wished she could reach out and touch the ancient characters. So soft were the lines of the sculptures, they created an illusion of movements of the gods and mythical creatures themselves. The rocks that surrounded the sculptures were purposely layered and stacked in a way that resembled ocean waves. Combined with the rapid outflow of water in the center, she could almost imagine the scene coming to life.

The majestic wall of the Palazzo Poli that served as the fountain's backdrop was equally impressive. On the wall, a statue flanked each side of Neptune. The one to his left symbolized Abundance, and the one to his right represented Health. Above them, the story of the fountain's origin was told in scenes of sculptures. Still higher up, a row of four statues stood, each of them representing one of the four seasons. At the pinnacle, Pope Clement XII's papal crest reigned over the entire city. As Tessa looked at this crown jewel of the fountain's façade, she realized, Anzio was over. It was truly over. The Germans and the Nazis did not win. This fountain was the proof. The glory and triumph that it represented still remained.

With a sigh of relief, Tessa returned her gaze to Neptune and his son. Looking at the sculptures, her thoughts turned naturally to Anthony. His body was no less powerful than these sea gods when he swam. As she remembered him rising out of the water after a swim back at Anzio beach, an irrepressible yearning rose from within her. Any moment now, Anthony would be here.

A familiar tug at her elbow distracted her thoughts. She knew right away who it was. The one she longed for, the one whom she thought endlessly of, was right before her eyes. He swept her into his arms and kissed her. Before the mightiest god of the ancient sea, before all the forces of nature and the four seasons, and all the souls of the world under the papal coat of arms, he kissed her to declare his love.

He took her hand and led her down the marble steps to the street. For the next three days, she would not have to count the hours until Anthony must leave. She would not have to worry about what dangers tomorrow might bring. For the next three days, their time belonged only to them.

They stopped briefly at the hotel to drop off her belongings. When they got there, Tessa was glad to see that Anthony had chosen a hotel with an impersonal atmosphere instead of a small, cozy inn. Among the whirl of guests, mainly British and American officers, and a few civilian reporters and special consultants attached to military operations, she felt inconspicuous even though there were not very many women here. The desk clerk, too, went about his business, paying little attention to anyone except when his service was needed. The only one keeping a watchful eye on them was the hotel's house cat. It lay like a sphinx on top of the reception desk, observing every coming and going while snubbing its nose at every person who passed. Tessa couldn't help noticing it. "What a grumpy looking cat."

"That's Galileo." Anthony smiled and put his arm over her shoulders. "He's old. The hotel manager said he's twelve."

As if he understood what they said, the cat blinked and proudly turned its head away.

In the hotel room, Tessa quickly changed her clothes and freshened up while Anthony waited. From the dresser, she glanced at him staring out the window. It was such a strange new feeling to be alone here with him. She felt excited, but awkward too. They hadn't seen each other since her birthday, and they had never talked about what happened that day at the underground shelter. What would the next three days be like now that they could be alone?

"Ready?" he asked and turned around.

"Yes." She picked up her handbag.

He took her to the Fagiano, a restaurant at the Piazza Colonna that served exclusively American officers and nurses. It had been so long since they had walked the streets together as a couple on a normal date. She tightened her hand around his and walked closer to him. Touched by her affection, he pulled her even closer and gave her a light kiss.

Ever thoughtful, Anthony had arranged a whole evening of activities for them. Dinner followed by a show at the Royal Opera House. A classical Mozart performance by a symphony quartet that he thought she might enjoy.

Back at Anzio, they had often talked about what they would do when the Allies captured Rome. What they wanted was so simple. So ordinary. A dinner and a show, and to spend time with each other. In the besieged hell of Anzio, this had been their dream.

Tonight, it was no longer a dream. They were doing everything they always said they wanted to do. They were together again. For a short while, they could leave all their duties and burdens behind. A night of music awaited them. The evening was going exactly how they had planned. And yet, it soon became obvious, this was not what she wanted.

And maybe, this wasn't what he wanted either. All through dinner, he wouldn't stop looking at her. His hand almost never left hers.

"Tell me more about the Montellos," she said, twirling her fork in her plate of pasta. "It must be a wonderful change to live in a house with a family after how you have been living the last few months."

"Wonderful doesn't begin to describe it." He held her hand from across the table. "I can't wait for you to meet them. You'll like them. They treat me like family."

A wave of laughter broke out from the table next to them. Apologetic, he looked at her, as though the noise was his fault.

She gave him a reassuring smile. Why were they out here? What she really wanted was to be alone with him.

After dinner, they walked hand-in-hand along the streets toward the Royal Opera House. Neither of them had said a word since they left the restaurant. All around them, merry groups of local girls and servicemen shuffled by.

Finally, he stopped and asked her, "Do you want to go back to the hotel?"

It was the same question that had been on her mind all night.

CHAPTER FIVE

BACK AT THE HOTEL, Anthony passed by the reception desk with Tessa without greeting the hotel receptionist or the British officer who was checking in. Manners were the last thing on his mind. He led her by the hand and hurried up the stairs into their room. Once inside, he could no longer resist the urge to take her. He pulled her into his arms and pressed his lips on hers. He wanted to smell her and feel her body against his. Ravenous, he unbuttoned her uniform and pulled her clothes off her while he removed his own uniform all at once.

Lying on top of her on the bed, he kissed her, tasting her lips and her skin. He was completely lost in the moment until he realized, this was the first time he had truly seen her naked.

Back in Chicago, he had seen her without clothes on once, when she stood naked under the moonlight before she walked into the lake and swam in the dark. That time, he didn't dare to look directly at her. All he saw were glimpses of her silhouette when she stood on the shore of the lake. Later on, she came up next to him, bickering with him without a thread of clothing on her body. Thoroughly embarrassed, he had turned his head and looked away from her.

And then, there was Anzio, where they had first made love. In the dugout underground, illuminated by nothing but his small flashlight, passion overwhelmed them and they made love with their uniforms on.

He stopped and knelt on the bed. She was the most beautiful girlfriend he could ever have asked for, and he had never looked at her in the nude. This could not be. He wanted to see her. All of her.

Confused when he stopped, Tessa kept her hand on his arm, but didn't question him. He moved his gaze from her face to her body. Every part of her was beautiful. Her body was a picture of perfection. He looked further down and fixed his gaze where he wanted to see her most. His heart throbbed in rapid pace at the sight.

Her face flushed red at the way he looked at her. Shyly, she closed her legs and turned her body away.

No! He put his hand on her, silently pleading for her to stay as she was. He didn't mean to be lewd, but he wanted so badly to see every part of her. He couldn't bear her pulling away from him.

She faced him again, staring at him as if trying to understand something. Then, her expression changed. He could not tell what thoughts had run through her mind, but her girlish embarrassment disappeared. She looked at him with deeper emotion, then rose to kiss him, soothing him with the caresses of her lips. When she reclined again, she took his hands and guided him down her inner thighs so he could see her, completely naked and exposed.

He didn't know what changed her mind, but when she gave herself over to his desire, he felt ecstatic. He wanted to embrace her and give her all the love he felt for her. He lay on top of her again and kissed her, on her lips, her face, her chest. As he kissed her, the rose pendant he had given her fell down her neck. Seeing the pendant, he felt an overwhelming wish to claim her, to do something that would make him feel she was all his.

Maybe it was the war. It had taken so much from him. His life, his dignity, his privacy, his sense of self. Even the clothes he wore and the food he ate didn't belong to him. The army determined and dictated everything. Until the war ended, until he had his life back, nothing belonged to him.

Except her. Here, Tessa was the one thing he could claim as his own. The war and the army could take his life away, or even hers, but he was the only one who could have her.

He ran his hands over every part of her, wanting not only to feel the softness of her body, but also to affirm that he was the only one who could touch her this way. But touching her was not enough. He needed more. He kissed her below her neck, inhaling the sweet fragrance of her rose perfume as he left on her skin visible red marks of love.

He knelt and looked at her again. This time, she yielded to him with no reservation. It excited him to see her open and exposed, to know that no part of her was off limits to him. He planted a kiss between her legs, inhaling the natural scent of her sex. He explored every inch of her body, stroking her inside and outside while he watched her shiver in pleasure. She almost turned away from him again, but this time, he wouldn't let her. He kept her in place and continued. He wanted to know what excited her. He wanted to see her respond to his touch. Her quickening breaths and moans were the most sensuous sounds he had ever heard. They set his body on fire. He could not withhold himself any longer. He needed to be one with her. Falling on top of her, he took her. Her silken warmness enveloped him, inviting him to release into her every emotion that had built up inside him since his life had been overtaken by this war.

Calmness settled into his mind as he held her under him. He felt renewed. Serene. Through her, he regained a sense of peace that he hadn't felt in a very long time. He kissed her lips one more time before he rolled off her to lay beside her. His mind finally at ease, he held her hand and relaxed into sleep. She was all his, totally and completely, in every way.

Lying on her side with Anthony's arms around her, Tessa opened her eyes. The room was quiet and it was still dark. Only the small candle on the coffee table provided a glimmer of light. They had fallen asleep and never put it out. She looked at the clock on the dresser next to her side of the bed. It was three past midnight.

Thump-pum. A light, muffled sound came from the wooden floor by the window. She looked in the direction of the sound. Galileo, the hotel's house cat, had climbed through their window from outside and come into their room. It strutted around like it owned the place, sniffing at their clothes which, in the heat of passion, they had taken off and strewn on the floor.

She looked at Anthony, who was sound asleep. Careful not to wake him, she turned to lie on her stomach and reached her arm out to the pompous cat. "Come here," she whispered. It ignored her at first, but then deigned to come and sniff her fingers before walking away to investigate the rest of the hotel guests' belongings.

Tessa pulled her arm back. Watching the flame of the candle flicker in the night, she thought of everything that had happened earlier, those sweet memories that paralyzed her and left her feeling breathless.

She remembered Anthony kissing her, hungering for her. She remembered the way he had looked at her when they were naked before each other. At first, she felt embarrassed. It was not that nudity bothered her. Growing up in the theater environment, she had seen actors and actresses use their bodies to express their characters. They skillfully used body language to practice their art. Watching them, she had learned that the body was a beautiful thing. After she became a nurse, she saw the body in a different way. She began to see it as something that she tended to, nurtured, and cured. She didn't consider the body as something she had to hide.

The way that Anthony had looked at her though was something different. He wanted to see her, all of her. He wanted nothing hidden from him. She had never shown herself this way to anyone. She felt so bare. So wanton. Her natural instinct made her want to turn away, but he held on to her. A pleading look of disappointment came into his face when she tried to conceal herself. There was so much yearning in his eyes, like she was denying him the last and only thing he had ever wanted.

At that moment, she looked at him, this beautiful person with whom she had fallen in love. She thought of all the dangers and miseries he had suffered. He had been in battle for so long in Anzio, out on the front, sleeping in the rain, the cold, or the snow. If that hadn't been bad enough, he had to watch his own men die brutal deaths day in and day out. The enemy was ruthless. His own army had no mercy. To both the Allied army and the enemy, he was disposable. The command expected him to carry on with his missions even if it meant he would be killed. He bore his burdens alone, with a company of men relying on him for their lives. His own life was always at stake.

When she thought of all this, she no longer had the heart to hold anything back from him. She abandoned her own feelings of modesty and all remaining sense of propriety. What he wanted was so little, compared to what had been asked of him. If this was what she could do for him, then she would give herself over to him. From this moment on, she would give him everything he would ever ask of her. She rose up and kissed him to reassure him. What they did tonight would be her declaration of love for him.

Her willing response excited him. She could see the fire growing in his eyes when he saw the full view of what he wanted to see. He laid a gentle kiss on her lips and caressed her, touching her everywhere and laying claim to every part of her. He took his time and explored her body, arousing in her sensations of pleasure she had never known. Even when the sensations became unbearable, he would not stop. He teased her, titillated her and imposed his will upon her to reveal to him all her physical reactions to his touch. He would not let her hide anything from him.

When he finally came into her, she was craving him, aching to become one with him. She wanted his body to melt into hers. She couldn't get close enough to him.

Remembering all this, Tessa smiled. While she indulged in her thoughts, she sensed Anthony stirring next to her. He brushed her hair away from her back to one side and kissed her bare shoulder. His kiss took her breath away. It made her body limp and tingle all over. She let go of herself and sank into the bed. She could feel his passion growing stronger. He wanted her again. Her breaths quickened as he slid his hand down her side and her leg. She loved the way he touched her. She loved that he needed her. She loved that he couldn't get enough of her.

Still behind her, he rolled on top of her back and, placing himself between her legs, entered her. Slowly at first, he pushed his way in, fulfilling her and removing all her feelings of void. His rhythm picked up, faster and faster and laden with desire. Not satisfied, he got up on his knees, pulled her hips up toward him, and plunged himself into her. She felt him reaching deep inside her. She loved what he was doing, the possessive way he took her body, and the voracious way he was making love to her. A primal, instinctive force was driving him. That force electrified her, swayed her. It overpowered her until a euphoric bliss subsumed her mind and all she wanted was to surrender herself to him.

How could she have known? Anthony, always so gentle, always so upright and in control, could be so rough, so demanding, and so untamed when they were alone.

Under his force, all her remaining inhibitions vanished. She wanted him to see all of her. Have all of her. She opened herself wider, thirsting to receive all of him. She felt his hardness thrusting inside her and his groin grating against her. His movements inflamed her and made her tremble from within. In a state of ecstasy, her whole body tightened. She grabbed the sheets beneath her hands as waves of spasms spread through every inch of her. The sensations rose to a height of rapture, propelling her to cry out for release.

Responding to her cries, he came at her until he reached his own climax and they both collapsed, breathless and spent.

Afterward, they lay next to each other, holding hands. Softly, he kissed her lips, over and over again until the flickering flame of the candle burned out and the orange glow of the wick extinguished in the dark of the night.

Standing in front of the mirror the next morning, Tessa gazed at her own reflection and put down the hairbrush on the dresser. She raised her fingers and touched the red marks peeking out from the collar of her bathrobe. A surge of excitement burst within her heart. She moved her hand from those reminders of intimate secrets to the rose pendant hanging around her neck. This was the best feeling in the world, to be in love.

Anthony came out of the washroom from his bath, wearing only a towel wrapped around his waist. He embraced her from behind and kissed her on the neck.

"What do you want to do today?" she asked.

"We can go visit the Montellos. They can't wait to meet you. Later tonight, maybe we'll go see the show we missed last night?"

"And tomorrow?"

"How about we get married?" He held up a small velvet box and opened it to reveal a pair of gold rings inside. Stunned, she turned around.

"I asked Mother to send these. I sent her a telegram before I went back to the front after I visited you on your birthday. They got here just in time, right before we got to Rome." He hugged her closer. "What do you say? Will you marry me?"

Not expecting this at all, she touched the velvet box and gazed at the shining golden rings. She had always thought that they would somehow live their lives together in the future, but she could not believe he was proposing to her, here, today. How long had he been thinking about this? "Are you serious?"

"Of course I'm serious. I wouldn't have done all the things I did with you last night if I wasn't serious."

His answer made her laugh. That was Anthony. Always responsible, always honorable. Before she gave him an answer, she couldn't help ruffling him a little. "You said you asked Aunt Sophia to send the rings after my birthday?"

"Yes."

She pushed his arms lightly off her and stepped away. "You don't have to do this."

"What do you mean?"

"You don't have to feel obligated to marry me because we made love." She turned her head so he couldn't see she was suppressing herself from laughing. "Perhaps that's what other girls would expect, but...do you remember what I told you back in Chicago that night by the lake? Remember I told you what kind of girl I am? Are you sure this is what you want to do? I love you, but I'd rather not marry someone only because he thinks it's the honorable thing to do."

"You think that's why I want to marry you?"

"Why?" She feigned ignorance. "What other reason could there be?"

He put the jewelry box down on the dresser. "It's not the only reason." He pulled her into his arms again and kissed her. "How's this for a reason?" He untied her bathrobe and took her to the bed. He started kissing her from her lips to her neck. As he caressed her body, he whispered, "Do you like this?"

"Yes." She giggled.

"How about this?" He began to make love to her.

She squeezed her eyes shut in delight.

"You like this too?" He pushed inside her again, rougher and more forceful this time.

"Yes…" She fell back and gave herself up to the force of his seduction.

"Will you marry me?"

"Yes…" She opened her eyes. "Wait! What? I did not…"

"Too late. You said yes. You can't take it back."

"That's not…I didn't say yes…"

"You just did. I'm not taking no for an answer."

"You can't…You tricked me!" Gasping, she tried to dispute him but was too aroused to argue.

"Will you marry me?" He drove deeper into her.

"Yes…" Yes, she wanted him to continue.

"Say it again." He continued, setting off all the senses of her body.

"Yes, yes..." Delirious and out of breath, she raised her hips to meet the fullness of his thrusts.

"Louder. I can't hear you."

"Yes!" She cried out as her body reached its climatic height.

She didn't know what question she was answering anymore. It didn't matter. Whatever he asked of her now, she would not be able to say no.

Joining her in the peak of their passion, he whispered, "I love you. I love you forever."

CHAPTER SIX

APPROACHING THE MONTELLOS' home, Tessa felt uncharacteristically anxious. Although Anthony had known the Montellos for only a few days, he was talking about them like they were family. She felt as if she was on her way to meet her boyfriend's family for the first time.

No. Not boyfriend. Fiancé.

Fiancé. She was still getting used to the idea. Everything was happening so fast, she had hardly any time to think. Right now, she had to get through lunch with the Montellos. She hoped she liked them, and they liked her. This was important to Anthony.

Her worries turned out to be unfounded. The moment she entered the Montellos' home, they welcomed her like family too.

Sonia was the first one to greet them. The little girl ran out of the house as soon as she saw them arrive. "Hi Tessa," she said, taking Tessa's hand. "We've been waiting for you. Anthony said you're beautiful. We couldn't wait to see what you look like."

"Anthony was exaggerating."

"No, I wasn't," Anthony said. "She is beautiful, isn't she?" he asked Sonia.

"Very!" Sonia said and led Tessa inside with Anthony following behind.

Although embarrassed, Tessa couldn't stop smiling at his open compliment.

Inside the Montellos' home, Signora Montello had already set lunch out on the table. As soon as they came in, the woman hustled everyone into the dining room, where a hearty meal awaited.

The Montellos were a merry bunch. While they ate, Tessa watched them talk loudly over each other. Their boisterous warmth was contagious. She could see why Anthony loved them.

One of them, though, was noticeably silent. Rocco, the small boy sitting across the table from her, didn't speak. Anthony had told her Rocco was deaf and could not talk. The boy ate quietly by himself, occasionally looking up to observe the others. She suspected that he could read lips. Sometimes, when someone said something funny or witty, he would smile. When someone said something disagreeable, he frowned.

Sensing her watching him, Rocco raised his eyes to meet hers. She smiled at him. He looked down at his plate, then looked up again and smiled back.

"Tessa dear," Signora Montello said when they finished their pasta. "I must apologize. You're an important guest. I wish I could have prepared a more elaborate meal. I still cannot find some of the food and ingredients I wanted. I can make a very good lamb dish, but there is no way to get meat."

"Oh, no, Signora Montello," Tessa said and wiped her lips. "This meal's great. Everything is delicious."

"Now, Anthony," the kind woman said. "Do you have any news to tell us?" She gave Tessa a big smile. "What did she say?"

"She said yes." Anthony put his arm around Tessa and pulled her close to him. The whole table broke out in cheers, and Tessa could feel her face burning up.

"Have you talked to my brother about finalizing the arrangements yet?" Signor Montello asked.

"I'm meeting with him this afternoon." With tender eyes, Anthony looked at Tessa. "We're getting married tomorrow."

Cheers erupted from the table again.

"You're all invited, of course." He looked around the table.

"We're so honored," Signora Montello said. "Thank you for including us in your special day. You must allow me to prepare a wedding dinner for you to celebrate afterwards."

"We'd love that," Anthony said. "Thank you."

"Tessa," said Fabia, Signor Montello's sister. "Has Anthony told you yet? Mia is a dress maker." She looked over at Mia, her sister-in-law. "We know the timing is too rushed for you to have a wedding gown made, but Mia has a few dresses at her shop you might want to look at."

A wedding gown? Tessa hadn't even thought of that.

"It has been a long time since Mia offered one of her fancy dresses to anyone. During the war, very few people bought clothes and she did mostly mending. But she has some nice ones she had made before the war. We would like to take you to her shop after lunch. You can see if you like any of her dresses."

Mia, who spoke limited English, smiled and nodded in agreement.

"Thank you," Tessa said. How could she say no to them? They had thought of everything. Everyone was so exceedingly generous. "I'd like that very much."

After lunch, Anthony took Tessa aside in the Montellos' family living room. "I'm sorry everything is so rushed. Our wedding shouldn't be so slapdash. You deserve so much more."

"No!" Tessa touched his face. "I'm thrilled. Really. As long as we're together, it's all that matters."

Her answer eased his concerns somewhat. "Do you want to invite anyone from the hospital?" he asked.

She would. Ellie immediately came to her mind. And Dr. Haley. Gracie too, since they were tentmates. "Can we invite Ellie, Gracie, and Dr. Haley?"

"Done," he said. "I'll go to the hospital on my way to my meeting with Father Lorenzo."

Tessa put her arms around him. She had never felt happier in her entire life. "Did you invite anyone?"

"I invited Warren to be my best man. He's on standby. We just wanted to make sure your answer was yes. I'll let him know later the wedding is on."

Tessa laughed.

"I invited Jesse too, but he declined."

"What?" Her heart dropped. Why would Jesse not come to their wedding?

"He said he doesn't like going to weddings. I really wanted him there, after everything he has done for us, passing messages for us back in Anzio and all."

Her heart sank further. Even if Jesse didn't like weddings, she still would have thought he would come to hers. Although they had never talked about it, she knew that at Anzio, he considered her a friend more than anyone else. His refusal to attend their wedding did not feel right. What was more, his refusal hurt. It surprised her she felt hurt.

"Tessa, are you ready to go?" Sonia came into the living room. Her older sister Sophia was right behind her. They were both ready to go with her to Mia's dress shop. Fabia, Mia, and

Signora Montello too had come in. Rocco followed them, stealing timid glances at Tessa.

"Yes, of course." Tessa let go of Anthony. She was still troubled that Jesse had turned down Anthony's invitation, but there was no time to think about this anymore. Everyone was waiting. She glanced at Rocco. "Anthony, what do you think if we ask Rocco to be our ring bearer?"

"That's a great idea!" Anthony said. "Sophia, would you help us ask him?"

"Certainly."

They looked over at Rocco. The sudden attention from everyone confused him. Sophia made a series of gestures with her hands to explain their request to him in sign language. When he realized what they were asking him, he broke into a huge smile. He nodded in acceptance and replied with a series of his own gestures.

"He said this is the best thing that's ever happened to him." Sophia interpreted for them.

Tessa went over to Rocco and gave him a hug, then turned to the Montello sisters. "Sonia, Sophia, would you do me the honor of being my bridesmaids tomorrow?"

The two girls cried out in delight. Happily, they each took one of Tessa's hands as they left to go to Mia's dress shop with the rest of the Montello women.

At the dress shop, Mia hung up several white dresses for Tessa to choose from. Signora Montello, Fabia, Sophia, and Sonia sat on the cushioned chairs and watched with eager anticipation. Tessa touched each one of the dresses, feeling their soft fabric. She could not decide which one she liked best. After wearing only her uniform for months, all civilian clothing looked gorgeous. Moreover, she wanted to look as beautiful as she could for Anthony on their wedding day. She held each one of the dresses, unable to make up her mind.

Mia looked her up and down, then picked out the one with an embroidered lace design. "This. Try this."

Tessa agreed and took the dress into the fitting room to try it on. In the mirror, the dress looked prim with its high collar. The princess seams, however, accentuated the shape of her waist, providing a sensuous contrast to the conservative neckline at the top. The capped sleeves and the yoked waist with a full skirt added dramatic flair. The effect was breathtaking. She loved this dress.

Back in the main room, the Montello women gasped in awe when she came out with the dress on. Signora Montello's eyes became teary, and Fabia pretended to faint.

"You look like a princess, Tessa," Sonia said.

Tessa smiled and looked at herself in the full-length mirror. She wished her mother was here. Her mother would have been thrilled to see her right now.

Mia brought her a matching pair of shoes, and said something to Fabia in Italian. Fabia interpreted for Tessa. "Mia said a daughter of a wealthy family ordered this dress to be made before the war. The girl never came to pick it up because her family escaped and left Rome soon after she ordered it. Then the war started, and a formal dress like this one had no use for anyone."

"It's a gorgeous dress," Tessa said.

"She said it's yours if you like it."

"Thank you."

Mia came behind Tessa and pulled on the looser parts of the dress. She marked those parts with pins and said in broken English, "Need to tighten waist and shorten the hem. I'll tailor this afternoon."

"Hold on," Fabia said. "You need something for your hair. We'll borrow one of Mia's hair clips." She opened the display case of custom-made accessories on the table, picked out a floral hair clip sewn with rhinestones, and clipped it into Tessa's hair. "There." She took a few steps back for everyone to admire the way Tessa looked. "Now it's perfect."

"Not yet." Signora Montello held up her hand and shook her finger. "One more thing." She took a jewelry case out from her purse and opened it to show Tessa a string of pearls. "This is something I own. It's our wedding present to you."

"Oh no, Signora," Tessa said. "This is too much. I can't accept."

"Yes, you can. A bride has to wear jewelry for her wedding." She put the string of pearls on Tessa, then held both of Tessa's hands to reassure her. "Please accept our gift. It's been a long time since something joyful has happened to us. The war has gone on for too long. Now we can finally celebrate. I think of Anthony as my American son, so you're like a daughter to me too. We are happy to be a part of your wedding."

She let go of Tessa's hands. Tessa turned toward the mirror and touched the necklace. Around the high collar, it made her look so elegant. "Thank you, Signora Montello. It's beautiful."

Signora Montello gave her a warm hug.

"What about the bridesmaids?" Fabia asked. "Mia, what dresses do you have for the girls to wear?"

Mia crossed her arms and looked at Sophia and Sonia. She then went to the back room and brought out two ocean-blue colored tea dresses. "Blue? You like blue?" she asked Tessa. "Blue like Anthony's eyes."

Delighted by the wonderful thought, Tessa gave her a big hug. "Thank you."

Tessa looked at all the gifts that they had bestowed upon her. The pearl necklace, the dress, the floral hair clip, and the bridesmaids' dresses. They reminded her of that old English rhyme.

Something old, something new, something borrowed, and something blue.

Blue like Anthony's eyes.

Jesse knew he should not have come to the hospital. He knew it would only cause him heartache. Ardley had said he was planning to propose to Tessa. He even invited Jesse to their wedding. Jesse could not see any reason why Tessa would decline, but still, he had to find out for sure. If she had accepted—or declined—the nurses at the 33rd would know.

When he saw Gracie and Ellie talking and their faces looking dour and upset, he held out a glimmer of hope. Could something have gone wrong? Was Ardley's plan derailed?

His hope was dashed in a flash. "She is so unfair," Gracie complained. "How can she do this?"

"Who are you talking about?" Jesse asked.

"Milton," Gracie said. "She wouldn't let us go to Tessa's wedding tomorrow."

Tessa's wedding. Jesse's heart sunk.

"She told us we could go when Lieutenant Ardley invited us earlier today, but she changed her mind when Dr. Haley said he was going too. That woman! She always gets neurotic whenever Dr. Haley might be around other nurses. Especially if Ellie might be one of those nurses."

"Gracie!" Ellie said. "That's not true."

Jesse barely heard what they were saying. Tessa had accepted Ardley's proposal after all. By tomorrow, Tessa would be married to another man.

What else did he expect? This was the inevitable outcome. Tessa loved Ardley. Fate had finally dealt him a losing hand.

"Don't look so sad, Lieutenant Garland," Ellie said. "Don't

feel bad for us. Maybe you can help us give our well wishes to Tessa?"

"No," Jesse said. "I'm not going."

"You're not?" Gracie's face changed from annoyance to hope. "You don't have to do that, Jesse. I know you want to go with me, but just because I can't go doesn't mean you shouldn't go." Although she said this, she could not hide her smile. "You'll have to tell Tessa congratulations for me."

"No," Jesse said. The world around him had darkened. His heart was embroiled in agony as he had never felt. "I have to go," he said and left the hospital.

Behind him, Ellie said, "He sure looked upset. I hope he's okay."

"Me too," Gracie said. "Poor Jesse. He must have really wanted me to be with him at the wedding. Say, do you think maybe he was planning to propose to me too?"

"I don't know him well enough to say, but I would be so happy for you if that's the case."

"That must be it," Gracie said. "That's why he looked so crushed. He must have wanted to propose to me at Tessa's wedding!"

CHAPTER SEVEN

THE NEXT MORNING, alone in their room in the hotel, Tessa put on the white dress that Mia had given her. She checked herself in the mirror and took a deep breath. Today was her wedding day.

So many people had put in a Herculean effort to prepare for the wedding. Yesterday, Mia had worked all afternoon to tailor the dress in time for her to wear it this morning. Back in Chicago, Uncle William had to make a series of hurried arrangements for their local parish to grant consent to Santa Lucia Church in Rome to officiate the wedding. Weeks ago, Aunt Sophia had had to send the rings and ensure they would arrive in time without delays.

The one who had made all these things possible was Anthony. He had set all the plans in motion without knowing whether she would say yes when he proposed. He had planned his proposal before he arrived in Rome, when he was still fighting a brutal war. He had asked Aunt Sophia to send the rings, without knowing whether he would make it out of Anzio. He did everything in reliance on nothing but hope.

She pulled her rose pendant out from under her collar and kissed it. How happy she was to marry someone like him.

Yet, the day was not perfect.

She took out a small photograph of her parents from the purse that Fabia had lent to her last night. She wished her parents were here. She wished Uncle William, Aunt Sophia, Uncle Leon and Aunt Anna, and Alexander were here. Even Katherine. She wished their entire family were here.

She wished her friends in Chicago could be here too. Ruby, Jack, Henry, and Nadine. Unfortunately, Ellie and Gracie couldn't be here. Captain Milton would not let them come. That woman! She couldn't stand seeing anyone be happy.

Dr. Haley could attend. He would be her only guest.

Tessa put her parents' photo back into the purse. Aside from her family, Jesse's absence was the one that troubled her the most. A hollow sadness crept into her heart when she thought of him. How could Jesse be so cold as to decline Anthony's invitation? It was as good as her own invitation. Why would he not join them on her most special day?

She took the angel amulet that Jesse had given her out of her uniform in the closet. The amulet shimmered under the light. She could not explain it, but she wanted Jesse to be near her today, even if he had refused to come in person. She put the amulet into the concealed pocket of her dress.

A knock on the door brought her out of her thoughts. It was Anthony. "Are you ready?"

"Yes. Come in."

He opened the door and entered. In his dress uniform, he looked sharp and dignified, but it was his expression that she would never forget. He looked mesmerized, stunned, as he stared at her.

She looked at him and smiled. He came up to her and touched her softly on her arm, as if afraid he might damage her. "I have the most beautiful bride in the world."

"You don't look so bad yourself, soldier."

"I have something you'll want to see." He handed her a telegram. "It came to the hotel this morning."

Dear Tessa and Anthony,

Congratulations! We are disappointed beyond words that we can't be with you on your wedding day, but know that we are with you in spirit. We will be thinking of you. With all our hearts, we wish you a bright and happy future together. When the war is over, we will celebrate again in London. Please write and let us know how your wedding day went, and send us plenty of photos.

— Love, Mother and Father

"From my mother and father?" Tessa asked. "How did they get the news so fast? We only decided to get married yesterday."

With a sheepish grin, he handed her another telegram. "I sent them a telegram to let them know that I would propose. I felt it was the right thing to do."

She took the other telegram. This one was addressed only to Anthony.

Dear Anthony,

If our other telegram has reached Tessa, that means she has said yes, and I am thrilled for you. I cannot be happier than to know that you are both happy and in love.

— All my best and love, Juliet

P.S.: If you do get married today, then the day I have always wished to postpone has finally come. How bitter a thing it is to look into happiness through another man's eyes. Nonetheless, I congratulate you. Be good to her, or you'll have me to answer to. — Dean Graham

Tessa put her hand over her heart. "My father! I'm sorry. He can be difficult like me."

"I'll have to worry about him later," Anthony took the telegram and placed it on the dresser, then offered to take her hand. "Shall we?"

She took his hand and, together, they left the hotel. Outside, Anthony's military jeep was waiting. His driver opened the vehicle door and beamed at them.

On their way to the church, Tessa watched Anthony. He looked so handsome, so sure of himself and what they were doing. Yes. She wanted to spend the rest of her life with him.

The entire way, he never let go of her hand.

She never wanted to let go of him either.

This was the right thing to do, to get married here, today. This was what they had to do in the midst of war, when everything could be taken away from them in an instant.

If life were normal, they would have held their wedding in London or Chicago. Their families would have arranged their wedding differently. If the wedding were held in London, her mother would have fussed over her all morning, and Tessa would not see Anthony until she arrived church as the bride. If it were in Chicago, Uncle Leon would have commissioned a couture wedding gown and insisted that she be married in it. Either way, their parents would have chosen an elegant and grand venue. They would have wanted to turn their wedding day into an occasion. The event might have even been reported by local newspapers. The wedding of the sole heir of the Ardley family in Chicago, or the daughter of the renowned actor Dean Graham in London, would no doubt have roused the interest of the gossiping crowd.

With the war, that kind of wedding was not to be. After everything she and Anthony had been through, and everything they had seen, all the fanfare was inconsequential. Here, all that mattered was that they had each other and could be with each other. In this mad, unpredictable world they were living, they could not afford to lose any time. With all the burdens they still carried, and all the travails they would still face, going to their wedding together this way, by each other's side, holding each other's hands, felt like the right thing to do.

The only tradition she regretted missing was having her father walk her down the aisle. She had made her choice. She was following Anthony and leaving her life in London behind. She wished she could've given her father the chance to symbolically see her off.

Together, Tessa and Anthony arrived at the Santa Lucia Church. Before getting out of the vehicle, Anthony gave her a solemn look. She understood his thoughts instantly. They had to cherish the moment. They had made it through Anzio, and neither of them had become a casualty. It was a blessing that they were still alive, so that their dreams could come true today.

"I love you," he said.

"I love you too."

At the church, Father Lorenzo was waiting by the entrance to greet them, as were Warren, Sonia, Rocco, and Sophia. While Warren shook Anthony's hand, the Montello children rushed up to Tessa.

"You look beautiful." Sophia kissed Tessa on her cheek and

took Tessa's purse. In exchange, she handed Tessa a bouquet of white roses.

Amazed, Tessa accepted the flowers. There were twelve stems tied together with a satin ribbon, all in full bloom. They looked as lovely as the ones that grew in the rose gardens at the Ardley's mansion. Sophia and Sonia, too, each held a small bouquet of miniature roses. Tessa couldn't imagine where the Montellos could have gotten these roses in this war-torn city. "Where did you find these flowers?"

"They're gifts from Countess Mary Gayley Senni," Sophia said. "She's American, from Pennsylvania. Her husband is Count Giulio of Rome. The flowers were delivered to our home this morning with this message." She gave Tessa a note.

— *For Miss Tessa Graham and Mr. Anthony Ardley, nephew of my dear friend Leon Caldwell. Congratulations.*

The message was signed "M.G.S." and affixed with the Senni family's noble seal.

"Looks like Uncle Leon arranged this," Anthony said. Tessa held the bouquet to her heart.

Father Lorenzo signaled the wedding party to enter the church, and the procession began. Inside, the Montello family had already taken their seats in the pews. Dr. Haley was there too. They stood up as the wedding party entered. Near the altar, a violinist performed the music of Bach's *Ave Maria*, joined by the church choir.

Tessa looked at the walls and ceiling of the chapel. In this church, where she had never been before, she was struck by how far she had gone from home since she had left London. With each step down the aisle, she was marching further and further away from her past. When she reached the altar, her old life would truly be behind her. In a few minutes, she would be making the biggest commitment of her life, and there would be no going back. This was her chosen path. She felt as if she was on the edge of a precipice, about to take a jump. She thought of her father and mother. She was leaving them behind forever.

Trembling, she reached her hand out to Anthony. He squeezed her hand and gave her the reassurance to proceed. She tightened her sweating hand around his, drawing on his strength to continue her steps.

They came to the altar, where Father Lorenzo took his place at the center. Tessa passed her bouquet to Sophia and knelt down, and Anthony did the same. While Sonia, Sophia, Rocco, and Warren took their seats, Tessa gazed up at the large cross hanging above Father Lorenzo, and the giant stained-glass windows behind him. She felt dwarfed by the grandeur. Taking a deep breath, she glanced at Anthony. For a moment, they held each other's gaze. He didn't appear nervous at all. He looked the happiest he had ever been. There was so much love in his eyes. Watching him, her anxiety disappeared. She reached her hand out to him again. As if they were of one mind, he reached out for her hand at the same time and held it for one last second before he let go and they bowed their heads in prayer.

"*Miei cari amici, siete venuti insieme in questa chiesa affinché il Signore possa sigillare e rinforzare il visto amore alla presenza di un sacerdote, ministro della Sua Chiesa, e di questa comunità...*" Father Lorenzo began the ceremony in Italian. As he spoke, Tessa sneaked a sideways glance at Anthony. His eyes were downcast, his demeanor earnest and serious. She lowered her eyes again while the choir performed another hymn.

When the Father began the homily, he handed Tessa and Anthony each a piece of paper. It was a copy of the sermon, handwritten and translated into English as Anthony had requested the day before. Anthony held on to the paper and tried to follow the homily by matching what the priest was saying in Italian to the words that he was reading in English. This was a sacred moment. He wanted to hear the Father's message. He wanted to remember to heed his words. He didn't want to ever forget their significance.

> *"Nella prima lettura di oggi, lettera ai Romani, Capitolo 12, Verso 12, sentiamo San Paolo suggerire ai romani di non scoraggiarsi di fronte alle difficoltà, ma di continuare a pregare Il Signore sarà con voi, ma delle difficoltà, inevitabilmente, arriveranno. Questo fa parte della vita umana. Oppure volte accadono cose sulle quali non abbiamo alcun controllo…"*
>
> — In our first reading of Roman's Chapter 12, Verse 12 today, we heard Paul advising the Romans not to give up when difficulties come but to keep praying. The Lord will be with you, but yet difficulties will come. It is part of our human condition, or sometimes things happen to us that we have no control over…

Anthony read the words. Like the Father said, there would be difficulties ahead. He had already seen what war entailed. But he vowed to himself and to God, for as long as he lived, there would be no difficulties that he and Tessa could not overcome. He would see to it. He would do all that he could to help them surpass all adversities in their lives. Whatever difficulties might lie ahead, he would keep on loving her. He promised in his heart that he would honor and protect her, and he meant to commit to his promises. He would memorize Father Lorenzo's every word, no matter what happened.

Whatever happens, I won't give up. He vowed to God and to himself before the altar.

"Amare, così come lo intende Gesù, è amare anche quando questo significa accettare di soffrire per il bene dell'altra persona. Questo è vero amore: amare per il bene dell'altro.. Perché Gesù ha detto: non vi è amore più grande di chi dona la propria vita per un amico…"

— Love, in the sense that Jesus means, is loving even when it means undergoing suffering for the sake of the other. That is real love, loving for the good of the other. For Jesus said, "No one has greater love than this, to lay down one's life for one's friends…"

Out of the corner of his eye, Anthony glanced at Tessa kneeling next to him. He remembered her showing up alone at the army base in Naples, looking for him. She had gone through unbelievable obstacles to find her way to him, leaving behind all the comforts of home and everyone else she cared about. It did not matter to her that she would face dangers, horrendous living conditions, and hard work. Long before today, she had already decided she would give her life for him. It was his turn to do the same. He vowed in his heart, he would bear whatever adversity, whatever hardship, as long as he could love her.

"Ricevete l'un l'altra come un dono, e ricevete il dono della vostra nuova vita come marito e moglie."

— Receive each other as gift, and receive the gift of the new life as husband and wife.

The vision of Tessa in her white dress this morning came to Anthony. The way she looked at him, the way she touched him, the way she moved. He smiled. That vision of loveliness was seared into his memory. He turned his head slightly to look at her. Under the light shining through the stained glass, she looked alluring, like a jewel that captured and reflected a thousand shades of light. He loved everything about her. Her beauty, her audacity and defiant spirit, her unwavering loyalty, her quiet aloofness, and the gentle compassion masked beneath. He had no doubts. Meeting her was the best thing that had ever happened to him. To be able to be with her for as long as they lived was the best gift he would ever receive in his life. He could not wait to start their new life together, with her by his side.

He bowed his head and made another prayer. He knew he was blessed. What other people hoped for, be it wealth, talent, or health, he had always had in abundance. He should be humbled and should not ask for more. But despite all that he already had, he dared to ask the Lord to grant him one more wish. He prayed that he and Tessa would have a long, happy future together.

"And now, I will conduct the next part in English." Father Lorenzo told the congregation when the sermon concluded. "Will the wedding party please rise?"

Tessa and Anthony stood up as the priest instructed, as did everyone present.

The Father then uncharacteristically broke his solemnity and said, "I hope you will pardon my bad English." A spark of humor twinkled in his eyes. Tessa and Anthony could hardly hold their smiles.

"Anthony and Tessa, have you come here today freely and without reservation, to give yourselves to each other in marriage?"

A lightness, like wind, rushed to Tessa's head. Her heart was skipping so fast, she could hardly breathe. She dug her nails into her palm to make sure this moment was real.

"I have," Anthony said, his voice firm without any hesitation.

"I have." The words poured out of Tessa from her heart.

"Will you love and honor each other as man and wife for the rest of your lives?"

"I will." They both answered at the same time over each other. Tessa let out a nervous laugh. Anthony beamed.

Father Lorenzo continued. "Since it is your intention to enter into marriage, you will now declare your consent before God and his Church. Will you please join hands?"

Anthony held out his hands and Tessa took them. For her, the moments that followed went by like a dream. All she could do was look at Anthony. Vaguely, she heard Father Lorenzo say to Anthony, "Repeat after me," but it was Anthony's voice that spoke to her.

"I, Anthony James Ardley, take you, Tessa Graham, for my lawful wife, to have and to hold, from this day forward, for better, for worse, for richer, for poorer, in sickness and in health, until death do us part."

Father Lorenzo directed her to speak. This was it. The seal of their love. "I, Tessa Evangeline Graham, take you, Anthony Ardley, for my lawful husband, to have and to hold, from this day forward, for better, for worse, for richer, for poorer, in sickness and in health, until…" She paused. She could not bring herself to say the remaining words of her vow, not with the war still going on. "Until…" she tried again, but could not. She didn't want anything to happen to him. She didn't want death to ever come. She didn't want them to be apart.

Everyone was now watching her. With the pressure mounting, she said instead the next words that came to her, "for all eternity."

It was against the Catholic church's rules to go off script, but she could not help herself. Father Lorenzo looked at her, surprised. Anthony looked outright bewildered. He tightened his grip on her hands. This time, his were the hands that trembled. But she would not apologize. With determination in her eyes, she looked at Anthony. He returned her gaze, his eyes filled with emotion and tenderness.

Father Lorenzo let her transgression slip and continued on.

"What God has joined, men must not divide." He opened the Bible and said to Rocco. "May I please have the rings?"

Rocco came forward with the wedding bands in a small jewelry box. Father Lorenzo put the rings on the Book and blessed them. He then held up the Bible with the rings on the open page and said to Anthony and Tessa. "You may place the rings on each other and repeat after me…"

Anthony picked up Tessa's ring and slid it onto her finger. "Tessa, take this ring as a sign of my love and fidelity." He repeated the words as instructed by Father Lorenzo. "In the name of the Father, the Son, and the Holy Spirit." Then, digressing from the script himself, he added, "Tessa, I love you for all that you are, and all that you will become. From the day I first held you in my arms, I have loved you, adored you, and cherished you. I will continue to love you for the rest of my life, and for all eternity."

When he said this, Tessa's eyes moistened. A teardrop fell down her cheek. She didn't expect him to go off script too. She didn't expect him to make such a dramatic declaration. In that moment, she knew that whatever the future might hold, she would always follow him wherever he went. She would follow him to the end of this world.

"Anthony, take this ring as a sign of my love and fidelity. In the name of the Father, the Son, and the Holy Spirit." She placed the other ring on his finger. As soon as she finished, he grabbed her hand, pulled her into his arms and kissed her. It was a kiss of unsuppressed emotions, a kiss that encompassed more than a thousand words of love, all conveyed in one moment in time.

The Father concluded the ritual with Holy Communion, blessings, and prayers. For the rest of the ceremony, Tessa could not stop smiling, and neither could Anthony. They were now bound to each other. Forever.

After the ceremony, they joined hands once again and

proceeded down the aisle. Outside, the Montellos were waiting. They cheered and showered them with rice when they exited the church.

And poor Dr. Haley. He finally had a chance to speak to them. "Congratulations. It was a beautiful ceremony."

"Thank you for coming," Tessa said to him.

Paolo, the Montellos' son, released a pair of doves into the air. The doves flew away, circling each other for a long time in the sky.

"Do you know what this means?" Signora Montello asked Tessa and Anthony.

"No," Anthony said.

"It means you two will be together for a very long time to come."

In the early evening, after a festive wedding dinner at the Montellos' home, Anthony and Tessa wandered and roamed the streets before they returned to their hotel. They wanted to leave behind memories of their footsteps on every street and every corner. This way, their presence today would become part of this ancient city's history.

On the Ponte Sant'Angelo overlooking the Tiber River, they paused to admire the view of the sunset behind the Vatican Basilica. The Ponte Sant'Angelo, the bridge of angels, was said to be the most beautiful bridge in Rome.

Tessa looked below at the sunset reflecting off the water flowing under the bridge. Today had been like a dream. She could not believe it was almost over. She wished she and Anthony could be free, and the current of the river could carry them away.

"Do you think the war will end this year?" she asked.

"Anything's possible." Anthony embraced her from behind.

"We've taken Rome. We've taken Normandy. We have to have faith."

"I just want us to be together."

"We'll always be together. You know why?"

"Why?"

He looked out to the horizon. "Because we got married in the Eternal City."

Part Three

DESPAIR

Part Three

CHAPTER EIGHT

IN AN ABANDONED BUILDING that was once a bar, Jesse sat on the floor in a drunken stupor with a group of four American soldiers. They were all grunts except him, but he didn't care. Right now, he didn't care about anything.

They had been here for hours. Maybe days. Exactly how long? No one was counting. Certainly not him. They were all too drunk to care. Two of them were so drunk, they had passed out.

Jesse leaned back against the wall as the others sprawled out around him. The bottle of liquor in his hand had dried up. He tossed it next to the pile of leftover food containers and empty liquor bottles. How many bottles had they finished? No one was counting those either.

"So this is it, boys," one of the soldiers said. His name was Loman. He had been griping nonstop for hours. "We're here finally. Rome! What a fucking let down. This is what I fought months and months for? To be drunk here with you bastards in this abandoned shithole?" The more he talked, the blotchier his face got. "Where are the parties? Where are all the women?"

"Shut the fuck up, Loman. Go fill out a T.S. slip and send it to the chaplain. Am sick of your bitching," said another soldier named Weaver.

"You shut the fuck up. I'm telling it like it is. We gave them Rome, and all them brass and bitches back home could talk about is Normandy. Fuck them, man! It's enough to make me wish they'll fail." The soldier named Loman gulped a mouthful of wine from the bottle in his hand. The wine dripped from the corners of his mouth as he drank. "Back in that shithole Anzio, they told us Rome was the prize. Every single fucking day, Petey and I swore we'd eat, drink, and fornicate like Roman emperors when we got here. When in Rome, know what I mean?" The loud snore of one of the soldiers asleep on the ground interrupted his tirade. He shoved the sleeping soldier awake. "Hey. Petey. Wake up, you fucking ass. You're snoring worse than a pig. You sound like a fucking Stuka."

Squinting, the soldier named Petey lifted his head. He grabbed the flask beside him, poured alcohol down his throat, and fell right back to sleep.

"Useless piece of shit." Loman kicked the sleeping Petey with his foot. "We had a bet going, Petey and I. Which one of us would be the first to bed a dozen ladies when we got here? Look at him. All talk and no balls. All he's done since we got here is sleep. You'd think he's in a fucking coma." Loman picked up his wine again and finished it to the last drop. "Garland. You got more booze? I'm out."

Jesse raised his eyes. His head ached and he could not think straight. He dug into his bag and pulled out a bottle of aged scotch. After a careless look at the label, he leaned his head back against the wall. "This stuff's too good to drink just to get drunk."

"Nothing's too good for drinking to get drunk," Weaver said.

"Gimme that." Loman grabbed the bottle of scotch from

Jesse, took off the cap, ready to chug. The liquor label caught his attention. "Talisker, aged 20 years... Shit, Garland. This is good stuff."

"I want some of that," Weaver said. Loman took a gulp and handed the bottle to Weaver.

"This is top shelf," Weaver said. Unlike Loman, he poured the scotch into a cup and took a slow sip, savoring the taste. "The wine tastes like piss water now." He kicked an empty wine bottle, and it rolled away on the floor. "How do you get this stuff?" he asked Jesse.

Jesse didn't answer, but lit a cigarette.

"This stuff's too good. We ought to make a toast," Weaver said.

"A toast to what?" Loman asked.

"A toast to the victory," Petey said, waking up from his stupor. "We conquered Rome."

"Victory my ass," Loman said. "Rome ain't no victory. It's just another fucking rest stop if this fucking war doesn't end. And from where I'm sitting, there ain't no end in sight."

"Loman," Weaver said. "I can't listen to you anymore. You're depressing as shit."

"Fine. A toast to Stalin then." Loman grabbed the flask next to Petey. "To Uncle Joe for kicking some German asses. If he crushes the Krauts before we do, then we can all call it quits."

"Fuck that," Weaver said. "I ain't toasting to no Russian victory. I've been fighting this war too damn long. If there's going to be any victory, it better be ours. I ain't putting my life on the line for the Ivans to get the credit."

"Our victory means you have to fight," said Loman. "All you've been doing is bitch about having to fight."

"No, I haven't."

"Yes, you have."

"You're drunk."

"No, I'm not."

"I have a toast," Jesse said, interrupting them. He took the bottle of Talisker back from Weaver and poured it into his cup. "A toast to the girl I love. Today's her wedding day." He held up the cup. "Here's to her living happily ever after." He drank the entire cup of liquor.

"Her wedding day today..." Loman said, "Wait, that means she's marrying someone else?" He leaned closer to Jesse. "Did she cheat on you?"

Jesse shook his head. He took a drag of his cigarette.

"She turned you down?" Weaver asked in disbelief. "A girl turned you down?"

Jesse stared ahead. He saw nothing but vacant space. No amount of alcohol could numb his senses. Giving up, he let his pain and anguish meld into a hopeless, bittersweet smile.

"She ain't worth it." Loman took the bottle of Talisker and poured another shot into Jesse's cup. "A woman ain't worth it," he slurred. "You don't need to be tied down with a girl. If I have women swarming around me the way they swarm around you, shit, I'd never get married." He raised the bottle. "A toast. To Lieutenant Garland. Here's to him forever being a lady's man, and to his stockpile of booze."

"Yeah!" Weaver said.

Even Petey sat up. He took the bottle from Loman. "To Garland."

While they cheered, Jesse lowered his eyes to the floor. "I'd marry her in a heartbeat," he said. His voice was so low, nobody heard him.

CHAPTER NINE

AN ERUPTION of laughter from the staff caught Fran Milton's attention as she came down the hospital corridor on her way to her meeting with Colonel Callahan. In the commons room, a group of young doctors and nurses had gathered. Brent Doyle, the new physician who had recently joined them, and Ellie Swanson were among the people inside. Doyle was telling his stupid jokes again.

"Two fish are in a tank. One turns to the other and asks, 'How do you drive this thing?'"

Another wave of laughter broke out. Annoyed, Fran scowled and continued walking. Brent Doyle's jokes were terrible. She couldn't understand why everyone thought he was funny.

Worse yet, he was dense. Fran wouldn't have found him so irritating if he wasn't thick as a block. Since they came to Rome, she had given him many chances to be alone with Ellie Swanson. If he had any sense, he would have gotten the hint by now and be pursuing Ellie. Couldn't he see that he and Ellie Swanson made a good, logical couple?

Instead, Doyle always drew a crowd. If he was assigned to

work with Ellie, somehow other staff members would end up working with them. If he and Ellie had time off together, he would inevitably turn it into a group outing. Time and again, he ruined every chance Fran had given him. The only thing that came out of Fran's efforts was that Aaron believed Brent Doyle and Ellie were an item. Aaron seemed to have come to terms with it too. When he saw Doyle and Ellie together, he would leave them be and withdrew from them.

Still, Fran worried. Aaron's misconception could only last so long. If Doyle didn't make a move soon, Aaron might get ideas again.

No. Fran hunched her shoulders. She couldn't let that happen. She had to figure out a solution, quick.

She entered the administrative office. Colonel Callahan was already seated at the table. She took a seat across from him. "Good afternoon, Colonel. Sorry to keep you waiting."

"Not a problem, Captain. I was early."

Fran shifted her glasses and opened the file in front of her. "We've set up the hospital as you requested last week. Three hundred beds, all ready to receive patients. Twenty-three beds are currently in use. Eighteen cases of common flu. Five local civilians and Red Cross volunteers with some illness or another, nothing too serious. We have no combat-related cases right now." She closed the file. "I guess all is going well for the Fifth Army."

"Yes," said Callahan. "Everything is going better than expected. I thought we'd see more German counter offensives outside of Rome going up north, but that hasn't happened. The Gerries are in full retreat. Thank the Lord."

"Indeed."

"Our next phase is to reorganize and regroup for Operation Anvil." He leaned forward and lowered his voice. "This is still a top secret mission. All details are strictly confidential. The information I'm telling you comes straight from army command."

Fran clasped her hands on the table and waited to hear more.

"We'll be taking the American troops out of the Allies' Fifth Army. Our Sixth Army Corp. will be replaced by the Brazilian Expeditionary Force. They'll be reassigned to the Seventh Army to join the Free French for our next attack in Saint-Tropez," Callahan said. "D-Day is planned for mid-August."

"That's six weeks from now."

"Yes. Of course, the 33rd and the rest of our evac hospitals will be reassigned to the Seventh Army too."

"That won't be a problem." Fran folded her hands. "With six weeks, we'll have plenty of time to work out all the logistics."

"Good," Callahan relaxed into his seat. "Outlook for our next offensive is good. From our intel reports, there is no major German defense stationed in the South of France. Conditions are favorable to us at the moment."

"That sure is good news after Anzio."

Rather than agreeing with her, Callahan took a deep breath and frowned.

"What is it?" Fran asked.

"All may be good here where we are, but things aren't going so well up in Normandy. We've taken a lot of casualties up north. It's a blood bath there. The army's falling short on fighting men and staff on all fronts. Conditions are getting critical."

"What about medical personnel? Are the hospitals up north sufficiently staffed?"

Callahan's frown grew deeper. "They need more support. We have enlisted medical corpsmen and nurses scheduled to arrive from Stateside. Problem is, they aren't arriving fast enough."

Fran stared at her hands. She tried to remain calm, but her mind was racing. "Colonel, may I make a suggestion?"

"Yes?"

"If the situation there is so urgent, why don't we divert some of the medical staff here up north now. We aren't engaging in serious combat right now. There's no point in having people here idled. The 33rd can transfer a number of nurses up to Omaha Beach. Maybe the evac hospitals can do the same too."

Intrigued, Callahan rubbed his chin and considered her proposal. Fran could tell he liked the idea.

"Wouldn't that create a personnel shortage for us here when we move to southern France?" he asked.

"You can arrange for medical replacements to be sent here. If our hospital will be stationed in Rome for six more weeks, the replacements can arrive with plenty of time to spare before Operation Anvil starts. In the meantime, our experienced nursing staff can give immediate support to the hospitals in Normandy. Doesn't that make sense?"

Callahan's lips curled into a half smile. Fran knew then he needed no further persuasion. "Great idea, Captain. We can transfer not just nurses, but other medical staff as well. I'll contact our medical HQ in Normandy. They'll be pleased. It'll be a relief for them, I'm sure."

Her eyes hidden behind her glasses, Fran nonetheless let a quick smile slip from her face.

"Before I do that, though," Callahan said, "do you want to run the idea by Colonel Haley first?"

"No need," Fran quickly dismissed the suggestion. "Colonel Haley won't be back from the medical conference in Naples for another week. I'm in charge of all personnel matters for 33rd while he's gone. As for the evac hospitals, I have no doubt they'll all do whatever is needed to help."

"That's true," Callahan said. "Command's been thoroughly impressed with our medical units' performance."

"I'll get everything moving straight away. No point in stalling. Any delay can be another life lost."

"Agreed. The sooner the better."

"The sooner the better," Fran affirmed with a professional, courteous smile. Her true satisfaction could not be seen behind her glasses.

Ellie Swanson.

Out of sight. Out of mind.

Standing by the window in the administrative office, Fran Milton sipped her cup of coffee while she looked out onto the street. She was in an unusually good mood. The medical department command's approval for the transfer of nurses to Normandy had come quickly. In just three days, arrangements for reassignment and transportation of personnel were already in place. The speed at which everything happened surprised even her. She could only surmise that the need for support and reinforcement on the northern front must be critical. It pleased her to know she was able to come up with a solution to provide some relief for their army's larger efforts.

On the personal side, she couldn't be more pleased to think that she could finally get rid of that annoying thorn in her side.

Ellie Swanson knocked on her door with Tessa Graham behind her. "You wanted to see us, Captain?"

"Yes, Lieutenant. Come in."

The two young nurses entered at her order.

"Have a seat," she told them. Ellie and Tessa each took a seat at the table.

Fran walked away from the window and sat down across from them. "I don't know if you've been keeping up with the news coming out of Normandy," she said. "If you have, you'll know that the Allied troops there are running into severe German counter-offenses. The First Army is in serious need of reinforcements, including nursing and medical staff."

Ellie and Tessa listened, exchanging a glance.

"In light of the situation, the army medical command has decided to reassign some of our personnel to the hospitals in Normandy to provide them immediate relief and support."

Tessa gripped the arms of her chair. The uneasy look on her face did not move Fran in the least. Fran had not forgotten the night when their medical unit was on its way to Rome. That night, Tessa had tried to persuade Aaron Haley to join Ellie Swanson by the campfire. She did not appreciate Tessa giving Aaron that kind of distraction. Tessa Graham, too, needed to be weeded out.

Keeping her voice detached and business-like, Fran continued, "The 33rd will be reassigning two nurses and six medical corpsmen. You'll both be transferred to the 51st Field Hospital attached the U.S. First Army."

Silence seized the room as if a gust of cold wind had passed through and the air had frozen.

"Captain...," Ellie said. "Do you mean...Are you sending us away?"

"No one is sending you away. You are being transferred because your service is more urgently needed somewhere else."

Speechless, Ellie sat stiffened in her seat.

Fran shifted her glasses. "Actually, Lieutenant Swanson, you might want to thank me." She softened her face with a patronizing smile. "For you, this is also a promotion. You'll be assigned to the position of deputy chief nurse for the 51st Field Hospital. You're now a first lieutenant. Congratulations."

The news did not bring any joy to Ellie. Disappointment spread across her face.

"I personally recommended you," Fran said. "Remember in Anzio when I put you in charge of the hospital when I went on leave to Naples? I was very impressed with your performance managing the nursing staff while I was gone. You did a marvelous job. It's time you take on a bigger role. Your promotion ceremony will be at 1600 tomorrow. Your achievement will be recognized before the entire hospital."

"Thank you," Ellie said, the reluctance in her voice belying her words of gratitude, "but…"

Fran looked intently at her, waiting to hear what she wanted to say. She had a ready answer prepared if Ellie dared to ask her to reconsider. But instead, Ellie asked, "What about Tessa? Does she really have to go too? She just got married. Lieutenant Ardley's with the Third Division. Can't we send someone else in her place instead?"

Fran gave Ellie a cold look through her glasses. Ellie's concern for Tessa fully convinced Fran that she had made the right call to send Tessa Graham away too. These two looked out for each other. She did not want Tessa to remain in case Tessa would act as a bridge between Ellie and Aaron after Ellie went away.

"Would you please reconsider for Tessa's sake, Captain?" Ellie asked. Tessa sat up and leaned forward. She looked from Ellie to Fran. Her hands tightened even more around the arms of her seat.

Fran's patronizing smile disappeared. Her stony expression returned. "What bearing does that have on our tasks at hand? There are thousands, millions of servicemen on active duty away from their wives. There are other military nurses separated from their husbands. Why should Lieutenant Graham be any exception?"

Lost for an answer, Ellie lowered her head and clasped her hands on her lap. Tessa's face turned white as a sheet.

"We're on a military mission, not a honeymoon," Fran said. "We're here to do our jobs. There are sick and injured soldiers in desperate need of help. I've given serious thought as to who to send for the reassignment. My decision is based on the army's needs, and I chose the most suitable candidates. The staff's personal concerns are irrelevant."

Tessa held on to the chair, tensed. Ellie stared at the floor, dejected.

"Lieutenant Swanson." Fran gave Ellie a stern look. "You're about to take on a new role. It's a role that will require an even higher sense of responsibility. The needs of the army and the hospital should always be your first concern. Not personal favors. You need to keep that in mind. That's my best advice to you."

"Yes, ma'am," Ellie answered meekly without looking back at Fran.

"Your new job is a good opportunity, Lieutenant. Don't waste it."

Angry, Tessa looked away to the window. Fran glanced at her and said to Ellie in a consoling voice, "I'm sending Lieutenant Graham too because I think you can use your own support. Your new position will be challenging. You and Lieutenant Graham are good friends. With Lieutenant Graham going with you, you won't be all alone." She smiled at Tessa. "Lieutenant Graham, you do want to support Lieutenant Swanson, don't you?"

The impossible question put Tessa in a bind. Ellie shook her head lightly at Tessa, but Tessa could only say, "Yes. I do."

"Good." Fran folded her hands, satisfied. "Departure is this coming Friday. You'll be joined by the reassigned medical corpsmen from our hospital and staff members from 15th Evac who are also being transferred. Be ready."

"This Friday?" Tessa asked. "That's the day after tomorrow."

Fran silenced her with an icy glare. Tessa held back and didn't say anything more.

"That'll be all. You're dismissed." Fran began reviewing a

file on the table to signal that their meeting had ended. Reluctantly, Ellie and Tessa got up from their seats and left the room. Fran ignored their departure without looking up. She couldn't wait for these two to be gone. Not just gone from her office, but gone for good. There would be no more distraction to Aaron from Ellie Swanson, and no more meddling by Tessa Graham.

Out of sight, out of mind.

Outside of Fran's office, Tessa shook with anger. She was so angry, she could not speak. Everything had happened so unexpectedly. She would have to leave Anthony. She could not believe this was happening.

"I'm so sorry, Tessa," Ellie said. "I don't know why, but I feel like this is all my fault."

"It's not your fault. I suppose they really do need help up in the north. I just wish we weren't the ones being reassigned."

"I know. You came here to be with Lieutenant Ardley. What if you try to contact General Castile again? Maybe he can help? Maybe he can halt your transfer?"

"No." Tessa started down the hallway. "I can't do that. When he assigned me here, I promised him I would always put my work as my number one priority. If nurses are needed in the north, I can't ask him to halt my transfer for selfish personal reasons. He won't like that, and I don't want to break my promise to him. Anyway, I'd be long gone before my message would even reach him."

They walked in silence. Not wanting Ellie to feel bad, Tessa said, "Congratulations. You're going to be a first lieutenant."

Ellie rolled her eyes. "I don't care about that. I don't plan on staying in the military after the war. I'm here to help our soldiers. The ranks mean nothing to me."

"Well, you'll be a deputy chief nurse."

"I'd rather stay here, to be honest. All my friends are here."

"I'll be going with you." Tessa smiled. "Milton said she's sending me to support you, and I want to do that. I don't want you to go off all alone."

"I'm sorry. I didn't mean that I don't want you to come with me, but I'll be fine. She didn't need to transfer you too. I can work here, I can work there. It's all the same."

Tessa stopped. It would not be the same. Dr. Haley would not be there. An urgent look passed over her face. "Ellie, we're leaving in less than three days. Dr. Haley won't be back from Naples by then. You won't even get to say goodbye to him."

To Tessa's surprise, Ellie didn't appear concerned. Instead, she smiled. "It doesn't matter. It was all wishful thinking on my part. He's already in a relationship with Captain Milton."

"Dr. Haley? In a relationship with Captain Milton? You must be mistaken."

"I'm not mistaken. She told me. He gave her a wooden heart he carved for her for Valentine's Day. She keeps it on top of her desk in her room."

"He couldn't have." Tessa felt sure Milton had manipulated the situation again. "I don't know why Milton has that wooden heart, but she had to be lying. He's not in a relationship with her. Dr. Haley likes you. I know he does. He practically told me."

"He told you he likes me?"

"Not in so many words, no. But he doesn't deny it when he talks about you. He worries he's too old for you. Maybe I should have told you, but I didn't want to interfere so directly. Besides, I thought he would rather tell you himself how he feels."

A gleam of hope came to Ellie's eyes, but just as quickly, it vanished. "It doesn't matter. I'm now with 51st. We're leaving in less than three days. Maybe it wasn't meant to be."

"Ellie…"

"Don't worry about me." Ellie put her hand on Tessa's arm. "You have to go find Lieutenant Ardley and tell him what happened. I'll be all right."

Uncertain about leaving Ellie to cope with the news by herself, Tessa hesitated.

"Go. You don't have much time."

Tessa agreed and took off. As she left the building, a lump rose in her throat. She couldn't bear the thought of leaving Anthony. She swallowed hard to hold back her tears, but the lump wouldn't go away. It choked and constricted her, souring her heart.

———

Anthony knew at once that something was wrong when Tessa showed up at the Montellos' home looking for him. Her face was as white as a sheet. She tried to speak, but instead of speaking, all she could do was stare at him while clutching on to him. Signora Montello, realizing that something terrible had happened, hustled her family out of the living room, leaving Tessa to talk to him alone.

"What is it?" Anthony asked. "What's wrong?"

"They're sending me away," Tessa said, her voice trembling. "Captain Milton. I can't be with you anymore."

"What? Hold on. Sit down." He led her to the sofa. "What are you talking about?"

"They're reassigning hospital staff to the medical units in Normandy. I'm being transferred. Captain Milton's sending me away."

The news struck Anthony like a thunderbolt. "How soon?"

"The day after tomorrow. I have to leave for Omaha Beach the day after tomorrow." She threw her arms around him. Pressing her face against his body, quiet tears began to fall down her face. "Why? After all we've been through. I did everything I could. All I want is to be near you. I'd do anything to be near you."

He put his arms around her. What she was telling him slowly sank in, but he still couldn't believe it. He thought they would finally have a break now that Anzio was behind them. He could not believe their time together would be cut short like this. He could not believe she would no longer be following him.

Worse, Tessa was being sent to another dangerous war zone. If they couldn't be together and near each other, then what was the point of her being exposed to the dangers of battle? She could've been safe at home. Her being here now was all wrong. What if something happened to her when she went away? "This is all my fault," he said. "You shouldn't be here in the first place. I got you into this."

"No." She looked up at him. "You didn't get me into anything. It was my decision to come. I wanted to be with you."

She said that, but he couldn't forgive himself. She risked her life to be with him, but he was always powerless to do anything for her. He could not protect her against the enemy raids when they were in Anzio. He could not protect her now when she would be sent to another dangerous place. As a man, there was never anything he could do to keep her safe. He felt useless.

"I just want to be with you." She held on to him. "Our wedding day was the happiest day of my life." She buried her face against his chest. Her tears were soaking his shirt. It broke his heart to see her like this. "I love you."

"I love you too," he said. But in his mind, he questioned what that meant. For all his love, he had no way to make things better for her. He wished he could tell her how sorry he felt that he couldn't do anything for her. He wanted to tell her how much it hurt him to think she would be away from him.

But he couldn't. She was already so sad. If she knew how bad he felt, it would only add to her burden and worries. He had no power to change their situation. The only thing he could do now was to be strong for her. He had to be strong for both of them. To keep their hopes alive. "Don't be sad." He stroked her arm gently and kissed her on the head. "This war has to end sometime. We will outlast this war. We have to because I want to give you many, many more years of happiness to come when we're together again. And I know we will be together again. We were married in the Eternal City, remember?" He wiped the tears off her face. "Promise me. When you leave, when we are far away from each other, no matter what happens, you won't give up hope."

She leaned against him, unable to utter a word.

"Promise me, you'll get through this. Please? Tell me you won't give up."

Through her tears, she nodded. "I won't give up."

He hugged her tighter. "I'll be thinking of you. Every day."

"I won't stop thinking of you."

"Yes." He put on a brave face. "We'll get through this war. We will be back together again. For all eternity." He gave her a firm kiss. Her faith now hinged on his words. He only hoped that what he said would be proven prophetic. It was all they had now. Hope.

CHAPTER TEN

THE VOICES of hotel guests stomping down the inn's hallway outside his room woke Jesse up from his sleep. He stared up at the ceiling. The fan hanging above him rotated around and around. For a moment, he couldn't tell if the fan was really turning or if it was his own head that was spinning. His temples were thumping with a splitting headache. His mouth and throat felt drier than sandpaper.

"G'morning, honey," Gracie mumbled next to him, half asleep.

"How'd you get in here?" He jolted up from the bed and pulled away from her.

"We came back together last night, remember?" She snuggled up to him. "I've been looking all over for you. Jonesy finally told me you were at the pub in this hotel. I found you, and we came back. You were so drunk."

Jesse fell back against the headboard. His head throbbing, he put his hand on his forehead. He had no memory of what happened last night. He grabbed his canteen on the nightstand and guzzled down the water. Gracie put her arm around him, but he dragged himself out of bed to the bathroom. In the bathroom, he wrapped a towel around his waist, turned on the faucet, and splashed water on his face, trying to clear his head.

"I haven't seen you all week," Gracie said from the bed. "I thought we'd spend more time together once we got to Rome. Where do you go all the time? I can never find you."

He continued washing up without answering her.

"I need you, Jesse. It'll be so lonely without Ellie and Tessa. I can't believe they're going to be gone."

Still wiping his face with a towel, he paused. "What do you mean they'll be gone?"

"They've been reassigned. That bitch Milton is sending them up to Omaha Beach to join the 51st Field Hospital. They're leaving tomorrow."

Alarmed, he came out of the bathroom. "Tomorrow? They're leaving tomorrow?"

"Tomorrow afternoon. They're leaving with three of our corpsmen and the nurses from the 15th who are being transferred too," she continued talking, oblivious to the shocked, urgent look on his face.

"I'll have to find myself a new tentmate when we go on our next mission. It's going to be so lonely without them. They're the ones I get along with best at the hospital." While she talked, Jesse picked up his trousers from the sofa and put them on. "Can't you come see me more after they're gone? I really hate being left all by myself…"

"Gracie," he interrupted her. "It's over."

She sat up in the bed. Confused, she asked, "What's over?"

He looked away, then stared directly at her. "Us. It's over."

"What are you talking about? Are you joking? Please don't joke about this."

He only stood there, emotionless.

"No," she said with a nervous smile. "You don't mean it. You can't mean it. We're going to get married, aren't we?"

Without responding, he picked up his uniform top and put

it on. She watched him, her eyes wide in disbelief. He finished dressing and walked toward the door.

"You're leaving? Just like this?" she asked

He looked down at his hand on the doorknob. He considered saying sorry, but apologizing felt false. If he were truly sorry, he wouldn't have started with her to begin with at all. Apologizing would only serve to cast himself in a better light, and he didn't deserve it.

"You can't leave me." She began to cry. "I love you."

Sadly, and not without pity, he smiled. *You don't even know me.* "I never said I love you."

"Wait! Jesse!" she cried out. "Don't leave. I don't understand. What went wrong? We can talk about this. Can't we talk about this?"

He turned the doorknob. Talking was pointless. He had been down that road before. The only purpose of talking was hope. There was no hope. "Goodbye, Gracie." He opened the door.

Seeing she could not change his mind, she became desperate. Sobbing, she picked up the small vase on the nightstand on her side of the bed and threw it at him. The vase missed him by an inch. It hit the door and fell to the floor, shattered.

He walked out without looking back.

———

At the school building where the 33rd Field Hospital was temporarily based, Jesse searched frantically for someone, anyone, who could tell him where to find Tessa. A nurse pointed him to the direction of Aaron Haley's office.

In Aaron's office, Tessa laid a sealed envelope on the doctor's desk. When she turned around, she found Jesse standing at the door.

"Jesse."

"You're leaving."

"You heard?" She looked at him with sad eyes. "Yes. I'm being transferred to the 51st to follow the First Army. The reassignment came yesterday. I wanted to tell you, but I didn't know where to find you." She smiled at him in jest. "Where've you been all this time? No one ever knows where you are. Are you up to no good again?"

He didn't respond to her joke. "You're leaving tomorrow."

"At 1300. I'm glad you've come here. I wouldn't want to leave without saying goodbye."

He remained standing at the door, as though afraid to come near her. Afraid to accept the inevitable.

"I wish you had come to my wedding. Anthony said he invited you. I was very disappointed you weren't there. I had to use the angel amulet you gave me as your stand-in."

He held on to the door frame, clutching hard to the wood. She could see the tension in his hands. "Jesse, are you all right?"

Ignoring her question, he asked, "This is goodbye then?"

"It's not what I want either," she said. "I'll miss you."

He walked toward her. His eyes full of anguish and more intense than she had ever seen them.

"Will you? Really?"

"Will I what?"

"Miss me." He put his hands on her shoulders.

She turned her head and glanced sideways at his hand on her right shoulder. Confused, she gazed up at him. Before she knew what was happening, he bent down and kissed her on the lips.

Too stunned to react, she stood there. His lips lingered on hers, full of yearning. His kiss, laden with unspoken passion so deep, deluged her to the core. His warm breath beseeched her like a torrent of desire, unfulfilled. When she realized what was happening, she tried to push him away, but he grabbed her hands and held her from moving away.

"What are you doing?" she demanded.

"I'm sorry. I had to do this. Just once, I want to know what it's like to kiss you."

She stared at him, dumbfounded. Still holding on to her, his grasp of her hands loosened. She started to object, but there was so much pain in his eyes. She couldn't bring herself to raise her voice.

"I love you," he said. "I've been in love with you since the first time I saw you." He ran his fingers softly across her cheek.

"No. This can't be. What about Gracie?"

"Gracie? I got close to Gracie because it was the only way I could get close to you."

She shook her head in denial.

"You know she means nothing to me. You know that."

"No," she said, still shaking her head. "You can't. I can't. Anthony…"

"Right. Anthony. The love of your life. The light of your world." He grabbed her hands again. "Can you honestly say you feel nothing for me? Nothing at all?"

She looked away from him. She didn't know how to answer him. Of course she had feelings for him. Next to Anthony, he was the person she felt closest to since she had come to Italy. Deep inside, she always thought they shared a kindred spirit. He never judged her, and she never judged him. Among the medical staff, he understood her, more than anyone else. During those miserable days in Anzio, she was always glad when he was around. He made life at the hospital more bearable. But what kind of feelings did she have for him? That was not something she had consciously thought about.

"Look at me," he said softly, drawing her to raise her eyes to meet his gaze.

"We have something," he said. "I feel it. You feel it. You just won't admit it. You won't even acknowledge it, but you know it's there."

His words brought forth so many unfathomable implications, she was afraid to even think what they might all mean.

"Can you say without a doubt we wouldn't have had a chance if you had met me first?"

She could neither admit nor deny what he said.

"I've only ever loved one person in my life, Tessa. That's you." He wrapped his arms around her. "I couldn't watch you get married to somebody else. I'm sorry I met you too late."

She knew the right thing to do was to back away from him, but he was so hurt. It hurt her to see him hurt. She could feel the rawness of his pain. In his arms, the tender warmth of his body engulfed her. She could hear the agonizing sound of his heartbeat.

"Goodbye, Tessa." He finally released her.

Shaken, she fell back against Aaron's desk as he walked away.

"I love you more than you'll ever know," he said before he disappeared out the door.

She watched him leave. When she recovered her senses, she thought back to all the times when they were with each other. How could she not see any of this? It was all so obvious now. Everything he had done for her. Every effort he had made to please her. Every excuse he had found to be around her. The way his eyes brightened whenever he saw her.

How much it must have hurt him to carry her messages to Anthony week after week, all for a ruse to be near her. Through it all, he upheld his word. He made sure she and Anthony could remain in touch the entire time they were in Anzio. Not once did he take advantage of their friendship to interfere with them. Not once did he say a single disparaging word about Anthony. Other than occasional harmless flirtations, he always remained honorable and proper around her.

She tried to think of what she could have done. Was there something she could have said to change anything? Could she have acted differently to save him from reaching this point of heartache and despair?

Nothing. She could not think of anything.

There was nothing she could do now either. She could not run after him. She could not console him. The only thing that could take away his pain was the one thing that she could not give him.

Remembering his kiss, she touched her lips. A long time passed before her mind cleared and she could leave the room.

———

Back in her quarters, Tessa found Gracie sitting on her cot, weeping. Alice, another nurse, was consoling her. Tessa could guess why Gracie was crying. But still, she held out the faintest hope that she was wrong. "What's the matter, Gracie?"

"He left me," Gracie said in tears.

"Who? What are you talking about?" Tessa asked, even though she already knew. Part of her still wished that none of this was real. She wished something else had made Gracie cry.

"Jesse. We're over," Gracie said, devastated and angry.

Tessa turned her face away. She felt guilty, even though she had done nothing to cause this.

"No explanation. No apology. All he said was, 'It's over.' Then he left. He said he never loved me." Gracie sobbed as Alice embraced her to comfort her.

"I'm sorry," Tessa muttered and quietly left the room. After what had happened, she didn't know what to say to Gracie. Anything she could say would be a lie. If she told her the truth, it would only hurt her even more.

Not knowing where she was going, Tessa kept on walking. She came to the stairs at the end of the hallway and went down to the main floor. She crossed the lobby and exited the hospital. She wanted to get away, to seclude herself, and to withdraw from being the source of everyone's distress.

Outside, people went about their business. Rome was once again a peaceful city. But the turmoil of her own world had only begun. A wild storm swirled within her. Everything inside had spun out of control.

She reached for the angel amulet in her pocket and took it out. The celestial whiteness of its surface epitomized the purity of love. She thought of Jesse's radiant smile. Her heart ached for all the pain he must feel.

She closed her hand around the amulet. "I'm sorry, Jesse. I already gave my heart to somebody else."

No one heard her words. Her whisper faded into the noise of the streets.

CHAPTER ELEVEN

On his way to the hospital in the late morning after returning from Naples, Aaron Haley stopped at the little café around the corner. Since coming to Rome, he had been coming here every time he wanted to take a break from work. The coffee served here was made with instant coffee supplied by the American Army, but the owner served it with chicory. The little trick added a woody, nutty taste to the beverage and made all the difference.

He had been thinking of a cup of coffee here on his trip back to Rome. His visit to Naples ended sooner than he had planned. The medical conference concluded ahead of schedule, and he was able to come back a day early. No one was expecting him today at the hospital.

Aaron took a seat at the small table by the front window. The cafe owner, a thin, balding man with a white mustache, recognized him right away.

"*Buongiorno, Dottore!*" the man greeted Aaron and brought him a coffee and a pastry.

Aaron politely accepted. He took from his bag a copy of the *National Geographic* he had brought back with him from

Naples to read while he drank his coffee. After taking a sip, he put the magazine down. He realized he would rather enjoy the moment instead. He didn't usually get to take his time to enjoy coffee and a pastry. Morning always began with a breakfast meeting with Fran Milton. His head would be filled with data and reports before his stomach got full.

This past week in Naples, he had been wondering if he shouldn't put an end to those breakfast meetings. The meetings began as a measure of efficiency to get their routine administrative issues out of the way before they started their daily work of treating patients. After the wretched ordeal of Anzio, he didn't want to take any good things in life for granted anymore. There had to be a better way to start the mornings, like a cup of coffee and a few moments of quiet reflection during breakfast before the day began.

He finished his coffee and bid the cafe owner goodbye, then continued on his way to the hospital. Behind him, two young boys followed, giggling. These boys lived around here. They had followed him every time he came to this cafe. Smiling, he strung them along until he reached the entrance of the hospital. There, he turned around and took out of his bag a chocolate bar for each of them. The boys ran up and took the treats.

"*Grazie, Dottore.*" They thanked him happily and waved goodbye.

He watched the boys shove each other in jest as they ran down the street. Once upon a time, he had wanted children. A lot of children. At one point in his life, he was sure he would be a father.

All that was so long ago. He no longer expected it. With the life he led, the chances of his becoming a father was unlikely. He had come to terms with it.

He stepped into the hospital.

"Good morning, Dr. Haley!" said the Red Cross volunteer

working at the reception desk in the lobby. "I wasn't expecting to see you."

"Good morning, Doris." He waved as he walked passed her. "The conference ended early."

In his office, stacks of files had piled up on his desk. A mountain of work awaited him. He went behind his desk and dropped his bag down by his chair. On the top of a file, a letter addressed to him caught his eye. He picked it up and opened it.

Dear Dr. Haley,

I regret that I won't have a chance to say goodbye in person before I leave. By now, you must have heard that Ellie, several corpsmen from our hospital, and myself have been transferred to the 51st Field Hospital in Normandy. I am very sad to have to leave the 33rd, but it is Captain Milton's final decision and cannot be changed. I want to let you know that I've learned a lot from you. It was an honour to serve with you. I hope we will meet again someday.

— Tessa Graham

Aaron reread the letter and tried to understand what had happened. Tessa left? Ellie was gone too? When did this happen, and why was the decision made without him?

Ellie…transferred…

Just then, Brent Doyle knocked on his door. "Dr. Haley." He entered. "I heard you're back. That's great because I wanted to ask you about a new idea I have. Since we're not too busy in Rome at the moment, what do you think if I set up a series of training sessions for the less experienced staff members to…"

"Dr. Doyle." Aaron interrupted him. "Do you know anything about Tessa and Ellie leaving the 33rd?"

"You mean Lieutenant Graham and Lieutenant Swanson? Why, yes. I heard they've been transferred to Normandy."

"You heard?" Aaron asked. Doyle had to know everything about this. Fran Milton said he and Ellie were now involved with each other. "What do you mean, you heard? Didn't Ellie talk to you about it?"

"No." Doyle shrugged. "She didn't say anything to me personally about it. There was an announcement about her transfer at her promotion ceremony yesterday."

"Promotion ceremony?"

"Yes. She was promoted to first lieutenant. She'll become the deputy chief nurse at the 51st Field Hospital up north. That's what they said in the announcement."

Aaron looked at Tessa's letter again. The news hit him hard, but it had to be worse for Doyle. "I'm sorry to hear that Ellie has to leave you, but you must be happy for Ellie for her promotion."

Looking confused, Doyle scratched his head. "I'm happy for her, of course, as much as everybody else. Swanson's a wonderful nurse. I don't understand, though. What do you mean you're sorry to hear she has to leave me?"

"Aren't you two seeing each other?"

"Seeing each other? No," Doyle denied, waving both his hands. "There must be some misunderstanding here. I'm not seeing Lieutenant Swanson. I don't even know her very well. Besides, I'm engaged." He took out his wallet and showed Aaron a photo inside. "This is Trudie, my fiancée back home in Charlotte."

Aaron looked at the photo. In it, Doyle had his arm around a young woman at a county fair. The young woman was holding up her hand to the camera, showing off her engagement ring.

"Don't get me wrong," Doyle said. "Lieutenant Swanson's a great lady, but our relationship is strictly professional." He closed his wallet. "Wait a minute. Is this what people think? You all think Swanson and I are an item?"

Aaron, too, was confused.

"No wonder then! I couldn't understand why..." A look of realization dawned on Doyle's face. He crossed his arms and started to think.

"You couldn't understand why what?" Aaron asked.

"I didn't know why Captain Milton kept pairing me and Swanson to work together. She even gave us time off together to go sightseeing and tour the city. I thought it was kind of her to do that, seeing I'm new here and all. It was okay the first couple of times, but after that, I didn't want to keep bothering Swanson, so I invited others to join us. Now that you mention it, maybe the captain misunderstood too. Maybe she thought she was doing us a favor to give us time alone. Well, good thing Swanson left then. Would've been embarrassing for her if we had to explain everything to everyone. I wonder how this misunderstanding got started..."

As Doyle continued to talk, Aaron's face turned progressively paler. He didn't want to believe it, but what had happened was all too clear to him.

Most importantly though, where was Ellie now? "Dr. Doyle, you said Lieutenant Swanson's promotion ceremony was yesterday. Do you know if she has left for Normandy yet? Is she still here?"

"She leaves today," Doyle said. "I believe she and Lieutenant Graham have left for the Lido di Roma Airfield. Doris at the reception desk would probably know. You can ask her. Gosh, I hope Swanson won't be upset if she ever finds out. Honestly, I never did anything to misrepresent..."

Without waiting for him to finish, Aaron rushed past him out of the room straight to the lobby to Doris' desk.

The driver sped over the roads toward the Lido di Roma Airfield outside of Rome. Although not far, only twenty-five kilometers away, the ride seemed excruciatingly long. Aaron felt as though it was taking forever to get there. He repeated in his mind over and over again what Brent Doyle had said, and what Fran had told him. He didn't want to believe Fran had lied to him, or that she had intentionally deceived him, but there was no other explanation. She had told him Doyle and Ellie were seeing each other.

He wanted to believe otherwise. He considered the possibility that Fran had made an honest mistake. She wouldn't go to this extent to manipulate him and the people around him, would she? Maybe she had the wrong impression about Doyle and Ellie, and she had meant well to give them a chance to spend more time with each other.

Fran was a longtime colleague. A trusted friend, despite her sometimes difficult personality and her temporarily misplaced affection for him. He wanted to give her the benefit of the doubt that everything was one big misunderstanding, but he knew that was not the case. Fran never concerned herself with the staff's personal lives. Even if Doyle and Ellie were really seeing each other, Fran would not have bothered to do them any favors by giving them time together unless work required it. Besides, she was an intelligent woman. She would have realized her mistake very quickly.

No. It was not a mistake. She had meant to manipulate everyone around her, including him. He had trusted her enough to never question her motives. When it came to Ellie, he kept doubting himself because of his age. All it took was for Fran to give him a reason to give up, and he easily surrendered his hopes. He convinced himself that Ellie would be better off with Doyle. And now, the scheme to pair Ellie off with Doyle having failed, Fran had decided to send Ellie away.

You fool, Aaron chastised himself. A desperate urgency seized him. He might never see Ellie again.

The jeep slowed down on the road behind several cars in front of him. He leaned out the window to see what was holding them up. Further ahead, a military truck loaded with supplies was trudging along at snail's pace and stalling everyone behind. Impatient, he checked his watch. He was running out of time. *Move!*

He wished he could make the vehicles move faster with his mind.

Finally, the road widened and the cars behind the truck were able to move into another lane and pass. He hoped he could still make it to the airfield in time. He didn't know what he would say or do if he caught up to her. All he knew was he didn't want her to disappear from his life.

At the Lido di Roma Airfield, the guard let the driver through the entrance and pointed them toward a Douglas C-47 Skytrain at the beginning of a runway out on the field. The driver drove toward the plane. When he stopped, Aaron got out of the jeep as quickly as he could. He spotted Ellie right away among the group of medical corpsmen and nurses who were leaving. She was with Tessa Graham, Tessa's new husband Lieutenant Anthony Ardley, and Captain Warren Hendricks. Aaron ran toward them. It no longer mattered how ridiculous he might look to be running after a girl like this at his age. All that mattered was that he did not miss her.

"Ellie! Ellie!" he called out to her. Everyone turned to look his way. Disregarding the curious stares, he ran up to Ellie. Ellie watched him coming toward her, stunned. Tessa, too, looked surprised, but she immediately pulled on Anthony's elbow and gestured for him to move away with her. They walked toward the airplane with Warren following behind them.

When they were out of earshot, Aaron took a step closer to Ellie. "I thought I'd never catch you. I thought I missed you."

"Dr. Haley," she said, still stunned. "Aren't you supposed to be in Naples?"

"I came back early," he said, excited and out of breath. "I came here as quickly as I could when I found out you're being transferred. I didn't want you to leave without letting you know…" He paused. He didn't know what he meant to say. Behind them, the airplane engine vroomed. The departing personnel began to board the plane.

"Letting me know what?" Ellie asked.

He took a deep breath. Letting her know what? What should he say? Where should he begin? "I, eh…"

She looked at him, perplexed.

The putters of the plane's propeller reminded him that he was running out of time. He looked into her eyes. "Letting you know that I would really, really like to take you out to dinner."

Ellie looked away, trying to suppress herself from laughing. He, too, felt silly and wanted to laugh.

She glanced up at him. "What about Captain Milton?"

"What about her?"

"Aren't you and the captain…" Her voice trailed off. He didn't know what she was hinting at. Warily, she said, "I saw a wood ornament in Captain Milton's room. It looks like one of your wood carvings. Did you ever give Captain Milton a gift of one of your wood carvings?"

"No." He didn't understand why she was asking about a wood carving of all things right now. "I never gave her anything. She did take a little heart I made for a GI once, but it had a chip on it and I was going to throw it away. Why are we talking about this? What does this have to do with anything?"

"She said it was a Valentine's Day's gift."

"It was. The GI needed a Valentine's Day gift for his fiancée. Since I chipped that one, I made him another one."

She broke into a smile and looked at him with renewed hope. He couldn't tell what Ellie was thinking. Maybe she wanted him to carve a heart for her? Maybe she wanted him to give her a gift, like the GI gave his fiancée a gift? Nervous, he said, "If you want, I'll make one for you."

Her face blushed. "That's not what I meant."

The last few of the transferred personnel were now climbing into the plane. "You still haven't answered me," he said. "Would you like to have dinner with me?"

This time, she laughed. "I'll have to check my schedule," she joked. "But yes. I would like that very much." Her eyes became teary.

He couldn't be happier. All he had done was asked her to dinner, but her acceptance implied so much more.

She turned and looked at the plane. "I have to go."

He wished she didn't.

"Write to me?" she asked.

"I'll write to you. Every chance I get."

She gave him one final smile, then picked her rucksack up from the ground and walked toward the plane. Halfway there, she turned around.

"Don't forget you promised me a date," he called.

"I won't." She continued on. His eyes followed her. At the plane's entrance, she looked at him one last time and waved goodbye.

Away from Ellie and Aaron Haley, Tessa embraced Anthony one last time before saying their final goodbyes. Earlier this morning, she had told herself she would not cry when she left. She didn't want Anthony's last memory of her to be one of a wailing mess. She wanted him to remember her happy. In his arms, she strained to hold back her tears.

"Take care of yourself, all right?" Anthony said, his voice ever so gentle. "Don't forget to write."

"I won't." Tessa took a deep breath. "You too."

"Remember, we're getting closer to the end every day. We're on to the Germans. It'll all be over soon." He gave her one last kiss and whispered, "Eternal City. Don't forget."

"I won't." She rested her head against his chest, feeling his warmth and his presence until time ran out. She could not believe he would be out of reach again. When would they see each other next?

"I love you." Unwillingly, he let her go.

"I love you too," she said. "Be careful."

He picked her rucksack up from the ground. They gazed at each other, their eyes expressing a thousand words that they could not say in the short moments that still remained.

"Don't worry, Tessa," Warren said. "I'll look after him for you."

Tessa squeezed out a smile. "Thank you, Warren. Goodbye."

"Goodbye, and Godspeed."

She looked at Anthony again. He looked right back at her. She tore away from his gaze only when she could delay no longer. Reluctantly, she walked toward the aircraft. When she reached the plane's entrance, she turned around. In that moment, she caught a glimpse of Anthony, looking as sad as she had ever seen him. He always held a positive, optimistic front when he was with her. Always trying to shield her from sadness and pain. He would only ever allow himself to show his own sadness when he thought she was not looking. She wished she could tell him that she knew how he felt too, that she shared all his sadness, fear, and despair. If only he could hear what she was saying to him in her heart.

She looked past Anthony and Warren and gazed at the airfield's entrance from beyond. There was no sign of Jesse. Part of her was relieved that he hadn't shown up. If he had, she didn't know what she would say to him or what would happen. It would be very awkward with Anthony here. Nonetheless, it didn't feel right to leave things the way they had ended yesterday. No matter what, she owed Jesse an answer. But now, she was leaving, and there was no time left for her to do anything about what had happened between them.

A storm raged within her heart as she climbed into the plane. She hadn't known before how much she had grown to care about Jesse.

Inside the plane, she dropped her rucksack on the floor and took a seat. Ellie came on board and sat down next to her. The door of the airplane closed, shutting out Anthony and tearing him away from her.

The airplane began to move. It accelerated down the runway until it took off and ascended into the air. From the windows, Tessa could see the limited view of the sky. A paralyzing sensation of weightlessness filled her body.

"Feels like we're on a roller coaster, doesn't it?" Ellie asked.

Tessa couldn't tell. This was her first plane ride. The new experience temporarily distracted her, and she was almost thankful for it.

The plane reached its target altitude and the passengers soon settled, searching for ways to pass the time. Seeing that Tessa was upset and wanting to keep to herself, Ellie took out a book to read, although she hadn't turned the page once since she had opened it. She stared at the words, smiling to herself. Tessa doubted that she even saw what was written on the pages. Clearly, she was thinking about Dr. Haley. At least she looked happy. It was so unusual to see Ellie lost in a daydream.

Tessa wished she could think of Anthony in the way Ellie was thinking of Dr. Haley, without all the tormenting sadness and emptiness. Perhaps she should be glad for the time she did have with Anthony, instead of dwelling on their separation. In Rome, they had created such beautiful memories. Those sweet memories of them walking down the aisle together on their wedding day and the magnificent sunset over the bridge Ponte Sant'Angelo that evening. In the heart of the Eternal City, they had vowed to be with each other forever.

No. She had no regrets. Even though they had to separate now, she did not regret that she had come to find him. If she had to, she would do it all over again. She would follow him to the end of this world. She would do anything to be with him. She pulled out her rose pendant to remind herself.

I love you more than you'll ever know.

The image of Jesse, full of pain, cut into her mind and broke her thought.

Jesse. Where was he now? What was he doing? She could feel his pain like her own pain. Her heart went out to him. Why did her pursuit of her own dream have to cause him pain?

Unable to think her way out, she looked around the aircraft's cabin. Sitting on her left, a medic was doodling on a stationery pad. He looked young, not much older than herself.

"What are you drawing?" she asked him.

"I'm drawing me." He showed her a sketch of a comical looking cartoon character with stuffed cheeks and an expanded waist. The character was falling backward with one leg kicking up in the air. Next to the character, he had drawn a large plate of spaghetti. Above the illustration, he had written, "Tyler eating his last Italian meal in Rome." Tessa took one look and chuckled.

"This was me eating dinner last night," the medic said. "I'm lousy with words. I don't write well. I'm better at drawing. I send drawings to my folks to let them know what I've been doing."

"I'm not very good with words either," Tessa said and looked more closely at the medic's drawing. "You're very talented."

"You like it? Here. Look at this one." He flipped the pages of the pad backward to show her another sketch. In that sketch, a private with droopy eyebrows and black loopy eyes had fallen asleep next to an empty bottle. Puffs of air were blowing out of his nose and mouth. An arrow with the words "Wild Turkey—stolen liquor" pointed at the bottle. "My buddy Owen, plastered," was written across the bottom of the page.

"Don't tell the brass, or I'll get into trouble." The medic, who was himself a private, gave her a conspiratorial wink.

"I won't." Tessa gave the pad back to him. "I draw too, but not comics like these. I don't have your sense of humor either."

"What do you draw?"

"I paint. I'm still learning the different styles and techniques, although I haven't painted since I was deployed. I hope to get back to it when the war's over. It's one thing I really miss doing."

"Sorry to hear that." The medic took back the sketch pad and held out his hand. "I'm Tyler. Tyler Renfield. What's your name?"

"Tessa." She shook his hand. "Tessa Graham."

"Lieutenant Graham."

"You can call me Tessa," she whispered. Tyler felt like someone she would have been friends with if they had met anywhere else.

Tyler hesitated, then shrugged. "Okay. Where are you heading? Do you know?"

"I'm joining the 51st Field Hospital."

"We'll both be with the First Army then. I'm joining the First Army's medical detachment. Where are you from? I'm from Philadelphia."

"London," she said. Then, glancing at her wedding ring, she added, "Chicago."

"You're from London and Chicago?"

"I was from London." She thought of Anthony's gentle smile. "Chicago's my home now."

"I see. Look, I'm almost done with my sketch. If you want, I can draw something for you to send home. Maybe a drawing of you on this airplane?"

"You would do that?" Tessa asked. "I would like that very much. Thank you!"

Tyler returned to his drawing. Alone with her thoughts again, Tessa twiddled her wedding ring on her finger and thought of Anthony. As the plane flew farther and farther away from Rome, her thoughts became more and more clear.

Chicago. That was her new home.

Chicago was where her heart belonged.

She took her own notepad out of her bag and began to write the hardest letter she had ever had to write.

———

On the ground, Anthony watched the aircraft's door slam shut, separating him from the girl he loved. The humming of the airplane engine grew louder. Soon, the plane rolled down the runway and lifted into the air. The sight of the carrier became smaller and smaller until finally, it disappeared into the faraway sky.

When would they see each other again?

"Come on, Ardley," Warren said from behind him. "Let's go."

They left the airfield and rode in silence back to Rome. With Tessa gone, Anthony was in no mood to talk. Thankfully, Warren didn't try to engage him in a conversation. Warren was a good friend that way. Whenever things fell to rock bottom, he would come around to Anthony, being near enough to give Anthony support, but keeping enough distance to not intrude upon him.

"Look, donut girls." Warren pointed to the small truck where two Red Cross volunteers were passing out donuts and coffee to the GIs. "Let's get some donuts."

"I don't know..." Anthony didn't want to. He had no appetite.

"Come on," Warren said. "We can't pass this up. We'll be back to inedible rations before you know it." He told the driver to stop.

Not wanting to spoil the fun for his friend, Anthony went along. The music of Harry James' "I'll Get by As Long As I Have You" played on the radio inside the truck. One of the donut girls came out and started dancing with the GIs.

"Hi there, soldier. Where're you from?" The other donut girl in the truck asked Warren.

"Chicago, Miss," Warren said. "Where are you from?"

"St. Louis."

"St. Louis? Oh no! Tell me you're not a Cardinals fan?"

"I sure am."

"Oh! Oh!" Warren put his hands over his heart. "I'm crushed."

"So am I," the girl laughed. "I guess there's no future for us. Here's a donut for you." She gave a donut to Warren, then turned to Anthony. "Would you like one too?"

"Sure," Anthony said, only to be polite.

"Here you go." She handed one to him. "And a cup of coffee for each of ya."

They took the treats and walked away from the truck. On the side of the street, an old woman peddling souvenirs in a cart smiled at them.

"Are those Roman coins?" Warren went over to her,

intrigued. "Will you look at that!" He picked one up and showed Anthony.

"You collect coins?" Anthony asked.

"My father did," Warren said. "My little sister and I kept his collection after he died." He picked up another one. "Amazing. It's the bust of Julius Caesar." He handed the coin to the woman. "I'll take this. How much?"

The woman held up five fingers, indicating fifty lire. Warren paid her and took the coin.

"A little on the expensive side, isn't it?" Anthony asked.

"Yeah, but just think how extraordinary this is. This coin's been around since 49 B.C. Besides, Bessie's going to love this."

"Bessie. Your little sister?"

"Yep. We'll add it to father's collection when I get home." He put the coin into his pocket. Watching Warren, Anthony was reminded that everyone else, including Warren, was separated from people they loved and cared about too.

He resolved in his heart that until this war was over, he would do everything he could to look out for everyone, to make sure they all could one day reunite with the ones they loved.

Part Four

MISSION: ORION

Part Four

CHAPTER TWELVE

ALTHOUGH TESSA HAD LEFT ONLY a few hours ago, the circumstances of war did not give Anthony any time to dwell on her departure. When he returned to his base, an order came for him to report to Colonel Callahan at once.

"We're moving on from Italy for our next phase of operation," Callahan told him. "Our next mission, code name Operation Anvil, is set to go. We'll launch our next attack in France on August 15."

His mind still on Tessa, Anthony did his best to push his personal thoughts aside and focus on the news and the tasks ahead.

"Our forces are mobilizing and reorganizing in Naples, Salerno, and Palermo. All American divisions in the Fifth Army, including the Third, will be reassigned to join the Seventh Army to push the Germans out of Southern France."

That would be less than six weeks from now. Anthony wondered if Captain Harding would recover well enough by then to lead their company. "Sir, how is Captain Harding? Will he recover in time to join us?"

"Ah, yes," the colonel said. "That's another thing I want to talk to you about. Captain Harding will no longer be with your company. It's Major Harding now. He's been promoted to direct the transfer and administration of replacement soldiers in Naples."

"We'll have a new company CO then?"

"Yes, you will." The colonel held out his hand. "Congratulations, Captain Ardley."

"Captain..." A moment passed before Anthony understood what Callahan meant. "Thank you, sir." He shook the colonel's hand.

"You earned it. Captain Harding gave you a glowing recommendation."

"He did?" Anthony found that hard to believe considering their strained relationship.

"We had several candidates under consideration. Major Harding thought you'd be the best choice."

While Anthony tried to take in the news, Lt. Dennison knocked on the door. Dennison was Company H's second lieutenant who had been held up with them back in the caves at Anzio. When they could not remain at the caves any longer, Anthony had put him in charge of leading the injured troops and Harding out of the caves and back to the army hospital.

Callahan invited Dennison to enter. "Captain Ardley, meet your new first lieutenant."

"Lee Dennison reporting for duty, sir," Dennison said to Anthony.

Anthony couldn't be more pleased. "Welcome aboard, Lieutenant."

Aboard the *U.S.S. Boyle*, Anthony took a walk through the decks to check on his men. The military vessel was sailing away from Italy. Rome was becoming a distant memory. The battle of Anzio was all behind him.

Operation Anvil was in full gear with all their battleships steaming ahead. In less than three hours, the Third Division would land in Saint-Tropez. The paratroopers had already taken off, targeting to launch the first wave of attacks to prevent a German counter-offensive from inland when the Allied infantry units landed on the southern coast of France. A battalion of military ships followed, ready and loaded with canons set to blast away the enemy before the infantry units set foot on shore.

On the upper deck, Anthony came upon two young privates talking quietly to themselves by the rails. Although he faced the same dangers in their missions, he always found it hard to look at the new recruits. They looked like stranded orphans, left on their own to fend for themselves in violent situations they could never have imagined. Worse, the recruits transitioned in and out so fast as the casualties mounted, he could never fully identify and account for everyone in his own company.

The two recruits quickly stood at attention when they saw Anthony coming toward them.

"At ease," Anthony said. One of the boys' faces looked familiar. "Ed? Edmond Ferris?"

"Anthony Ardley?" Edmond Ferris blurted out before noticing the silver bars on Anthony's uniform. "Sorry. I mean, Captain Ardley."

Anthony remembered now. He and Edmond had gone to the same academy back in Chicago, except Edmond was three years younger. Edmond was on the school's swim team too. They didn't know each other well back then because Edmond was only a sophomore and Anthony was already a senior. Afterward, Anthony went to college, and they hadn't seen each other since. "When did you get here?" Anthony asked.

"Three weeks ago," Edmond said. "I was shipped straight here from Camp Dover. Him too." He pointed to the recruit next to him.

"What's your name?" Anthony asked.

"Ross, sir," the other recruit said, clearly nervous. "My name's Percy Ross."

Anthony smiled to put him at ease. "Ed and I went to the same high school," he said, more fondly than he should. Seeing someone from back home, he momentarily reverted to his civilian self. "How are your parents?" he asked Edmond. He had met both of Edmond's parents at past swimming competitions.

"They're good," Edmond said. "Thanks for asking."

He would have to write and tell his parents about this, Anthony thought. Edmond's mother served on several charity committees with his own mother, and their fathers had occasional business dealings together.

"Captain Ardley and I were on the swim team together," Edmond said to Percy, "He was captain back then too."

Yes. Captain. Captain of the swim team. Anthony could remember the day they won the state championship. That former life felt so far away. His role as captain here required him to carry a much greater burden.

A new thought occurred to him. These two boys had no battle experience. What responsibility did he have to prepare them for the horrors they were about to see?

He recalled the time when he himself had arrived as a fresh recruit. Back then, Harding had sent him to lead a dangerous mission, even though Anthony had never fought a real battle. Trusting, naive, and eager to prove himself, he was ready to do whatever anyone asked. Until Wesley explained it to him, he didn't realize that Harding had considered a fresh, inexperienced recruit like Anthony as dispensable, and had planned to use him as a human shield and to distract the enemy.

What would Mr. and Mrs. Ferris think if they knew Edmond was under his command? Would they trust him with their son's life? The gravity of his responsibility as their captain struck him hard.

"Who's your platoon leader?" Anthony asked Edmond.

"Sergeant Oliver, sir."

That was good to know. "You're with me too then. Sergeant Oliver and I will be bringing the first wave of men on shore. When we get to the beach, try to follow me and stay close to me. Get across the beach as fast as you can and stay alert. You too, Percy."

"Yes, sir," they answered.

"Get some rest while you can. We'll be landing soon." Anthony started to leave.

"Captain," Edmond called out after him. Anthony looked back.

"It's good to see you again," Edmond said.

Anthony acknowledged him and walked on. He hoped both of those boys would make it out okay. He hoped he could be the captain worthy enough for them to follow his command and to risk their lives.

Arriving near the shores of Saint-Tropez, Anthony led his company in climbing off the ship into the LCTs. Their reconnaissance planes had returned, and the locations of the enemy outposts had been transmitted to the naval command. The amphibious attack was about to begin.

Furious roars of American naval cannons sounded all around them. The blasts were soon joined by the rocket boats showering missiles across the stretch of beach. The missiles detonated the mines lurking under the sand, curtailing the dangers the enemy had planned for the infantry, but also reminding them of the peril that awaited them.

The LCT that carried Anthony and his troops sailed forward. Standing close to the front, Anthony made every effort to keep his mind alert. From the outside, he looked every bit the officer in control. No one except him knew the rapid pumping of his heart, or the beads of sweat dripping down his scalp underneath his helmet. His tension rose with the choppy bumps of the LCT cutting through the wakes.

Not too far from him, Ed Ferris and Percy Ross huddled on the landing craft's floor. Ed's face was as white as a sheet. Percy was throwing up, either from seasickness or terror, or both.

"Stay close to me." Anthony put his hand on Ed's shoulder. Too stressed to speak, Ed stared at him with his mouth agape.

Oddly, the enemy on land still did not return fire.

The LCT came to a stop. Anthony stepped into the water. Back when he landed in Anzio, they had gone into the attack at the height of winter. At least this time, the water was not freezing cold.

As with Anzio, their landing seemed unobstructed. Only random cracks of gunfire greeted them. The enemy defense appeared to be non-existent.

Could they be this lucky again? Had they caught the Germans by surprise?

Anthony shouted for his men to rush forward. They had gone only a few steps onto the shore when the explosions swelled up from the ground. Their naval rockets had not been able to clear out all the mines, and now, their infantry soldiers were setting them off.

Between the blasts, Anthony heard the howl of a familiar voice. He turned around just in time to see Ollie step onto a mine. The explosion thrust Ollie's body up into the air. He flopped down onto the ground with blood streaking all over his face. Only stumps remained where his legs used to be. The sergeant had breathed his last breath.

With no time to give thoughts to the dead, Anthony turned his attention away from Ollie's body and scanned the land ahead. The beach ran inland to a field. He could not see any spot where the enemy could conceal their gun posts. His biggest threats were the mines. The blasts of mine explosions continued, and he knew more of his men were being killed.

Still, they could not remain in place to avoid the mines. They would be standing targets if they didn't move. And they had to secure the beach, fast.

He took a step forward, tiptoeing lightly even though he knew it would not do any good. The mines would detonate with just a few pounds of weight. With each step, he took a deep breath, hoping his next step would not be his last. This was worse than walking on eggshells. His heartbeat went into overdrive. His uniform was soaked in sweat.

Finally, he reached the green field at the end of the beach. He leapt into a drainage ditch for cover. Ed and Percy jumped in after him. They had stayed close to him, just like he had told them when they were on the ship.

Still catching his breath in relief, Anthony signaled the men behind him to head toward the farmhouses beyond the fields.

"Those farmhouses may be enemy strongholds," he said to Ed and Percy. "If they shoot at you, you put them down before they put you down. You have your guns. Use them."

Nervously, Ed clutched his rifle. Percy looked like he wanted to vomit again.

"Move!" Anthony shouted. He jumped out of the ditch and sprinted ahead. As soon as they began to run across the field, a sniper began shooting at them from a second-story window of the farmhouse closest to them. Quickly, Anthony dashed behind a large pile of wood and aimed. Ed and Percy followed. Before Anthony pulled the trigger, Ed stood up, exposing himself in the open, and shot down the gunman behind the window. The kill surprised even Ed himself.

"A lucky shot, sir," Ed said.

Next to Ed, Percy sat on the ground, trembling with his rifle in his hands.

Popping sounds came from the farmhouse again. Another sniper had taken over and replaced the fallen German soldier. Anthony ignored Percy, aimed again and fired. The rest of their men joined in. The scant number of enemy troops could not defend themselves and were soon subdued.

Leaving behind a group of soldiers to take over the farmhouse, Anthony led his troops toward the next house. This time, the enemy soldiers did not put up a fight. Their leader exited the house holding a piece of white cloth. The rest surrendered with their arms raised above their heads.

Anthony could not believe how easy this had been. Within hours, they had raided all the houses and barns in the area, and cleared their target sector. They had captured more than eighty German prisoners. Their swift victory exceeded all expectations.

When the battle was over, Anthony went to the old barn where Ed and Percy's platoon had chosen to bunk for the night.

"You doing all right?" he asked.

"Yes, sir," Ed said.

Percy was not doing so well. He sat on the floor, disoriented.

"Is he okay?" Anthony asked Ed.

"He's frazzled, I guess…"

Anthony understood. He felt sorry for Percy, but at least Ed was taking everything in stride. "Get some rest. We'll be moving again tomorrow."

"Yes, sir," Ed said, his eyes full of admiration. Anthony did not know how to handle being admired. Of course, he wanted his men to respect him. In fact, their respect was necessary for him to carry out his duty to command. But admiration? He felt flattered, yet overwhelmed. He felt an urge to live up to what Edmond saw in him. "Ed," he said, "it'll all be okay. We got your six."

"I know." Ed showed not a trace of doubt. "Thank you, Captain."

Anthony returned to the farmhouse where his company had set up its temporary command post. There, Lee Dennison had already accounted for all of their casualties. Fox, their reliable young sharpshooter, came in with a stack of K-rations.

"Have you seen Jonesy?" Anthony asked.

"I saw him go off back toward the beach," Dennison said.

"Does he know about Ollie yet?" Anthony had to ask. His own spirit dropped as he remembered the sight of Ollie's corpse after the mine blew up.

"Yeah," Dennison said. "He didn't take the news very well…"

Anthony was afraid of that. The news must be killing Jonesy. "Does anyone know where he is?"

"I do," Fox said, his ashen face revealing the sadness they all felt. "He's in one of the decoy pillboxes behind the beach."

Anthony knew what he had to do. He took a bottle of water and one of the dinner rations Fox had brought in, and went out to look for Jonesy.

In a pillbox, Jonesy sat on the ground, listless. Ollie's rucksack lay beside him. He remained slumped even when Anthony entered and made no attempt to get up.

Anthony came closer. Jonesy was crying. He had never seen Jonesy cry before.

Ollie...

There was nothing Anthony could say that would make Jonesy feel better. Ollie and Jonesy were close like brothers. They had fought together for over a year. In war, nothing was tougher than seeing your friend killed. Anthony felt horrible himself. Ollie was a good soldier, and he didn't begrudge Anthony for being an inexperienced officer back when they were in Sicily. It was such a waste, for Ollie to live through Anzio only to die here. Watching Jonesy, Anthony wanted to sit down and mourn too. But he couldn't. A full company of men depended on him. And right now, he had to get Jonesy back to a functioning state. He pushed his own sentiments aside and squatted down next to Jonesy. "You okay?"

Jonesy didn't answer. He looked utterly drained and defeated.

"You gonna spend the rest of the night here?"

Jonesy stared into space with bloodshot eyes. Tears continued to roll down his face.

"Do you need anything?"

The first sergeant remained silent.

As much as Anthony wanted to let him grieve, there wasn't much time for that. He needed Jonesy to recover. Having lost Ollie, he needed Jonesy more than ever. Their lives depended on it.

"You can stay here for the night." Anthony put down the water and the box of rations he had brought with him. "Do what you have to and get it all out of your system. Tomorrow, we got jobs to do. I need you to get your act together, all right?"

Jonesy's face twisted as if he was in agony.

"You have to pull yourself together," Anthony said, as sympathetically as he could but remaining firm at the same time. "I expect you and your platoon to be ready and prepared when we move out tomorrow. You got that, First Sergeant?"

Jonesy turned his head and looked away.

"Report to me at 0800. That's an order." Anthony got up. The best thing he could do for Jonesy now was to give him things to do. Keep him busy and divert his attention to something else. Otherwise, his grief would only grow. It would eat at him and make him more depressed.

Anthony left the pillbox. Good thing Jonesy didn't see how Ollie had died. Anthony himself would not get much sleep tonight. Not with the sight of Ollie's dismembered body and blood-soaked face still vivid in his mind.

CHAPTER THIRTEEN

WHEN ANTHONY ARRIVED at the regiment headquarters, he had expected to see Colonel Callahan for another briefing. Operation Anvil had gotten off to a good start. The Seventh Army had taken over the beach of Saint-Tropez in just one day. Casualties were minimal. Their mission's success had boosted the troops' morale, and they had all the momentum to win.

Whether they would win remained to be seen. Back in Anzio, their landing had been equally successful. No one could have foreseen the long, drawn-out battle that followed. If Anzio had taught Anthony anything, it was that a perfect landing was not a battle won. Not yet.

He entered the headquarters' main meeting room and found, to his great surprise, the person waiting for him was not Colonel Callahan. "General Castile."

General Castile stood tall with his arms behind his back, his commanding air of authority as indomitable as ever. Still, Anthony was happy to see him. General Castile was the one who had driven him to excel back when he was still at training camp. Later on, the general had made it possible for Tessa to join him in Italy.

Anthony couldn't believe the general was here and had summoned him. The last time he saw General Castile, Anthony hadn't even been deployed.

"It's been a while, Captain," General Castile greeted him and made a point of noticing the silver bars pinned on Anthony's uniform. "You've done well."

"Thank you, sir." Anthony tried to keep his expression straight and respectful, but he couldn't help letting a smile escape. It was hard not to be flattered by a compliment coming from General Castile.

"I'll get right to business," General Castile said. "Operation Anvil's going as well as command had hoped. The Germans are in a state of flux. Their communications and defense here are broken. We think up north is where the heavy fighting will be."

Anthony was glad to hear that. While he sympathized with the troops in northern France, he did not want his own men to suffer again what they had experienced in Anzio.

"But we aren't taking any chances. The Seventh Army will continue to drive its way up." General Castile walked over to the map on the desk. "We won't make the same mistake we did in Anzio. We won't give the Germans any chance to mobilize and throw another counter-attack. The Seventh Army troops will drive west immediately to Toulon and Marseille, then onward to Montélimar. We're going to take the entire southern region." He circled his pen around the region the Allied forces planned to occupy. "The Free French Army has already moved into Toulon and Marseille. Their guerrilla attacks are taking a toll on the Germans. When our boys arrive, we should be enough to drive the Germans out."

"That's good news, sir," Anthony said. "My company and I are ready. What do you need us to do?"

Castile opened a folder on the table and showed him several photos. Anthony recognized one of the men in the photos right away. Klaus.

What did the army want with Klaus?

"Do you recognize this man?" General Castile asked.

"Yes, sir. Major Heinrich Klaus. Wehrmacht star commanding officer." Anthony remembered his last encounter with the man, when Klaus had gotten away in Cisterna. "We've had several confrontations with him."

General Castile nodded. "I want you to lead a strike team to pursue Klaus. Capture him."

Klaus again? Anthony didn't understand. Back in Anzio, their company had gone after Klaus because Captain Harding had a personal vendetta against him, but for what reason would the U.S. Army want to go after him?

"Sir, may I ask why?"

A grave look overtook General Castile. "We may look like we're winning the war here, but none of it will matter if Hitler succeeds with his weapons program." Castile handed Anthony a set of confidential documents titled "Amerika Bomber." "One of Hitler's secret weapons is a strategic long-range bomb that can be set off from France to reach as far as New York, and possibly beyond. We believe this weapon is still under development. But if he succeeds, and his bombs reach American soil, you can imagine the consequences."

Anthony flipped through the "Amerika Bomber" report, and came to a page that listed Hitler's intended targets. General Motors, Indianapolis. Chrysler, Detroit. Alcoa, Tennessee, and at least sixteen other locations. All were manufacturers of American aircraft parts. Plus, New York City. Anthony felt a chill running up his spine. American cities could be destroyed.

"We need to find out as much information as we can and stop this program," Castile said. "Hitler has a select group of

Wehrmacht commanders who have access to his weapons program information. These commanders are strategically placed to launch the missiles from different locations in Europe. Heinrich Klaus is one of them."

Anthony recalled the times he had come face-to-face with Klaus. "You want me to find him?"

"Yes." Castile looked dead serious. "The army is setting up strike teams to search for all the key targets who may be privy to the information we need. We want you to lead the team that targets Klaus. The code name for your mission is Orion. You will choose who to assign to your team from your company. We'll provide you with support units under your command as you need."

Wary, Anthony picked up one of the photos. Klaus's icy, serene eyes stared back at him.

"Think you're up for the job?" General Castile asked.

"Yes," Anthony said. He didn't relish the thought of having to go after Klaus again, but General Castile had come in person to give him this mission. It showed how much the general favored him. "I'll do my best, sir."

General Castile's expression softened. He glanced at the ring on Anthony's finger. "How's Lieutenant Graham?"

"Tessa?" Anthony didn't expect General Castile to ask about her. "Fine. She's fine, sir. Thank you for asking."

"She's an impressive young lady."

The general's compliment filled Anthony with pride. He could see a note of affection in Castile's eyes when the general spoke of her.

"I had reservations about placing her near you," Castile said. "I worried she might be a distraction. I'm glad my concerns were unfounded."

"She's not near me anymore, sir," Anthony said. "She's been transferred north to follow the First Army."

"Really?"

"There's been a reassignment of medical staff to cover the personnel shortage in Normandy."

"I see. Well, we all have to do what we have to until the war's over."

"Yes, sir," Anthony could only concur. The general had already indulged him and Tessa once by helping her come to join him in Italy. He wouldn't think of asking the general to do them any more favors.

"That'll be all, Captain." General Castile straightened his face once again. "Remember, Orion's mission is a top priority. Colonel Callahan will work with you to assemble your team and get you all the support you'll need." He paused and looked Anthony in the eye. "Don't fail me."

"No, sir. I won't," Anthony said.

"One more thing," Castile smiled. "If all goes well, I'll see what I can do to arrange a pass for you and Lieutenant Graham to meet up before Christmas."

Thrilled, Anthony wished he could tell Tessa right away. The general's offer was the best news he had heard all day. "Thank you, sir."

"Or," the general sighed, "God willing, the war will be over before then, and you won't even need it."

In the medical truck driving away from Saint-Tropez to join up with the Orion strike team, Jesse stared out to the fields. He and his squad of medics had been chosen by Anthony to join a new mission code-named Orion. The trucked rolled along with the medics in high spirits. Morale of the men of the Third Division remained high after the success of Operation Anvil. For Jesse though, the world had never felt bleaker. A dreary wasteland had taken over his heart.

He unfolded the letter in his hands and read it again.

Dear Jesse,

This is the hardest letter I've ever written in my life. I've started more than a dozen times. Each time, I've had to stop and start over. I am no good at talking about things. I don't know if what I say in this letter will be enough, but I will try. I will try my best. I want you to know that.

It would be easier if we could pretend that what you told me was a joke. If we could lie to ourselves, we could dismiss everything you said and did as another one of your womanising stunts. We could pretend nothing serious happened and never speak of it again. I guess that would make things easier for me, but that wouldn't be fair to you, would it?

After all those months in Anzio, I should have known. I don't know why I didn't see it. Maybe I willfully did not want to see. I don't know.

When I think back to the first time we met, and everything we've experienced in between until the day you said goodbye, I know that, in the vast scheme of things and despite all the crazy, horrible things happening around us, I am glad I met you. I have known from the moment I first saw you that you have a beautiful heart. You have a star that shines from within you. It is bright and it outshines everyone and everything around you. It was so dazzling, I couldn't look away. Behind your facade, beneath the false persona you want everyone to believe was real, I see a soul untouched by the evils of this world. To be loved by you is a precious gift. I don't take this gift lightly. I will always cherish your feelings for me.

But you must already know that I cannot return your feelings. I dare not look deeper to find out how I feel. Nothing good will come of it. If I discover that I have no feelings for you, it will only hurt you. If I discover that I do have feelings for you, it won't change the fact that I am also deeply, deeply in love with Anthony. I'm married to him. I've made a promise to commit my life to him. My heart is with him, and I never want to be without him. I cannot love two at the same time, and knowing that I have feelings for more than one will only hurt everyone. It is better for all of us to leave everything the way it is. Is this cowardly of me? Maybe. Still, I think it is for the best.

What I know for certain is that, had fate been different and destiny had put you in my life instead, my life would have been wonderful in a different way. While I cannot accept what you have to offer me, the loss is entirely mine.

There is one small thing I want to do for you. I have decided I will never dance the tango again. The last time I danced the tango, it was with you. I will give you my tango. My last tango will always be yours.

I wish I could do more in return for your love. It pains me that I cannot because I never wanted to see you hurt. I am sorry.

While I am glad that Anzio is behind us, I will forever be thankful that our lives have crossed because of it. Despite all the atrocities that had happened there, when I look back, I will always remember you as one of my best memories.

You will always be in my thoughts. Wherever I am, I will always be wishing you well.

— *Tessa*

The medical truck continued on. Jesse folded the letter and put it back into his pocket. He had lost count of how many times he had read it.

But you must already know I cannot return your feelings.

Hopeless. Everything was hopeless from the start.

Had fate been different and destiny had put you in my life instead, my life would have been wonderful in a different way.

Fate. Yes. Of course. Fate had always been good to him, except for the one time when it mattered to him.

I am deeply, deeply in love with Anthony.

Anthony. Why did Anthony have to come into her life before him?

I don't want to be without him.

Those words pierced him like a dagger through his heart. He felt his heart dripping blood. He felt his insides shredded to pieces.

The box of medical supplies bounced and shook every time the truck hit a bump on the road. How many times had he mended the wounds of men and used those supplies to stop others from bleeding? The joke was on him. Nothing in the box could stop his own bleeding. Nothing could put the pieces of him back together.

When I look back, I will always remember you as one of my best memories.

Already, she was talking of him as a memory in the past. Was there no room for him in her present? No room at all?

The voice of the gypsy woman in Naples came back to him.

You're her guardian angel.

He laughed bitterly to himself. How? How could he be her guardian angel? They were hundreds of miles apart. They probably wouldn't see each other ever again. What could he possibly do for her now?

She'll know how important you are to her. In time.

Would she? When?

Fool. He was an utter, hopeless fool.

Why was he taking seriously the words of a vagrant gypsy?

The vehicles carrying Anthony and his men sped down the rocky road leading to Montélimar. Since the Orion strike team assembled and departed Saint-Tropez a week ago, he had been chasing Klaus. After the Free French Army defeated the Germans in Toulon and Marseille, Klaus had fled to join the German forces in Montélimar. The city was a German stronghold. If they let him reach there first, it would be that much harder to capture him. The strike team had to make good time if they wanted to catch the elusive German commander before then.

They had passed Toulon and were coming out of Marseille when Anthony's driver slowed the vehicle.

"Captain, look," the driver said. A straggling group of American soldiers was walking ahead of them. As the Orion convoy came closer, the America soldiers stopped and moved to the side of the road.

"Pull over," Anthony told his driver. The driver pulled up next to the soldiers, a group of five privates. Anthony needed to find out who they were. Every so often, lower-ranking soldiers would purposely get lost to get a break from fighting. He needed to make sure these boys were not ducking their duties.

"What are you all doing here?" Anthony asked. "Where's the rest of your unit?"

The five soldiers exchanged glances. One of them, a private first class and the highest ranked of the group, stepped up. "We're with the 142nd, sir. We are heading to Montélimar. We're…," he gave Anthony a sheepish smile, "we're a bit lost, sir. Our company ran into some Germans and we got separated."

So these boys were with the 36th Division. Anthony knew the 36th was heading to Montélimar. "Have any of your division units arrived yet?"

"Maybe, sir. We don't know. Our company went through a lot of hills on our way here. We weren't able to communicate with the other units most of the time. We had to slow down and walk a lot, too, 'cause of the terrain, and we kept running out of fuel."

Anthony looked behind him. His own headquarters vehicle was full. There was no room to fit anyone else with Fox, Ed

Ferris, and Jesse, along with their radio operator and their team's French guide, Remy, all on board. The jeeps behind them carrying Jonesy and the rest of the soldiers on the strike team were full too. Only the supplies and artillery trucks still had room.

"We're going to Montélimar," Anthony said to the straggling soldiers. "Get into one of the supplies trucks in the back. You can ride with us till we get to the city."

"Yes, sir," the private answered. "By the way, sir, we've been seeing more and more Germans since we got into this area. They're hiding everywhere. We should be careful."

Anthony nodded. The soldier was right. They were entering German occupied zones. Just because it was quiet now didn't mean danger wasn't around the corner.

The privates walked away to the back of the Orion convoy. After they had all gotten into the supplies truck, Anthony motioned for his driver to continue, then called out to their radio operator. "Check with command. See if they have any info on German troop movements further up. See if our recon planes spotted anything."

"Yes, sir," the radio operator answered. While he tried to communicate with their regiment, Anthony sat back and looked at the road ahead. He worried that they might be running out of time.

Hours passed as the Orion convoy continued its way to Montélimar. For Jesse, the torturous boredom of the ride was enough to kill all his senses. No one in the vehicle was talking anymore. They had been riding for so long, all conversation had dried up. He wished there was some way he could relieve the monotony and doldrums.

The truck rolled along the bumpy country road, tossing the

passengers up and down on the hard flat beaten seats. To escape the discomfort, Jesse closed his eyes and let his mind return to a night far away from where he was now. A night in Naples where tango music filled the air. A night when Tessa shared with him the one and only thing she had now promised to dedicate to him. Their tango dance.

If they ever saw each other again, he would hold her to her promise. He would make her dance with him no matter what.

The vehicle came to a sudden stop at a path leading into the woods. Next to the path, the corpses of several French soldiers lay on the ground. Jesse wondered how long these bodies had been there.

"Is this the only way to go?" Anthony asked their French guide. From the front of the truck, Anthony pointed to the path leading into the woods.

"It's the fastest and most direct way," the French guide said. "If we go around the forest, we'll have to go another thirty kilometers from here. A long detour east, and we'll have to pass through a lot of twisty roads and hills."

Anthony turned his sight toward the path, then at the road ahead. "We'll go through the forest," he said to the driver, then turned to their radio operator. "Tell everyone behind to move as fast as they can through the woods. And watch out for snipers."

"Yes, Captain," the radio operator responded and turned on their radio. The convoy moved on. From the back of their truck, Jesse watched Anthony talk to the driver.

Lucky bastard. Jesse turned his eyes back toward the road. There was a time when he had genuinely enjoyed Ardley's company. Ardley was almost a friend. Someone with whom he could have a thought-provoking conversation about things that the other men in the army didn't know much about, like books, philosophy, science.

If only they didn't love the same woman.

Good thing Ardley got promoted. His promotion gave Jesse a good excuse to distance himself. Now a captain, Ardley couldn't get too close to someone below his rank.

Better to keep their distance. The last thing Jesse wanted was to hear Ardley talk about Tessa.

Ardley had no idea though. For someone so competent and intelligent, Ardley was naively trusting of people he believed to be his friends. When he picked Jesse to lead the medical squad for the Orion strike team, Jesse almost wanted to shake the guy awake. It would've been funny if it wasn't so ironic. The newly minted captain hadn't the faintest clue that he had put his life in the hands of someone who had already betrayed his trust.

It was hard, having to see Ardley day in and day out, all the while wondering what could be if this person wasn't around. What if Ardley didn't exist?

Jesse glanced at Anthony again. What if, by some cosmic arrangement of the universe, he got a chance to find out?

Not liking where his train of thought was going, Jesse forced himself to put these questions away. Farther away in the woods, bodies of dead soldiers lay spread across the ground. Out of boredom, Jesse took out his binoculars to see whether they were French or American soldiers. Through the lenses, he caught the glimpse of a body not more than thirty feet away on the ground trying to get up.

"Stop! Stop the car," Jesse shouted to the driver in the front. The vehicle came to a quick halt.

"What is it?" Anthony asked.

Jesse held up his binoculars toward the woods. The man on the ground, obviously wounded, had fallen over again. "Someone's alive."

Everyone in the vehicle looked toward the injured soldier. Through his binoculars, Jesse could see the soldier was American. "He's one of ours!"

"Some of the 36th units must have passed through," Fox said.

Anthony stood up from his seat and looked out at the direction of the wounded soldier. Everyone in the truck waited nervously for his response. Each man braced himself for the worst, in case Anthony called on him to go save the wounded man.

Jesse looked through the binoculars again. The soldier was crawling. It seemed he had injuries to his legs. There was no way the man could escape without help. Jesse lowered his binoculars and waited for Anthony to give his order, but Anthony still hadn't said anything. Jesse could see Anthony was conflicted. The anxiety among the troops intensified as they waited to see what Anthony would do.

"Ardley…Captain," Jesse asked in a low, pleading voice, "won't you send someone to get him?"

Anthony turned away from the sight of the wounded man. "No. He's too far away. There are snipers hiding out there. I won't risk any of you getting killed." He sat back down on his seat.

Jesse looked out to the injured man and reached into his pocket for his lucky seven dice. Before Anzio, before Tessa, he would've volunteered to take the chance to bring the injured soldier back. He would've insisted on it.

That was then. Back then, his life was an open auction, good for a trade with any other life more worth living than his own.

Not anymore. His life had a purpose now. He couldn't play dare with the Fates like he used to. He had someone important to live for. As long as he was alive, he lived for her.

He closed his hand around the dice. No. He couldn't risk his life. There was always a chance…

"I'll go," said Ed Ferris, the new replacement. "Captain, let me go get him. I can run fast."

"I said no," Anthony refused. "You'll get yourself killed. Sergeant," he said to the driver, "get moving."

The driver drove on. A grim and solemn mood now settled on everyone riding in the back of the truck. Jesse looked around at all their faces. Clearly, everyone felt like a louse for leaving behind one of their own. They must be wondering too. If they were ever injured and needed help like the soldier back there, would their own army leave them behind?

The injured soldier diminished from their view. Helpless, Jesse looked on. His guts were all knotted up. He felt so powerless. He couldn't change the wounded soldier's situation. He couldn't change his own situation.

The pops of sniper shots cut through the air before they had gone far. Behind them, the private first class from the straggling group of soldiers from the 142nd had run out to try to retrieve the wounded soldier. Another sniper shot knocked him to the ground, killing him instantly before he could reach the man he had tried to save.

"Tell everyone behind to keep moving!" Anthony shouted to the radio operator.

Jesse slumped down in his seat. He felt so tired. Tired of it all. Tired of everything.

Fox made a wisecrack. "Guess we're not 'out of the woods' yet."

No one laughed. The convoy drove on with Ed Ferris staring back at the woods, in shock at the instant slaughter of the private who could have been him.

CHAPTER FOURTEEN

Late in the afternoon, Fran walked into the 33rd Field Hospital's makeshift administrative office and unexpectedly found Aaron standing behind the typist giving out instructions while she prepared a document. Aaron and the typist both looked up when Fran entered, then returned to their work without acknowledging her further.

Feeling awkward, Fran stood in place. She crossed her arms and hugged the folder she was holding tightly against her chest as though it could shield her. It didn't. Everyone seemed to be ostracizing her.

This wasn't fair. She had done nothing wrong. She was only doing her job when she reassigned staff members to the hospitals up north.

She gathered her composure and walked over to Lieutenant Dillard, a matronly looking nurse who handled administration and logistics, and put the file she was holding on Dillard's desk. "Here you go, Lieutenant Dillard. I've reviewed the staffing schedule for next week. I see you've downsized the number of nurses for each shift. Why?"

"We haven't had as many patients, Captain," Dillard said.

"Our landing here has been so smooth. Most of the boys are here because of the flu, not because of combat injuries. I thought we should give our nurses some time off while we can. They've all been working so hard this year."

"Nonsense," Fran said, raising her voice. She wanted Aaron to know that she had really come to the administrative office for a work-related matter and not because he was here. Another part of her also wanted him to be aware that she was here, doing a good job as always. "We have to be prepared at all times. We're still at war. Things can turn disastrous without a moment's notice. We can't risk being short-staffed."

"I did put at least two people on call per shift."

"That's not good enough. Redo the schedule and staff the hospital the way we normally do."

Dillard dropped her shoulders and picked up the file. "Yes, Captain."

While they talked, Aaron left the typist and headed toward the exit. Fran watched him, wanting to speak to him but unsure how. "Captain." He gave Fran a cordial acknowledgment as he passed her. She stood rigid, unaware that she was twisting the pen in her hand over and over.

"Is there anything else, Captain?" Dillard asked.

"No. That'll be all," Fran said, barely paying Dillard any attention. She gathered her wits and quickly left the room. Everything had changed completely since Aaron returned from Naples. The good rapport she had had with him was gone. He had become aloof and distant. They no longer had breakfast meetings every morning or afternoon tea at the end of the day. They never worked alone together anymore. He had invited Dr. Bernstein, another high-ranking surgeon, to assist with hospital supervision. If he must meet with her, he would always invite Dr. Bernstein to join as well.

He never asked her how her day was going either anymore.

She couldn't understand. How did everything turn out this

way? Ellie Swanson was gone. Everything should have returned to the way it used to be. What went wrong?

No doubt, Aaron was displeased with Ellie Swanson's departure. Fran knew he thought she should have consulted him first. She was prepared to explain her decision, and to help him understand the military's dire need for support up north, but he never asked her about it. He wouldn't give her a chance to defend her decision.

Even if he held a grudge against her for sending Ellie away, he couldn't possibly think that he still had any more chances with Ellie Swanson, could he? Swanson was now so far away.

Back in her own quarters, Fran took off her hat and loosened her collar. There was nothing she could do for now. Aaron needed time, that was all. He hadn't gotten over the idea that Ellie was no longer here. He'd come around. At least this was what she told herself.

And if he didn't come around...Well, if he was determined to give her the cold shoulder, then it would confirm all the more that what she had done was justified. Why should he get a chance with Ellie, when Fran herself couldn't get a chance with him? Why should Ellie Swanson be able to waltz into the hospital, and without the slightest effort, take away the only man Fran had ever wanted in her life? Why should she let Ellie Swanson take it all away, when this was the one time that she had entertained the prospect of sharing her life with another person?

She lifted the blanket folded on top of her cot and picked up the chipped wooden heart she had taken from Aaron.

Let all three of them be losers then. She didn't have to be the only one losing out. They could all bear the same pangs of disappointment.

"Tessa! Tessa!" Tyler Renfield called out to Tessa at the mess hall, where she was writing a letter to her parents. "So glad I found you." He sat down across from her, excited. "I only have a few minutes before catching my ride back to the front. I wanted to show you this." He put his sketch pad in front of her. "You can send it to Captain Ardley."

She glanced at the sketch. It was a comic drawing of her sitting inside the airplane cabin, looking pouty and grumpy. Next to the illustration, he had written, "Tessa leaving Rome and Anthony."

"Here. See?" He flipped to the next page. "This is the second one." The sketch on the following page showed an exaggerated illustration of her holding out her arms and blowing kisses of little hearts, with "Tessa when Anthony's letters arrive" written across the top of the page.

"I'm not sending him this," Tessa said. "You made me look ridiculous."

"You have to send it. He needs to know how much you miss him."

"No! You're terrible." She looked at the drawing again. Her indignant amusement changed to sadness.

"What's the matter?" Tyler asked.

"Nothing." She put down her pen. "I just haven't gotten any letters from him in weeks."

"They'll come," Tyler said. "Mail's been really slow for everyone. I haven't gotten any letters from my folks either. I'm sure he's written you lots of letters by now."

Tessa gave him a grateful smile. What Tyler said was true. Mail had been exceptionally slow since they had arrived in northern France. Sometimes, she felt almost cut off from the rest of the world. The First Army was constantly on the move. Unlike Anzio where the battle had stalled in a single location, the army units here never stayed in one place long enough for the mail to get to her.

Actually, mail delay was the least of their problems. Since the First Army battalion's breakout at Saint-Lô, their troops had been moving so fast that the evacuation hospitals could not keep up. At one point, the infantry's front line had extended as far as a hundred and fifty miles ahead of the closest evac hospital. The army could not transport patients there in time for immediate surgeries. To accommodate the changing circumstances, the medical command had moved all the field hospitals as far forward as they could behind the infantry troops. The field hospitals were now giving treatments and performing surgeries that had been given and performed only at the evac hospitals before.

At the fast rate they were moving, Tessa could not be sure where she would be at the end of each day.

Right now, she was in Falaise. The First Army had liberated this town a few days ago. Unfortunately, their swift victory did not lighten the damage caused by the war. On her way here, she saw entire villages destroyed. Ruins, rubble, and abandoned army equipment lay in piles as high as buildings, obstructing the roads. Thousands of dead human and animal bodies spread all over the streets, attracting swarms of flies and maggots that reveled in the stench of decaying flesh.

Anthony must be seeing the same things where he was too. On the table, a copy of the Stars and Stripes featured the headline, "Seventh Army Takes Toulon, Marseille." The paper reported that the Seventh Army was also advancing in southern France at rapid speed.

Maybe, like he said, the war would come to an end soon. She could only hope.

While she was thinking, Ellie had come to join them. "Tessa, Tyler."

"Lieutenant Swanson," Tyler greeted her back.

Ellie gave him a quick smile, then said to Tessa, "I need your help."

"Yes?"

"There's a new patient in Ward 8. I'm having a hard time getting any of the nurses to look after him."

"Why's that?"

"They're afraid of him," Ellie said. "He looks intimidating."

Tessa and Tyler looked at each other, perplexed. After all the horrific things they had witnessed in this war, what more could intimidate the nurses?

"He's got tattoos."

"Half the guys here got tattoos." Tyler laughed. "Every navy guy's got some on his skin. I'm thinking of getting one myself. A tattoo of a K-ration. Right here." He pointed at his stomach.

"Be serious." Tessa slapped him lightly on the arm.

"His tattoos are different," Ellie said. "There are also rumors that he's the son of a mafia boss. I don't know if this is true or not. Anyway, the women are uncomfortable going near him. I don't want to force anyone. I'd take care of him myself, but I've got so much work on my hands. I have to arrange to transfer the patients with contagious diseases out of here and finish up the reports on the ones with battle fatigue so they can be evacuated." She looked pleadingly at Tessa. "I really do hate to put this on you, but do you mind?"

"I'll do it," Tessa said without hesitation.

"Thank you," Ellie said, relieved. "His name is Victor Cardozo. Everyone calls him the Blade. You only have to administer his treatment. You don't have to do anything more than that."

"Leave it to me," Tessa assured her. She was curious to find out how frightening this man might be.

"I'll see you both later then." Ellie gave Tessa another look of gratitude and took off.

"I better get going too," Tyler said. He tore the two

drawings he had made for Tessa from his sketch pad and gave them to her.

She made a face at him, feigning displeasure at the way he had depicted her. "Goodbye. And be careful."

"You be careful," he said. "Watch out for the Blade." He made a face too, pretending to be afraid.

She shook her head and watched him leave. Smiling, she folded his sketches into her own notepad and left the mess hall to go to Ward 8 to check on her new patient.

Housed temporarily in an old French hospital, Ward 8 appeared no different than any other patients' ward set up by the 51st Field Hospital. The advantage of being in an actual hospital building was that they could put the patients on real beds rather than easily movable cots on the floor. Today, the ward was no more overcrowded than usual. Everything appeared normal. Tessa scanned the room for the patient she had come to see. Her eyes swept over the soldiers who were playing a poker game in the first row of beds near the entrance, to the ones in the back who were neither sick nor injured, but were exhausted by battle and had come to sleep. On the other side of the room, a gravely wounded soldier groaned.

She continued to look around until her eyes settled on a man with a broad face and thick lips. Right away, she knew he must be the Blade. A large man, he had the rough, low-class look of someone who had spent a life in the company of people on the wrong side of the tracks. Shirtless, the raw strength of his bulky, muscular arms and shoulders laid bare on full display. He sat on the bed like a dangerous predator, ready for a hunt. Or a kill.

Tessa approached him. Like an animal in the wild, he immediately sensed Tessa's presence. His eyes, sharp and penetrating, picked up every trace of movement in his vicinity like the eyes of a hawk. By instinct, he reacted to anything that presented itself as a threat or a challenge…or a potential prey.

Wary, but undeterred, Tessa walked toward him. Up close, she could see why Ellie had mentioned his tattoos. Tattoos were common among soldiers. Many of them liked to brand their unit's insignia on their bodies as a badge of honor. Often, they liked to pierce onto themselves sentimental symbols and images of bravado too. Graphic illustrations of women in seductive poses were also commonplace.

The body art tattooed on the Blade was something else. Tessa had never seen such depictions of the grotesque. A large image of a slit inked in deep red ran down his chest over his heart like a savage cut that had ripped open his body. Emerging from the slit, a haunting demon threatened to tear his way out. The demonic image was accompanied by another tattoo on his arm, which depicted an open mouth with long, saw-like teeth, covered in blood.

Nonetheless, neither of these images came close to being as gruesome as the one on the right side of his abdomen. The tattoo was designed around an old gunshot wound. It was an ugly wound with coarse, scaly scars. Rather than hiding what remained of the former injury, the tattoo showcased the wound by portraying those scars as the scaly eyelid of a reptile. In the center, a pupil of a pinkish yellow shade was added on the wound itself to give off the appearance of real open flesh. The entire image was revolting.

No wonder the nurses didn't want to come near him. Poor Ellie. She had enough to deal with already, getting used to working in a new hospital and learning to manage the medical staff. She didn't need more trouble like this man.

Tessa walked to the end of his bed. The least she could do for Ellie was to take the problem of this vulgar man off her hands.

"Sergeant Cardozo." She picked up his medical charts hanging on the end of the bed. She could sense him watching her, observing and studying her. Ignoring his attention, she flipped the blanket off him to reveal his legs. She then took one direct look into his eyes and proceeded to straighten his leg and unwrap the bandages around his thigh.

Her boldness surprised him. Intrigued, he asked, "What's your name, sweetheart?"

"It's Lieutenant Graham to you," Tessa corrected him.

Cardozo sneered. Tessa did not react, but continued to apply medication to the wounds on his leg. When she finished, she looked casually at the tattoo on his abdomen. He clasped his hands behind his head and leaned back to show it off, waiting for her to squirm. Instead, she reached out and rubbed the pinkish yellow spot. Her unexpected action startled him and he flinched.

"What?" Tessa asked. "Does it still hurt? Should I put some medication on it? Or maybe I should stitch it up?"

"Hurt?" he snorted. "That little wound's nothing."

Tessa touched the wound again, this time to examine it. "It's an old wound," she said. "You got it before the war."

He didn't deny it. As Tessa proceeded to wrap his leg with clean bandages, he asked, "You're not afraid of me?"

In fact, she wasn't. She could tell that this man had an unusually strong instinct to survive. As a nurse, she was one of his keys to heal and survive. Calmly, she replied, "Afraid of you? Why? Should I be? Why should I be afraid of you when I'm the one helping you heal?" She filled a syringe with morphine. "You should be afraid of me." She gave him a mischievous smile and showed him the needle, then inserted it into his vein.

When she finished, she gathered the medical equipment and walked away. Behind her, Cardozo muttered, "Son of a gun."

CHAPTER FIFTEEN

TWENTY MILES OUTSIDE OF MONTÉLIMAR, the Orion strike team convoy slowed down and pulled to the side of the road. To Anthony's disappointment, they were unable to catch up to Klaus before reaching the city. And now, an order had come for them to halt and wait. In Montélimar, the 36th Division had been battling the Germans for days. More 36th units were still on their way. The army command had instructed Anthony to hold position until the 36th made a breakthrough.

The task force settled into an abandoned house in the back of a field away from the main road. Coming into the area, Anthony could imagine how scenic this place must have once been. To get to the house, they had to pass an old vineyard. He could almost see the wine growers harvesting grapes beneath the sun shining on what could have been a picturesque landscape. If such an idyllic setting had existed, the war had ruined it. The people who had lived here had long since disappeared. Across the vineyard, brown weeds and wild grass intertwined and tangled with old grape vines. All were dry and dying under the heavy summer heat.

His unit had reserved for him a bedroom on the second

floor as his sleeping quarters. On the old bed, Anthony sat down and removed his boots. The bed wobbled. He would have to take it easy or it might fall apart. He sighed and dropped his body onto the mattress. The stale and musky smell from the mold on the walls was stifling. He would have to keep the windows open for the night.

As bad as the conditions were, he already had it better than everybody else. The other officers on the strike team had to share rooms or sleep on the floor. The higher ranking soldiers had taken over the main rooms, and the junior soldiers had to camp in their pup tents outside. Before they could rest, they had to dig themselves foxholes for their own safety.

The perks he enjoyed as captain didn't come without a price. It was lonely being the leader of the highest rank. He had to be mindful to keep his distance and never socialize with the men he commanded. Everything he did, he had to do alone. He read alone, ate alone, rested alone. Even the ranked officers he used to be friendly with, like Garland, had distanced themselves from him since he had become the CO.

Battling loneliness day after day was a tough fight in and of itself. How he wished Tessa was here.

An unexpected knock on the door interrupted his thoughts. "Come in."

Edmond Ferris nudged the door open. He looked unusually nervous. "Captain…"

Anthony sat up. "Yes?"

"I should report this to my squad leader, but I'm afraid…"

"Afraid of what?"

"It's Percy. He shot himself in the foot."

Percy Ross. The replacement who had joined his company the same time as Ed.

Great, Anthony thought. Just what he needed right now. Cowardly quitters choosing to bow out without carrying their share. Still, he wanted to give the boy the benefit of the doubt and make sure. "Was it an accident?"

"Acci... An accident?" Edmond asked, as though he had never thought of this.

Anthony looked pointedly at him, waiting for his answer.

"Yes, sir. It was an accident."

Anthony scowled, but decided to give Edmond another chance to come clean. "Ed. I'm asking you again. Was it an accident?"

Ed hunched his shoulders. "No, Captain. It wasn't an accident."

Anthony let out a heavy sigh. Ed stole a glance at him. "Anthony?"

"Where is he?" Anthony asked.

"In our foxhole. At the back of the house next to the pile of farm equipment."

Exasperated, Anthony put his boots back on. Army or not, Ed had come to him. He couldn't refuse to help someone he knew from back home. "Go find Lieutenant Garland and meet me there."

Ed went away in relief.

Drawing on his last bit of energy, Anthony went outside to the foxhole shared by Ed and Percy. At the bottom of the dugout, Percy cowered on the ground. Blood trickled out of the bullet hole at the toe of his left boot. When he saw Anthony, his whimpers grew louder.

Anthony crouched down at the top of the foxhole. "You know there will be a penalty for this," he said to Percy, not to scare him, only to tell him the fact.

Ed and Jesse arrived. Jesse took one look at Percy. Like Anthony, he showed no sympathy. He jumped into the foxhole and grabbed Percy by the ankle. Percy bawled out.

"Hold still and be quiet," Jesse said, but Percy would not stop crying.

Ignoring Percy, Anthony asked Jesse, "You'll handle it from here?"

"Sure."

"Get him back to the hospital as quickly as you can. Take a driver but keep this quiet. We don't need anyone else getting the same idea."

"Got it."

Anthony stood up, ready to leave, except that Jesse was staring oddly at him. He couldn't make out why Jesse was staring at him this way. "Everything okay?" he asked.

"Yeah. Everything's fine." Jesse returned to the task of fixing up Percy.

Anthony started to walk away, but Percy cried out to him. "Captain! I'm sorry. I'm really sorry. I can't be here. I don't want to be here. I don't want to fight a war."

Without answering Percy's cries, Anthony walked on. Of course the boy didn't want to be here. Anthony didn't want to be here either. Neither did the wounded soldier they had left behind in the woods, nor the young private who had run out to try to save him but was shot dead himself.

There was nothing Anthony could do for any of them. The only thing he could do, that he did do, was to order his men to leave the wounded soldier and the dead private behind. It was a decision he would have to live with for the rest of his life.

More than a week into the battle, the siege in Montélimar had done nothing except to bring both sides into a stalemate. From the reports Anthony had received, the 36th Division was bombarding the city with everything they had. The Germans, though, refused to let up. The enemy had increased their counter-offensive. More Panzer divisions had come to reinforce the fight. On the outskirts of the city, where the Orion strike team was positioned, Anthony could hear fierce explosions and gunfire going off at all hours.

To secure a victory, the Allied command had decided to send the Third Division here to join up with the 36th. Orion's mission was temporarily put on hold. The command had directed the strike team to rejoin their company to engage in the continual assault on Montélimar. When Warren and Lt. Dennison arrived with their unit, Anthony was glad to see their familiar faces. From what Anthony had heard, Dennison had been doing a fine job leading their company while Anthony pursued Klaus.

Warren also brought with him good news. "The 36th broke the Krauts' perimeters. They're trying to trap the Germans inside the city. Won't be easy though. The Krauts will do everything they can to keep a route clear for evacuation."

"Any news on Klaus's whereabouts?" Anthony asked.

"We got it from the Y-service he's in charge over on the north side of the city."

"That makes sense," Dennison said. "The north's where they're trying to maintain their escape routes."

"Yep." Warren opened a map and pointed to Crest, a small town north of Montélimar. "There's a stronghold of Panzer units right here. If Klaus wants to get away, he can go here for backup."

"We'll have to capture him before he makes his way there then," Anthony said.

"If we can capture him, he'll be a goldmine of intel." Warren's eyes gleamed with excitement at the thought. "But your priority now is to lead your unit to join the attack. Command is very clear on that."

"We'll do both," Anthony said. "Whatever it takes." He wasn't trying to talk big either. Since the Orion mission began, the Amerika Bomber report was always on his mind. The more the Allies pushed ahead, the more desperate the Germans would become. There was no telling what they would do if they were pushed to the brink. In the worst case scenario, Hitler might set off his long-range bombs. As long as Klaus was at large, the risk of a disastrous attack on the American homeland would continue to exist. If that happened, Anthony didn't know how he could live with himself.

———

The next day, Anthony set off toward Montélimar with his company at dawn. Their order was to lead the reinforcement of Third Division tanks and artillery units into the city to link up with the 36th Battalion. As they approached the city, they came upon a scattered group of 36th Division soldiers attempting to hold a blockade against the German troops striking out from inside the city's walls. The blockade was faltering. Enemy shells pounded and smashed against them, setting their light tanks and armored cars on fire. The unit's own self-propelled guns, whatever was left of them, could not match the German Panzers.

As soon as Anthony and his company were within range, a runner from the group under attack ran up to his jeep. "We're collapsing, sir. Our infantry platoons are wiped out. The engineers battalion's fighting in their place. We can't hold much longer."

Anthony surveyed the scene ahead. He hadn't expected to engage in a battle here, nor was he prepared to have to take on tactical command. His original order was only to act as the highest ranking officer to bring reinforcements to the 36th battalion command. Now, he had to make a call.

Next to him, Jonesy said, "We got enough men and weapons to take the Krauts out."

Anthony agreed. "Go back and tell your units we're taking over from here," he said to the runner.

"Yes, sir." The man took off in a hurry.

After he left, Anthony said to the radio operator riding with him. "Tell Dennison to pull all units into position. We're going in."

"Yes, sir."

Accompanied by the Sherman tanks, Anthony commanded their units to move forward. The Germans were putting up a good fight, but he felt confident their own troops could overpower them. Surveying the grounds, he shouted orders to his troops, passing on observations to the armored units and guiding them through the radio operator to forge ahead. The might of American weapons gave them the edge. Their arrival brought on a storm of gunfire and bullets that their enemy could not defend against. In short order, the German forces disintegrated. Everything was looking good.

"Captain," the radio operator shouted, relaying the information given from the troops ahead of them. "They've got hostages!"

"Hostages?" Anthony asked. That was bad. The Germans must have captured the locals in the city. "Civilians?"

"No, sir. Our own men."

Alarmed, Anthony stood up from his seat and looked ahead with his binoculars. Two Panzers emerged to meet them head on. The Panzer that was leading the way had three American soldiers tied to the front. The enemy was using their American POWs as human shields.

Damned Krauts! Anthony winced. This was low.

"Captain?" The radio operator asked. "What now?"

Angry, Anthony continued to stare into his binoculars.

"Captain!" The radio operator urged him again. "The tank units asked what you want to do."

He lowered his binoculars. Sweat dripped from his head inside his helmet.

"What's your call, Captain?" Jonesy asked. "We can't retreat now."

Jonesy was right. Any hesitation, and the Germans might find an opening to inflict more casualties on them.

Without taking his eyes off the men tied to the Panzer, he said, "Tell them to fire." The words came out of his mouth like dead weight.

The radio operator began to transmit the order.

"Tell them to aim as low as they can," Anthony added, his voice lame and feeble. He could hardly convince himself that the attempt to avoid hitting the victims would work.

Next to him, Jonesy turned his head, unable to look.

Boom! A shell struck the Panzer, annihilating the enemy along with the American soldiers set up to be killed. Out of respect, Anthony kept his eyes on the three men he had chosen to sacrifice. At the least, he should bear witness to the consequences of his order.

Sorry. He said over and over again in his head. *I'm so sorry.* He wanted to throw up.

The battle raged on, leaving behind all those who did not survive. Eventually, the American units pushed the Germans back, forcing them to retreat while the reinforcements Anthony had brought rolled into the city. As he passed the disabled Panzers, he saw the bodies of the American POWs who were killed at his order laid limply on the enemy tank. He felt his center had turned into a sinking hole. He had told the tankers to aim low, but…those men didn't stand a chance.

Inside Montélimar, the entire city was burning.

Bombs and grenades exploded left and right. The sounds of explosions mixed with the haze of smoke, filling the city with a miasma of darkness. Mounds of debris on the ground burned in flames, unleashing fumes that stung Anthony's eyes. The heat of fire everywhere oppressed him. The ghosts of the men killed at his command smothered him.

Carcasses of dead horses littered the streets along with blackened human corpses. For all the death and destruction he had already seen, Anthony still could not numb himself to the casualties. The smell of charred skin, singed hair, and burnt flesh nauseated him.

Everywhere, vehicles were burning. Buildings were burning. The train station was burning. Montélimar was a boiling inferno.

When the battle finally ended and the Germans made their retreat, Anthony felt as if the battle had not only wrecked the city, but also his soul. Early on when he joined the war, he had resolved to do everything he could to protect his men. As he rose in rank, he thought he would be in an even better position to save them from harm. That had not been the case. The more power he had, the more often he had to give them up for sacrifice. He loathed this burden. By what authority was he empowered to determine any man's fate? What right did he have to decide who lived and who died?

He watched the American troops march the captured German soldiers away. When this war was over, if the Allies could claim victory as they did here today, surely the world would deem his actions justified. His own conscience, however, was another matter. From whom could he seek forgiveness? Not the wounded soldier he had left behind in the forest, nor the private who had run out to save him. Not the soldiers who the Germans had tied to the Panzer to use as human shields.

He reached his hand up to touch Tessa's cross. His cross. The burden of the cross had never felt heavier.

"Captain!" Fox, the young sharpshooter from his company, came up to him. "We found Klaus! First Sergeant Jones found the Kraut's HQ. Klaus got away, but we know where he went."

Quickly, Anthony switched his thoughts to focus on the task at hand. "Good. Gather the strike team and tell Lieutenant Dennison we're taking off. Tell them Orion is on."

CHAPTER SIXTEEN

DOWN THE ROAD away from Montélimar, Anthony led his squad toward the small town of Crest. The rest of the Orion strike team followed. By now, Warren, too, had joined them. This was the only road between Montélimar and Crest. If they moved fast enough, they might be able to capture Klaus before he reached his reinforcements.

"If the Y-service reports are correct," Warren said as they sped along, "Klaus is looking to gather the Panzer units at Crest and push on to Lyon. The German command wants him to join and direct the German forces there."

"Too bad for them," Anthony said. "He's not going to make it to Lyon." He looked directly at Warren. "We'll get him."

Anthony wasn't boasting. When Klaus left Montélimar, he had taken a route separate from the rest of the Germans in retreat. With his stealthy escape, he likely believed he had gotten away from the Americans. As far as he knew, the Americans had diverted all their attention to pursue the troops he had left behind. If he was under a false sense of security, the Orion strike team would have a better chance of catching him by surprise. The only thing that worried Anthony was the time.

It was late afternoon already. They only had a few more hours before it would get dark. If they failed to find Klaus before evening set in, he could escape in the dark.

Just as Anthony thought, Klaus had let his guard down. The strike team's forward squad reported that Klaus and his men had stopped at a farmhouse. Losing no time, Anthony organized his troops for a raid. This was the closest they had come to achieving their mission. They could not make any mistakes.

The troops of the strike team surrounded the house, rotating in groups as they moved closer. Anthony watched. Why weren't there any Germans on guard outside the house? Did Klaus know they were here? Were he and his men watching them from inside the house? Something didn't feel right. Anthony took a deep breath. Gunfire could go off any minute.

To his surprise, a large sheet of white cloth dropped from the farmhouse's second story window.

"They're surrendering?" Anthony asked in disbelief.

"Without even a fight," Warren said. "I can't believe it."

"Could be a ruse."

The strike team halted. Wary of the enemy's intentions, Anthony watched for Klaus's next move. The door of the farmhouse opened. A lone German soldier walked out, holding a white flag. He held his other arm in the air. Jonesy, Fox, and Edmond, who were closest to him, quickly moved in and captured him. One by one, the German troops exited the house, surrendering with their arms in the air.

"Let's see what's going on." Anthony walked toward them. Warren followed.

The last man to exit was Major Heinrich Klaus, the man they had been after. Unlike the German soldiers under him, he walked out of the house with his arms by his side. Fearing he might be armed, Fox and Jonesy raised their rifles at him, as did the other strike team members behind them. Their hostile reaction did not faze Klaus. Calm and composed, he walked toward Anthony, looking neither nervous nor defeated.

"*Keine Bewegung!*" Jonesy shouted to stop him from getting too close to Anthony. "*Hände hoch!*"

Klaus glanced at Jonesy, then spoke to him in English in the voice of a superior. "Is this how you talk to a high command officer? Don't worry. I'm unarmed." He opened his palms to show he was not holding any weapons. Jonesy and the other soldiers, however, would not lower their guns.

Klaus ignored them and said to Anthony. "Captain Ardley. Pleasure to finally meet you."

The German's greeting caught Anthony off guard. He did not expect Klaus to know who he was.

"I know you've been after me for some time now, Captain Ardley," Klaus said.

Not wanting to let on what he didn't know, Anthony kept his face blank.

"You have your intelligence, and I have mine," Klaus explained anyway. Anthony's attempt to hide his surprise didn't fool him.

"We have to take you in," Anthony said.

"Of course you do. You've captured me. At the rate we're going, your team would have caught us before we could get away." He looked around at the Orion strike team soldiers surrounding the house. "We're outmanned and outgunned. It's better this way, don't you think? No need for unnecessary bloodshed. I don't want my men to die any more than you want yours to. Isn't that right?"

Anthony wouldn't answer, but Klaus was unnerving him. He needed to do something to stop Klaus from playing mind games with him. He eyed Jonesy to signal him to frisk their prized prisoner. Jonesy got the order and began searching Klaus's body up and down.

Klaus scowled, his face indignant. "Respect is a two-way street, Captain Ardley. I'm sure you're aware of that. You treat our officers well, we'll treat yours well if you are ever captured." He looked Anthony in the eye. "Just remember that."

Not wanting to engage him, Anthony refused to respond.

"He's unarmed," Jonesy said.

Relieved, Anthony sized up the rest of the German prisoners in their custody. They numbered about fifteen men. What should he do with them? Should he take them back to Montélimar now? Or should he ask command in Montélimar to send more troops to guard them on their way back?

The sky dimmed. Night was falling.

"Captain," Warren said to Anthony. "Can we speak?"

Anthony walked with Warren farther away from the prisoners and the strike team.

"We need to find out everything Klaus knows as soon as possible," Warren said. "He might have vital information about the German troops' next move. Let's get him back to command before the Germans find out we've got him."

Anthony looked over at Klaus, then the group of German prisoners. "It's too risky traveling with this many prisoners in the dark. We don't have enough men as guards. If we run into more German troops on our way back, we might lose them. We can't risk losing Klaus."

"What do you want to do?"

"I think we should hold them here. We'll radio command to send another squad at least. We'll take them back to battalion tomorrow."

"Tomorrow?" Warren said in disbelief. "We can't wait that long. Command's going to want to know everything he knows, now!" He leaned closer to Anthony and whispered, "We've got to get everything he knows about the Amerika Bomber. That's why you're here, remember?"

The Amerika Bomber. Warren was right. Finding out what information Klaus had about Amerika Bomber was mission critical. Could they securely bring Klaus and all the German soldiers back to Montélimar at night? They would have to keep the headlights off to avoid drawing enemy attention. But what if they got lost? He looked back at the road they had followed to get here. This was unfamiliar territory. They'd have to be very careful finding their way back in the dark. Could his men handle it?

Anthony glanced at Klaus again, then at his men. Jonesy was still pointing his gun at Klaus. Jonesy might be up for it. Fox would do whatever he ordered. So would Edmond. Edmond had adapted very quickly since joining the company. He had learned the ropes about how to fight and survive in only a few short weeks. He was brave too. He wouldn't hesitate to do what was needed to win the battle and save his brothers-in-arms, just like the private who had run out to save the wounded soldier Anthony had left behind in the woods.

Like the private who had run out to save the wounded soldier...

He couldn't put Edmond at risk like that.

"No," Anthony said. "It's too risky. I don't want to put our men in any more danger if we don't have to. We can wait till tomorrow morning."

"We can't wait," Warren said. "We're losing time. If the Germans know Klaus's been captured, they'll change their plans. Everything Klaus knows might become useless."

Still thinking of the private who had died saving the wounded soldier, Anthony remembered the three soldiers tied to the Panzer. Montélimar had been a long, exhausting journey. Did he have it in him to order his troops to put their lives on the line one more time?

He felt Klaus's penetrating gaze on him. Anthony stared back. Klaus gave him a cold but cautionary smile.

No need for unnecessary bloodshed. I don't want my men to die any more than you want yours to.

Anthony didn't want to push on. Klaus was making him stressed and agitated. "Let's wait. One night won't make any difference."

Warren disagreed. "It could mean a world of difference. It could mean winning or losing this war."

Anthony could not bring himself to do what his friend wanted. His mind was exhausted.

Frustrated, Warren said, "Fine. I'll take Klaus back then. You can bring the rest of the prisoners back tomorrow."

"But…"

"You don't want to travel with a group in the dark. I understand. I'll take him. Just lend me your driver. We'll be able to travel faster with just one jeep, and we'll be less conspicuous. It's the best option."

"I can't let you do that. That's too dangerous."

"It's not up to you," Warren said. His voice was more resolute than Anthony had ever heard. "I'm the intelligence officer. This is my call. There's too much at stake. You've done your job. Now I'll do mine."

Anthony wanted to persuade him otherwise, but Klaus was still watching him, observing him. The German commander's unshakeable gaze irritated him.

"Fine." Anthony relented. He didn't want to argue anymore. "Take him back. Take my driver. Tell command to send us more troops tomorrow."

"Will do." Warren left him and walked toward Klaus and Jonesy. Anthony followed to organize his team to restrain the prisoners and to settle in for the night. As Warren walked Klaus away with his pistol pointing at the prized prisoner, Anthony could still feel Klaus's eyes on him. Although he didn't want to admit it, Klaus impressed him. He had seen Klaus in action several times already. The German had an extraordinary clarity of mind. He could always calculate what should be his next move regardless of what threat he was under.

The German's exceptional abilities weren't all that Anthony admired. He and Klaus shared something in common. Klaus admitted there was no way he could've gotten away from the Orion strike team. The Americans were known to observe the Geneva Convention. His decision to surrender ensured the safety of all the German soldiers who were with him. Whatever Klaus might be, he was a leader who looked out for his men.

The strike team soldiers took the other German prisoners away. The last to follow was Jonesy, who smiled at Anthony and held his fingers up in a V sign.

Anthony smiled back, but he felt uneasy. Something didn't feel right. The end to their mission came too easily. He couldn't shake the feeling that everything was not over. Maybe it was just exhaustion. He tried to put his anxiety away as he went inside the farmhouse to check if Klaus and his men might have left any valuable information or weapons behind.

While Anthony surveyed their loot, a commotion broke out outside. He could hear his driver shouting at the top of his lungs and the others yelling back. Anthony hurried outside. "What's going on?"

"Captain Hendricks, sir!" His driver shouted. "Captain Hendrick's been shot!"

"What?" Anthony demanded to know.

"Klaus got away. I was already in the driver's seat and I'd started the engine. Captain Hendricks was coming and he tripped. Klaus grabbed his pistol when he fell. I tried to save him but by the time I got out of the jeep, Klaus had already grabbed him by the neck and pointed the gun at his head. He threatened to kill Captain Hendricks if I didn't turn the jeep over to him. So I did." He paused to catch his breath.

"What happened?" Anthony shouted.

"Klaus got in the car, then he shot Captain Hendricks anyway. Then he drove away."

Anthony's ears started ringing. He ran toward the field where the jeep that Warren had gone to had been parked. The other soldiers followed. Warren was lying on the ground. Jesse was kneeling next to him but not doing anything. Anthony ran over to them. Seeing the stream of blood down the side of Warren's head, he felt goosebumps on the skin of his arms. His legs weakened and he knelt down next to them. "Warren!" He shook Warren's body. "Warren! Warren!"

Only Warren's lifeless eyes stared back at him.

"He's gone," Jesse said.

Gone? They were talking only a moment ago. Anthony pulled Warren's body up and held him. How could this have happened? How could he have let this happen under his watch?

This is all my fault. Anthony thought back to their conversation before he agreed to let Warren take Klaus away. If only Warren had listened to him….*No!* If only he had tried harder to convince Warren to stay. *Damn it!* Why didn't he try harder? He should have tried harder. He knew Klaus was a dangerous man. He should've known better than to let Warren take the risk.

The sky darkened. Jesse pulled out his flashlight and turned it on. The light caught something shiny on the ground. Anthony picked it up. The Roman coin that Warren had bought for his sister had fallen out of his pocket.

Anthony closed his hand around the coin. Somewhere back in Chicago, a little girl was waiting for her big brother to come home. His heart sank. "I'll make sure she gets it," he whispered to Warren. His heart seized with pain knowing Warren could no longer hear him.

"I'll take it from here," Jesse said.

Anthony let go of Warren. With another soldier's help, Jesse carried Warren's body away. Everyone else moved away too. Why did he give in to Warren? Why didn't he insist harder? Why didn't he think of telling Warren to tie Klaus's hands before they got to the jeep? After everything he had seen of Klaus, why didn't he realize the man was still lethal even when he wasn't armed?

Klaus. There was no need to kill Warren. Without his pistol, Warren could not have harmed him.

Anthony looked around him. He wanted to make Klaus answer for what he did. But night had come. There was no way to find the murderer in the dark.

With heavy footsteps, Anthony trod back to the farmhouse. Jonesy watched him enter like he was watching a hurricane about to hit.

Anthony knew what Jonesy was thinking. There would be hell to pay when battalion command heard about this tomorrow.

The command was the last of Anthony's worries. He didn't need command to tell him what he had to do. Orion was back on a mission.

And from now on, their mission was personal.

Part Five

THE HIGH VOSGES

Part Five

CHAPTER SEVENTEEN

November 2, 1944

Dear Tessa,

Another winter is coming. Has it really been another year already? It feels to me like we just got out of the winter in Anzio. Here where I am, the mornings are so chilly. I feel bad for the soldiers who fought in Anzio. None of us want to live through another winter season like that again. I think it'll start to snow soon. I hope the winter jackets and uniforms will come before the snow starts.

I still think about Warren a lot. I've seen many people die since I joined the war, but often when I close my eyes, I see Warren's body there on the ground. I keep asking myself, why is he dead? Just two years ago, we were in school together. Both of us had our futures ahead of us. He'd changed so much from when I first met him. He'd become a man of strength and confidence. What kind of life would he have lived if he had survived the war? What kind of work would he have chosen? What if he could have done great things? He was quite shy when it came to girls, but he was a good guy. Surely a nice girl would see that. He would have been a great husband. A great father. He has a little sister whom he loved. I wonder if she knows yet her brother has died. She will be heartbroken, I'm sure.

There are ideals we are here to fight for, but I can't help but doubt when I think of him, dead. Uncle Lex died for his ideals too. In the end, will any of it make any difference? I still try to hold on to the hope that Warren hasn't died in vain. I'd like to believe that what we are doing here will make a difference, but I can't find any answer anywhere.

I'm sorry, I must be bringing you down with all these depressing thoughts. I wish I knew where you are now. What are you doing? Did you get my letters? I received a new batch of letters from you yesterday. Without you, I feel like a patch of dry weeds, wilting under the harsh weather and trampled upon by callous footsteps. Receiving your letters for me is like getting an infusion of water, air, and sunshine. A word from you gives me life again. I cannot tell you how much I miss you.

I love the drawing of you on the plane. Thank you for sending it. I'll have to meet Tyler someday. I wish he could draw me too so you can see what I looked like when you left. I was so sad. Not a day goes by that I don't think about you. I will never be complete without you.

I've told you already (if you got my letters), General Castile came to see me when I was in Saint-Tropez. I can't thank him enough for getting us passes to see each other in Paris before Christmas. It's good news that Paris is liberated. I long for the day when I will see you.

Tomorrow, we move forward again. I'm tired. We traveled many miles today. Be good, and take care of yourself.

Love you always and forever, — Anthony

READING ANTHONY'S WORDS, Tessa felt heartbroken. It pained her too that Warren was dead. He was good friends with Anthony. Anthony must be so sad now. Away from him, there was no way for her to share his sadness and burdens.

Another winter like Anzio, Anthony said in the letter. How she wished he didn't have to suffer such a bad experience again. How much longer did this war have to go on? When would it all end?

Not soon enough. She checked her watch. Right now, she had to go tend to her patients. Reluctantly, she put away the letter and headed to Ward 8, the ward which nurses now always tried to avoid because it currently housed the man named Victor Cardozo, otherwise known as the Blade.

"Why do they call you the Blade?" Tessa asked the surly patient while she tended to his wounded leg. She noticed that he had followed her order to remain fully dressed at all times. She didn't tell him, but his compliance pleased her. His repulsive tattoos upset too many people on the medical staff. His menacing stare was enough to make the nurses shudder. The tattoos, they could do without.

Instead of answering her, the Blade asked, "You ever played darts?"

"Yes."

He pulled a small steel knife with a cord grip from under his pillow. Curious, she waited to see what he would do. He tossed the knife up into the air and caught it when it dropped. "I don't throw darts. I throw knives." Before she could react, he aimed and threw the knife straight ahead. The knife zipped across the room, brushing the air next to a patient on the other side, and struck the wall. Startled, the patient shouted a dozen curses at him.

"Good heavens!" Tessa exclaimed. "Don't do that. You almost killed someone."

"No, I didn't," the Blade said. "If I wanted to kill him, he'd be dead." He climbed off the bed, even though Tessa was still in the middle of wrapping new bandages on his leg. "You asked. So I answered your question." He staggered across the room and retrieved his knife. "I never miss."

"Don't ever do that here again," Tessa said.

He glared at her, but abruptly changed his expression to an agreeable smile. "Okay. But only because you say so, Lieutenant Graham." He sat back down on his bed to let her finish.

Tessa started wrapping his leg again. This patient. He sure was a handful. "Is it true what they say? That you're with the mafia?"

"Is that what they say?" he asked her back. "You shouldn't ask me these questions. There are things you'd be better off not knowing."

"Really?"

He smiled and tossed the knife in his hand. "You want to know how many German throats I've cut with this knife?"

Not wanting to give him the satisfaction of baiting her, Tessa didn't inquire.

"Better you don't know." He leaned back in his bed, waiting for Tessa to pry more.

She wouldn't. "Fine. I don't care to know. I'm not impressed with people who like to brag." She picked up the used medical supplies and placed them onto a metal tray.

"Tessa. Tessa!" Tyler entered the room waving a note in his hand. "Lieutenant Swanson asked me to give you this."

Tessa took the note from him. When she saw what it said, she looked up in disbelief. "I'm going to Paris!"

"Uh-huh." Grinning, Tyler nodded and affirmed the news. "A three-day pass to see your honey. Direct order from General Castile himself."

Interrupting their excitement, the Blade asked, "Who's going to attend to me if you're gone?"

"You'll be released by then," Tessa said. "Or maybe you'll just have to start being nice to the other nurses."

The Blade grunted. "Your husband better be good to you, or I'll give him a good beating."

"He'll give you a good beating," Tessa said, indignant.

"Tessa. Look what else I got?" Tyler opened his sketchbook to show her a letter kept inside. "Your friend Ruby wrote me."

"She did?"

"She sent me her picture! See?" He turned the page to show her a photo. It was a professionally taken portrait of Ruby. "She's a real doll."

Tessa picked up the photo. How she missed her friend. "Yes. She's very pretty."

"Should I send her a picture of me? What if she doesn't like the way I look?"

"You look fine." Tessa gave Ruby's photo back to him. "I already wrote to her all about you. She'll like your look just fine."

"But what if she doesn't? No girl's ever written to me before. What if she doesn't like the way I look and stops writing to me?"

"She's not shallow like that. Stop worrying."

"Maybe I should send her this instead." He flipped the pages of his sketchbook and showed her a drawing of himself stuffed in an army-issued winter jacket with his hair all messed up.

Tessa laughed. "Maybe you can take a picture next to the Blade. He looks so scary, you'll look good next to him for sure."

The Blade folded his arms and grunted.

"By the way, Tyler," Tessa touched his shoulder. "We're short on blood. Do you mind donating again?'"

"Not at all," Tyler said without hesitation. "I'll go now." He waved goodbye and took off.

After he left, Tessa said to the Blade, "Why don't you ever give blood? You've got more than enough to spare."

"No one ever asked," he said.

"Okay. I'm asking now. Would you? Please?"

The Blade sat up, swung his legs to the side of the bed, and started putting on his shoes.

"Where are you going?"

He stared at her as if the answer was obvious. "To give blood."

"Now?"

"Yes. Now. You want me to go later?"

"No. I mean. I'm surprised, that's all." Tessa softened her voice. "You were waiting for somebody to ask?"

"No. I'm doing it because you asked."

"What difference does it make who asked?"

He looked at her with all seriousness. "You asked me if I was in the Mafia. Where I come from, we live by a code. If someone looks out for you, you look out for them. If they need something and ask, you do everything you can to help them get it, even if your life is on the line. That's how we know who's a friend and who's not." He slapped his thigh where Tessa had tended his wounds and startled her, but he continued. "You look out for me. I'm bound to do what you ask."

He got up. With all sincerity, he said to her, "I needed help, and you came to my aid. I'll always remember that." He headed out of the room, leaving Tessa speechless and bewildered.

CHAPTER EIGHTEEN

IN THE MORNING, Anthony summoned his officers for another briefing in the abandoned schoolhouse where the company was currently stationed. A copy of the Stars and Stripes lay on the table. Its front cover headline, "Montélimar Clear of Enemies," was nothing more than an afterthought for those who had gathered here. Beneath the headline was written, "Seventh Army pushes Germans three hundred miles north in rapid speed." Even though they had been part of the army that had brought forth this victory, no one in the room gave the subhead a second glance. What held their attention right now were the surveillance aerial photos showing their next objective.

Anthony circulated the photos among Dennison, Jonesy, and Beck. The insurmountable terrain of the High Vosges, a chain of mountains seventy miles long and about forty miles wide, already depressed their morale. Cloaked by dense clusters of trees and forests, the Vosges mountains served as a thickly wooded fortress for their enemy. To cross the German border, Anthony's company would have to break through this monumental barrier. An order had come for him and his company to march with their regiment to the High Vosges to a hidden location where their command believed Klaus was positioned.

Looking at the photos, disillusion and fatigue set in on everyone's faces. This would be a repeat of Anzio, a battlefield where the enemy would have all the tactical advantages, while the Allies would suffer every pitfall in the treacherous landscape. Fox was the only one unaffected. He had been promoted to sergeant to replace Ollie, and was doing his best to take everything in stride so as not to disappoint anyone.

"Let's move." Anthony ended the briefing with a simple command.

For the next four days, he led his company to embark on their new journey toward the mountains. He felt wearier than ever as they trekked through the hilly farmlands of Moselle through heavy rain, fog, and wind. The muddy roads kept slowing down the tanks and mortar vehicles, forcing them to fall behind even though they were supposed to lead the way. The rising elevation, which broke the land into large hills, delayed them all further as they came closer and closer to the Vosges foothills where they began the hardest part of their climb. Anthony and his company were the first among their regiment units to come near the top.

Close to the hilltop, a soldier slipped and fell. "Fucking mud. I should get a purple heart if I break my leg on these shitty roads."

"Sure," his buddy laughed. "Maybe you'll fall down the mountain and break your neck, and they'll give you the Medal of Honor."

Anthony heard them and smiled. If a soldier slipping on mud was their only casualty, he would take that any day. He relaxed somewhat. The coast seemed clear. If there had been German troops positioned at the top, they would have hurled grenades and bullets down at them already. He wondered if their streak of luck would last.

"Captain," Jonesy said to him. "We should send up some scouts. See if the Krauts left any traps on the other side."

Anthony gazed back down the slopes they had climbed. He estimated the distance from the top to the base to be about three hundred meters. There could be snipers or machine gun nests hiding in waiting. Chances were, the enemy had planted mines too. "Agreed. Go ahead. See if anyone wants to volunteer."

"I'll go." Edmond, who had overheard them, volunteered at once. "I can lead them, Captain."

Anthony and Jonesy exchanged a glance. Jonesy shrugged. Anthony surveyed their surroundings to gauge the risks. The rain had stopped. There was no concern as to visibility at the moment. On these slopes, the trees were spread out. The landscape was mostly open fields with bushes. In case of an ambush, they could probably manage and come to the scout team's rescue.

"I can do it, Captain," Edmond said.

Anthony knew Edmond was eager to please him. Since they had crossed paths again in the army, Edmond's admiration for him had only grown. Anthony didn't play favorites, but he did have a soft spot for Edmond. He nodded and said, "Help Sergeant Jones gather a squad."

Eager to proceed, Edmond took off.

"Ed," Anthony called out to him. "Be careful. Don't take any risks you don't have to."

"Don't worry, sir. I won't." He flashed Anthony a smile.

After the scout team left, Anthony gazed down the hill. He could see the Sherman tanks and mortar vehicles still on their way, as well as another infantry company coming up behind them. He told his radio operator, "Send a message to command and let them know we've reached the top of the hill."

"Yes, sir."

The men in their unit settled down for a lunch break. Anthony found a spot away from his troops. He finished his meal quickly, and tried to get a moment to rest himself. If Warren had been here, he would at least have had someone to talk to.

"Captain! Captain!" Waving his walkie-talkie, the radio operator came running to Anthony.

Languidly, Anthony asked, "What is it?"

"The Krauts! They're coming up the other side of the hill! The scouts say there's a battalion of them."

"What?" Anthony jumped to his feet. A battalion? How could this be? He didn't see any enemy troops when he surveyed the other side of the hill earlier.

Anthony sprinted as fast as he could to the peak of the hill. The radio operator ran after him, panting and trying to catch up. Jonesy, seeing them racing in a sudden hurry, dropped his lunch and joined them.

From the peak of the hill, they saw a swarm of Panzer tanks and German mortar cars emerging up the other side. Hundreds, maybe a thousand, of Wehrmacht soldiers were marching up toward them from below a spur. The scouts had made their way down the spur, but hadn't seen the Germans coming up the other side until it was too late. By then, the Krauts were already halfway up the hill. They hadn't spotted the scouts yet, but they were too close. The scouts had nowhere to hide.

"Holy Mother of God," Jonesy said.

"Jonesy!" Anthony shouted. "Get the anti-tank unit up here. Get Dennison! Get everyone up here into position." He turned to the radio operator. "Tell the scouts to come back, now! Pronto!"

As Jonesy rushed off, the radio operator screamed into the walkie-talkie. Anthony took out his binoculars and looked down the other side of the hill. The scouts had turned back, but not fast enough. The Germans were moving faster. The gap between the scouts and German battalion narrowed.

"Come on," Anthony muttered, urging the scouts to move. His grip on the binoculars tightened. Several of their own regiment's anti-tank vehicles had now reached the peak. Dennison had organized their company to line up in position. Jonesy ran back to Anthony and the radio operator.

"Captain. Regiment command said you should give the signal to fire when the Germans are in range."

Anthony checked on the scouts. They were scrambling to come back. He watched them climb. Climb for their lives. Behind them, the enemy moved closer. The Wehrmacht snipers had spotted them and had begun shooting at them. One of the scouts got hit and fell over.

"Captain," Jonesy said, his voice low and grave. "We can't let the Krauts get any closer."

Anthony knew that. He didn't need the reminder. Right now, their position at the top was the only advantage they had. If they let the Krauts reach the top, the Krauts would be able to shoot down the hill at the rest of their units that were still on their way. The enemy would wipe them all out.

"Now's the only chance we got," Jonesy said. "We can smite them from here."

Anthony took a sweeping look at the view below, searching for Edmond among the scouts. It was impossible to tell who was who down there.

"We need to shoot, Captain," Jonesy said, his voice getting desperate.

Horrified, the radio operator said, "But Sergeant, our guys are still down there."

"There's no time. We can't wait."

"They'll all be killed if we open fire."

"Captain?"

"Captain, no!"

The radio signal went off. The operator answered. Meekly, he looked at Anthony. "The anti-tank unit wants to know if they should shoot."

Anthony tensed. He stared down the hill. "Tell them to fire."

The radio operator passed his order on over the phone. His face scrunched like he was being fed poison as he spoke.

In no time, the American tank destroyers began their bombardment of the enemy below. Their shells struck their targets and, one by one, the Panzers flared up in flames. Clouds of black smoke burst into the air. The American anti-tank guns were holding the Germans off as more heavy weapons units made it up the hill to join them. Aware that their position was their only advantage, they fired bombs and rockets relentlessly down at the enemy. Soon, everything below was caught in a barrage of explosions. The scout team was lost in the crossfire.

Lying on the ground, Anthony held on to his Tommy gun. He couldn't pull the trigger. The vision before him was a massive blur. What was he doing? Shooting at Ed?

"Captain!" Jonesy yelled. "They're retreating!"

Anthony felt dazed. He didn't hear him.

"Captain! They're retreating!" Jonesy yelled again. "The Krauts are falling back! The Krauts are falling back!"

Anthony scanned the hillside from left to right and top to bottom, hoping for any sign that Edmond and the other scouts had survived. Down below, the Germans withdrew. It had been a stroke of luck that Anthony's company had made it to the top first. The outcome would've been unthinkable if it had been the other way around.

The American mortar vehicles and troops advanced cautiously down the hill to claim the terrain and establish perimeters. Anthony lowered his binoculars and slumped his shoulders. He looked again at the destruction across the field below. Where were his scouts?

I can do it, Captain, Edmond's voice echoed in Anthony's ears.

Anthony's body shook. His insides felt all torn up. He clenched his fists around his binoculars, wanting anything solid to hold on to. He felt as though he was losing the ground under him.

Ed, it'll all be ok. We've got your six.

Anthony squeezed his eyes shut. What were Ed's last thoughts when he looked up the hill and realized his own brothers were firing at him? What crossed his mind when he realized his own captain, his idol and his friend, had abandoned him to die?

Ed. How could he ever face Edmond's parents if he ever made it home?

When the battle was over, Anthony gave his report as usual to the regiment command. Command was pleased with him. With his help, they had vanquished the enemy. The American army had claimed the hill as their occupied sector, and the area was now safe. To Anthony though, none of this could make up for the void he felt for what had happened to the scouts.

"Well done, Captain," Colonel Callahan said to him. "Could have been a disaster today. You deserve a commendation for what you've done."

Anthony did not reply. He deserved nothing. An award was the last thing he wanted. He did not need a reminder of having given the order to kill his young friend. "If there's nothing else, sir."

"You may go," Callahan said. "And, Captain, you saved a lot of lives today."

Anthony took his leave. He found no consolation in Callahan's praise. What he really wanted to do was to hole himself up alone somewhere and let his mind go blank. He had reached his limit. He didn't want to think about the war or the military anymore.

Outside the colonel's tent, Anthony passed by the crowds of soldiers and moving vehicles, busy establishing their base. He went toward the squad working for the graves registration unit. "Did we find any of the scouts?"

"Yes, sir," the squad's leader said. "Everyone's accounted for."

"Any survivors?" Anthony was afraid to ask. The squad leader shook his head. Some of the dead bodies that the graves retrievers had brought back were piled on the ground. Anthony did not see Ed's body among them, but he decided not to ask anymore. If they had found Ed's remains, he would rather not see it. He left and started toward his own tent, but changed his mind and headed toward the medical detachment unit instead.

Inside his tent, Jesse leaned back against his bag, trying but unable to find a good way to sit upright. He pulled his blanket up over his legs. The cold ground and thin cot provided little comfort. Giving up, he took out his flashlight to reread the only letter he had ever gotten since he was deployed. He had read this letter so many times by now, he had memorized every word. Regardless, he took in each sentence carefully, searching for meanings between the lines that he might have missed. Again, the words only pierced his heart.

You will always be in my thoughts. Wherever I am, I will always be wishing you well. — Tessa

What good did that do?

While he was deep in thought, Anthony pushed open the flap of his tent. "Garland."

Anthony's voice startled him. Without giving away a hint of betrayal, Jesse folded the letter, careful not to damage it, and put it back in his inner pocket.

"You got anything strong? And I mean strong." Anthony came in and huddled next to him.

"For you?" He threw Anthony a surprised look. Ardley was not one who ever came to him asking for booze.

"Yes."

Noting the seriousness on Anthony's face, Jesse took a silver flask from his bag and passed it to Anthony. Anthony didn't even ask what it was. He took a swig. Then another. And another.

"Whoa!" Jesse held down Anthony's arm. "Easy there. I'm not taking any responsibility if you get plastered and everyone gets killed tomorrow 'cause you're here flipping your wig."

Ignoring him, Anthony took another mouthful. He picked up a stone and threw it down hard.

Jesse turned his head and looked away. Earlier, after the Germans retreated, he had tried to look for the scouts, hoping against hope that some of them might have survived. What he did find, he would rather not remember.

"When Ed first joined the company, I told him we'd look out for him. 'We've got your six,' I said to him." Anthony took a big gulp from the flask. "I lied. I dealt his death sentence."

"Friendly fire," Jesse said. "Happens."

"Friendly fire happens by accident. I ordered the tanks to shoot."

"You weren't shooting at him. You were shooting at the Krauts. He was in the way."

Anthony scoffed, "At least there'll be one thing I can be thankful for if I don't make it out of this war. I won't have to see his folks. I don't know how I'll ever show my face around his parents again."

"Don't say things like that," Jesse snapped, surprising

Anthony with his strong reaction. "Don't joke about that. What do you think would happen to Tessa if you don't make it out of this war?"

Reminded of Tessa, Anthony looked even more guilt-ridden. "It wasn't just Ed. It's the others too. I ordered our troops to fire when the Krauts tied our own to their tank and made them their human shields. I left a wounded soldier behind for dead back in the woods. You were there. You asked me to send someone, and I refused."

"You did what you had to."

"Did I? I don't know what's right or wrong anymore. I don't know if I can go on. I didn't sign up for this. I didn't come here to kill our own people."

"And if you didn't do what you did, more of us would've been killed. Don't beat yourself up over it."

Anthony wasn't convinced. He held up the flask to drink another shot, but Jesse's first-aid bag caught his attention. "I should've signed up to be a pill roller like you. What you do, it's so...humane. The whole damn world has gone insane. You guys are the last vestiges of humanity. I envy you. I'm part of the insanity. I shoot, I maim, and I kill people. You get to patch them up, bring them back to life, and make them all better. Can I trade places with you?"

Thum-pum. Jesse's heart flipped. "Be careful what you wish for," he said under his breath.

Barely hearing him, Anthony continued. "You know what really infuriates me? Klaus. We weren't going to harm him. He didn't have to kill Warren. In fact, why don't the damn Krauts just give up? Why did Warren have to die? No one had to die. The Krauts can stop now."

"It's war, Ardley." Jesse tried to console him. "If everyone gave up, we wouldn't be at war."

Jesse's words had no effect. Anthony's mind was off on something else. "Klaus and his kind are the problem. You don't know the man like I do. He likes to play mind games. He and his kind aren't just fighting a war. They want to test us. Push us over the edge. That was why they tied our men to the Panzers. That was why Klaus killed Warren. I'm gonna get that sonofabitch if it's the last thing I do." Anthony drank the last of the alcohol in the flask and gave it back to Jesse.

Jesse took the flask. The way Anthony was talking troubled him. "Do you know who you sound like?"

Anthony stared at him, perplexed.

"You sound like Harding. I'm not saying the Krauts are the good guys, but you're seeing malice where it doesn't exist. We're at war, Ardley. Klaus and his kind are doing whatever they have to do to save themselves, the same way we are trying save ourselves."

"No. You don't understand," Anthony said. "I've dealt with Klaus. I've come across him face-to-face more than once. The man has no feelings. He's a cunning, fighting machine. He'll take every chance he can to inflict harm."

"Listen to yourself. You need to get some perspective. If we're stuck in a cave again, I hope Dennison won't have to ask me to order you to stand down."

Anthony paused. Jesse could see from Anthony's face the conflicting thoughts wrestling in his mind. "Let it go, Ardley." He slid down and pulled the blanket over himself. "Go to sleep. Don't obsess over Klaus."

"I can't let it go. What about Warren? I owe it to Warren."

"Hendricks is dead," Jesse said, his teeth chattering from the cold. "It doesn't make any difference to him whether you get Klaus or not. I suppose getting Klaus might make you feel better."

"You're saying I shouldn't try to get Klaus?"

"I didn't say that. Go ahead. Get Klaus. That's your job. Just don't think it matters to Hendricks either way."

"I don't believe that."

"You should. Revenge, justice. Whatever. Doesn't matter. You're taking it all too seriously. If you ask me? Do your job. Then go home." Jesse reached into his bag and pulled out a small bottle of whiskey. "You want more?"

Anthony ignored his offer. "No. I can't agree with that." He got up off the ground. "I owe it to Warren to get the man who killed him. I won't let him die in vain," he said and left the tent.

Jesse watched him leave.

Ardley. Idiot.

He scooted back into his cot and pulled the blanket higher to cover his shoulders.

Klaus. Who cares? If he were Ardley, the only thing he would care about would be to stay alive. Going back to Tessa would be the only thing that would matter for him.

CHAPTER NINETEEN

IN THE THICK forests deep in the Vosges, Operation Dogface was in full swing. Along with the Third Division, Anthony and his company had held their position while the 45th cleared the sectors around Brouvelieures, and the 36th launched an attack in the areas surrounding Bruyères. With German forces diverted, the true mission of Operation Dogface was about to begin. The Rock of Marnes would lead the Seventh Army's main offensive to push through the Vosges toward Saint-Dié and launch a surprise all-out attack along route N-420.

For Anthony and his strike team, their mission to capture Klaus was seamlessly incorporated into the plan.

"Go past Les Rouges-Eaux north of N-420," Colonel Callahan told Anthony when he gave Anthony the secret location of Klaus's whereabouts. "That's where his command post is. If he hasn't escaped yet, you'll find him there. Dennison and the rest of your company will take Highway D-7 and cut off his escape route. You and your strike team will go after him."

"Yes, sir." Anthony knew that this time, he had to succeed.

When they had let Klaus get away back in Montélimar, his entire unit had had to take the fall for it.

"We've got him cornered," Callahan said. "Good luck, Captain. We're counting on you."

Anthony could feel the pressure mounting. The command thought they had taken all the necessary measures to capture the German major. They did not know the true extent of how shrewd Klaus could be. Anthony didn't blame them. One could not know what an extraordinary soldier Klaus was without dealing with him in person. Klaus had demonstrated he could turn a situation around in the most tenuous of circumstances. He had done it without blinking an eye. Whether he was under siege or captured, he always remained cool and calculating, and somehow always found a way to save himself.

"Captain Ardley. Pleasure to finally meet you." The way Klaus spoke, one might have thought he was meeting Anthony over dinner. He had thrown Anthony off guard by revealing that he had known all along about Anthony and his team's mission.

Not this time, Anthony made up his mind. The pressure to get Klaus didn't come only from command. He wanted to do it for Warren too. This time, Anthony swore, he would make Klaus answer for what he had done.

A light armored vehicle carrying the forward observers led the way as Anthony and the Orion strike team trekked up the steep hills. The low hum of their mortar vehicles followed not far behind. They weren't far from Klaus's headquarters now. Today, their target was within reach.

Along the way, Anthony looked out for the slightest rustle of leaves and the faintest crackle of tree branches. Here, they had to be cautious. The Vosges was Satan's fun house. In these forests, the slightest error could spell death for all of them.

They had come a long, treacherous way. The roads up the High Vosges followed along the Moselle River. The river diverged into canals, ditches, and streams that crisscrossed the mountain plains. Climbing up the mountains, they had waded through frigid water with ice frozen on their uniforms. And that was only the beginning.

For days, heavy rain poured, sometimes mixed with snow. Not a moment went by when they weren't freezing and wet. When they finally reached higher elevations and water was no longer there to torment them, the mountains doled out a new array of obstacles to perpetuate their misery. All the roads had become narrow and steep. Getting the tanks and mortar vehicles up the slopes had been an exercise in pure frustration. Sometimes, their convoy would go a long way up the paths, only to come to a dead end in the middle of nowhere. Other times, they would come upon large roadblocks of fallen trees, placed there intentionally by their enemy to obstruct their advance.

If their vehicles did pass the roads, there would be dense thickets of trees and shrubs to further test their will. Riding in the vehicles, the soldiers could not see through the trees and bushes to strike their targets. At the same time, the vehicles themselves would become easy targets for the enemy camouflaged in the foliage. So rather than the tanks protecting the infantry, the infantry had to spread out to patrol the surrounding area to protect the tanks from being ambushed.

The infantry soldiers on patrol had to be on constant lookout. Tripwires, snipers, machine guns, Panzers, and self-propelled armory were hidden everywhere, waiting for them. Danger came not only from the ground, but also from above. Without warning, machine gun bullets would shower down from the tops of the trees. The forests were filled with lethal hidden weapons and booby traps. One small erratic move was all it took to set them off.

For those who were lucky enough to survive through the forest, the landmines buried under the mountain plains would be there to greet them when they came out of the woods.

In the High Vosges, no place was safe. No one was safe.

"Sir, we're coming close," Fox said. As always, he was walking with Anthony. They had been climbing this mountain all morning. Like a squire ready to guard and protect his leader, Fox remained close by his side. Klaus's command post was not far ahead past the next thicket of trees further up the slopes.

Mindful of the perils surrounding them, Anthony kept his eyes and ears alert. A burst of wind blew through the chilled air, and the tree branches swayed. A startled bird screeched and flew off. The sudden flapping sound of its wings made everyone's heart jump. Mumbles of profanity and nervous laughs followed.

Before they were done breathing a sigh of relief, *Boom!* A shell blasted into the top of the trees above the armored vehicle leading their way. A hailstorm of burning shrapnel and splintered wood sprayed down at the men below. Their shrieks of pain were answered by more shells blasting into the top of the forest. The troops scattered and ran for cover. The cyclone of enemy machine gun bullets continued as they raced to brace themselves against the closest trees to avoid being hit by the deadly shell fragments falling from above.

In the confusion, Anthony dashed up the slope to a safe spot behind a tree. Through the acrid smoke, gunpowder, and deafening explosions, he saw the German Tiger tank higher above them that was causing all the mayhem. The Tiger tank kept on shelling until the Orion strike team's own destroyer fired its gun and the Tiger tank blew up.

The horrifying shelling had stopped, but the strike team and the enemy soldiers were now caught in a deadly gunfight. Near him, rifle shots snapped down from the slope above.

Jonesy, Fox, and everyone else near them were pinned to the ground. One of his soldiers tried to return fire. In return, a sniper's bullet zipped down and hit him, killing him instantly.

Anthony winced. Behind a bush, Fox fired in the sniper's direction. Another round of gunfire ensued, but Jonesy and his squad still could not move. Anthony looked up the slope, searching for a way out. Concealed behind a wall of oak trees, the sniper's vision was obstructed. Making as little movement as possible so as not to draw the sniper's attention, Anthony moved higher up into a thick row of fir and scuttled toward a boulder near the sniper. From behind the boulder, he pulled his pistol from his holster and aimed. When the sniper raised his gun again toward Jonesy's squad, Anthony pulled the trigger and fired. His bullet hit the sniper in the head, and the man fell backward behind the trees.

Anthony threw a grenade into the oak trees, in case there were other snipers up there. The grenade exploded. For a brief moment, he thought the threat had subsided, but a round of machine gun bullets came firing in his direction. Behind the dead sniper, the woods thinned out. Anthony could see the German machine gunners guarding Klaus's command post from behind a barricade of tree logs.

He looked down the slope. Jonesy, Fox, and the others were now pinned down by the machine gun behind the barricade. The machine gunners were showering bullets at them as they tried to climb up. Anthony was the only one far enough up the slope to try to take the machine gunners down.

There was no time to think. As fast as he could, Anthony sprinted toward the barricade and lobbed a grenade, then another one for good measure. The grenades went off. Several men behind the barricade howled. The machine gun fire stopped.

Cautiously, Anthony walked up the slope to the barricade. Beyond where the trees thinned out, he could see Klaus's command post. An underground bunker well-concealed by the rise of the natural landscape and camouflaged behind soil, weeds, and leaves.

"Jonesy, Jonesy," he said into his walkie-talkie.

"Captain," Jonesy's voice returned.

"I found it. Klaus's command post. Bring everyone up." He gave Jonesy the coordinates and took a few steps toward the path to the command post. Could Klaus be in there?

Should he wait for Jonesy and the rest to catch up?

Below, Jonesy had gone back down the slope. The strike team and their support units were still battling the German troops below.

Klaus was not one to wait for his own death and do nothing. He had to know the American troops were on to him and his own troops were faltering. Every minute lost was another minute for Klaus to make his attempt to get away.

Warren.

"You're not getting away this time," Anthony muttered under his breath and started toward his target.

Clutching his Tommy, Anthony came to the edge of the woods not far from the bunker. He stared at the entrance and ran through in his mind the possible ways to capture Klaus. Behind him, the rustling sound of leaves made his heart jump.

"Stop," said a voice behind him.

Anthony's heart plunged as soon as he heard the voice.

"Hands up. Drop your weapon."

Lowering his arms, Anthony felt his whole body sinking. *This can't be. How can this be?*

He dropped his Tommy and raised his hands.

"Turn around."

Having no choice but to comply, Anthony turned around. Klaus's crystalline eyes and the barrel of his Luger were all Anthony could see. He still had his pistol in his holster, but he could not pull it out with the Luger pointing at him.

"Here we are, Captain Ardley. Just you and I. Curious, isn't it? Are you chasing me? Or am I chasing you?" Klaus smiled at him. The smile sent a chill down Anthony's spine.

Refusing to back down, Anthony looked Klaus in the eye. No. He would not give Klaus the satisfaction of seeing his fear. If this was the end, then he would at least stand up to his enemy until the end.

"You didn't think I would just sit around and let you hunt me down, did you, Captain Ardley? Maybe I overestimated you."

Defiant, Anthony said nothing. His eyes remain fixed on Klaus. Cold sweat dripped down his back.

"You don't talk much, do you, Captain?" Klaus said. Even now, he was speaking as if they were only having a friendly chat. His demeanor, though, showed his true intent. He watched Anthony, his eyes clear and alert. "You should've killed me when you had a chance. Your mistake was being too greedy. It wasn't enough that you got me. You wanted information from me," he said with a condescending smile before his lips hardened. "I would've never given you and your brass any information. Not about the Amerika Bomber. Not about anything else. If you were smart, you should've gotten rid of me, and we wouldn't be here today."

"That's not how we operate," Anthony said. "We don't kill unless we have to. Unlike you." He still remembered Warren's dead body lying on the ground.

"Ah," Klaus said. "You're telling me you had mercy. Captain, we're at war. Mercy is not a good thing in war. It's a defect. A weakness. You should know that. Next time, don't give in to mercy. How unfortunate though. You won't have a next time." He raised his Luger and pointed it at Anthony's head. "You'll forgive me, I hope. It's nothing personal. But next time, you might be pointing your gun at me, and I can't risk that."

Anthony took a short, deep breath. In a moment, his entire life flashed before him.

Tessa.

He closed his eyes.

"Drop your gun." A voice came from behind Klaus. Anthony opened his eyes in surprise. Jesse was pointing a rifle at Klaus. Klaus turned his head slightly sideways to see who it was.

"Drop your gun or I'll shoot," Jesse said.

Klaus glanced at Jesse and the red cross banner around his arm. "Medic. Are you sure you know how to handle your gun? Got to be careful with that, or you might hurt someone. We wouldn't want that now, would we?"

Jesse didn't answer him. Klaus turned his gaze back to Anthony. "Captain. Looks like today's your lucky day after all."

"Quit stalling and drop your gun," Jesse warned again.

"Okay, okay. Take it easy, medic. Let's not have any accidents." Klaus bought his arm gingerly to his side, crouched down as if to put his gun on the ground, and quickly turned toward Jesse. Before either Anthony or Jesse could see what he was doing, Klaus raised his Luger and fired a shot at Jesse. On reflex, Jesse pulled the trigger of his rifle as he fell back. The shot hit Klaus's arm as he lurched sideways and dropped his gun.

"Jesse!" Anthony shouted. He grabbed his Tommy off the ground and aimed it at Klaus while Klaus fled into the forest. He fired but Klaus ran and disappeared into the mass of trees.

"Garland! Garland!" Anthony ran over to Jesse. Blood was spilling out of the left side of Jesse's chest. Anthony pressed his hands on the wound and tried to stop the bleeding.

"It's no use," Jesse said. He grabbed Anthony by his collar and pulled Anthony toward him. "Ardley. I want you to listen to me."

"Jesse," Anthony said. "Hold on!" Anthony pressed harder on Jesse's chest while blood oozed over his hands.

"No. Listen to me," Jesse coughed, choking on his own blood. "Ugh!" He groaned and struggled to talk. "My whole life, I've loved only one person. One person." He pulled Anthony closer. "Tessa. She's the only one...the only girl I've ever loved, and I can't do anything about it because she's yours." He choked again. Blood dripped out of his mouth and spots of blood splattered over Anthony's chin and collar as he spoke.

"She loves you. She thinks you're her everything. The only thing I can do for her that you can't is to look out for your sorry ass. So I swore to myself, if you ever get hurt, I'll do everything I can to get you back to her. I haven't let you out of my sight since we left Rome." He looked at the wound on his chest and laughed. "This wasn't what I had in mind."

Anthony listened, too stunned to respond.

"The lady or the tiger, Ardley."

"What?"

"The lady or the tiger, remember? We talked about this."

The Lady or the Tiger. Anthony remembered now. The first time he met Jesse. Jesse who said he wouldn't do anything for love. Jesse who thought the princess should have killed the maiden rather than send her lover to either the lady or the tiger.

"Guess you're getting the lady." Jesse laughed. Anthony watched with a falling heart as Jesse coughed. "You have to stay alive, all right?" Jesse took his lucky seven dice out of his pocket and placed them on top of Anthony's hand. Anthony stared at him, confused.

"For luck. To keep you alive." He smiled. "You stay alive no matter what. You do what you have to but get through this war. Get through it and go back to her. Nothing else matters.

Nothing. You hear me?" His voice growing weaker. "If you die, she'll be very sad. Don't make her sad."

Unable to stop the bleeding, Anthony watched Jesse's life seep out of him. "Jesse!"

But Jesse couldn't hear anything anymore. As the world slipped farther and farther away, he felt calm. Serene. Shrouded by a comforting sense of peace. Everything was now behind him. Whatever wrong he had done in the past, whatever pain he had caused, whatever inexplicable reason had brought him onto this earth, and to whatever or whomever he owed his life, his debt was paid. It felt like spring again. A new beginning, and all he felt was love. In his last vision, he saw Tessa, smiling at him.

His eyes closed. His hand that was holding Anthony's collar dropped to the ground.

In shock, Anthony picked up the lucky seven dice. What happened?

Jesse…in love with Tessa…

Jesse…took a bullet and tried to protect him. If Jesse hadn't come to his rescue, Klaus would have killed him. He would be dead now. Anthony's hands trembled at the thought.

But what about Jesse? He didn't want Jesse to die for him. He wanted to bring Jesse back to life.

"Jesse!" He picked up Jesse's shoulders and shook his body, wishing he could wake him, but there was no response.

"Captain," Fox called out to him. "Captain Ardley."

Devastated, Anthony held on to Jesse's body. Fox came closer. "Captain! What happened?"

"Klaus got away," Anthony said. He put the lucky seven dice into his pocket.

Fox looked around. "Captain, we should go."

Not heeding Fox's warning, Anthony touched the blood stain on Jesse's uniform where the bullet had struck him in the chest.

Jesse, in love with Tessa. Did she know?

If she knew, how would she feel now knowing Jesse had died for her? For them?

"Captain. Let's go. We should keep moving," Fox urged him.

Anthony picked up Jesse's body and carried him over his shoulders back down the hill. The weight of guilt bore down on him like a colossal mountain.

The High Vosges. It was an unforgiving place.

REUNION IN PARIS

Part Six

CHAPTER TWENTY

A FEELING of déjà vu overcame Tessa as she placed the farewell letter on Aaron Haley's desk. Hadn't she already done this once already? She looked around and found herself in the doctor's office at the 33rd Field Hospital. She was back in Rome.

Someone was watching her. Who? She turned around. Jesse. Standing by the door, he seemed so close, yet so far away. "This is goodbye then?" he asked.

He looked so forlorn and alone. She wanted to go to him and console him. Inexplicably somehow, she could not move. Her feet felt stuck to the ground.

He came toward her. He still looked sad, but there was no more anguish in his eyes. In its place was a distant look of acceptance that she could not understand.

He put his hands on her shoulders. "Will you miss me?"

His voice was so tender, she wanted to hear him whisper in her ear.

"Yes," she said. "Yes, I'll miss you."

He smiled and stroked her cheek.

"Don't go." She didn't know what came over her. In the moment, all she wanted was for him to stay. She would do anything to keep him from leaving. "Please don't go." She touched his chest and unbuttoned the top of his shirt.

He took her hands and stopped her.

She reached up on her toes and tried to kiss his lips, but he put his hands on her shoulders again and gently pushed her back.

"Please, Jesse. Stay."

He smiled again and let go of her. She watched him walk to the door. She wanted to run after him, but her legs were stuck like rock. She could not move. When he reached the door, he turned around once more. "I love you more than you'll ever know."

And then, he was gone.

"Don't go. Don't go," she whispered over and over again, but he was gone.

The winter sun peered through the windows, signaling the start of another day. In these forest regions near the Belgian Ardennes, snow had already arrived. A heavy mist had set in outside while the nurses slept. Under the gray sky and dim light of the quiet dawn, Tessa woke up from her dream. Her nose felt cold from the room's frosty temperature after a night spent in this unheated stone building where the hospital staff had set up their temporary quarters.

Her mind still foggy, she looked around. The other nurses in the room were still asleep. She turned from her side to her back and stared up at the ceiling. More awake now, she remembered what day it was. Today, she would leave for Paris. A rush of excitement sprung up in her heart.

Almost immediately, the vivid memory from her dream flashed through her mind and slashed her feeling of elation.

I love you more than you'll ever know.

Jesse's voice resonated in her mind. The details of the

dream came back to her. In her dream, she had tried to unbutton his shirt and kiss him.

Why did she dream about Jesse this way? She wouldn't do that. How disconcerting. On the night before she was leaving to go see Anthony too.

But in her sleep, she had felt them, those feelings she had for Jesse when she tried to kiss him. In her dream, she had yearned for him to stay. That yearning was still with her, and so strong too.

Trying to shake off the awkwardness brought on by the dream, she got up, grabbed her face towel and toothbrush, and went to the washroom. On her way, she couldn't help feeling a pang of guilt.

It was a dream, she told herself. *You can't control what you dream.* She did her best to put it out of her mind.

The train pulled into Gare du Nord station shortly after two o'clock. Her heart filled with anticipation, Tessa stepped off the train onto the platform.

Paris. The City of Love.

Her heart was bursting with excitement. Four months had passed since she and Anthony had last seen each other. To have three days with him in Paris was a dream come true.

The city bus took her down the Boulevard de Sébastopol toward the Latin Quarter. Paris was a familiar place to her. She had come here many times with her parents when she was a child. For Anthony, this would be his first visit. She planned on being his tour guide. In America, she always felt he knew more about everything than she did. This time, she would get to show him where everything was and what everything was about.

There were so many places she wanted to take him. They

would go to all the major tourist sites, of course. There were other, lesser-known places too, like the Shakespeare and Company bookstore on Rue de l'Odéon, where her father liked to go. It was the same bookstore the writer James Joyce had frequented. She wondered if the bookstore was still there. She wanted to take Anthony there. He would be fascinated.

She got off at the bus stop across from the Seine River. On her way to the hotel, she passed by a fashion boutique, where a beautiful satin dress was on display in the window. Its color, azure blue, captivated her. She stopped to look at it, and saw her own reflection in the glass. She looked so grubby in her ragged army uniform. In an instant, she made up her mind and went into the store.

"*Bonjour.*" The girl working at the store greeted her.

"*Bonjour. Puis-je voir cette robe?*" She pointed to the blue dress in the display window. The French classes from her St. Mary's days had some use after all.

"*Bien sûr. Venez s'il vous plaît.*" The sales girl brought Tessa the dress and led her to the back of the store. Holding the dress by the hanger over her body, Tessa looked into the full-length mirror. The dress reminded her of the blue sky on a clear summer day.

Blue like Anthony's eyes.

"It's stunning," she said, more to herself than to the sales girl.

Not understanding Tessa's words, the sales girl smiled and pointed to the fitting room. "*Voulez-vous l'essayer?*"

Worried that she might soil the dress, Tessa shook her head. "*Pas besoin. Je vais la prendre.*" The dress looked about her size. She would just have to take the chance that it would fit. She turned to the mirror one more time. She couldn't wait to see Anthony's face when he saw her in this dress.

In the train car reserved for the army officers, Anthony sat in the corner of the last row of seats as far away as he could be from the other passengers. Only one other lone officer sat across the aisle from him, reading a book. During the entire ride, Anthony kept to himself, wanting to be left alone.

The rattling sounds of the train traveling across the tracks pounded his head like a hammer. Outside the window, the scenic countryside swished by before he could catch its full beauty. Not that it mattered. He could not enjoy the view. He turned his gaze away from the window. The claustrophobic interior of the train gave him no escape.

He opened his palm and looked at the lucky seven dice. Their chain dangled from his hand and swung to the motions of the moving train.

"My whole life, I've loved only one person. One person."

Jesse, the man to whom Anthony now owed his life, said he had loved only one person.

"Tessa. She's the only one...the only girl I've ever loved."

Why? Anthony kept asking himself. Why did Jesse do it? Why did he risk his life to save him?

Jesse could've let him die. If he loved Tessa, why didn't he let Klaus kill him? If Anthony was gone, Tessa would be free.

No one has greater love than this, to lay down one's life for one's friends.

When he married Tessa, this was a line in his wedding vow. His vow. How did this happen? How did his vow become an act of love to his wife demonstrated by another man?

Anthony tightened his fist around the dice and struck his fist sideways against the train car's wall. The sound of the punch startled the officer sitting across the aisle. The officer glanced at Anthony, then turned his attention back to his book.

Left to his own thoughts again, Anthony clasped his hands and lowered his forehead onto his fists. The chain of the dice dangled from between his palms, reminding him of the debt he could never erase.

How could he go on with Tessa now, knowing that Jesse had wanted her too? Did it not matter what Jesse wanted?

Part of him felt angry. If Jesse hadn't saved him, he wouldn't feel so guilty about being with Tessa, his own wife.

If Jesse hadn't saved him, he wouldn't be alive to be with Tessa.

Unable to clear his thoughts, Anthony buried his head in his hands. The rattling of the train grew louder and louder, hounding his mind.

If he hadn't run after Klaus alone, could Jesse's death have been avoided? Should he have waited for the rest of his troops and the backups to arrive before heading toward the clearing?

A mountain of guilt weighed down on Anthony.

Why wasn't there any way to undo everything? What could he do now to make everything right?

CHAPTER TWENTY-ONE

In the hotel room, Tessa checked herself in the mirror. In her new blue dress, she felt like a pin-up movie star. Not since her wedding day had she looked so fresh and pretty. Anthony would be so surprised.

She picked up her bottle of rose perfume and sprayed a light layer on her neck. Anthony loved it when she wore her rose perfume.

All ready, she waited for him in the sitting area. The flicker of the candle on the small table in the center of the room danced like the beats of joy in her heart. Anthony should be here any time now. She fiddled with her rose pendant and imagined the moment when they saw each other again.

At last, a knock. Her heart raced as she opened the door.

She thought Anthony would take her into his arms, sweep her off her feet, and kiss her the moment he saw her. Instead, he held his distance from her. His ashen face and his sorrowful eyes confused her. She had never seen him look so disheartened before, not even on their worst days in Anzio.

"Anthony?"

He walked into the room and dropped his rucksack on the floor. The warmth of excitement Tessa had felt earlier came to a dead stop. A disquieting silence filled the room. Something truly awful had happened. What could have brought Anthony down this way?

"Anthony?" Tessa closed the door and came near him. "What's wrong?"

Anthony took a dog tag out of his jacket and put it on the table. A chill shot up Tessa's spine, sending goose bumps to her arms. Whose tag was this? Why was Anthony showing her a dog tag?

Warily, she reached out to pick it up. Before she had it in her hand, she could see the name imprinted on it. Her hand froze. She looked at Anthony, but he turned and looked the other way. She took the tag, hoping against hope that her eyes were wrong. They were not. The name on the tag was clear and could not be mistaken.

"The man I've been chasing, Klaus," Anthony said in a low voice, "he had his gun pointed at me. I was supposed to catch him, but instead of catching him, he caught me and he was pointing his gun at me. He was going to kill me."

Tessa put her hand on the table to steady herself.

"I should be dead now, but Jesse saved me. He was following me. I didn't know he was following me. No one else was. He saw me going off alone. He picked up a rifle from a dead soldier and followed me. When Klaus got me cornered, he tried to get Klaus to let me go and threatened to shoot him if he didn't.'"

She held up the dog tag. The cold piece of metal lay in her hand, a cold reminder of his death.

"Klaus played us. He pretended to put his gun down but he shot Jesse. Jesse shot him back, but he got away. And then..." Anthony swallowed and couldn't go on. Tessa came closer to him, but he pulled away. "I couldn't save him. I tried but I couldn't save him."

Tessa closed her eyes, but could not stop the flood of tears.

"He said he loved you."

She looked up.

"He said you're the only one he ever loved. He said he decided to look out for me because you loved me. He said looking out for me was the only thing he could do for you that I couldn't."

Tessa pulled out a chair and collapsed into the seat. Silently, she cried while holding tight onto Jesse's dog tag.

Anthony watched as Tessa cried her silent tears. Tessa had shown no surprise when he told her that Jesse had feelings for her. Her pain on hearing the news of his death was beyond that of an ordinary friend. Anthony didn't want to think this, but he wondered. "Did you know?"

"Know what?"

"Did you know he loved you?"

Rather than answering the question, she cried even harder. There was no doubt that she knew.

"How did you know?"

"He told me."

Anthony's heart sank. She had never said anything about this. How long had she known? What really went on between her and Jesse back in Anzio? How did it get to the point where he would die for her?

"Did anything ever happen between you and Jesse?" Anthony was almost afraid to ask.

Tessa held her hand to her face. He could see she did not want to answer this question. "He kissed me. Once."

Anthony felt his world falling apart. Nothing, it seemed, was what he understood it to be.

"I didn't kiss him back." Tessa jumped from the chair and grabbed his arm. "He caught me by surprise. He told me he loved me and then he kissed me. I was caught off guard and I didn't kiss him back. You have to believe me. I told him I love you."

She told him she loves me.

But what about Jesse?

"You told him you love me. If I wasn't here, could you have fallen in love with him?"

Tessa didn't answer. That was enough for Anthony to know what he wanted to know. If she had said no right away, perhaps everything would still be all right. Perhaps he could live with himself, if he knew that Tessa would not have loved Jesse anyway had Anthony himself been the one who died. At least then, his own survival and love for Tessa would have had no bearing on Jesse's hopes. But she didn't answer right away. She had to stop and think.

"You could," Anthony said. His own heart in pain, he smiled. Jesse did not have to give up and die. If he hadn't tried to save Anthony, he would have had his chance with Tessa.

"No. No, Anthony," Tessa pulled his arm in vehement denial. "I love you. You know I love you."

Her denial now made no difference. "That bullet had my name on it. It should've been me who died. If I had died, you could've fallen in love with him, and he would've deserved you."

"No, Anthony. Don't say that. I don't want you to die. I don't want to be without you."

"You would rather he died instead of me then?"

Speechless, she could not respond. She held on to his arm, her eyes filled with despair.

Don't make her sad. Jesse's last words.

Remembering those words, Anthony loathed himself even

more. Jesse would not have asked Tessa such an impossible question. "I'm sorry. That's a cruel question and I'm not being fair." He noticed her dress for the first time since he arrived. "You look so beautiful tonight. Too bad Jesse can't see how beautiful you look in your dress."

"No. No. No." Tessa sat back down. "This isn't real. This is not real." She shook her head. "You said he threatened to shoot the man who tried to kill you."

"Yes."

"This isn't real. You got this wrong. This can't be. Jesse wouldn't take a gun to anyone. I know he wouldn't. He can't kill. It's against his conscience. He can't kill." She said this with full faith and conviction. It was clear to Anthony, her feelings for Jesse ran much deeper, even if she herself didn't know it.

"Maybe so," he said with a bittersweet smile of defeat. "But he would kill for you, and he died for you."

Tessa broke down and buried her face in her hands.

"I'd like to think I would do the same for you if I had to," Anthony said. "But how can I ever prove it? I'll never be able to prove this to you or to myself." He took a step back away from her. "I don't know why I'm here today and he's not. He deserves you. After what he did, I can't compare."

"You don't have to compare. You don't have to prove anything. I love you."

"But you could've loved him. Everything could've been his. Should've been his."

Tessa tried to speak, but she couldn't. She didn't have to say anything though. Anthony understood. He understood completely. Neither of them could say that Jesse's love for her made no difference. They could not say that their love for each other was all that mattered. Their love came at the cost of Jesse's hopes, his happiness, and his life. Nothing felt right. Tessa put her face in her hands again and cried.

Looking at her, Anthony wanted to console her. But what could he say? Tell her he was sorry? Tell her not to be upset? How could he ask her not to mourn the death of the person who had saved his life? How could he say he was sorry, when he already hated himself for not feeling sorry enough. Earlier, when she opened the door to greet him, he felt glad and relieved that he had lived to see her again. He hated that he felt glad, when someone else had to die in his place. Worse than that, he had indirectly brought about Jesse's death. He made the mistake of going after Klaus alone. His feelings of guilt ate at him like rotten vermin chewing away at his flesh from the inside.

He didn't want to feel happy. He didn't want to feel glad he had survived. He didn't want to be happy with Tessa without thinking of what Jesse had sacrificed.

Still holding Jesse's dog tag, Tessa looked deflated and lost.

He felt wrong being here. He could find no way to commiserate with her. She was in her own world, one where Jesse occupied her mind. Anthony felt his own presence was an intrusion. He picked up his rucksack and quietly left the room. He didn't know if she had noticed him leaving. She didn't come after him.

Not knowing where he was going, he left the hotel and wandered aimlessly through the streets. A myriad of thoughts ran through his mind.

Jesse didn't think about himself. He didn't think twice about dying for her.

Tessa said Jesse kissed her. A vision of Jesse embracing her and kissing her invaded his mind. The vision felt like a stab in his heart, and he hated himself for feeling hurt. Jesse was dead. How could he be jealous of a dead man?

Jesse had given his life so Tessa could be with the one she loved. He, Anthony, on the other hand, couldn't even spare Jesse for giving her one kiss?

The more Anthony thought about it, the more unworthy he felt. He was not half the man that Jesse was.

He walked farther and farther away from the hotel. Tessa deserved a worthier man. He didn't know if he could face her again.

———

For hours, Anthony rode the bus. He didn't know where the bus was going, and he didn't care. He didn't know where he wanted to go. Passengers came and went. GIs, Parisian civilians, he paid no attention. He felt displaced in a world that was moving on. He shouldn't be here.

Why was he still here? Why was Jesse gone?

Why was Warren gone? Ollie and Jim Darnell too. And Wesley. Why were they all gone?

Why did he get to live and they didn't?

I can do it, Captain. He remembered Edmond's confident smile as he walked down the hill to his doom.

Edmond. The officers tied to the Panzer when they entered the battle in Montélimar. The injured soldier left behind in the forest, and the private who had tried to rescue him. Every one of them remained vivid in Anthony's mind. How could he ever make it up to them? How could he make it up to Jesse?

He couldn't stay in Paris. He couldn't be here, enjoying his life when they were all dead. He could not let them die in vain.

He had to go back. The Allies had to win this war, or all of them would have died for nothing. He had to do everything he could to help win the war.

Above all, he had to get Klaus. For Warren. For Jesse.

His mind made up, he got off the bus at the stop closest to the USO headquarters, where he went to write Tessa a letter. When he finished, he gave it to a staff administrator for delivery to her at the hotel, and left for the train station for the next train back to the Vosges.

The train would not arrive until 0600 hours the next morning. Anthony lay down on the wooden bench on the platform to catch some sleep. Deep into the night, the temperature dropped to freezing point. He shivered and pulled his jacket tighter. There was an inn nearby the station, but he didn't want to go. What was a little cold compared to what happened to the ones who had died? Anyway, by now, he was used to being outside in the winter. All he wanted was for the train to arrive to take him back to where he could pay back what he owed everyone.

Off and on through the night, he thought of Tessa. How could he carry on with her without regard for Jesse? Every time he thought of her, he felt like he had wronged Jesse.

He kept seeing Tessa happy in Jesse's arms. Jesse kissing her. Jesse walking away with her. The troubling images kept him awake, and he twisted and turned on the bench, unable to reconcile all the conflicting thoughts battling in his mind. The few hours' sleep that he did have were plagued by dreams. Dreams of all those who were now gone. Dreams of people and faces he could not forget.

Alone in the hotel room, Tessa lay on the bed, holding her angel amulet close to her face. Anthony was gone. Yesterday, while she was lost in grief, he had left the hotel and didn't come back. He didn't say goodbye. All he had left behind was a short letter he had sent from the USO headquarters.

Dear Tessa,

I am returning to the front. I owe it to Jesse to get the man who killed him. I will not rest until I get Klaus. Jesse deserves you a hundred times more than I do. If I can win him justice, and I know that he can rest in peace, maybe then, we will be able to get on with our lives. I can see now that you care greatly for him. I will do everything I can to avenge him for you. Maybe then, I will be truly worthy of your love.

— *Until then, Anthony*

Tessa left the message on the table after she had read it. She didn't care to read it again. Anthony. How stupid. How could he think he was not worthy of her love?

She clutched her angel amulet tighter. Tears fell from the corners of her eyes, soaking the pillow beneath her face.

Will you miss me?

"Yes. Yes, I miss you. I miss you very much."

Jesse couldn't hear her.

Life. How fragile it was. Gone. Like the wind, Jesse was gone. To another side where she couldn't see and couldn't touch. The dead and the living, separated by an invisible wall through which no one could pass.

Why did fate have to play this cruel trick on them? Why did she and Jesse have to meet when she was already in love with Anthony? How was she supposed to feel now, knowing how deeply Jesse had loved her? Could she have done more for him when he was alive?

Jesse was so alone. So misunderstood. She knew in her heart that she was his only true friend. If only time could turn backward. She wished she could go back in time to tell him he was not alone. She wished she could tell him that she, at least, understood him and cared about him. It was all too late now.

What about Anthony?

Anthony.

"If I wasn't here, could you have fallen in love with him?"

Anthony looked devastated when she didn't tell him no.

How could she explain to him that she didn't answer because, when he asked her that question, her memory of her dream the night before had sprung to her mind? She couldn't answer because she remembered that in the dream, she had tried to kiss Jesse. The sudden memory made her pause. She didn't know what to make of it.

But it was only a dream. A stupid dream over which she had no control. After that, she had tried to tell Anthony she loved him, but it wasn't enough. She had hurt him.

"Anthony," she whispered through her tears. He couldn't hear her either.

What if something happened to him? What if he was killed too, and she never had the chance to tell him how much he mattered to her? She didn't want to lose him.

The thought hit her like a lightning bolt. She had to tell him. She had to let him know. She had to write to him. Drawing on all the strength she had, she got up and went to the desk, and began writing.

Anthony,

I am so sorry you had to find out everything about me and Jesse this way. What a burden you must have carried on your way to Paris to deliver the news to me. I can imagine what you must be going through now.

I know nothing I say will change anything in the past. I only ask that you do not doubt me. I don't want to answer the question of whether I could love Jesse if you weren't there, because I don't ever want to be in a world where you aren't there. I chose you. Wherever you are, my heart is yours. It has always been yours. Remember, in Rome? You told me then, whatever happens, don't give up. I'm not giving up on us. I won't give up.

Come back.

I love you. I vow to love you for all eternity.

Come back to me.

— Yours always, before and forever hereafter, Tessa

KAMPFGRUPPE PFEIFFER

Part Seven

CHAPTER TWENTY-TWO

A TROOP of three hundred German soldiers, now prisoners of war, marched down the streets. In his jeep, Anthony passed them without giving them a look. The German prisoners to him were but an afterthought. He was after only one man.

Since returning to the Vosges, he had been on a relentless pursuit of Klaus. Following the Seventh Army pushing forward to the German border along the Rhine, he led the Orion strike team and advanced through village after village, searching for the man who was the pillar of the enemy's defense in the south. The man who was responsible for Warren's and Jesse's deaths.

Deep in these mountains, Klaus had left his footprints everywhere. From the propaganda flyers dropped from the sky to the radio broadcasts to the Germans hiding in foxholes on the ground. He called for his troops not to surrender, to take their last stand and fight to their last man. His rallying calls spurred the German troops to keep on with their fanatical resistance.

Beyond the noise and fervor, the German forces had regrouped. The enemy had sent new armies and Panzer units to reinforce their troops along the German West Wall. Known also as the Siegfried Line, the West Wall was a defensive barrier that stretched three hundred and ninety miles from Switzerland to the Netherlands. It was made up of a network of hundreds of interlocking links of pillboxes, trenches, and observation posts, fortified by acres of mines, tripwires, and tank traps.

The West Wall was said to be invincible. No army in history had ever defeated an enemy defending the Vosges.

Undaunted, Anthony pressed on. The West Wall might indeed be invincible, but if he could take down the tallest tree in the mountain, if he could pierce a hole in the wall, it might cause a crack that would lead the wall to crumble. That was why he must get Klaus.

When he did get Klaus, perhaps then, the lives of all those who had died would not be in vain. Perhaps then, he would have finally done enough to be worthy of being alive again.

His driver took him back to the command station, a large open tent in the rear where he spent most of his time now when he was not out on the field. He poured himself a cup of coffee. A cold breeze blew past him, bringing with it flurries of snowflakes drifting in the air.

Back in Chicago, the night of New Year's Eve two years ago, light flurries of snow were dancing in the air when he and Tessa walked along the Michigan Avenue Bridge. That night felt like a lifetime ago.

He took her letter out of his pocket. He had had the letter for two weeks, but he hadn't opened it. He wasn't ready. Not yet. If she told him in the letter that she loved Jesse and that she felt any regrets, he didn't know if he could still hold himself together and do what he had to do.

When he got Klaus. When he had repaid Jesse for the sacrifice of his life, and made it up to Tessa for the loss of Jesse, he would go back to her and take back what belonged to him.

Only then.

In the nurses' quarters, Tessa mindlessly sketched the illustration she had made on her notepad while her fellow nurses gathered around a small portable stove to fend off the chilly temperature. One of them noticed her sitting on her cot by herself and called out to her, "Tessa, want to come over here where it's warmer?"

Tessa smiled and politely shook her head. She returned to her drawing. Sketching had become her new pastime. Tyler had suggested it last week when he came by the hospital.

"If you can't paint, why don't you make pencil sketches like me?" he asked her.

"I'm not funny like you. I don't know how to draw humorous comic characters."

"Then draw something serious. Draw something meaningful to you."

She agreed to give it a try. The more she sketched, the more she was hooked. Everything she found difficult to say in words, and all the emotions she felt but could not express, took on tangible forms in her sketches.

She darkened the edge of the horizon over which the sun set on Anzio beach. On the beach, she shaded the tiny silhouettes of the young couple looking out to the sea.

"Look at the sea, Tessa. Look how vast and beautiful it is. What we have ahead is this sea. It won't change. The war can't take it away."

The war can't take it away.

Those were Anthony's words. She had to hold on to these words. She had to believe that no matter what happened in this war, it couldn't take away their love. Having faith in what Anthony himself had said was all she could do to maintain hope after what happened in Paris.

"We have to be like the sea. Try our best and hold on to who we are.

The sea, the things that are beautiful, those are what we have waiting for us."

Could they really hold on to who they were? Could they go back to loving each other as they did? She stopped her drawing. Where was Anthony now? Had he received her letter yet? Why hadn't he written back? Did he remember these words that he had told her back in Anzio? She needed to hurry and finish this sketch and send it to him. Maybe it would remind him of all their dreams.

She flipped back to the sketch she had drawn a few days earlier. The sketch was one of Jesse the way she remembered him, dashing and radiant under the evening sun in Rome.

Jesse.

A sharp pain cut through her heart.

Her thoughts were interrupted when Ellie entered with a parcel along with a stack of papers. Mail! The nurses sitting around the portable stove rushed toward Ellie. Everyone hoped they had gotten letters from home. Anxious, Tessa went over to join them. One by one, Ellie distributed the V-mail. Nothing. Nothing for her. No word from Anthony.

Heartbroken, she returned to her cot. In two weeks, it would be Christmas. Last Christmas, they had hoped the war would be over by now. She never imagined that everything would turn out like this.

Ellie came over and asked, "Are you okay?"

Tessa tried to smile, but couldn't.

Ellie sat down next to her. "I heard the war's going very tough for the Seventh Army. I'm sure Anthony has written to you. It's probably just mail delay."

Maybe, but deep inside, Tessa doubted that this was the case.

"Look." Ellie showed her the parcel she had brought with her. "I got a Christmas package from my parents." She opened the parcel. Inside, there were canned meats, salami, cookies, candy, books and magazines, even socks and mittens. An envelope, already opened, lay on top of the goods. Tessa noticed the sender was Aaron Haley. She glanced at Ellie. Ellie's face turned red. Quickly, she moved the goods around in the parcel to conceal the letter. "I asked my folks to send me gifts to pass out to the troops. Why don't we go to Honsfeld? We can give some of these to Tyler and the boys in his medical battalion who are resting there. I bet they'll be thrilled to get some Christmas presents."

Tessa agreed. She could use a diversion, and delighting Tyler and his friends could lift her spirits too. She put away her sketches and notepad, and left with Ellie for Honsfeld, the little village that was the 99th Division's rest center.

Outside the nurses' quarters, the Blade and another soldier drove by in a jeep. They noticed Tessa and Ellie trying to catch a ride and pulled up. "Going somewhere, Lieutenant Graham?" the Blade asked.

"Yes. We need to go to Honsfeld," Tessa said.

"What do you know? We're heading that way. Hop on in."

Tessa climbed into the vehicle. Ellie joined her in the backseat and gave the Blade a nervous smile. Like most of the other nurses, Ellie was uncomfortable around the Blade.

They closed the jeep's door. The driver, a staff sergeant with a small frame and a crew cut, stepped on the gas pedal. *Vroom.* The jeep's engine propelled the vehicle forward, jerking the passengers out of their seats.

"Sorry," the driver said.

"Don't mind Cohen," the Blade said. "He's still learning to drive."

"I know how to drive. I'm just not driving the Army way. It's counterintuitive, like everything else with the Army." Cohen drove on.

Ellie watched Cohen talk back to the Blade, who was nearly twice his own size. Her expression eased and she relaxed into her seat. "Sergeant Cardozo, Sergeant Cohen, I have candy." She took two chocolate bars out of her parcel. "Would either of you like some?"

"Candy bars?" the Blade laughed. "No thanks, Lieutenant Swanson. But if you have any spirits, we'd take those."

"Oh. No," Ellie said. "I'm afraid I don't have any liquor unfortunately."

While they talked, Tessa stared out at the trees lining the road. The thick forest filled with evergreen trees seemed to be hiding sinister secrets unknown to the human world. The gray gloomy clouds shadowed the eerie mist of fog hanging in the air. The entire scene made her uneasy. She felt isolated. She had an odd feeling that they shouldn't be here.

"Hold it. Stop," the Blade said, his voice cautious.

Cohen stopped the jeep. The Blade remained still as a rock, listening for sounds. They looked around but saw nothing unusual.

"Is something wrong, Sergeant Cardozo?" Ellie asked.

He held up his hand, indicating for her to be quiet. His behavior made Tessa nervous. The Blade had the instincts of a wild animal. He could sense anomalies in his surroundings like no one else.

"Something's not right," he said. "Why are we the only ones here? Where are all the others? There should be 99th vehicles coming up and down these roads."

Tessa's own senses rose in alert. The Blade was right. It had been a while since they had seen other U.S. army vehicles. Honsfeld was only a few miles away. Why wasn't there army traffic coming in and out of that little town?

"Let's go a little further and see," the Blade said. "But get off the main road." He pointed to a dirt trail leading into the forest. "We'll take the back road instead. I want to see what's going on."

"We're going in there?" Cohen said, about to make a joke, but thought better of it and drove on. Cautiously, he took them onto the dirt road into the forest, where they were less conspicuous. The Blade's eyes darted around in every direction as they moved forward, scanning the area around them like a panther on a hunt. The rest of them fell quiet. Not a sound could be heard except for the low humming of the jeep's engine and the occasional cracks of stones beneath the tires.

"Stop," the Blade said when they came upon an area with a patch of bushes. Cohen halted the jeep. The Blade trained his eyes on the bushes. "Bastard's not shooting. I wonder why." He grabbed his rifle. "Stay here." He told everyone, then got out and headed toward the bushes aiming his rifle, ready to shoot.

Holding her breath, Tessa watched him. As far as she could see, there was nothing in the bushes. Everything was quiet and still.

"Come on out, hands up," the Blade said, still aiming his rifle.

Lightly, the bushes swayed. Tessa's heart skipped. Ellie jumped in her seat and she grabbed Tessa's hand.

"Don't shoot." A voice whimpered from behind the bushes. "Please...don't shoot."

Tessa recognized the voice before she was able to see the person in hiding. "Blade! Don't shoot!"

His gun still pointing at the direction of the voice, the Blade held his fire. A figure emerged slowly from behind the bushes. "Don't shoot. It's me! It's me!"

"Tyler!" Tessa shouted and jumped out of the car. Ellie and Cohen, too, followed.

Tyler rose with his arms up. Tessa could hardly recognize him with all the dirt and mud smeared on his face and uniform. The Blade lowered his rifle.

"Tyler!" Tessa ran up to him and grabbed his arm. "Tyler, what happened?"

Tyler fell to his knees and sobbed. "They're gone. My entire company's gone." His voice was shaking so badly, it was hard to make out his words. "The Nazis came and killed everyone."

They listened to him, stunned.

"It was so early. The sky was still dark. I was with a buddy of mine from infantry. He was on guard duty on the first watch. I stayed up to keep him company. We saw a tank and a formation of men moving in, but they were moving so slow, we couldn't make out who they were. We called the company HQ but all the lines were jammed and we couldn't get through. Then daylight broke and we started to see what was happening. They weren't just Wehrmacht soldiers. They were Nazis." He broke down again. Tessa knelt down and put her hand on his back. Her touch calmed him and he stopped crying.

"They moved into the entire village," he went on. "We didn't see them coming. They came into the town from every direction. There were Panzers and SS troops on every street, every entrance, every road. They had paratroopers dropping down too. I don't know where they all came from. I don't know how they got to Honsfeld without us finding out. Honsfeld's supposed to be miles from the front line. The Nazis snuck up on us at night, and then they were everywhere. Everywhere."

Hearing him recount the events, Ellie and Cohen turned ghostly white. Tessa, too, felt frightened. Only the Blade seemed unaffected. "What happened then?" he asked Tyler.

"We started to fight, me and my buddy. We were on the second story of the house and there was no way for us to get out, so we fired from the window. I'm not even a combat soldier! I only had his pistol. It was useless. We were completely outnumbered. We saw our troops coming out of buildings with white flags and arms over their heads. They surrendered."

Ellie covered her mouth. Tessa looked at Tyler, aghast.

"That's not all," Tyler continued. He was in tears again. "The SS came into our building. I knew then it was over. They took us outside and made us line up with the rest of our troops. They took all our stuff. Our wallets, watches, rings. They marched us down the streets and then, and then..." He was bawling so hard now, he couldn't finish.

"Then what?" the Blade asked.

"I heard gunshots going off behind us. I thought it was a skirmish. I thought someone was retaliating and not giving up without a fight. But then a Panzer drove by us and a man sitting on top of it fired at us. I saw his face. He looked me in the eye, and he shot at me like I was a target."

Ellie lost her balance and took a step back. Tessa hugged Tyler, thankful and relieved he was not dead.

"He missed," Tyler said. "The bullet hit my buddy next to me. He fell and knocked me over, and we both fell into the ditch next to the road. He fell on top of me. I turned to look at his face, and he was dead. His blood spilled all over me. Then I just lay there with his body on top of me. I played dead. I guess the SS thought I was dead too. I heard more shooting. More bodies fell into the ditch. That was when I realized they weren't taking us prisoners. They were shooting us. They killed us."

"Oh, Tyler," Ellie cried out.

"I lay there for a long time. Maybe hours, I don't know. I didn't dare to move. I was scared out of my mind. The Nazis moved on and I was still afraid to move. I didn't know what to do. Then, I couldn't take it anymore. I got up and ran away. I was lucky no one saw me. I didn't know where I was going. I just ran and ran away from the town until I got here. I heard you coming and hid behind the bushes." He fell into Tessa's arms and sobbed.

"It's all right. You're with us now," Tessa let him cry on her shoulder while she looked at the Blade to see what they should do.

"We have to turn back," the Blade said. "Let's get out of here."

Tessa squeezed Tyler's shoulder. "Come on." She led him toward their jeep, her arm still around him to give him support.

Solemnly, they got back into the vehicle. Tyler was calm now, but it was not a good calm. He had the look of someone who was in shock. No one said a word, and Cohen drove as fast as he could. Tessa could feel everyone's fear around her, only they didn't dare to say it out loud.

The jeep came out of the forest at the end of the dirt trail. As soon as they came out, they found themselves face to face with a small convoy of Waffen SS troopers heading up the main road. Unwittingly, they had come into the Nazi troopers' direct view. There was no way to hide.

Cohen tried to turn them around, but it was too late. The SS troops caught up to them and surrounded them. They raised their rifles. Tyler tugged Tessa's arm. His face was white as a sheet. "That's him," he said, looking at a man sitting in an officer's vehicle. "That's the man who shot at me and killed my buddy."

Tessa turned her gaze in the direction where Tyler was looking. A tall man in a Nazi commander's uniform got out of his car and walked toward them. A young SS soldier who looked about eighteen followed closely behind.

"Are you sure?" she whispered.

"I'd recognize him anywhere."

The Nazi commander stopped about ten feet from their jeep. The young SS soldier walking with him shouted in English, "Drop your weapons and get out of the jeep."

Ellie froze in terror. Tyler grabbed Tessa's arm more tightly and stared at the Nazi commander with petrified eyes, but the Nazi commander didn't seem to recognize him.

"Get out of the car. Now," the young SS soldier shouted.

Cohen, the driver, was the first to move. He stepped out of the jeep. The Blade got out after him. Tessa elbowed Tyler, signaling him to move. Unwillingly, Tyler got out of the car. Tessa took Ellie by the hand and led her out.

"*Schwestern. Schwestern*," some of the SS troopers mumbled when they saw Tessa and Ellie. They seem surprised to see women among their prisoners. Tessa exchanged a glance with the Blade and walked up next to him. Once their prisoners were lined up, the young SS soldier shouted something in German at the other troopers surrounding them. In response, two of the troopers came and began searching the male prisoners.

"Show your identification papers," the young SS soldier ordered. Except Tyler, whose papers were already confiscated earlier, the Blade, Tessa, and Ellie all took out their papers to hand them to him.

"Where are your papers?" the young SS soldier shouted at Tyler.

"I lost them."

"You lost them? You're lying."

"He's not," Tessa raised her voice. "He's not lying."

The young SS soldier turned to her, unsure how to respond to an American nurse.

"He doesn't have his papers. They're lost," she said. "You can take mine." She gave him her own identification papers. Looking a bit flustered, the young SS seized the papers from her hand. While he examined her papers, she noticed the Nazi sig rune symbol on the right patch of his collar, and the single pinstripe of a private first class on the left.

The Nazi commander came closer, and the young private gave him the identification papers he had collected from their

American prisoners. Tessa raised her eyes to see what the commander looked like. Blonde, blue-eyed, clean cut and shaven, he was actually good looking. He had the kind of face that would charm people anywhere. In his gray tunic uniform, he even looked regal.

As handsome as he was, Tessa sensed something about him that repulsed her. She didn't know what it was, but she felt disgusted looking at him. She checked the marks on his collar. Like the private, he wore the sig rune insignia on his collar too, as well as a rank insignia of four diamond-shaped pips with a single pinstripe.

The SS commander flipped through the American prisoners' papers with little interest until one caught his attention and he scowled in disgust. "Cohen. Which one of you is Cohen?" He glared at Tyler, then the Blade, then at Cohen himself. None of them responded. The commander walked up to the Blade. "Are you Cohen? You must be him. You're the Jew, aren't you? You're the ugliest thing I've ever seen in my life."

Not showing any reaction, the Blade glared back at the German Nazi with defiant eyes. Although the Nazi commander was tall, the Blade was a big man and stood even taller than his enemy.

"No," Cohen said, breaking the tension between the Nazi commander and the Blade. "He's not Cohen. I am," he stuttered.

The Nazi commander squinted. "Well, why didn't you say so earlier, you disgusting, filthy scum?" he shouted in Cohen's face. Cohen cowered. Already a small man, he looked puny next to the Nazi.

His admission didn't move the Nazi commander in the slightest. "I almost killed the wrong man because of you." The Nazi pulled out his Luger and shot Cohen in the forehead. Cohen's eyes widened, and he fell dead on the ground. Ellie cried out and fell against Tyler. Tyler held her up, but his own eyes were bulging in terror.

The Blade lunged toward the killer. Without thinking, Tessa reached out and pulled him back. "No," she whispered to him. Against his instinct, he stopped. His anger seethed as he breathed. His chest heaved like a mad lion ready to jump and attack.

The killer swept his eyes over the remaining three of his prisoners. "Now what are we to do with the rest of you?" He stepped in front of the Blade. "You sure are one ugly piece of work. I didn't think I'd ever see someone uglier than a Jew. Are you even human? How do you live with yourself?"

The Blade sneered.

"I should probably get rid of you too." The Nazi studied the Blade up and down, seemingly fascinated. "On the other hand, you ugly turd, you're the perfect specimen to remind my men why the world would be ruined if we let you Americans win. I think I'll keep you around for a while." He wrinkled his nose in disgust, then glanced quickly at Tessa, barely acknowledging her existence, and passed his attention over to Ellie. His eyes lingered on Ellie's golden-blonde hair.

Disturbed by the way he was staring at her, Ellie turned her face away from him. He chuckled. It was the most perverse chuckle Tessa had ever heard.

Lastly, the killer took a disinterested look at Tyler. Noting the red cross banner on Tyler's sleeve, he asked, "We can use the medic and the nurses. Do you have medical supplies in your car?"

Tyler was too frightened to answer. The young private shouted an order to the troopers, and several of them began to search the Americans' jeep. They confiscated their prisoners' guns and equipment. Another one brought over a tool to siphon petroleum from their jeep's tank. When they took Ellie's

Christmas parcel away, Tessa wanted to lunge at the Nazis herself.

When they finished, the Nazi commander said something in German to the young private and went back to his vehicle. The young private directed several troopers to tie up the Blade and Tyler by their hands. They debated among each other while glancing at Tessa and Ellie, but ultimately decided not to restrain them. The young private then pointed his rifle at the prisoners. "Move."

Having no choice, Tessa and the others began to walk. With the enemy's rifles pointing at their backs, they followed the SS convoy and walked into the unknown.

CHAPTER TWENTY-THREE

FORCED by the Waffen SS troopers, Tessa walked for hours with her friends until the sky began to get dark. She did not know where she was or where they were going. Eventually, they arrived at a tiny village, or the remnants of what was once a village. Earlier bombings had flattened most of the houses. Even the ones that were still intact had shattered windows, roofs that were torn apart, and damaged walls. The Nazis were the only ones roaming the streets. There were no civilians in sight. The people in the village had evacuated long ago.

The SS convoy that captured them came to a halt. Two Nazi guards made them sit down on the side of the road. Hungry and thirsty, Tessa and her friends waited. She felt fear like she had never experienced. She didn't know what would happen to them, and no one would tell them anything. The Nazis would do anything they wanted to them.

After a while, the young SS private who had captured them reappeared. He shouted an order to the guards in German. In response, the guards motioned for the prisoners to stand up. The private and the guards took them to a house and forced them to walk down to its cellar. The cellar was not lit except for two small candles on an old wooden table with rotted legs. The sour smell and the damp air only further reminded them of the hopeless situation they were in.

The private ordered them to turn over their personal belongings. One by one, he confiscated their wallets, watches, and every other valuable item they carried. He took away Ellie's bracelet and the Blade's cigarettes. The Blade wore several large silver rings. When the private collected those too, Tessa reflexively covered her ring finger with her right hand. She wanted to take her wedding band off and conceal it somehow, but the guards were watching them. She couldn't make any movement without their notice. Desperate, she squeezed her hands. She did not know what to do.

The private came to her next. Tentatively, she gave him her wallet.

"Your watch," he said. She took it off. When she unclasped her watch on her right wrist, he stared straight at her wedding ring. She felt she was about to cry.

To her surprise, the private only took her money and her watch. "Take your ring off and hide it," he whispered so that only she could hear. He moved his body in front of her to block the SS guards from seeing what she was doing.

Quickly, she took her ring off and put it in the inner pocket of her jacket. The private moved on to Tyler, who had nothing on him as all his belongings had already been confiscated earlier. Tessa watched the private, still surprised but breathing easy for the first time since they had been taken prisoners.

When the private had taken all their valuables, he led the guards up the stairs, leaving Tessa and her friends alone in the cellar.

After the cellar door slammed shut, Ellie let herself fall on Tessa's shoulder. "My Lord! I think I'm going to faint."

Tessa put her arm around Ellie. "What are we going to do?" she asked the Blade.

The Blade crossed his arms. "I guess we'll stay here for the night."

Before they could say more, heavy footsteps stomped down the stairs. The private and the guards had returned, this time with the Nazi commander. "What kind of idiotic arrangement is this?" he shouted at the private, not in German but in English. Clearly, he meant for his prisoners to hear what he was saying.

He made a big show of scowling at the private and the guards, then said to Ellie, "Fräulein! You must excuse my men's callous behavior. They are brutes. I assure you, you're our guest." He looked around at the walls. "This dingy cellar is no place for a lady."

Ellie tensed. She slid her feet back slightly, but in this confined space, there was no way for her to retreat from him. The Blade moved a step closer to her.

"Come." The Nazi commander smiled at her. "Let me take you to a more comfortable place. You can spend the night there."

"I..." Ellie said, her voice quivered. "Thank you for the offer, sir, but I'm fine staying with my friends."

Nervous for her, Tessa grabbed Ellie's hand. Ellie was trembling.

The Nazi commander laughed. "Fräulein, I'm not asking you to spend the night with me. Or is that what you have in mind?"

Ellie's face turned deep red.

"I'm staying in a nice house with my Belgian hosts," he said, speaking more like an amorous suitor in pursuit of a woman than an enemy captor. "They're very pleasant folks. I assure you, you will enjoy their company. They have a fireplace, a warm bed. You'll be a lot more comfortable there."

Too fearful to refuse outright, Ellie looked at her friends. Tessa tightened her hold of Ellie's hand, in fear of what might happen to her. The Nazi kept smiling. His cordial smile looked ridiculous given the reality of the situation they were in.

Ellie gathered her nerves and said, "Commander..."

"Pfeiffer."

"Excuse me?"

"The name is Pfeiffer. Jans Pfeiffer. *Oberst* is my rank." He came within inches of her. "But you can call me Commander. I like that."

Ellie drew back, but was too afraid to blatantly refuse him. Keeping her own voice sweet to avoid offending him, she said, "Commander. Your offer is very kind, but I wouldn't feel right leaving my friends here while I go off to somewhere more comfortable. It wouldn't be the honorable thing to do. You're a commander. You understand that."

Pfeiffer took a quick look at Tessa, Tyler, and the Blade. "All right. Your friends can come too." He leaned into Ellie. "See. Contrary to what you might think, I am a nice man."

Ellie forced herself to smile. Pleased with himself, Pfeiffer laughed and left, yelling something to the private and the guards as he walked back up the stairs out of the cellar.

The guards raised their rifles at their prisoners. "You heard him," the private said. "Move. All of you."

They departed the cellar and followed after him.

The SS brought them to a house not too far away. Inside, a boy who looked no more than twelve was kindling the wood in the fireplace. He jumped when they entered. The young private who led them here ignored him. A guard pointed to the stairs and motioned for them to go up. The boy watched them pass by. Behind him, Tessa caught a glimpse of an old man lying in bed through the open door to a small bedroom. The boy hurried in there when he heard the man coughing.

Leaving the boy behind, they followed the guard upstairs to a room which was divided into two parts by a double door. The guard signaled Tyler and the Blade to use the straw mattresses on the floor, then pointed at the part of the room behind the double door for Tessa and Ellie. After that, he locked the doors and disappeared.

Alone by themselves again, Tessa opened the double door. There was nothing in there besides more straw mattresses. She tried to open one of the windows, but it was stuck.

"That won't help," said the Blade. "There are guards all around this house."

"What should we do?" Ellie asked. "What do you think they'll do to us?"

"We'll take it one step at a time," he said. "They'll probably take us to a prisoners' camp."

"I don't think they will." Tyler went to one of the mattresses and sat down, depressed. "These people are inhuman. They killed my entire company. They killed Cohen. They'll kill us too."

The Blade's face darkened. Tessa knew then the true extent of the danger they were in.

The door opened again. The SS private came in, carrying a plate of black bread and butter, which he set down on a small table against the wall. The boy they had seen downstairs followed with a tray holding a coffee pot, a jug of water, and cups. He placed them next to the food, then left the room.

On his way out, the private said, "The Oberst quarters in a bedroom downstairs. I suggest you all don't try to make any trouble, if you know what's good for you." The entire time, he avoided looking directly at them.

"What's your name?" Tessa couldn't resist asking.

He paused. He turned his head around slightly, but stopped short of looking at them. "Oskar," he said, and locked the door, leaving them trapped again.

They ate the food in silence. Afterward, they tried to sleep. In the cold room, Tessa could hear Ellie shifting and turning. Her own thoughts went to Anthony. Did he know she was missing yet? He must be so worried if he did. And her parents. When would the army notify her parents? They would be heartsick when they found out.

Tyler said these people killed his entire company. What if they killed them too? The reality that she might never return home sunk in. She thought of her mother and father in London. Her Uncle William and Aunt Sophia back in Chicago, and Ruby, Jack, and Henry. Even worse than being scared, she feared she would never see them again.

Nobody knew where they were.

Anthony.

She reached for her rose pendant. So clear was her memory of his face and his smile. She could remember the way he walked up to her when she came to his base in Italy. He was so shocked, and so happy to see her. She could feel the warmth of his chest, his kiss, and his touch.

Remembering her wedding ring, she took off her necklace and put the ring on it before she lay down again.

I want to see you again. She kissed the ring and the pendant.

I want to see you. She called out to him in her mind, a call into the void where no one could hear.

The next morning, the boy came again and brought them more bread and coffee. A Nazi officer came too, and questioned them one by one. Afterward, a guard came and ordered them to follow him.

"You. Stay." He pointed his rifle at the Blade, and indicated for him to remain in the room. Tessa did not want her friend to be separated from the rest of them, but they were compelled to do what they were told. She followed the guard downstairs with Ellie and Tyler. In the living room, the boy was feeding soup or porridge to the old man sitting by the fireplace. When the old man had finished eating, the boy pulled his blanket up over his body. Tessa tried to make eye contact with the boy, but he quickly looked away.

Walking along outside, the guard did not appear hostile. Still, her fear would not subside. There was no telling what these people might do. These were Nazis.

They arrived at a barn that housed the injured SS troopers. At once, it became clear they were brought here to work. Their appearance surprised the Nazi medical staff and patients. A slight commotion ensued. Some of the medics glared at them with suspicion. Others looked at Tessa and Ellie with great curiosity, exclaiming "*Schwestern.*" The Nazi troopers had reacted this way yesterday too when they caught them. Tessa was once again struck by how surprised these men were to see female enemy prisoners.

The guard spoke to the doctor in charge. The doctor eyed them once over, then said to Ellie. "You're the ranking officer?" He spoke good English.

"Yes," Ellie answered.

The doctor pointed to a group of men huddling on one side of the barn. "You three can start with changing their dressings. Clean their wounds. Supplies are over there." He showed them a stack of boxes and walked away.

Ellie indicated to Tessa and Tyler to get started, but Tyler would not move. "These people killed my entire company. For sport. Not at war."

Ellie's voice softened. "I know how you feel, but we have to do this. We have no choice. And we ought to do this. It's our job to save people." She tugged him gently on the arm. "Come on." Grudgingly, he acquiesced and started helping the enemy wounded.

While she worked, Tessa took in the scene. The patients greatly outnumbered the medical staff. With only one doctor and a limited number of medics, all of whom looked exhausted and overworked, many injured people were waiting for a long time for their turn to be treated.

She began to busy herself. Once she got started, she was glad to have something to occupy her mind. For now at least, the tasks before her distracted her from thinking about anything else. Every so often, she checked on Ellie and Tyler. Ellie, back in her element as a nurse, almost looked like she had forgotten she was a prisoner of war. She tended to each of the wounded, even smiling at them. Tyler, on the other hand, kept a grumpy face as he methodically treated the Nazi patients.

At noon, the doctor gave them a short lunch break. More black bread and coffee. The bread no longer tasted as good as it had last night when they were ravenous. The lukewarm coffee provided no satisfaction either.

"Maybe we'll be okay if they realize we're doing our best to help them," Ellie said, trying to brighten their spirits.

"I wouldn't count on it," Tyler said. "I bet they'll get rid of us when we're no longer useful to them."

Tessa touched her chest to feel her ring and her rose pendant hidden under her uniform. All she wanted was to see Anthony again. She would never ask for anything else if she could be granted this one wish.

When their day was over, the guard took them back to the house. The boy was in the kitchen, and Tessa could hear him chopping vegetables. The old man was still sitting by the fireplace, half asleep. A light sheen of sweat covered his forehead. Struggling to breathe, his pale lips dropped open, letting out short spurts of shallow breaths.

Displeased by the sight, the guard wrinkled his nose at the old man. "Take him back to his room," he yelled at the boy. "Oberst will be back soon."

The boy stopped what he was doing and hurried to the old man. The old man stirred and bowed over.

"Sir," Ellie said to the guard. "He looks ill." She went to the elderly man and placed her hand on his forehead. "He has a high fever. He needs help."

"We don't have any medicine to spare for him," the guard said. "And you should mind your own business."

"Please," she said. "Let us try and take care of him. I can make him feel better."

"I said mind your own business," the guard shouted.

The front door opened and Pfeiffer walked in. Everyone became silent all at once. The guard stood at attention. Pfeiffer stared at all of them, his eyes cold like steel until he saw Ellie. "What's going on?"

"The old man is sick, sir," Ellie said. "We'd like to attend to him. We can help him."

"I told them to mind their own business," the guard said.

Pfeiffer held up his hand to shush the guard and smiled. Tessa remembered this same perverse smile from when they were first captured.

"Please, Commander. Let us help him?" Ellie summoned her courage and asked.

Pfeiffer came closer to her. She looked away to avoid his gaze.

"And if I grant you your wish, how will you thank me?"

Ellie tensed. Pfeiffer laughed when she didn't know how to answer.

"Tell you what, Fräulein. Your friend here can take care of the old man." He tossed a dismissive glance at Tessa. "Why don't you join me for dinner? I see our Belgian friend's got a nice hot meal cooking." He smiled at the boy and went into the kitchen. When he came out, he held up a bottle of wine to show Ellie.

Bewildered and scared, Ellie didn't know what to do. She looked at Tessa, who was equally uncertain.

"Go! Get the old man to bed and take care of him," Pfeiffer said to Tessa. "Get us our dinner," he said to the boy. "I'm hungry."

Tessa helped the old man onto his feet. The boy watched her bring the old man to his bedroom, then hurried back into the kitchen.

"See, Fräulein? Everything's fine." Pfeiffer lifted a lock of Ellie's hair, admiring it as she shuddered. "Have a seat." He invited her to the table and opened the bottle of wine.

Ellie sat down across from Pfeiffer. In the bedroom, Tessa helped the old man lie down on his bed. On purpose, she left the bedroom door open to keep an eye on Ellie.

Pfeiffer poured himself a glass of wine, then noticed Tyler and the guard standing by the stairs. "Go," he said to the guard. "Take him upstairs. You brutes get out of my sight."

The guard poked Tyler with his rifle. Worried, Tyler looked back at Ellie several times as he walked up the stairs until he couldn't see her anymore. In the bedroom, Tessa tried to put the old man in a comfortable position. The boy came in with a basin of warm water and a small towel.

"Thank you." Tessa smiled at the boy. "What's your name?"

"Mathias. Mathias Zegher."

"Hello, Mathias. I'm Tessa. Tessa Graham."

Mathias smiled back. "He's my grandfather."

She wiped the sweat off the old man's face with the towel. "Do you know what's wrong with him?"

Mathias shook his head. "Will you make him better?"

"I'll try my best." She wished she could do more, but without medicine, there was not much she could do. The boy sat down on the bed next to his grandfather and touched the old man's arm.

"Where are your parents?" Tessa asked.

"They died in a bomb raid. After that, everyone in the village left. My grandfather's too sick, and we couldn't leave."

"I'm sorry."

Mathias stroked his grandfather's face. The boy looked so helpless, Tessa wanted to give him a hug.

"I have to serve the Oberst his dinner." He got up and left the room.

Tessa examined the old man. His pulse was weak and his breathing sounded congested. She suspected he might be suffering from the flu or pneumonia. She wished she had proper medicine and equipment to help him. All she could do was to try to make him more comfortable. When he fell asleep, she went back out to the living room.

In the living room, she found Pfeiffer slumped over on the table, asleep. His bowl of potato stew barely touched. Ellie sat stupefied in her chair, staring at him. Her bowl of potato stew also untouched. Mathias stood by the kitchen entrance, too afraid to come out.

"What happened?" Tessa asked.

"I don't know," Ellie said. "I guess he's drunk."

Tessa came over to the table. Snoring slightly, Pfeiffer was sound asleep. She picked up the wine. There was still a quarter bottle left. "What a lightweight."

Ellie cracked a smile for the first time since they returned to the house. Mathias still didn't know if he should come out of the kitchen. The kitchen gave Tessa an idea. "Mathias, is there any food left? I'm hungry too."

"Yes. I'll get you some stew."

"No," she kept her voice nonchalant. "You go check on your grandfather. I'll help myself."

"Okay."

Tessa went to the kitchen counter. She opened the cabinet doors and checked what was kept inside. As discreetly as she could, she pulled out the counter drawers one by one. Her heartbeat and breath quickened when she discovered the drawer with cooking utensils. She brushed the knives with her fingertips. This was her only chance. She rummaged through the silverware until she found a sharp knife that could fit in her jacket.

"Grandpa's asleep." Mathias' voice startled her. "Do you need help?"

"Sure." She turned around and smiled at Mathias. "Can we bring some food to my friends upstairs? I'd like to eat with them."

"Yes." Mathias took several bowls out of the cabinet and filled them with stew. While he prepared the food, Tessa returned to the living room and said to Ellie, "You might as well eat, or you're going to be hungry all night."

Less frightened now that Tessa was with her, Ellie crammed down her now cold potato stew. Mathias brought out more bowls of stew and a jug of water. Tessa thanked him, and she and Ellie proceeded to bring the food and water upstairs. The guard raised his gun when he heard their approaching footsteps.

"Can you let us inside?" Tessa asked as casually as possible.

The guard eyed them up and down with suspicion, but nonetheless opened the door and let them into the room. When they entered, the Blade and Tyler jumped to their feet. The guard locked the door behind them.

"Are you all right?" Tyler asked.

"Yes," Tessa said. "Here's some food for you." She laid down the tray of potato stew. While she, Tyler, and the Blade ate, Ellie collapsed onto one of the mattresses. "I was so scared," she said with huge relief.

"We need to get away from here," the Blade said. "I have a bad feeling about Pfeiffer. He's evil. I can feel it in every fiber of me."

"Don't talk like that," Tessa said. "You're frightening Ellie." She took the knife out of her pocket. "Look what I got."

The Blade's eyes livened when he saw the knife.

"Shhhh." Tessa put a finger to her lips. "You have to be careful with this. If they find this on you, they'll kill you."

"You don't need to tell me." He took the knife from her. His spirit and vigor returned, like a hawk that had found its wings again.

"Are you two sure about this?" Tyler asked.

"No," Tessa said. "I'm not sure about anything. But if we have a chance to escape..." She exchanged a glance with the Blade.

The Blade understood. He smiled back at her. "If we have a chance to escape, we'll take it."

CHAPTER TWENTY-FOUR

IN THE WEEK BEFORE CHRISTMAS, the 33rd Field Hospital followed the Third Division and arrived at Strasbourg. All morning, Aaron had scoured the city's famous Christmas market, searching for ornaments to decorate the Christmas tree for the medical staff. The market had begun as early as 1570. It was one of the oldest Christmas markets in Europe. Scores of American soldiers were wandering around the stalls, looking for gifts to send back home. The Free French Army had liberated the city last month, and the Allies now occupied this beautiful place. It had survived the war and German occupation intact and was once again a picturesque scene of peace and civilization. With the war still going on, he couldn't have asked for a more pleasant place to spend the holidays.

Strolling down the streets back to the hospital, he marveled at medieval churches and the black-and-white timber-framed houses. He felt as if he had been transported to an old world of fairy tales, to a land of magic. Everywhere, beautiful young girls in Alsatian costumes walked the streets, extending their welcomes. He could almost forget the turmoil of the present time.

In the spirit of the holidays, he and his staff had decided to decorate the patients' wards. The best part was the Christmas tree. All winter, the forests had been their bane. Now, for once, the forest was giving them something to enjoy. He had brought a bag full of ornaments back from the Christmas market. As he expected, the nurses were thrilled when they saw what he had gotten. They spent the afternoon decorating the wards, and putting baubles and trinkets on the Christmas tree. When they finished, the staff urged him to place the star on the top. Humbly, he agreed and did so to their delight. The nurses and staff cheered, and the patients applauded and laughed. In their celebration, no one noticed Fran Milton on the other side of the room.

On the other side of the room, Fran glimpsed Aaron and the merrymakers out of the corners of her eyes while she examined a patient's medical chart. She hardly noticed when Dr. Bernstein, one of their senior colleagues, came up to her. "Captain, my wife sent me these graham crackers. Would you like some?" He offered her graham crackers on a plate.

"No, thank you."

Cheers erupted from the group by the tree again when a corpsman brought in gift-wrapped packages. Fran watched Aaron arrange the packages under the tree. Noting the sadness in her eyes, Bernstein asked, "Why don't you join in the fun?"

She looked away from the group back to the chart in her hands. "Christmas is just another day to me. I don't have time for anything trivial. We have too many patients to attend to."

"I don't celebrate Christmas either. It doesn't mean we can't get into the holiday spirit. Truth be told, we all can use some happy distractions."

"If everyone's distracted, who'll be around to make sure our work gets done?" She hung the chart back on the patient's bedpost. "I'm giving most of the nurses a day off on Christmas. I'll be on duty personally so they can enjoy their time off. The problem is, people don't always appreciate the ones who give the most." She looked pointedly at Aaron.

Bernstein looked toward Aaron and the nurses. The festive mood in the room was brought to a halt when Colonel Callahan entered. The staff stopped their activities. The colonel ignored the formality and approached Aaron right away. From his heavy strides and grave expression, Aaron could tell that something serious had happened. Bernstein and Fran looked at each other. They both walked over to the colonel and Aaron to find out what was going on.

"I'm sorry to bring you the bad news, especially now," Callahan said to Aaron, and looked at the rest of the nurses. "Ellie Swanson and Tessa Graham have been reported missing."

The news turned everyone speechless.

"What do you mean, missing?" Aaron asked.

"They're MIA. They were last seen at their field hospital a week ago. No one has seen them since."

The nurses let out a collective gasp. Fran glanced curiously at Aaron. His face had turned stone white.

"What happened to them?" Aaron demanded to know.

"Command up North is doing their best to try to find them. That's all I know."

The nurses hugged each other. Some began to cry.

"I'm sorry for the sad news, but I thought you'd all want to know," Callahan said. "We're notifying their families now. Rest assured, the army will do everything they can. No one wants the news of women being taken prisoners to travel back home. That'll keep the pressure on command to find them."

"Find them?" Fran said. "That's only if you assume they're still alive." Everyone stared at her, stunned and indignant at her cold, emotionless reminder. "What?" she asked. "I'm speaking the truth. Anything could've happened. We should be prepared for the worst possible outcome."

"No," Aaron said, his voice full of distress. "Colonel, you have to find them."

"We'll do everything we can," Callahan promised again.

Aaron looked at the floor. The news had sent him reeling. Fran knew what she had to do. Later, when he had had a chance to think through what must have happened to the missing nurses, she would have to help him prepare for the worst. She would have to be there to see him through when the loss of Ellie Swanson became inevitable.

For days, the Nazi troops remained in the small village. Tessa had no idea what their captors were up to or why they had chosen to stay in this area. From the sounds of artillery shells that went off nearby sometimes, she speculated that the Nazis might be engaging in combat with the Allied troops. Their front line seemed to shift constantly. The distinct sounds of American weapons and German artillery fire came from all different directions. Every day, she prayed that the Allies might come storming into the village to their rescue.

She also guessed that the Nazis were in combat because of the continuous number of wounded soldiers delivered to the makeshift hospital. Every morning, the SS guard would bring her, Ellie, and Tyler there to work. Their captors' medical staff had been stretched beyond their limit, and they took full advantage of their captive prisoners' help.

In the evenings, she and Ellie would take turns caring for Mathias' grandfather. Ellie tried to persuade the German doctor to give them medicines for the old man. The doctor refused at first, but in the end gave them a two-day dosage of decongestants. He would not spare anything else. They could hardly blame him. The hospital was running desperately low on supplies. As the old man's condition worsened, they wondered what would happen to Mathias if his grandfather died.

Thankfully, they hadn't had to deal with Pfeiffer again. The ongoing battles must have been intense, as he was constantly occupied elsewhere. By the time he returned to the house each night, they were usually already locked in their rooms. He only returned early once, when Tessa and Ellie were attending to old Mr. Zegher. That time, he returned with another officer. They spoke in German, and neither Tessa nor Ellie understood what they were saying. The Nazis drank while they talked. The more they talked, the more agitated Pfeiffer looked. After the other officer left, he slumped over drunk on the table.

Tessa checked his liquor bottle. Again, it was unfinished. "Lightweight." She laughed with Ellie.

Those few days almost gave them the illusion of safety.

Almost.

The evening began as usual. While Ellie and Mathias prepared dinner, Tessa attended to Mr. Zegher. The old man was suffering and his condition was worsening, but he never complained. She helped him sit up on his bed and showed him her angel amulet. His eyes shone. His face softened as though he felt comforted. She let him hold the amulet while she gave him a glass of water. When he finished drinking, she helped him lie back down on the bed. He put the amulet next to his pillow.

"It's pretty, isn't it?" She pulled the blanket over him.

The door slammed open. Pfeiffer stormed in with Oskar and several of his men behind him. Tessa rushed out to the living room to see what was happening and to make sure Ellie and Mathias were okay. To her surprise, the SS guards had caught another American soldier. Oskar had his rifle pointed at him. The American soldier was shocked to see Tessa and Ellie too.

Pfeiffer shouted something in German, and two troopers stomped upstairs. Within minutes, they had brought Tyler and the Blade down with them. Pfeiffer shouted again. One of the troopers went into Mr. Zegher's bedroom, forced him out and sat him down at the table. Mathias ran over to him.

"This one!" Pfeiffer pointed his Luger at the newly captured American soldier. "This one killed one of ours." He stomped up to the Blade. "And now, he's going to pay for it." He glared at Tyler, and Tyler took a step back. Pfeiffer turned his eyes on the Blade. "What do you say?"

The Blade didn't answer, but kept his face expressionless. Pfeiffer shouted a series of orders. Oskar pushed the American soldier about ten feet in front of the Blade, while another guard grabbed old Mr. Zegher and Mathias, and forced them to stand a few feet to the right of the American soldier.

Pfeiffer turned to the Blade again. "You are going to make him pay for what he did. I'm giving you a gun. You can either kill this bastard for killing one of us," he pointed at the American soldier, "or you can kill these two imbeciles right here." He switched and pointed his gun at Mr. Zegher and Mathias.

Ellie cried out. Distracted by her reaction, Pfeiffer shouted to a guard, "Take her upstairs." The guard took Ellie by the arm and marched her upstairs.

"Give me a gun," Pfeiffer said to another guard after Ellie was gone. The guard handed him a handgun. Pfeiffer put it on the table. "You, Sergeant, are going to decide which one of them you want to kill. Your comrade, or these two." The guards raised their rifles and pointed them at the Blade.

"I won't do it," the Blade said.

"If you won't do it, I'll do it. I'll kill them all."

The Blade looked at the three people in front of him. Tessa could see his fury rising.

"Go on. Take the gun," Pfeiffer said, not letting him off. "But don't even think about pulling any stunts. Because if you do," he pulled Tyler against him and pointed his Luger at Tyler's head, "if you try anything, your friend here is going to die. You wouldn't want that now, would you?"

The Blade's face turned tight as a rock. Watching Pfeiffer, Tessa felt her own fury flaring up inside her. Mathias started to cry. Struggling to stand, his grandfather put his arm around the boy's small shoulders. The American soldier looked at them, then at the Blade.

The Blade picked up the gun from the table as though it was a poisonous snake. His eyes moved from the American soldier to the old man to the kid.

"Sergeant," Pfeiffer said. "We don't have all night."

Slowly, the Blade raised the gun. His grip on the gun was loose and limp. Tessa had never seen him look so powerless. Mathias buried his face against his grandfather. The old man held on to his grandchild and closed his eyes. The American soldier raised his gaze to the Blade and nodded. It was a subtle gesture, barely noticeable, but Tessa saw it. The Blade fired several times at the American soldier, and the soldier fell to the ground.

Mathias cried out in fright. The Blade stood frozen with his arm still out, his eyes blinking rapidly as though he was trying to wake up from a trance. A guard grabbed the gun out of his hand.

Pfeiffer released Tyler and pushed him away. "Now, get moving," he shouted. As he passed by Mathias and Mr. Zegher, he said to his men, "Take them outside and get rid of them."

"What did you say?" the Blade asked.

"I said get rid of them."

"You said I got to decide who dies."

Pfeiffer walked back to him. "I said you got to decide who you would kill. We're leaving tonight. I have no time or patience to deal with a sick man and a child."

"You don't have to take them. Leave them here."

"Leave them here? Sergeant, you should know better than that. They know who we are. They've heard everything my men and I have said. I am not leaving them here for one of your people to find out anything about us."

The Blade watched in horror as a guard dragged Mr. Zegher away. Mathias, crying, tried to hold on to him. Another guard pushed Mathias along.

"Thank you for the fine show," Pfeiffer said to the Blade before he left the house. "I did enjoy watching a big, ugly turd like you squirm."

Tessa and Tyler could only look on, helpless.

A gun shot went off outside, followed by another. Tessa squeezed her eyes shut. At this moment, all she wanted was to be away. Away from here. Away from everything.

"We're moving on," Oskar said to Tessa and Tyler. A guard brought Ellie back downstairs. She looked at the dead American soldier on the floor and covered her mouth in horror.

"Let's go," Oskar said, leading the way. Their two guards marched them out of the house.

Outside, Tessa turned her head away from the direction where she had heard the gunshots. She didn't want to see the Zeghers' remains. Hunching her shoulders, she put her hands into her pockets and squeezed her fists in silent anger. With her hands in her pockets, she realized something was amiss. "Wait! I left something behind."

The guards ignored her. She pleaded with Oskar. "Please, I have to find it." Without waiting for his response, she ran back inside the house to Mr. Zegher's bedroom.

In the bedroom, she searched for the amulet all over his

bed. Last she saw, it was next to the pillow, but it was no longer there. In a panic, she flipped the blanket over. Nothing either. She pushed aside the pillow and found her angel amulet underneath. She grabbed it and let out a huge sigh of relief. As she calmed down, she noticed the barrel of a gun protruding from under the pillow where the amulet was. She lifted the pillow slightly and found a small handgun.

She could not believe this. The Zeghers were hiding a handgun, right under the Nazis' eyes. Her heart pounding, she took the gun.

"You need to come now!" Oskar called her from the living room. No time to think, she put the gun and the amulet into the pocket of her jacket.

"Yes. I'm coming." She came out of the room.

At the same time, Pfeiffer walked in. He was about to say something to Oskar when he saw her. Her presence surprised him. He eyed her from head to toe. His stare made her nervous, but she looked back at him.

"What do you have in your pocket?" he asked.

She froze. Her heart was beating so fast, she felt like it would jump out of her throat.

"I asked you a question."

Without thinking, she took out the angel amulet. He took it, glanced at it, and gave her a derisive look. "No God or angel can save you now," he sneered. "The Führer is your only God, and I'm your only savior." Laughing, he put the amulet into his pocket. No longer interested in her, he spoke to Oskar. Tessa watched him, her fury rising. Pfeiffer paid no attention to her as though she didn't exist, but her eyes never left him. Looking at him, she felt a storm of rage.

"Let's go," Oskar said to her when he and Pfeiffer finished talking.

She ignored him. Her eyes remained on Pfeiffer, who was

leaving the house. "I want it back," she said to the Nazi commander.

Pfeiffer stopped, surprised she dared to talk to him, let alone make a demand of him.

"I want it back," she repeated, her voice firmer than before.

Unused to being challenged, he looked at her with renewed interest. "You mean this?" He took the amulet out of his pocket and dangled it in front of her.

"Give it back to me."

"Why? Why is it so important?" he taunted her. "Did your boyfriend give it to you?"

She only looked at him, her eyes as icy as his were steely. They stood glaring at each other. She refused to back down.

He smiled. The sinister smile that disgusted her from the start. But then, a flicker of unease appeared on his face. The amulet seemed to make him uncomfortable. He shifted his eyes away from her to the amulet, then tossed it back to her. She caught it and wrapped her hands tightly around it.

"Cheap piece of junk," he muttered and walked out of the house. She held the amulet to her cheek. Tears of relief rushed out of her eyes as she caressed it with her face.

O HOLY NIGHT

Part Eight

CHAPTER TWENTY-FIVE

In the early morning, the SS truck came to a stop. "*Auf!* *Auf!*" the guards yelled. Tessa opened her eyes. They had come to another village, and the sky was barely lit.

The guards hustled them out. Following their orders, Tessa got out of the truck. Her mind still groggy from the few hours of miserable sleep during the ride. She didn't know what time it was or where they had taken her, but she was too tired to care. She walked with her friends by her side. The SS guards followed closely behind them. The frosty air stung the skin on her face. White fog escaped her mouth every time she breathed. She licked her lips. She could really use a glass of water.

They came to a medieval looking church surrounded by a stone wall about four feet high. The guards told them to stop. One of them went inside and returned with a nun.

"I'm Sister Margaux," the nun said to Tessa and Ellie. "This is our convent. You'll be staying with us the next three days."

"What about my friends?" Tessa moved closer to Tyler and the Blade.

"This is a convent. The men can't stay here."

"Where will they go?"

"I don't know."

"No." Tessa took a step back. The Blade stepped forward next to her and Ellie. The guards immediately raised their rifles and stopped him.

"Please, Sister. Don't separate us," Tessa begged Sister Margaux. "Please ask the guards not to separate us." The nun only lowered her head.

"They'll be fine." Oskar approached and spoke from behind them. "Don't worry. They'll be quartered in another building." He spoke to one of the guards. The guard signaled Tyler and the Blade to move on. Reluctantly, they continued walking.

"Let us go with them," Tessa said to Oskar.

"You'll be more comfortable in the convent," Oskar said. "The sisters will take good care of you." Tyler, the Blade, and the guard turned the corner of the street and disappeared from sight. "The day after tomorrow is Christmas. I'll bring them back here then. You can spend Christmas Day together," Oskar reassured her.

"Please. Come this way." Sister Margaux said and began walking back to the convent. The SS guard signaled for them to move. Ellie followed them, but Tessa turned to Oskar once again. "What will you do with us? Where are you planning to take us?"

"When we arrive at the next town, there will be a train station. From there, you will be taken by train to a prison camp for Americans."

"A prison camp?" Ellie stopped.

"There are injured American soldiers there. You can assist with treating them."

Ellie relaxed, but Tessa remained suspicious.

"Follow me, please," Sister Margaux requested again and led them toward the entrance of the convent. Tessa stared back at Oskar one more time. His face betrayed no emotion. He looked like the perfect soldier. Once they went inside the gate, he turned around and walked away.

When they reached the entrance of the convent, the SS guard left. Sister Margaux took Tessa and Ellie through a narrow corridor to the kitchen, where a girl of about seventeen was cooking a pot of soup on the stove. The nun invited Tessa and Ellie to sit down, and the girl served them each a bowl of hot soup and bread. Tessa took a seat. A pang of hunger hit her stomach when the smell of the soup filled her nose.

"Go ahead. Eat. You must be hungry," Sister Margaux said.

Unable to hold back any longer, Tessa picked up the spoon and devoured the food. Ellie, too, could not resist. Despite her apprehension, Tessa was glad for the meal. The soup was the best thing she had eaten since they were captured. She wondered where the Nazis had taken the Blade and Tyler. She hoped they were given a decent meal too.

While they ate, the girl poured them each a glass of water. "This is Tilda, my helper," Sister Margaux said. The girl smiled. "When you're done eating, she will take you for your baths."

"A bath?" Tessa asked, her voice guarded.

"We want you to be comfortable. That's why you were brought here. It's highly unusual for the soldiers to capture female prisoners. They don't mean to mistreat you. We'll give you a clean change of clothing to wear while we wash your uniforms."

Remembering the gun, Tessa slid her hand below the table into her pocket. "I want to keep my jacket." The curtness of her voice stumped the Sister.

Nonetheless, the nun smiled. "Of course. Our winters are cold. American-made outerwear must be very warm."

Tessa returned to the food and avoided her eyes.

"Please don't worry," Sister Margaux said. "You're safe here with us."

After they had eaten, Sister Margaux took them to their room. The room had nothing except a desk, a chair, and a small table between the two beds. A jug of water with two cups and a lamp had been left on top of the desk. There was no item of luxury or convenience, but Oskar was right. This place was comfortable compared to the straw mattresses back at the Zeghers.

Remembering the Zeghers, Tessa bowed her head and said a silent prayer for Mathias and his grandfather. She was in a convent. If God was out there, maybe He could hear her.

Afterward, Sister Margaux let them take turns for their baths. Tessa had been worried that her ring and the gun would become exposed. Luckily, Tilda left her to her privacy after showing her to the washroom. Tessa took the gun out of her pocket to see if it was loaded. Two bullets.

She wondered if she should hold on to the gun. When she took it at the Zegher's, she had acted on the spur of the moment. She had no idea what she meant to do with it. Here in the washroom, there was no place for her to dispose of it without anyone finding out. She could not risk anyone discovering that she had a gun.

Quickly, she closed the cylinder, and put it back into her jacket. As she did, her fingers brushed against her angel amulet. Poor Mr. Zegher. He adored the amulet. And Mathias. That endearing child. Anger seized her again. The scene of their last moments remained fresh in her mind.

Pfeiffer. He was a monster.

She had not forgotten what Tyler had said. Pfeiffer killed Tyler's entire company.

She decided she would keep the gun. Neither the Blade nor Tyler was with them. In the worst-case scenario, she would use it to defend herself and Ellie. There was no telling what Pfeiffer might do. If their situation worsened, having a gun to protect themselves might be worth the risk.

In the convent, Tessa felt more like a prisoner than she had in the Zeghers' house. All day long, she and Ellie were locked in their room with nothing to do. Sister Margaux and Tilda had come twice to bring them their meals. Beyond that, the Spartan details of the dark room were all that occupied them.

"I wish they would let us go take care of patients," Ellie said. When the Nazis made them work at the enemy hospital, they actually had a semblance of freedom of movement and also something to keep them busy.

Sitting on her bed, Tessa closed her eyes and tried to pass the time by playing all nine of Beethoven's symphonies in her head. She was up to *Symphony No. 6* when the heavy thud of a man's footsteps, accompanied by the shuffling sounds of Sister Margaux's habit, interrupted her. Their door unlocked. The nun let Oskar in, then quietly withdrew from the room. Tessa and Ellie sat up on the edge of their beds, waiting for him to speak.

"How are you?" he asked. "Did you sleep well last night?"

Tessa didn't answer. What a strange question to ask his hostages.

"Yes. Thank you." Dear, sweet Ellie. Even now, she could not help but be nice.

"I'm glad to hear that, Fräulein. The Oberst doesn't want you to be uncomfortable." His comment made Ellie uneasy, and her face flushed. What he said next, though, surprised them. "If you want to write a letter home to your families, I can help you send it." He put a stationery pad and a pen on the desk. "I can deliver it to the Red Cross. They can send it for you. You can send one letter each."

She could write a letter home? Tessa could not be sure if his offer was for real.

"It will be censored, of course," Oskar said. "But you can let them know you're safe. We'll be leaving for the next town the day after tomorrow. Our headquarters are based there. I will send your letters for you when we arrive."

"Thank...thank you," Ellie stammered. She was as amazed as Tessa. "I...thank you very much."

Oskar broke into a smile for the first time since he had become their captor. Feeling bolder, Tessa asked him, "Why did you become a Nazi?"

His smile disappeared. He looked her in the eye. "Because it is the only way I can help unite the German people in the world. When we're united, we're invincible." His face became stern again, and the room fell quiet.

"You honestly believe that?" Tessa asked.

"Honestly and completely."

She looked back at him, challenging him. She wanted to believe he was lying. She tried to search for the slightest hint of a soul beneath his cool front, but he did not break. His eyes only revealed further his deep conviction.

"I've seen what we can do," he said. "Before the Nazis came to power, the German people were divided. Because we were divided, we fell to the mercy of our conquerors. We were oppressed because we weren't united. With the Nazis, we became a united front. We have food. We have jobs. Our young people are healthy. Everything is better because of us."

Tessa wanted to dispute him, but he continued. "The first

time I went to a rally, I was fourteen. I saw our potential. Our destiny. There were thousands of us, single-minded and unified. And we are strong. We bring glory to our fatherland. The world was ready to destroy us, but we prevailed. I saw what we could become with my own eyes."

"And what have you become? Killers of an old man and a child."

The question did not trouble him. "They were weak. They are better off eliminated."

"Mathias wasn't weak. He was young."

"He was weak by extension. His country didn't protect him. His family didn't protect him. He could not have grown up strong by himself. He was not German. We cannot take care of him. It is better this way."

His words gave Tessa chills. Oskar was no different from Pfeiffer after all. Ellie cowered and raised her hands to cover her lips. Tessa glanced at her, then looked at Oskar again. "What will you do to us? Are we weak too? Will you eliminate us?"

His expression eased somewhat. "As I already said, you will be taken to a prison camp. When your country surrenders, we will send you home. The Führer has great plans for us. We will dominate Europe and Russia. America just needs to stay out of our way." He opened the door. The distant voices of a choir flowed into the room. Although Tessa could not understand the language, she recognized it was the familiar tune of "O Holy Night."

"Tomorrow is Christmas," he said. "In the afternoon, I will bring your two friends here. You can have a meal and spend the afternoon together."

The offer hardly cheered them after what he had just said to them.

"I should warn you, the Oberst's tolerance has a limit. Do

not do anything to cross him. We have no plans to harm you. Do as you're told. Do not do anything to cause trouble, and you'll be all right." He left and closed the door. The sound of the lock reminded them of their true predicament.

On her bed, Ellie sat back against the wall. She curled up and wrapped her arms around her legs. "Can we sing a song? Let's sing a song." In a low, lonely voice, she began.

O Holy night
The stars are brightly shining
It is the night
of our dear Savior's birth

Numb and lost, Tessa joined her.

Long lay the world
In sins and error pining
Till He appeared
And the soul felt its worth

Louder they sang. How much Tessa wished the lyrics of the song could somehow erase all the horrors and atrocities of this world.

A thrill of hope
The weary world rejoices
For yonder breaks
A new and glorious morn

Fall on your knees
O hear the angel voices
O night divine
O night when Christ was born

O night
O night, o night divine

Tessa reached for her angel amulet. No one could hear them. Their lone singing voices echoed down the empty corridor. Their pleas for deliverance went ignored and unheard.

CHAPTER TWENTY-SIX

At the 33rd Field Hospital, Aaron watched and listened as a group of nurses and medical staff sang Christmas carols to the patients. The group had dubbed themselves the 33rd Christmas Choir, and had invited the army band to join them. On this afternoon of Christmas Eve, they moved from ward to ward, spreading the holiday spirit to those who could not participate in the festivities planned by the army.

Halfway through their performance, Aaron departed. He walked down the hallway to a large window and looked outside to the snow drifting down. Two weeks had passed since Colonel Callahan had come to tell them that Ellie and Tessa Graham had gone missing, and yet there was still no news of their whereabouts.

Regret. How he regretted all the time and chances he had lost. If he hadn't been so hesitant in approaching Ellie, he and Ellie might have been together, and Ellie and Tessa would not have been sent away so easily without his consent.

"The odds are slim," Fran said. He didn't notice she had walked up next to him. "You should prepare for the worst."

He turned around.

"If they could be found," she said, "the army would've found them by now. There are only two possible outcomes that explain why they haven't found her."

He ignored her and looked back out the window. He thought of Ellie's smile when she turned to look at him before boarding the plane to Normandy. No. That could not be their last goodbye. She was out there, somewhere.

"Even if she's still alive, you might never find her again. There's no telling where the Germans would take her."

"Why are you telling me this?" he asked without looking at her.

"I'm worried about you, Aaron. It's better if you don't keep your hopes up. Chances are, you'll be disappointed. It's better to be prepared."

"Yes. That's always the most important thing to you, isn't it, Captain? To calculate and be prepared."

Seeing she could not sway him, she chose not to answer his question. "Merry Christmas, Doctor." She collected herself and walked away.

Paying no attention to her, he searched for the sunlight between the clouds. In the past, he had let this woman discourage him. He had reasoned himself into believing he was too old to pursue the girl he loved. He had given up all too readily whenever Fran goaded him with ideas that affirmed his false beliefs. Not anymore. He knew better now. Love was not about reason, or planning, or being prepared. To love someone was to have faith. To take chances, to hope, and to accept the outcome, good or bad.

As long as there was still hope, he would do everything he could to keep that hope alive.

On the day before Christmas, the Orion strike team moved into Strasbourg just in time for the holiday dinner planned for the Third Division. In the mess hall crowded with arriving troops, the strike team searched for the soldiers from their company who had already arrived in the city before them. To everyone's delight, the kitchen staff had planned a surprise sit-down dinner instead of a buffet spread. From the fine wines down to the elegantly printed menus resting on their plates, no effort was spared in giving them a full-on fine-dining experience.

Passing by the crowds, Anthony went to the kitchen. He asked one of the cooks for a box of B-rations, then quietly headed out the exit.

"Captain, you're leaving already?" Fox asked as Anthony passed him. Anthony acknowledged him and continued to walk away.

On the streets, American soldiers roamed the city, searching for parties and dances in local restaurants, or hurrying on their way to join civilian families to enjoy a home-cooked meal. Anthony waded through the people reveling in festivities, back to the inn where he was staying.

The inn was quiet and deserted when Anthony returned. Everyone had gone out to celebrate. Even the innkeeper was nowhere to be found. Only the fire burning in the fireplace provided a tepid bit of warmth. He went into the kitchen, brewed himself a pot of coffee, and sat down at the table to eat his army-rationed dinner. When he finished, he took the letter that Tessa had sent him out of his jacket. He had been carrying the letter for weeks without ever opening it. She had not sent him any more letters after this one. Her silence could only mean one thing. She must have realized she should have chosen Jesse. He feared that the unopened letter would only confirm this.

He had tried to write to her, but every time he picked up his pen, he was lost for how to begin. There was so much he wanted to say to her. He wanted to tell her he still loved her, but compared to Jesse's great act of sacrifice, anything he could tell her felt like a consolation prize. He couldn't begin to write about their hopes for the future, when any talk of future plans felt like another bullet in Jesse's chest.

He put the letter back into his jacket. He wasn't ready to read what she had written. He didn't want to find out for certain that she loved somebody else.

Outside the window, flurries of snow floated in the air. Soon, the snow accumulated on the ground. The peaceful scenery gave him the only solace he could feel on this night.

What was Tessa doing now? Was she celebrating Christmas with her hospital? Or was she working near the front line, and Christmas was just another day of tired battles?

Was she thinking about him, the same way he was thinking about her?

He threw the empty B-ration cans into the garbage and left the kitchen. The front door of the inn opened and Colonel Callahan walked in. Anthony didn't expect to see him. "Colonel?"

"Captain Ardley," Callahan said. "Lieutenant Dennison said you might be here. May I have a word with you?"

"Of course, sir," Anthony said. The colonel's deferential tone confounded him.

"It's Lieutenant Graham. I'm sorry to tell you the news. She's missing. She's been missing for almost two weeks."

"Lieutenant Graham...you mean Tessa?"

"She and Lieutenant Ellie Swanson are both missing," Callahan confirmed, his eyes filled with sympathy. "I've been waiting for you to arrive so I could give you the news."

Missing... Anthony's heart almost came to a stop. Tessa had

gone missing, and he was only finding out about this now? "Did you say two weeks? Why didn't anyone tell me earlier?"

"You were on a mission. We didn't want to distract you and jeopardize you or your men's lives. There's nothing you can do anyway."

Anthony felt utterly helpless. Doing his best to withhold his anger, he asked, "What happened?"

"She was last seen with Swanson outside their field hospital in a region near the Ardennes. No one has seen them since." Callahan walked closer to him. "The army has searched the entire area around the hospital, but unfortunately they haven't found anything yet."

Shaken, Anthony tried to imagine what Tessa might have been doing the day she had disappeared. What could have happened to her? Where did she go? He wanted to run off and look for her. "We have to find her."

"Of course. We'll do our best. I've already telegraphed her family."

Anthony fell onto the sofa near the fireplace.

"Will you be all right?" Callahan asked.

Anthony nodded.

"I'm very sorry," Callahan said. "I'll let you know first thing if we have any news." He gave Anthony another sympathetic look and left.

Alone, Anthony tried to make sense of the news. He wanted answers, but none would come. There was no sound in the room except the crackling of the wood burning in the fireplace. The heavy whiteness of the snow outside had buried the tranquil scenery from his sight.

He grabbed his service cap and jacket, and went outside. He didn't know where he was going. He only knew he wanted to go somewhere, to do something.

The snow came down harder and heavier. Snowflakes fell

on his eyelids, and the blistering wind stung his face. He drew in deeper and deeper breaths as he plodded on.

How could he have been so wrong? She was missing. Perhaps in danger. Possibly dead. None of these scenarios had ever occurred to him. All along, he thought she hadn't written because she no longer loved him.

She was wallowing in tears when he left her in Paris. Afterward, he couldn't overcome his fears to write to her and let her know how much he still loved her. What if he never saw her again? Would that be their last memory of each other? What had he done?

Don't make her sad. Jesse's words echoed in his mind.

He had failed Jesse. All he had done was make Tessa sad. He was a poor, wretched excuse for a husband.

He came to a public square before a large cathedral. The monument stood tall and majestic above all the other buildings in the surrounding streets. He followed the cathedral's lights to the faint singing voices of the choir. He walked closer to the entrance, but could not move on. He felt unworthy to go any further. In front of the closed doors of the cathedral, he felt shut out.

He fell to his knees. The snowstorm had turned into a blizzard. The cathedral towered mightily over him, mocking his insignificance.

What do you want from me?

No answer came. Silence dominated the empty public square except for the voices of the choir coming from within the church.

Scenes of all the battles he had fought swarmed his mind. He saw the rivers he had passed, and the mountains he had crossed. Up until now, he had held out hope he would prevail.

If Tessa was gone, what was left for him to fight for?

The monument of God gave him no sign, no answer.

I've done everything I could. I've done all that you've asked. What more do you want from me?

Snow fell on his shoulders and the top of his cap. The choir had stopped singing. There remained only the howling sounds of the wind. Howls of pain in the dark of the night.

CHAPTER TWENTY-SEVEN

IN THE LATE morning while Tessa was drawing sketches on the stationery pad Oskar had brought them, Sister Margaux came to their room. This time, instead of bringing Tilda, she had brought along a guard.

"Merry Christmas," she said. "Come along. Your friends are waiting."

"Our friends?" Tessa asked. "Do you mean...?"

The sister smiled and nodded. Ellie jumped out of her bed, elated. Oskar had said he would let them spend Christmas day with Tyler and the Blade, but they didn't count on it happening.

They followed Sister Margaux and the guard down the winding corridor to a room on the opposite wing of the convent. Sister Margaux unlocked the door and let them inside. In front of a small fireplace, Tyler and the Blade were seated at a table waiting for them.

"Tessa!" Tyler got up immediately when they entered. "Lieutenant Swanson!"

"Tyler!" Tessa went to the table. "Blade!" The Blade wouldn't say anything in front of the guard, but she could see the relief in his eyes when they came in. "Are you both all right?"

"Yes," Tyler said. He and the Blade too were cleaned up and dressed in clean uniforms.

Tilda and another nun Tessa hadn't seen before brought in trays of hot food and water. Sister Margaux signaled them to place the food on the table. "Enjoy your afternoon. We'll be back later for the gentlemen." She led the guard and the other women to the door. "Merry Christmas." She closed and locked the door.

"I've been so worried about you two," Ellie said once the nuns and the guard had left.

"We've been worried about you." Tyler sat back down at the table. "Food! Good, I'm starving."

They sat down and began their meal. At first glance, it seemed like a meager offering with only a piece of bread, potatoes, and a small cup of soup. The gravy, however, had small bits of meat, which they all knew was a holiday treat.

"Did they treat you all right?" Ellie asked.

"Not bad, all things considered," Tyler said. "They locked us in a room in some kind of office. Every morning, an officer would come and question us. A different one each time. Well, mostly, they questioned Sergeant Cardozo. We didn't tell them anything of course. They let us shower once." He slurped the last of his soup. "What about you? How's life in the convent? Have you decided to forsake civilian life to take up the habit yet?"

"You can still joke." Tessa punched him in the arm. He laughed and took a bite of his bread.

"I'm glad to hear they've treated you well," Ellie said. "They've been unusually nice, don't you think? Maybe it's the holiday. Maybe they're feeling the holiday spirit."

"They're not," the Blade spoke for the first time since they had arrived. "I don't trust them. The war must not be going well for them. I think they're being nice because they want information, and they think we have it. That's their tactic. Treat us well and fool us. When they realize they're not getting anything out of us, they'll try something else."

His reminder cooled their momentary excitement. "I'm telling you all the truth." He shoved a fork into his potatoes and continued eating. Tessa had lost her interest in the food. The Blade had good instincts. If he thought they were in danger, then most likely, they were.

"We need to get away," the Blade said.

"Get away? How?" Tessa asked.

"We should try to escape. Now. Right now is our only chance."

"Escape?" Tyler asked. "What?"

"We're alone here. It's Christmas. I watched the streets when they took us here. The Nazis are in their mess hall eating and drinking. Hopefully, they're drunk out of their minds. There's no one patrolling the area. The nuns are busy praying or doing God knows what they do on Christmas. We're in a convent. They think we're locked in." He lowered his voice and glanced at the door. "There's no one guarding us outside this room."

"How do you know?" Tyler asked.

"I heard their footsteps when they left. Four sets of footsteps. They're all gone."

Tessa's heartbeats quickened. Escape. Maybe they could escape!

"But we're locked in here," Ellie said. "How can we get out?"

The Blade pulled out from his jacket the knife that Tessa had stolen for him back at the Zeghers. "I can pick the lock." He looked around at them. "What do you say? Are you all with me?"

Tessa looked at the door. Suddenly, the door became a

gateway to hope. It was the only thing standing between them and their freedom. "Blade." She took the small pistol out of her pocket. "Look what I got."

The Blade stared at her and the gun in shock. "Where did you get this?"

"From the Zeghers. I found it under old Mr. Zegher's pillow right before the Nazis made us leave their house."

The Blade exhaled in disbelief and took the pistol and put it in his pocket. "Son of a gun."

"Tessa!" Ellie looked like she wanted to faint.

"They would've killed you if they had found out!" Tyler said.

"I took it on the spur of the moment. I had no way of getting rid of it without them knowing."

"You must have been out of your mind."

"Never mind all that now," the Blade said. "We need to get out of here."

"What if we get caught?" Ellie asked.

"You're caught now. You're safe in the convent maybe, but they won't let you stay here forever." He said pointedly to her, "You've seen the way that filthy Nazi Pfeiffer looks at you. What will you do when Tyler and I leave, and he decides he wants more?"

She put her hands to her face.

Tessa pulled on her ring on her necklace and rolled it between her fingers. She looked up. "I'm in."

Following her lead, Tyler joined them, but with hesitation, "I'm in too."

Tense and worried, Ellie asked Tessa, "Are you sure?"

"I want to see Anthony again," Tessa said, still holding onto her ring. "I'm not letting them take me to the prison camp. If they take us there, I might never see him again. You want to see Dr. Haley again too, don't you?"

Ellie lowered her eyes. "I'll do whatever you all decide."

"Good," said the Blade. "Finish your food. We have precious little time, and we might not get to eat another meal for a long while."

Quickly, they finished their meal. While they ate, the Blade went to the door and listened for sounds. When he was sure no one was outside, he began testing what he could do to open the lock. "Got it!" The lock turned with a light popping sound. "Ready?" he asked. They all got up and went toward him. He pushed the door open a crack. The door creaked, and Ellie squeezed her eyes shut. Tessa felt so nervous, she could hardly breathe.

The Blade pushed the door open wider, just enough so he could sneak a look outside. "All clear." He opened the door and walked out. "Let's go."

They followed him, hustling but trying to stay as silent as possible. "Do you know where you're going?" Tyler whispered to him.

"We'll go back the same way they took us when we came in. Weren't you paying attention when you came in?"

"No."

"You're useless."

The Blade led them down the corridor past a small prayer room, where a gathering of nuns was praying inside. They kept going until they came to a stairwell. At the bottom of the stairs, there was a wooden door that opened to the outside. The Blade turned the doorknob. To their surprise, a guard was stationed there. He raised his rifle, but the Blade grabbed him and strangled him with a chokehold. The guard struggled, then his body went limp, and the Blade let him slump to the ground. Ellie took a deep breath and looked away.

"I'm sorry," the Blade said to her. "We have no choice." He checked the dead guard's body and found a Luger, which he kept. He then picked up the rifle and handed it to Tyler. "You know how to use this, right?" It was not a question, but a command.

Tyler gulped and nodded. He looked like someone had force-fed him a nasty medicine.

The Blade took the Zegher's small pistol out of his jacket and gave it back to Tessa. "Keep it." He winked at her. "It's your souvenir. I hope you won't ever have to use it."

Tessa nodded and put the pistol back in her pocket.

The Blade took a quick survey of the yard outside. Just as the Blade had said, there was no one patrolling the area near the convent. "If we can get out of here, I know the way to get us to the road that would take us back to the village where the Zeghers lived. The Nazis already cleared out of that area. We can keep going west from there. The First Army's pushing east to the German border. If we're lucky, we'll be able to find them." He pointed ahead to the stone wall surrounding the building. "The wall's low. We can climb over it. But we have to move fast."

Tessa knew what he meant. They were about fifty feet away from the wall. There was no place to conceal themselves between where they were and where they needed to go.

"Let's move." He started toward the wall. The rest of them followed. Behind the wall, past the rows of abandoned houses, lay their path to freedom. If they could reach the wall, they would have a chance.

Tessa took a deep breath of the frosty air as she hustled across the yard. The clouds were dull and gray. Tessa hoped they would remain inconspicuous under the gloomy overcast skies. She looked at the area ahead of her on her left, then her right. Still no one.

She quickened her steps. They had gone as far as twenty feet. She was almost sure they would make it when someone shouted behind them. "Stay where you are!"

They froze. Her heart pounding, Tessa turned and saw Oskar standing by the door from where they had escaped.

"Turn around." He pointed his rifle at them. "Drop your guns."

Slowly, they turned around. Petrified, Tyler let his rifle fall to the ground. The Blade tightened his fist around the Luger.

"Drop your gun," Oskar warned again and aimed his rifle at the Blade.

The Blade scowled and tossed down the Luger.

Standing close together, they waited to see what Oskar would do. Oskar glanced at the dead guard on the ground. "Why didn't you listen to me? I told you not to make any trouble, and you'd be all right. But you wouldn't listen."

Sister Margaux and a group of nuns came out to see what all the shouting was about. When they saw the dead guard and Oskar pointing his rifle, they stayed back in fear.

"Get the guards," Oskar said to Sister Margaux. In shock, she failed to respond. "Get the guards!" Oskar shouted. The sister ran away as she was told. The rest of the nuns huddled and whispered. Tessa noticed a package of cakes that had been dropped on the ground next to Oskar's feet.

"I brought those for you," Oskar said, following her gaze. She slid her eyes up and look into his. "It was a Christmas present."

Sister Margaux returned with two guards. Oskar signaled the guards to march them forward.

"Where are you taking us?" Tessa called out to Oskar.

"You tried to escape. And you killed a guard. I have to report this to the Oberst." He walked ahead of them.

"Please, Oskar. Please. No."

"I have to."

Forced by the guards, they walked on. Behind them, the nuns hugged each other. Some began to cry. Sister Margaux crossed her heart as she watched them leave.

The guards took them back to the building where the Blade and Tyler had been held. In the locked room, they sat in silence. Suddenly, the door unlocked and swung open. Pfeiffer entered with Oskar and two guards behind him. He took a sweeping look at his prisoners. Without saying anything, he tossed his head to signal his men. The two guards pulled the Blade and Tyler up from the floor.

Tessa jumped up and shouted, "Where are you taking them?"

"They tried to escape," Pfeiffer said. "Not only that, they killed one of my men. They will be executed."

"No!" Tessa and Ellie both cried.

"He didn't kill anyone," the Blade said and looked at Tyler. "I did."

"Doesn't matter. You both are the reason why one of my men is dead."

The guards pushed the Blade and Tyler along. "No!" Ellie grabbed Pfeiffer by the arm. "Please don't. Please don't kill them. We won't try to escape again."

He paused. His face twitched, as though he was conflicted.

"Please, Commander," Ellie pleaded. "I beg you. Please don't kill them."

He hesitated. Still angry, his chest heaved up and down as he breathed, but his eyes wavered. "Fine. This one stays." He pointed to Tyler. "Take the other one outside."

"No!" Ellie cried and looked desperately at the Blade.

"He killed my man. He cannot go unpunished."

The guard let go of Tyler and pushed him. Tyler stumbled forward while Tessa caught him and kept him from falling. The guards took the Blade by the arms.

"Blade!" Tessa cried out.

The Blade smiled at her to give her his last goodbye. His

face then tightened as the guards led him away. "Blade," Tessa cried again.

"I hope you will remember my act of mercy," Pfeiffer said to Ellie and left the room. Tessa glared at Oskar, her eyes questioning him, but his eyes showed no emotion. He looked away and locked the door.

THE ANGEL AMULET

Part Nine

CHAPTER TWENTY-EIGHT

COMING upon a wooden bridge across the canal, Anthony gazed out to the other side at the enemy stronghold he and his battalion were tasked with breaking through. On the west bank of the Rhine River, the German forces had formed a pocket of resistance forty miles wide and thirty miles deep. This heavily fortified section ran from northwest of Colmar, down to the towns of Cernay and Mulhouse. It served as Hitler's last line of defense against the Allies crossing into Germany from the southern end of the West Wall.

"So this is it." Jonesy came up next to him. "The infamous Colmar Pocket."

Yes. The Colmar Pocket. Facing this impassable half circle which exasperated the Sixth Army's entire chain of command, Orion's mission could not proceed until their army could open a way into the enemy territory.

Anthony pulled out his binoculars. Along this area of the West Wall, lines of pillboxes went on for miles and miles like they would never end. Intercrossed like a spider web, each pillbox was designed to protect and be protected by multiple other pillboxes to the left, right, front, and behind. If one came under attack, machine guns from the other ones would return fire at the attackers from every other direction.

Another death trap, Anthony thought as he put away his binoculars and led his company forward. The cycle of another battle had begun all over again.

How many more mountains must they cross? How many more battles must they fight? Who were all these new boys and men marching beside him who had come to replace the ones who had fallen? He didn't know most of them, and yet, their very lives depended upon every decision he made.

He didn't want to be responsible for them anymore. It was such a burden. All he wanted was to leave and go look for Tessa. Or, if she was no longer alive, then let him crawl into a foxhole somewhere and never come out again. He had no more strength to carry these men through.

They marched across the bridge. The night descended. He gave orders for the company to set up camp and rest for the night. The tank units were behind and still needed to catch up to them tomorrow.

On the field, men dug for hours, unable to make more than a dent in the frozen earth. There would be no luxury of foxholes in this frigid terrain. The clumping sounds of shovels weakened to light picks at the ground. The picks fizzled into faint kicks against the hardened soil as soldiers gave up digging and now only hoped to keep their feet warm. There would be no sleep for the weary. The freezing cold kept everyone awake through most of the night.

A dreary layer of gray clouds spread over the sky at the crack of dawn.

"Captain," the radio operator woke Anthony. "We got an update. The tank and mortar units can't cross. The bridge is too unstable. It won't hold."

Anthony looked across the river. Behind the bridge that

they crossed yesterday, a line of Sherman tanks, painted white for camouflage in the snow, stood useless on the other side.

"How long will it take them to get over here?" he asked.

"The bridge engineers are working on it. A day maybe?"

"Maybe?"

"They said tomorrow morning, but they can't guarantee it. They'll try to add support to the bridge first. If that doesn't work, they'll build a new bridge."

Jonesy and Dennison had woken up. The radio operator went to give them the situation update.

"Sir," the radio operator returned to Anthony. "We got another message. Command wants us to keep going."

"Keep going?" Jonesy asked. "With no tank and armor support? How do they expect us to break in there?" He looked toward the enemy bridgehead. "We'll get chewed up. We might as well be throwing eggs against a pride of lions!"

Leaving his men to the usual vent and gripes, Anthony walked to the edge of their campsite. Snow had come last night while they tried to sleep. A thick blanket of snow as high as his knees covered the wide meadow plains through which they must pass to reach their next target.

Command wanted them to keep going.

How did one keep going when there was nothing left inside him.

In Aaron's office, Fran stood watching as he cleared all his personal belongings from his desk. His commission with the hospital had come to an end. To the entire staff's dismay, he had announced he would not stay. He had decided to go north to look for Ellie Swanson.

How had this happened? Her hopes, her dreams. The life

she had envisioned after the war. How did everything turn out so different from what she had wanted?

"These are all the records I've kept for the hospital." Aaron picked up a stack of files on his desk. "I've briefed Dr. Bernstein on everything he needs to know. He'll make an excellent chief superintendent. If you need anything, I'm sure he'll give you his full support."

A stack of hospital records. This was all they had between them after the three years they had worked side by side? "I didn't think you'd leave," she said.

"Why not? My commission's over."

"Do you actually think you'll find her?" She pushed the files back down. "You'll be looking for a needle in a haystack."

He let go of the pile. "I have to try. She was seen in a convent close to the German border. I'll never forgive myself if I don't at least try and find her."

"This is absurd," Fran said. "What about your work here? You're giving up everything you've accomplished for a girl. Is it worth it? Does she deserve everything you're doing for her?"

"You don't understand, Captain. You never did." He stepped away from her and his desk. "It's not about how much I give up and how much I get in return. It's not about what she does or doesn't deserve. It's just something I want to do." He picked up his bag. "Good luck, Captain. It was an honor serving with you."

He left the office and didn't look back. Not once.

Angry, she shoved the pile of records off the desk. The papers flew across the floor, turning it into a mess.

For the first time, Fran Milton did not care if the files were in the wrong order.

In the old wooden barn where they were being held, Tessa sat on the floor, staring into space. She didn't cry after the Nazis took the Blade away. There was no need to cry. She would be joining him soon. Before long, Pfeiffer and his henchmen would decide they wanted her gone. Maybe they would punish her for trying to escape. Maybe Pfeiffer would want to kill somebody because he was in a bad mood. Or maybe, the Nazis would simply decide they no longer wanted to drag their prisoners along with them, the same way they had decided not to take Mathias and his grandfather. No law or boundary applied to these men. They did whatever they wanted. After everything these men had done, Tessa harbored no illusions about her fate.

Next to her, Tyler sat with vacant eyes while Ellie slumped against a stack of hay. Neither of them had said a word since they were brought here. If they had any hope of escape, that hope was now gone. The Nazis would not let them out of their sight again.

The guard at the table yawned. Every now and then, he would throw them a glance. A stern glance to keep them on their toes, and to remind them who was in charge. It was almost as if he was playing a game. Tessa refused to look at him. She wanted no interaction whatsoever with him. Her open antagonism might get her killed sooner, but she didn't want to cower in front of these people and beg for their mercy. Defying them with her silence, she turned the angel amulet in her pocket over and over and over. The mindless, repetitive motion was all she could do to shut out the world.

The barn door swung open. Pfeiffer barged in with a bottle of liquor in his hand. Repulsed by the sight of him, Tessa turned her head and looked away.

"Out," he ordered the guard.

The guard jumped to his feet.

"Go patrol the woods."

"Oberst…"

"I said out!"

The guard picked up his rifle and left. Pfeiffer sat down at the table and poured a shot of liquor into the cap of his canteen. "Fräulein," he said to Ellie. "Won't you join me?"

Ellie's eyes widened in panic. She looked at Tessa and Tyler, searching for help. But when they looked back at her, she came to the realization that Pfeiffer's infatuation with her was the only thing left that was keeping them alive. Tessa and Tyler's lives were in her hands. Knowing this, the fear in her eyes disappeared, replaced by a look of stern determination. She got up, brushed the hay off her clothes, and walked to the table.

"Sit next to me, won't you?" Pfeiffer pulled out a chair next to him. He was so eager, he almost fell over his own chair.

Ellie sat down. Her face exhibited no emotion.

He pulled closer to her. "I'm sorry about your sergeant. I did what I had to. You understand that, don't you?"

Ellie remained still as a statue.

"I have to do what's best for my people. I have to protect my own. I'm not a bad man. I do what I do to preserve the best of humankind. Can't you see?" He leaned closer to her face. She cringed and moved her chin slightly away. "I have a house in Rottach," he said. He almost sounded timid. "It's not far from Munich. It's up on the hill and overlooks the lake. When this war's over, if you like, I want to take you there. It's a beautiful place."

Ellie neither accepted nor refused. Pfeiffer poured himself another shot of liquor. "This is a fine bottle of whiskey. Rare and hard to get these days." He showed her the label. She raised an eyebrow and took a quick look.

"Would you like some?"

She shook her head.

"You don't drink?"

Watching them, Tyler's face twisted and flushed with anger. Tessa turned the amulet faster and harder as she turned her attention away from them to the bottle of liquor on the table. She had seen this type of whiskey before, but where? She focused her eyes on the label, trying to remember. Yes. It was a fine bottle indeed. In the 33rd Field Hospital's underground storage where the medical supplies were kept back in Anzio, Jesse had come to her with one just like it.

"Unless, like all the other girls, you can't hold your liquor."

"Who says I can't hold my liquor?"

Jesse. She remembered now, the way he had looked at her with his captivating eyes. So dark and intense. How blind she had been. She thought he looked at every girl that way. She took the amulet out of her pocket and caressed it softly with her thumb.

"How do you get your liquor supply anyway? What do you do with it? Drink it yourself, or pass it around to the other soldiers?" She remembered asking him.

Not bothered by her string of questions, he had only smiled. His dashing smile was as clear to her as yesterday.

"I trade them for what I need to get for our boys. Sometimes, I'd even offer to share it with the woman I love."

The warmth of his voice, so out of reach.

A cold draft passed into the barn. Feeling the chill, Tessa curled her freezing toes inside her boots and stared at the direction from where the draft had come. The barn door was unlocked. It squeaked open and shut as the night wind blew. No one else seemed to have noticed.

"You're shivering," Pfeiffer said to Ellie, his voice starting to slur. "You should have some." He offered the whiskey to Ellie again. "It'll keep you warm. It'll relax you." With hesitation, he put his hand on hers. Ellie's lips quivered, but she didn't pull her hand away.

A wave of nausea hit Tessa in her stomach. Tyler couldn't

watch anymore. Subconsciously, he had wrapped straws of hay around the palm of his hand. The hay was wrapped so tightly around his fist, his knuckles had turned white.

The barn door creaked open with the wind. Through the crack, Tessa peered outside into the darkness.

Anthony. He was out there. If she were to see him again, she had to find a way to escape. There was no one left to help her.

Quietly, she felt for the small gun she had hidden in her jacket. The barn door remained ajar.

Pfeiffer held the drink up to Ellie's face to let her smell the whiskey, but she shook her head. Ellie wasn't one who liked to drink.

Gracie didn't like to drink either. *"Gracie can't drink. She has no tolerance. Not like you."*

No, Jesse. Not like me.

Tessa turned her eyes back to the table. His face flushing from the alcohol, Pfeiffer had dropped all pretense of decorum. He whispered to Ellie in a mix of German and English, his lips only inches away from her neck. "Have a drink with me," he coaxed her. Clearly uncomfortable, Ellie tried to push the liquor away without upsetting him.

Lightweight. Tessa sneered in her mind. Even she could outdrink him.

Get him drunk, a voice urged her from within. She squeezed the amulet and put it back into her pocket, then said out loud to Pfeiffer, "I'll drink with you."

The sound of her voice startled him. He squinted at her, as though he had forgotten she was in the barn.

"I'll drink for Ellie." She got up off the ground and went over to him. Without waiting for him to react, she took the drink from his hand.

Bottoms up, Jesse. She emptied it with one swallow. "Give me another one."

His interest piqued, Pfeiffer poured her a shot. "You want

more?" He gave her a sly, condescending smile. "Be careful. This is strong."

"I know it's strong." She looked him in the eye and finished the next shot. The liquor went down her throat like electricity through a lighting fuse. Emboldened, she picked up the bottle, refilled the cap, and held it toward him. "Your turn."

The Nazi snickered. He downed the shot, then turned the cap upside down to show Ellie that he hadn't left a single drop. Tessa watched his eyelids droop as he laughed.

"Have you had enough?" She poured another shot from the bottle. "Don't force yourself if you can't handle it."

"Are you insulting me?" He grabbed the cap from her and downed it. "You next." He handed the cap back to her.

"Tessa!" Ellie shook her head at her.

Not worried, Tessa took a seat across the table and poured herself another shot. Sipping the liquor, she asked, "Oberst. Tell us. What are your plans when the war's over?"

"My plans?" He mused on the question. "I'll continue the great work of building the German empire, of course. You'll see. You'll all see. We'll be the strongest race among all humankind. For myself though…" He gazed at Ellie. "A family. Children. Beautiful, strong, healthy children." Ellie looked away, but his smile grew wider.

While he talked, Tessa filled the cap to the brim with more liquor. Unsure of what Tessa was trying to do, Ellie gave her a puzzled look. Tessa motioned to her to offer the drink to Pfeiffer. Although unsure of Tessa's intent, Ellie nonetheless did as Tessa prompted.

"Thank you." Pfeiffer took Ellie's hand and drank the liquor she was giving him. "You have such beautiful hair. Like gold." He lifted a lock of her hair and smelled it, then closed his eyes and dropped his head onto his arm on the table.

Tessa's heart pounded. This was it. Now was her chance. She moved her hand into her pocket and felt her gun.

Do it. Her mind was telling her. *Do it now.* She closed her hand around the gun. She didn't know if she could take someone's life.

Another draft of wind blew in. The barn door creaked again. It was now or never. She got up and walked behind Pfeiffer.

"What are you doing?" Ellie asked.

"I'm getting us out of here." She took the gun out and pointed it at the back of his head. Ellie let out a small cry.

Tyler jumped to his feet. "Tessa!"

Tessa held up the gun. Her hand trembled and her whole body shook.

"Tessa, wait!" Ellie said, in shock.

"We can't wait. This is our only chance. The door's open." Tessa tried to steady the gun with both her hands. "I'm not going to die. I'm going back to Anthony." She took a deep breath.

On the table, Pfeiffer stirred. He opened his eyes. When he saw Ellie's frightened face, he turned his head. Fury rose when he saw the gun. Shaking, Tessa took an involuntary step back. Pfeiffer lurched at her. Tessa hardened her heart and pulled the trigger. The power of the shot thrust her backward and threw her off her feet. The bullet struck Pfeiffer in the head, and he dropped and fell onto the table. Blood oozed down his menacing face. Ellie cried out and fell back into her seat. Shocked, Tyler stared at Pfeiffer. The Nazi monster was dead.

Tessa's hands, arms, and her entire body shook. Her ears rang from the blast of the shot. She killed him. She killed another person.

"What's going on here?" Oskar slammed the barn door open. Before anyone else could react, Tyler lunged at him and grabbed his rifle. In their struggle, a shot went off. The bullet hit Oskar in his neck. Blood spurted out from his throat and he fell to the ground. By the time Tessa reached his body, he was already dead. Tyler stumbled backward, aghast.

Their scuffle brought Tessa back to her senses. She closed Oskar's eyes. "We killed them. We have to run. Now." She stuck her gun back into her pocket, picked up Oskar's rifle, and gave it to Tyler. "Take it."

Tyler accepted the rifle, still too shocked to speak. Tessa grabbed Ellie by the arm. "Come on."

Without knowing where they were going, they ran out of the barn. In the dark of the night, they raced down the trail away from where the Nazis had set up camp.

Foolish! Tessa thought as she ran. How could she be so foolish? The Blade would never have tried to escape without a plan. She had no plan. Where would they go? She didn't even pay attention to the roads when the Nazis drove them here.

Distracted by her rash of thoughts, she tripped. "Ahhh!" she yelled and fell to the ground. Her knees banged against the hard, frozen earth. Her angel amulet slipped out of her pocket.

"Tessa!" Ellie ran to help her up while Tyler turned back around toward her. She ignored them and reached for the amulet. In a frenzy to retrieve it, she knocked it further away and it rolled down the ditch on the side of the road. "No!" she climbed after it.

"Tessa!" Tyler cried. "We gotta run!"

"I dropped my amulet. I have to find it."

"We don't have time."

"Tessa, forget it. Let's go!" Ellie pleaded.

"I can't. You two go without me." Tessa slid down the ditch. On her hands and knees, she searched frantically for the amulet. Where was it? How could she lose it? She wanted to cry.

Ellie and Tyler looked at each other, then jumped into the ditch with her. "What does it look like?" Tyler asked.

"It's celestite," Tessa said.

"It's what?"

"It's a kind of gemstone," Ellie said. "It's white."

"White? Great. We're looking for a white gemstone in patches of snow."

In desperation, Tessa felt the ground with her hands. In front of her, the moonlight reflected off a piece of shining object. The amulet! "I found it!" She snatched it up, but Tyler pushed his hand over her mouth and muffled her. He shoved her with such force, she fell onto her back against the ground. She tried to speak, but he hushed her with his eyes and shook his head. He had pushed Ellie down too, holding Ellie still with his other hand over her mouth.

Tessa's heart nearly stopped when the hums of a utility vehicle passed by above them on the road. They lay still against the ground for a long time, too afraid to move even though the vehicle had driven away. Finally, Tyler let go and collapsed. "That was fucking close."

Regaining her breath, Tessa held the amulet against her heart. Her heart was still beating out of control.

"They would've seen us if we weren't down here, right?" Ellie asked. Neither Tessa nor Tyler answered. The idea was too terrifying to think about.

"Let's move along the ditch and see how far we can go," Tyler said.

In the ditch, they continued on their way. Slower and more cautious this time. When daylight broke, they came to an empty stable. Too tired to go on, they went inside. In a corner, they huddled together and crashed asleep.

CHAPTER TWENTY-NINE

COMING to the edge of the Colmar forest, Anthony led his troops down the path toward Schlenzingen, a small German village less than a mile away.

How he had made it this far, Anthony did not know. Since the news of Tessa's disappearance, he had lost the drive to go on. Victory, escape, survival. What did it matter? He had come to war with the hope of fighting for a better world, but how would his world be better if she was gone?

While his own hopes dwindled, the Allies continued to make gains. After his battalion's arrival at Colmar, the Seventh Army had succeeded in pushing past the German West Wall. No outside forces in history had ever broken through this invincible military fortress. The Germans were failing. As the number of their troops diminished and their ammunition and supplies were depleted, the tactical advantage of the West Wall's web of intercrossed pillboxes was neutralized. The enemy could not match America's military prowess.

The prospect of winning the war gave Anthony no solace. The one thing that kept him going now was Klaus. As fate would have it, the army's latest intel had reported that Klaus had retreated this way. With the Orion strike team and his entire regiment behind him, his job was to capture the German commander once and for all.

Anthony welcomed the order. He wanted to get Klaus. He wanted to make Klaus pay for all the damage he had caused. He would make it his life's mission to get the German scoundrel. For Warren. For Jesse.

After that?

If he couldn't find Tessa, or if she was dead, the thereafter wouldn't matter anymore.

The Orion strike team marched out of the woods into a long field covered with a thick layer of snow. There was no sign of life anywhere except for a little empty shack standing at the clearing at the end of their path. A gust of wind blew past as Anthony observed the area with his binoculars. At first, all he saw was a sheet of white. But something was off. The snow-covered plain seemed to be rolling. It reminded him of what the beach looked like when the tide moved in. The whole ground seemed to be moving.

"What in the world...," Jonesy exclaimed. He, too, was looking out into the field with his binoculars. As the movement closed in, the threat soon became clear. Advancing toward them were eight Tiger tanks, all painted in white. The tanks were followed by a formation of marching soldiers. One hundred of them, maybe two hundred. Anthony could not tell. So well camouflaged in their white winter uniforms, they blended into the landscape like waves in a white ocean.

"Bring our mortar units up!" Anthony shouted. The enemy's surprise attack had thrown his company into a sudden emergency. Two American tanks and an artillery tractor pulled out of the forest. A machine gun squad rushed to quickly set up the lone artillery tractor by the little empty shack. The infantry soldiers moved up immediately, bracing for the fight.

A blast blew past above Anthony. The treetops behind him

exploded, taking with it the machine gun squad beneath before they could finish unloading their shells. The force of the explosion flipped the artillery tractor to its side and obliterated part of the shack. Remnants of the shack flared up in flames. The surviving soldiers near the tractor dove away and ran for their lives.

On the ground next to Anthony, the radio operator shouted into the radio receiver, "We're under attack! Repeat: we are under attack! We need reinforcements."

The American tank returned fire and cleared a line of enemy soldiers. The hit made barely a dent in the oncoming German troops. Another wave of soldiers moved up and replaced them from behind. A Tiger tank fired a shell and disabled their Sherman. Not finished, the enemy released a second shell. The Americans' other tank, too, blew up. A slew of American soldiers now lay dead on the ground. Snow and smoke clouded everything, and the scene descended into chaos. The battalion of enemy troops advanced closer to them.

Jonesy lunged toward Anthony. "We can't fight this. We need more heavy weapons."

"Agreed. Get everyone the hell back into the forest!"

While Jonesy led their troops back into the woods to escape, Anthony fired his Tommy at the oncoming German troops to hold them off.

"Captain! Go!" Jonesy shouted.

Anthony dashed away after Jonesy. When he ran past the burning shack, a hunch made him look back. He darted behind a tree and peered out through his binoculars.

Impossible! Driving an officer's car behind the waves of white-clad German infantry was the man he had been looking for. Klaus!

He looked into his binoculars again to make sure. A high command officer should not be out front on the battlefield. Yet there he was.

Anthony could not help feel a grudging respect. Klaus was, after all, a worthy opponent. Like Anthony, Klaus protected his men. He had done so when he surrendered his troops back in Montélimar. Here, he would fight alongside his men and lay down his life with them.

Nonetheless, he had killed Warren and Jesse. And for that, Anthony would give his life to avenge them.

In that moment, Anthony also knew. He would have to kill Klaus. Even if he could capture the man alive, this German officer would never disclose any secrets to his enemy. Klaus would give up his own life before he would let his men and his country fall.

Dennison, their company XO, ran up to Anthony. "Captain! We have to fall back."

Anthony looked at Dennison, then the shack. The shack was shattered except for the partially blown walls still burning in flames. The bodies of the former machine gun squad lay like dead fish on the ground. Amidst the ruins, the machine gun remained, undamaged. A pile of ammunition lay next to it. The squad had been killed before they ever had a chance to use them.

"Go back," Anthony shouted to Dennison and started toward the machine gun.

"Captain!"

"I said go back."

"No! I'm not leaving you here."

"Leave! Look after everyone. That's an order!"

Dennison hesitated. His disbelieving eyes glared out from his gunpowder-smeared face.

"I said go!" Anthony yelled.

Dennison squeezed his fist, then ran the other way.

· · ·

The machine gun stood pointing at the enemy. Anthony jumped behind it, aimed it at the group of enemy soldiers coming toward him and fired. The spray of bullets sent those soldiers crashing to the ground.

He paused and looked through the binoculars, searching for Klaus. The heat of the burning flames in the shack behind him thawed his blood and ignited in him a second wind. He fired at another cluster of men. Concealed by smoke, the enemy did not see him. His adrenaline rising, he swept his gun at the lines of enemy soldiers, sending a blaze of bullets into the menacing sea of white.

He continued to search for Klaus. A surge of rifle fire spewed from behind the trees. The rumbles of Sherman tanks grew louder and louder. *Good.* The cavalry had arrived. His regiment had regrouped and had returned to launch a counter offense.

Anthony fired again. The sputters of the machine gun mixed with rifle shots zipping between the two sides. Unable to detect Anthony's position amidst the noise, the enemy's infantry soldiers fired in the direction of the forest. One of the shots struck the disabled artillery tractor. The forest wind blew, carrying with it a waft of gasoline leaking from the broken gun carriage.

Volleys of shells began to drop from the sky. Anthony looked up. Air support. The American planes had come and were dumping weapons from above. The bombs hit the ground and exploded, creating heavier screens of smoke that further shielded Anthony from the enemy's sight.

The German formation began to break. From the disarray, Klaus's vehicle emerged, driving closer and closer to Anthony until it was within a hundred yards of where he stood.

Anthony's heart pounded. This was it. Now was his chance.

He aimed the machine gun at the man who had come to represent all the destruction in his life. Could this be the end?

Would he finally end this war for himself and his men if he took out this man?

Could it be true that this was all he needed to do to take this unshakable German major down? Just aim and shoot?

He pulled the trigger. A succession of pops rattled off. In a split second, Klaus tipped over, stunning his men around him. Alarmed, they blazed their weapons in every direction. The roar of a Sherman tank answered their fire, followed by more American shells falling from the sky. Klaus's platoon disintegrated. Anthony released a final splash of bullets at the ones trying to escape until they dropped and their shouts and screams ceased.

On the field, the Tiger tanks retreated. The noises of battle tempered out and waned. Only distant sounds of gunfire still rang.

The stench of gasoline fumes churned Anthony's guts. No air. The smoke constricted his lungs and choked his throat. Dizzy, he dropped to the ground. The open eyes of a fallen soldier stared at him. The dead man's mouth had frozen open like a crazy grin.

Delirious, Anthony smiled back, then laughed. His laughs turned to cries as tears spilled and soaked his face. He was done. Klaus was dead. Warren and Jesse could rest in peace.

The fire that was burning the shack spread, engulfing the area around him. The flames would soon reach the trail of gasoline leaking from the tractor and the stack of artillery that had fallen out of it. Detached, Anthony watched the fuel leak along the snow-covered ground. His tears stopped.

Hot. He felt hot. His uniform was drenched beneath his jacket. He whipped open his buttons. Vaguely, he could sense the growing fire around him, but he was too drained of energy to get up. Everything around him felt surreal.

He closed his eyes, ready to sleep. Let him fall into a deep sleep from which he would never have to wake up. *Wesley. Darnell. Ollie. Warren. Ed. Jesse.*

Tessa.

Let this be his turn. He didn't want to carry the burden anymore.

Is this what I gave my life for? A voice pierced his mind and jerked him out of delirium.

Where did the voice come from? He pulled his knees close to his body. A tiny, hard object dug against his hip. He pushed it out of his pocket. Jesse's lucky seven dice.

You have to stay alive.

With a trembling hand, Anthony picked up the dice.

You stay alive no matter what. You do what you have to but get through this war. Get through it and go back to her. Nothing else matters.

Anthony clutched the dice and bent his head. The corner of Tessa's letter jutted out from the inner pocket of his jacket and poked his chin. The envelope, crumpled with creases, was still unopened. He was afraid to open it. What if she had realized she had made a mistake not choosing Jesse?

If you die, she'll be very sad. Don't make her sad.

With clumsy fingers, Anthony opened the letter. Tears filled his eyes again as he read her words.

Wherever you are, my heart is yours. It's always been yours. Remember, in Rome? You told me then, whatever happens, don't give up. I'm not giving up on us. I vowed to love you for all eternity. Come back. Come back to me.

It was him. It had always been him. She had never wavered.

I'm not giving up on us, her letter said.

Come back to me. He heard her voice calling out to him.

For all eternity...

At their wedding, Tessa had vowed to love him for all eternity.

Had he forgotten that when he married her, he had made a

promise at the altar that he would never give up, no matter what happened or what difficulties lay ahead?

He blinked his eyes to stop his tears and forced himself up.

I won't give up on us either. He put the dice and letter into his jacket. *I'll never give up.*

He pushed himself off the ground. Step by step, he made his way to the dirt road that led to the forest. He had just reached the road when a gunshot went off behind him. At first, he didn't feel anything. Next, warm wetness seeped over his left side. Then, a searing pain.

He turned around. A boy in a white Wehrmacht uniform had his rifle pointed at him. How old was he? Twelve? Thirteen? The boy looked shocked. His arms and rifle were shaking.

Anthony hardened his heart, pulled out his pistol from his holster and shot the boy dead. One more count of guilt against him in this endless trial of misery.

Struggling to breathe, he pressed his hand against his wound. So exhausted was his mind, he could no longer think. He walked on, feeling as though he was in a trance. Behind him, the fire reached the spilled gasoline and the tractor exploded. The power of the blow knocked Anthony down. His helmet fell off and rolled away.

Sprawled on the ground, he could not move. The bullet torched his stomach like molten iron. The drumming of his own heartbeat pounded against his ears. Was he dying? He closed his eyes. The snow on the ground next to his mouth melted, wetting his face.

Come back.

He curled his fingers and grabbed the snow under his hands.

Come back to me.

Tessa's voice called out to him. He struggled onto his knees.

The cross she gave him dangled from his neck. He grabbed it and held onto it.

I won't give up on us. Not as long as there is still a chance she's alive. I won't.

With his other hand, he took out the lucky seven dice. "For luck," he said to himself, and put their chain over his head around his neck. With every last ounce of strength, he pushed himself onto his feet. The cross and the dice swayed as he walked on.

"Captain! Captain!" Fox's voice came somewhere from the edge of the forest.

Anthony raised his head. "Captain!" Fox's face appeared, he thought. He wasn't sure. Everything was blurred and fuzzy. His legs gave out. His head whirled and he fell to the ground.

CHAPTER THIRTY

VOICES. Anthony woke to voices of people he couldn't recognize. The voices buzzed all around him. They came from the patients in the next beds and their attendants in the next rows. He opened his eyes. Blurry rows of wounded soldiers lay around him. The cots appeared to shift. The patients seemed to be moving around and around in circular motions. Even his own body felt like it was floating and spinning.

Discombobulated, Anthony tried to lift his head, but fell back onto the pillow. All his strength had left him. He tried again. This time, he succeeded in lifting his back slightly off the bed. As he bent to get up, a sharp pain shot up from his side.

"Captain Ardley!" A nurse on duty came to the side of his bed.

Gasping for breath, Anthony lay back and waited for the pain to subside. "I feel like the room's spinning."

"It's the anesthesia. You've had major surgery. Try not to move. I'll get you some water." The nurse turned to go fetch him water.

"Wait. Please," he said, his voice barely audible. "What happened?"

"You were shot." She touched him lightly on the shoulder. "Don't worry. You're okay now. We'll take good care of you."

He loosened his body. His side hurt every time he breathed. Memories of the snowfield slowly returned to him. Klaus. The burning remains of the shack. The German boy.

Tessa…Where was Tessa?

He wanted to ask the nurse, but his last bit of energy left him, and he faded back into sleep.

The stable door opened and a rush of cold air blew in, waking Tessa from her sleep. She forced her eyes open while Tyler and Ellie stirred. The lone silhouette of a woman stood in the blinding sunlight pouring in from outside. Instinctively, Tyler grabbed the rifle. The woman standing at the door screamed and held up her hands.

Quickly, they got up. "Let's go," Tessa said. They had been discovered. This was bad news. "Let's get out of here."

Pointing his gun at the woman, Tyler led Tessa and Ellie toward the door.

"So sorry." Ellie apologized as they passed her.

"Wait," the woman followed them outside. "Out there. Danger." She looked out to the open field.

They stopped. Tessa exchanged a glance with Tyler. He, too, was uncertain.

The woman pointed at herself. "Anke." She pointed to a small cottage behind the stable, which they hadn't noticed last night. "My house."

"Is she inviting us to her house?" Tyler asked.

Ellie smiled and took a step toward Anke, but Tessa pulled her back. "Maybe it's a trick."

Anke looked to the open field outside. "Out there. Soldiers. War." She pointed at the cottage again. "My house. No soldiers. Only husband."

Still hesitant, they looked at the cottage. The woman was speaking the truth. There was no military vehicle, or vehicle of any kind, anywhere in sight. The only sign of life they could see was the smoke rising from the cottage's chimney.

"My house," Anke said again. A lock of her graying hair had fallen out of her headscarf. "I have food."

Against her will, Tessa's stomach grumbled. Tyler's resolve, too, weakened at the mention of a meal. Ellie dropped her guard and approached Anke, "Thank you. I'm Ellie. These are my friends. Tessa. Tyler."

Anke gave them a warm smile. Tessa still could not be sure if she could trust the woman, but her hunger was now directing her mind.

"Come this way." Anke started down the path. They followed her to the cottage, where a man with a thick grey beard was chopping wood. When he saw them with his wife, his mouth dropped and he raised his ax. Anke held up her hand and spoke to him in German. He furrowed his eyebrows, confused, then lowered his arm.

"Husband. Fritz," Anke said to them, then waved for them to go inside her house. Dumbfounded, Fritz watched them enter his home.

The warmth of the hearth enveloped them as soon as they walked in. In the fireplace, a pot of soup simmered. The aroma of slow-cooked mushrooms and onions hit Tessa's nose and her stomach growled. She had forgotten when she had eaten last.

Anke nodded toward the table. "Sit."

Tessa, Ellie, and Tyler each took a seat. Tessa felt horrible now for having suspected Anke earlier. She gave Anke an uneasy smile. Anke returned her smile and pointed to the red cross band on Tessa's arm. "Medical."

"Yes," Tessa said. It didn't occur to her that Anke had noticed.

Anke filled three bowls with the soup from the pot and put them on the table along with several pieces of bread. "*Suppen.*" Without further prompting, Tessa, Ellie, and Tyler began devouring the food.

As she ate, a lump grew in the back of Tessa's throat. Her eyes welled up and a tear fell from the corner of her eye. She had never been so hungry before. Like a starving animal, she wolfed everything down. Tyler and Ellie were doing the same. No wonder Anke wasn't afraid of them. They didn't look frightening, they themselves looked terrified.

VICTORY EUROPE

Part Ten

CHAPTER THIRTY-ONE

"WELL, at least it seems the Nazis treated them well," said Culkin, the Salvation Army volunteer who had been driving Aaron around. "Don't give up hope yet, Haley. Now we know they're with the Kampfgruppe Pfeiffer. The First Army is catching up to them. We'll keep following their trail. We'll find them."

Aaron hoped so. He looked to the road ahead. Thanks to an old friend at the Arm Med in charge of liaising with civilian volunteers, the Salvation Army had taken him as a volunteer after he had left the 33rd Field Hospital. They had brought him to Bonn, where the First Army had picked up news that Ellie and Tessa had been seen there as prisoners of war when Kampfgruppe Pfeiffer passed through. As soon as he heard, Aaron knew he had to get there. He would dedicate his life to finding Ellie, if it was the last thing he did.

The Salvation Army truck passed a road sign pointing south reading "Cochem 80km." The nuns at the convent in Erftstadt near Bonn had said the Nazi unit was heading in this direction, so Tessa and Ellie were still alive when the Nazis left Bonn. But were they all right now? Pfeiffer had massacred all of the Allied troops in the towns and villages along his path. It was a miracle that Ellie and Tessa had survived all the way through Bonn.

Nonetheless, the First Army was rapidly gaining ground. The German defense was faltering within their own heartland. If the American troops could catch up to Pfeiffer in time, the army might find them yet.

Meanwhile, Aaron prayed, let the miracle last.

In the three weeks since their escape, Tessa, Ellie, and Tyler had remained in hiding with the German country couple in their house. While there, Tessa learned that they were at a place near Cochem, a tiny German town on the western border of Germany. She tried but couldn't discover why Anke and Fritz had made the decision to shelter them. With Anke's limited English skills, they could not communicate. However, Tessa knew the couple had taken on a great risk to their own safety by harboring Americans. What Anke and Fritz did was beyond ordinary kindness. They reminded her that there was no barrier to compassion among people, even in times of war.

Anke and Fritz were generous too. The German regime had not been able to provide for its people for a long time. Anke and Fritz had few resources to spare. What meager food they had, they shared with Tessa and her friends. Tessa could only hope that she would be able to repay the couple someday for everything they did.

Anke had an old German–English dictionary for children. While Tessa and her friends stayed at their house, Anke would sometimes use the dictionary to look up words if they had difficulty understanding each other. It had pictures that accompanied some of the words. Tessa tried to look up the word "enemy" once, to ask Anke if she was worried that

Americans were her enemy. The word was not included in the dictionary.

Finding the word missing from the pages, Tessa couldn't help feeling the irony. She looked at Anke and Fritz, who were sitting at the table with her. The meaning of enemy wasn't something she could easily define anymore.

One thing Tessa had gathered was that the couple missed their son. On the wooden shelf by their window was a picture of a young man in a Wehrmacht uniform standing proudly in front of the Brandenburg Gate. "Your son?" Tessa asked the kind woman.

Anke smiled. "Frederick." Her eyes showed a mixture of joy and pain.

"Is he with the German Army?"

Anke looked away sadly and shook her head. "No more. Frederick no more."

Tessa had a feeling that Anke and Fritz regretted the war. Regardless of sides, the war had left everyone caught in its wrath with their own private anguish which others could not help to relieve.

Watching Anke, Tessa wondered what her parents must be thinking, not knowing where she was. They must be so worried. She wished she could reach out to them and let them know she was okay.

And Anthony. Where was he now? Was he okay? She prayed for his safety every day.

When the news came on the radio that the Americans had taken over Cochem, Ellie broke down and cried. This was what they had been waiting for, a way home.

After they heard the news, they decided to go to Cochem and report to the American troops. Anke and Fritz kindly offered to go with them to make sure they would not get lost.

Following Anke and Fritz, Tessa, Ellie, and Tyler walked for three miles along the rural path. They had no other way to get there. Fritz had a car, but it had been a long time since he had access to any fuel. Anke told them they had had an old horse, which had died before the war reached them. She was thankful for that, because the horse might have suffered if it had been taken away by the German army.

They came into town, hopeful yet nervous until they saw the convoys of American jeeps. As they tried to explain to the First Army unit who they were, a Salvation Army vehicle drove up.

"Ellie!"

Ellie and Tessa looked at each other. The voice sounded familiar.

"Ellie! Ellie!" Aaron Haley called out. "Tessa!"

"Dr. Haley?" Ellie asked. Tessa, too, could not believe it. Doctor Haley should be with the Seventh Army in the South.

Aaron Haley jumped out of the car and ran toward them. "Ellie! Ellie, is it really you?"

"Dr. Haley!" Ellie cried. Leaving behind all her worries as to propriety, she ran into his arms, unable to stop crying her tears of joy.

At the U.S. Army's General Hospital in Paris, Anthony reclined in his bed and stared into space. Music was playing on the radio, but he could not tell one song from another. The songs blended together into nothing but background noise. His interest would pique when the news came on with reports about his own company's movements, but even those did not hold his attention for long. Safe in the hospital in an Allied occupied zone, everything that was happening on the battlefront felt remote and unreal. He didn't know how war and peace could coexist this way in the same world.

At lunch, he picked up his tray from the serving queue

and sat down in a quiet spot. His abdomen still hurt when he moved that part of his body, but he didn't mind. In a way, he appreciated the pain. His scar was a badge of honor no medal could ever match. Every time he felt its pinch, it reassured him that he, too, had paid his due. Every twinge stripped away a little more of his guilt. Moreover, it reminded him he was still alive, that he could still feel pain. It was a small price to pay, compared to the sacrifices of those he still remembered.

Lost in his own reflections, he did not notice when an unexpected visitor came to him and sat down at his table.

"General Castile." Anthony quickly put down his fork and tried to stand up.

"At ease, Captain. No need to stand up."

Anthony sat back down.

"How are you?" the General asked.

"Good, sir. Thank you."

"The doctor said you're well enough to be released."

Anthony knew this was coming. He supposed he had recovered, even though his wound was still raw. What hadn't recovered was his psyche. His mind was an empty wasteland. He had no will to go back into battle. He had no more fire within him to wage a good fight. He dreaded what the general might say next.

The general had something else in mind. "I've got good news. I wanted to deliver it myself and I came as quickly as I could. We've found Lieutenant Graham."

"You found her?" Anthony could not be sure if he had heard right. "Did you say you found her? What happened to her? Is she okay?"

"Yes. We've found her. She's safe and she's fine."

Anthony's lips quivered. He didn't want to cry in front of the general but he could no longer control himself.

"She was captured by a Nazi unit along with another nurse

and a medic," Castile said. "She escaped and was hiding with a German family outside of a small town called Cochem."

"Where is she now? Can I go see her?" Anthony's face was wet with tears, but he no longer cared. Tessa was alive. She was alive. That was all that mattered.

"She's at an army rest area in Liège. She's being processed. We have to make sure she's in good health, and we have to interview her about what happened to her when she was with the Nazis. If she has any important information, we need to know."

"Can I go see her?"

"Of course." The general smiled. "That's why I'm here. She's been through a lot. She'll be relieved from commission. She's going home."

"Home? Chicago?"

"Home to London. That's where her parents are, isn't it?"

London…

"You've been through a lot too," Castile said. "The Orion mission is over. Klaus is dead. It's time you got a break. You'll be on furlough starting tomorrow. Perhaps you would like to go to London?"

Anthony nodded. Yes. He wanted to go to London. He would go anywhere in the world to see Tessa.

"We have recruits arriving at our bases in Gloucestershire. There's an opening for an instructor. Someone with extensive battle experience like you can set a good example."

Gloucestershire? Training? What was the general saying? Anthony could not understand.

"When your furlough is over, you'll be reassigned to Gloucestershire. It'll be your job to train new recruits and get them ready."

"I'm not going back to Germany?" Anthony asked.

"You're not going back to Germany."

A deep breath of relief escaped Anthony. He felt the

weight of the entire world had been lifted off him. It was over. His war was over.

London.

After all that had happened, and all that could have destroyed everything they had, he and Tessa had both come out alive. He would see her again.

CHAPTER THIRTY-TWO

WHEN AARON WOKE up in the morning, he hadn't the slightest clue what he should do with himself. His wedding was still hours away. What should the groom do in the hours before the wedding?

Here, in the foreign city of Liège, now a U.S. Army occupied zone, there was no one to tell him what he should do with himself before the wedding. Some of the volunteers at the Salvation Army had joked that as the groom, all he needed to do was to show up at the altar. Joking aside, he could never take his wedding that lightly. It was a rare blessing—a gift—to find love at this juncture of his life. He had almost given up, not to mention how the war had reared its ugly head and nearly taken his dream away. No. He would not take this day lightly.

But how should he approach the day? Shouldn't he be doing something? Sitting here alone churning in anticipation was torturous.

If the wedding were held at home, and he were getting married in normal times back in America, maybe he would know better what he should be doing. Maybe there would be guests to greet. His sister Cecilia and her husband would be with him for sure, as would his nieces and nephews. Maybe they could have told him what to do.

Stop! He told himself. He felt ridiculous. He wasn't a young man anymore, and this wasn't a party. He was a doctor. An esteemed professional highly regarded by his community. He should handle his wedding with solemn dignity. The nervous anticipation with which he awaited his wedding was unbecoming of someone of his age and stature.

But no. His bride…the thought of her brought a rush of joy to his heart. He gazed out the window of his hotel room to the house across the street where his bride was staying. How fortunate he was to have found her, in war and in life.

He checked his watch. The time had arrived. He straightened his clothes and walked outside. The war was ending. He could sense it. The world was entering a new era, and so was he. His future was no longer a monotonous passing of years with no significance. There was so much to look forward to. A jolt of energy ran through him. He couldn't remember the last time he felt this vigorous and alive. He couldn't wait for the next chapter of his life to begin.

In the room that had been turned into the bridal suite, Tessa helped Ellie put on her wedding gown. It was sewn together with pieces of silk fabric recovered from fallen parachutes. The women from the Salvation Army had done a work of wonder putting it together so quickly.

"You look gorgeous!" Tessa gave Ellie a hug, then quickly pulled away. "Oh no, I don't want to mess up your beautiful dress."

"Don't be silly." Ellie embraced Tessa again. "This is the happiest day of my life. I'm so glad you're here. It means so much to me and Aaron to have you be a part of our wedding."

"I'm glad to be here too," Tessa said. "Anyway, I can't miss your big day since you and Dr. Haley have decided to rush your wedding date to include me."

"I don't mind the rush. We don't want to wait anymore. If we've learned anything from what happened to us, it's that we have to seize every moment and not let happiness pass by us. Aaron and I were too hesitant for too long. If we hadn't been so lucky, we could've lost our chance forever." Ellie took Tessa's hands. "You saved me, and now he and I can be together because of you. Thank you, Tessa. Aaron and I owe you everything."

"Don't give me all the credit. We got through it all together. You would do everything you could to save me too," Tessa said. She hadn't forgotten how Ellie had almost sacrificed herself to please Pfeiffer in order to protect her and Tyler. "We have Anke and Fritz to thank too, for taking us in."

"Yes," Ellie said. "I'll never forget them. Bless their hearts. We have so much to be thankful for, don't we? Everything could easily have gone wrong for us. We might have never made it back. From now on, we'll have to remember to make every moment count."

Make every moment count. More than ever after their ordeal with Pfeiffer, Tessa knew how easily she and Anthony could have lost everything they had. When she saw Anthony again, she would do everything she could to cherish every moment they would have together.

In the small chapel, beams of sunlight shone through the window down to the army chaplain, who was reciting the familiar vows.

"Will you, Aaron Haley, take Ellie Swanson, as your lawfully wedded wife, to have and to hold, from this day forward, for better, for worse, for richer, for poorer, in sickness and in health, until death do you part?"

"I do," said Aaron, who could not take his eyes off his bride.

"Will you, Ellie Swanson, take Aaron Haley, as your lawfully wedded husband, to have and to hold, from this day forward, for better, for worse, for richer, for poorer, in sickness and in health, until death do you part?"

"I do."

At the altar behind Ellie, Tessa felt the joy of the day filling her entire being. Tyler, who was serving as the groomsman, couldn't stop grinning in his spot behind Aaron. How lucky they all were, to be here today. Her only regret was that the Blade did not make it out alive to be here with them.

"With this ring, I thee wed." Aaron picked up the wedding ring from the open Bible and put it on Ellie's finger.

Ellie did the same. "With this ring, I thee wed."

Tessa gazed at her own wedding ring, which she had put back on her finger after their escape from Kampfgruppe Pfeiffer. Anthony should be in London by now. She would be leaving for London tomorrow too. Very soon, they would be able to see each other again.

Tomorrow could not come fast enough.

CHAPTER THIRTY-THREE

WITH HIS RUCKSACK slung over his shoulder, Anthony walked down the unfamiliar tree-lined street, searching for the address written on the small piece of paper he held. He counted the building numbers until he came to the small gate of a charming double-fronted red-brick house. There, he stopped and hesitated. The front door of the house was only steps away.

He tightened his fingers around the small piece of paper. How he wished he didn't have to meet his in-laws all by himself for their first meeting. It was so odd to think they were his family. He had never even met them, and yet, they were the dearest people to his wife. He hoped they would like him. Juliet probably wouldn't be a problem. From the way his father and Uncle Leon had talked about her, she sounded like a warm and caring person. Tessa's father was a different matter. Anthony had heard from both rumors and his own family that the highly-regarded actor Dean Graham was not an easy person with whom to get along. He hoped he could impress Dean. It was the only way that Tessa would be happy. He didn't want

Tessa to have any misgivings or regrets when he took her back to America after the war was over.

He walked up to the front door, took a deep breath, and rang the doorbell. Shuffling sounds of footsteps approached, and the door opened. A blonde woman with emerald-green eyes greeted him.

"Good afternoon," Anthony said.

"Anthony?" The woman stared at him. She looked somewhat shocked.

"Yes. Are you Juliet? I mean, Mrs. Graham?" Anthony asked. He didn't know why she was looking so strangely at him.

"Anthony!" Juliet put her hand over her heart. "I'm sorry, you must be Anthony Ardley, William's son. For a moment, I thought I saw Anthony Browning." She smiled. "Leon told me you look like our Anthony Browning, but I didn't expect... Never mind. Pardon my manners. Please come in. You can call me Juliet. Dean and I've been waiting for you. How was your journey? Are you tired?"

Anthony's mind eased with Juliet's warm welcome. He followed her into the house. The art deco design of the front room, furnished with dark mahogany wood furniture and a red carpet, was much bolder in style than the parlor of his own home in Chicago. Posters of West End theater productions hung above the sofa and display cabinets, providing a colorful contrast to the cream-colored walls. An entire collection of the works of William Shakespeare lined the shelves of the bookcase. In the center of the room, a man was playing music on a beautiful antique grand piano.

The man stood up when they entered. He bore a striking resemblance to Tessa and carried the same air of aloofness. But unlike Tessa, he exuded a unique, attractive energy. His presence filled the room, overshadowing everyone and everything else that shared his space. He watched Anthony without showing any emotion. Anthony felt a distant barrier between them.

"Dean!" Juliet walked over to the man, seemingly oblivious to the tension emanating from her husband. "Anthony's here." She smiled at Anthony. "Anthony, this is my husband, Dean."

"Hello, sir," Anthony said. The man did not respond, but continued to stare at him. Anthony had never seen anyone with eyes so piercing and yet so captivating. He felt like he was being examined under a bright spotlight.

"Take a seat, Anthony," Juliet carried on. "Make yourself at home. You must be tired and hungry after your long journey. I'll go get us some tea and sandwiches. When I come back, I want to hear all about what happened to you since you got to Europe. I have so many things I want to ask you about Tessa." Juliet turned to her husband. "Dean, would you please keep Anthony company? I'll be right back."

Anthony wished Juliet would not leave them. Dean Graham still hadn't said anything. Anthony felt he should try to break the ice. He acknowledged the man again. "Mr. Graham."

Dean came closer. His expression was stern. There was nothing welcoming in the way he was looking at Anthony. Anthony braced himself. He still wanted to make a good impression on Dean, but this was not going to be easy after all.

"I'm not pleased with all that's happened recently," Dean said. "It's bad enough my daughter went to war to run after you. Then our worst fears. We got the news she was missing. Do you know how worried Juliet and I have been? We had no idea what happened to her. Juliet was devastated. As if that wasn't bad enough, we found out she was taken prisoner by the Nazis."

Anthony swallowed hard. Hearing the way Dean Graham recounted the events of the past months, he felt guilty. It was terrible indeed what Tessa had had to go through, all because she wanted to be with him.

"So, what have you to say for yourself?" Dean asked.

"I'm very sorry, sir."

"Don't call me sir. I'm not in the military."

"Sorry sir, I mean, Mr. Graham." What should he call this man? "I, too, am very sorry for what happened to Tessa. I never, ever wanted her to be harmed."

Dean crossed his arms. "My daughter went through hell because of you."

Not wanting to appear disrespectful or upset Dean any further, Anthony stared down. He wondered if it might appease Dean if he apologized again. But then, he changed his mind. Instead, he looked up and faced Dean. "I regret what happened to her, Mr. Graham, but I have no regret that she and I are together."

Dean looked furious now. If looks could kill, his eyes would be shooting arrows, but Anthony decided he had to hold his ground. He was Tessa's husband. However displeased Dean Graham might be, the man would just have to accept this fact and make peace with him. "I love your daughter. I will never regret that, no matter how you feel about it. As for what happened to her, I will make it up to her. I will do whatever I can to love her and make her happy for as long as I live." He waited for Dean to berate him some more, but instead, a sparkle gleamed from Dean's eyes.

"Dean!" Juliet's voice broke their standoff. She had reentered the room with a tray of tea and sandwiches. "Are you giving Anthony a hard time? Stop it. He's our guest."

To Anthony's surprise, Dean broke into laughter. "I was just playing with him," the actor said and offered Anthony a handshake. "Come on, Anthony. Put down your bag and take a seat. Have some tea. I'd think twice about the sandwiches though. Juliet's culinary ability has been called 'questionable' on kinder days."

"Dean! We're greeting our son-in-law and you're making disparaging remarks about my culinary skills. How rude." Juliet put the tray of tea and food on the coffee table. "I make fine sandwiches. Do have some, please, Anthony."

Confused by Dean's temperament, Anthony hesitantly sat down. Dean showed not a trace of the fury he exhibited only seconds ago, although he could still feel the man scrutinizing him.

"Don't mind him, Anthony." Juliet gave him a cup of tea. "What did you say to him, Dean? He looks all pale. The poor boy came a long way to see us. Couldn't you at least try to be nice?"

"I needed to know if Tessa has put herself in good hands," Dean said. "You missed it, Juliet. Our son-in-law made the most heartfelt declaration of love for Tessa." He beamed at Anthony.

Anthony put his tea down. He felt his face burning up. What a brash thing he had done. He openly declared his love for Tessa in front of her father.

"Don't listen to anything he says, Anthony." Juliet handed him a plate of small sandwiches. "A lot of times, he's acting and putting on airs. It's an occupational illness."

"Yes, my dear. It is my occupational illness." Dean pulled Juliet toward him and kissed her on her cheek. "That's why I married you. My illness gets worse and worse every day, and I need a nurse to look after me."

Dean and Juliet continued to tease each other. No adult couple Anthony knew ever behaved so dotingly with each other in public. Watching them, he was reminded of something Tessa had said back in Chicago.

I've never seen anyone more passionately in love than my parents. When I fall in love, I want to be just like them.

Yes. It would be a great thing if he and Tessa could remain so in love too when they grew older.

Feeling more at ease, he took a bite of a sandwich. The taste of fresh bread and jams set off his appetite. He hadn't realized he was this hungry. He eagerly took in every morsel while he tried to answer Juliet's questions about his trip to London, his furlough, and his next army assignment. When he finished eating, Juliet asked him, "Would you like to freshen up and take a rest? Let me show you to the guest room."

He glanced at Dean, who gave him a sharp but approving look before turning away to sit down at the piano. Once Dean began to play, Anthony understood why Tessa had always said that she couldn't play the piano as well as her father. Dean was practically a virtuoso. Anthony had never heard a more hauntingly beautiful performance of Beethoven's "Moonlight" sonata than the one he was hearing now.

"Come on," Juliet said to Anthony. He picked up his rucksack and followed her. When they reached the top of the stairs, Juliet paused. "Before I take you to the guest room, would you like to see Tessa's bedroom?" She placed her hand on the doorknob of the first room on the left.

"Yes," Anthony said. How amazing. Here, pieces of Tessa's past were slowly revealing themselves. He had not realized how much there was to discover when he embarked on this trip.

Juliet opened the door and let him in. Tessa's bedroom was not what he imagined. Back in Chicago, she had kept her room bare and impersonal. She stayed there like a permanent guest. If she had moved out, there would be little trace of her or her memories. This room, in contrast, was filled with reminders of a life left behind. The interior walls, covered with yellow wallpaper with a daffodil pattern, gave the place a warm, cozy feel. A Victorian-style desk lamp with a pearl-embroidered lampshade sat on top of the dresser. A teddy bear lay on the little sofa seat. This was unexpected. Anthony had never thought of Tessa as someone who liked toys.

"This is Rudy." Juliet picked up the teddy bear and handed it to Anthony. "She loved Rudy. When she was young, there were times when I had to work the evening shifts and Dean had to perform at night. She had a nanny, but I knew she felt lonely without Dean and I. Rudy was the one who made her happy and kept her company."

Anthony looked at the bear. It made him feel a little sad. Tessa had never behaved like a child since she arrived in Chicago. Seeing her room now, he realized how quickly Tessa had had to grow up after she had left London.

As if she understood his thoughts, Juliet put her hand on his arm. "But she has you now."

Pleased by her words, Anthony put the teddy bear back and walked up to the small chest of drawers with a model sailboat on top.

"Dean got her this sailboat for her thirteenth birthday," Juliet said. "Tessa was a difficult one to buy gifts for. She never liked girlish toys. She did like this boat, only I never thought that by the next year, she would sail away from us."

Hearing Juliet's sad voice, Anthony almost wanted to apologize.

"But if she sails toward a life of love and happiness, then it's all that Dean and I could hope for." Juliet walked over to the bed and placed her hand on a folded patchwork quilt with a pattern of interlocking circles. "This is our wedding present for you and Tessa. The double rings intertwined represent the bond between a husband and his wife. I hope you like it."

Anthony came closer to look at the quilt. How thoughtful of them. He barely knew Juliet, but he could feel how much she loved him already as part of the family. "Thank you. It's a wonderful gift. Thank you very much."

Juliet smiled. "Now let me show you to the guest room. I would put you in here, but Tessa's old bed is too small for you."

Anthony took one more look at the room before following Juliet out. Seeing Tessa's old room, he felt close to her again. He couldn't wait till she returned.

"By the way," Juliet said, "I hate to do this to you. It's your first night in London, and I wanted very much to welcome you with a special home-cooked meal, but I received a message from the hospital earlier. They're short-staffed this evening. I need to go in and help."

"That's all right. I can take care of myself."

"You won't have to do that." She opened the door to the guest room. "Dean will take you out."

Anthony stopped. Dinner alone with Dean? He still wasn't sure what his father-in-law truly thought about him. Taking care of himself would be a more preferable plan.

Dinner with Dean Graham by himself.

Tonight would be a very long night.

On their way to dinner, Anthony felt even more awkward than when he had first arrived at Tessa's home. Dean hadn't said a word the entire time they had been walking. Unsure of what his father-in-law was thinking, Anthony did not know what he should say or do. He considered starting a conversation, but Dean didn't seem interested in discussing anything. He walked with his head down and his hands in his pockets. All Anthony could do was follow along.

Tessa was often silent too when they were alone. But whereas Tessa's silence made him feel a quiet sense of peace, Dean's silence made him feel agitated. He had never thought he could meet someone even harder to please than Tessa.

They came to a small Italian restaurant called, simply,

Trattoria. A large, bald man greeted them at the door. "Mr. Graham!"

A smile escaped from Dean. "Good evening, Bruno." Without being led, Dean went straight to a table by the window with a view to the street. "Bruno owns this restaurant," he said to Anthony.

Anthony acknowledged Bruno with a polite nod.

"Haven't seen you in a while, Mr. Graham. How's the missus?" Bruno gave Dean and Anthony each a menu.

"Juliet's well. Thank you. She sends you her regards. She says she's sorry she can't be here this evening." Dean glanced at Anthony with a huge smile on his face. "Bruno, would you please bring out the best bottle of wine you have tonight?"

Bruno raised his eyebrows. "Sure. What's the occasion?"

"Bruno, meet my son-in-law, Anthony Ardley."

Anthony held the menu, surprised to hear Dean referring to him as his son-in-law in such a warm voice.

"Your son-in-law?" Bruno asked. "You mean…Tessa? Little Tessa is married?"

With a mischievous smile, Dean sat back in his seat to watch both Bruno's and Anthony's reactions.

"Well, good heavens! Aren't you lucky, young man." Bruno slapped Anthony on the back, and held out his hand. "Congratulations."

"Thank you, sir." Anthony shook his hand.

"You need to stop calling everyone 'sir,'" Dean said. "And stop sounding so terse all the time. We're not your military superiors. We're your family. Even Bruno. He's like family too. We've been coming here to eat since before Tessa was born."

"Uh…right." Anthony chuckled at himself and relaxed.

"I'll tell you what." Bruno took the menu out of Anthony's hands. "Forget the menu. I'll make something special for you tonight."

"There's no need for you to take to the kitchen yourself, Bruno," Dean said.

"Of course there is. I insist," Bruno said. "Little Tessa's husband is here? You bet I'll cook. I'll make her favorite spaghetti dish with my own special recipe." He winked at Anthony and left for the kitchen.

Left alone with Dean, Anthony found his father-in-law observing him again. Unsure what Dean hoped to see, but still hoping to gain his approval, Anthony straightened himself in his seat.

"I used to bring Tessa here for dinner whenever Juliet had to work in the evenings," Dean said. "This is our table." He appeared lost in his memories. Anthony noted the tender expression on his face. It must have been hard for him to send his daughter to America and be separated from her for so long. Surely, Dean must have hoped for the day when Tessa would return to London. And now, Anthony had come to take Tessa away.

Anthony lowered his head, unable to look Dean in the eye.

"I remember one time," Dean said, "Tessa told me a boy from school wanted to marry her. A boy named Philip. She was only ten years old." He smiled. "She always sat there across from me, right where you are sitting now. That day, she sat there with her legs crossed. Her hair tied back in a ponytail. She looked all serious, like a little adult."

Anthony wondered how Dean felt now, seeing him in the same seat where Tessa used to sit.

"She said Philip told her he wanted to marry her when he grew up. I asked her if she agreed. She said no. She said she couldn't marry Philip because he didn't know who Hamlet was. I watched her eat. I was just glad thinking it would be far into the future before the day would come when someone would really want to marry her."

Feeling awkward, Anthony thought Dean would tell him

how displeased he was that his daughter was now in fact married, but Dean only looked out the window. Across the street, a queue had formed in front of the grocery store.

"Britain's going through a very tough time," Dean said. "People are in good spirits because we're getting good news about the war, but there will be tough times ahead." He looked away from the window back at Anthony. "Our economy is suffering after so many years of war. It will be a long time before Britain can recover."

"I'm sure it will in due time, Mr. Graham."

"Be that as it may, Tessa will have a better future in America."

America? "Mr. Graham…"

"She's my daughter. I want only the best for her."

The best for Tessa. Dean was implying…being in America was the best future for her?

"Tessa is not an easy one to be around," Dean said. "She's like me. We can be stubborn and arrogant."

"Not at all, sir."

"Nonsense. You don't have to deny it. I know my own daughter."

"Right," Anthony said. He couldn't seem to say anything right in front of Dean.

"By the way, stop calling me 'sir' or Mr. Graham, will you? Why don't you call me Dean?"

Glad for Dean's offer of conciliation, Anthony smiled.

Dean took a booklet from the inner pocket of his jacket and gave it to Anthony. It was a used copy of the script of *Twelfth Night*. "I've performed this play many times, in different roles too. This was the script I used the first time I was cast in the play. That was many years ago."

Anthony took the script. Its corners were wrinkled and the pages were worn. Dean must have read it often, and kept it for years. Anthony opened the cover. Inside was a message,

To Anthony, my beloved son-in-law. Some are born great, some achieve greatness, and some have greatness thrust upon them. I'm proud of you. — Dean

Holding the gift, Anthony couldn't even think of the right words to say to thank him.

"I'm lucky Juliet would put up with me," Dean continued. "And Tessa's lucky now she's got you to put up with her. How she was able to find herself an impressive young man like you, I'll never know."

What Dean said came as a total surprise. Did Dean just call him an impressive young man?

"Take good care of her, will you?" Dean asked.

"Of course." Anthony broke into a smile. "I wouldn't think of doing anything less."

Dean nodded. For the first time since they had met, Anthony felt he understood the man. As difficult as his father-in-law might seem, he was liking him more and more.

───────────

On the crowded platform, Anthony stared at the empty tracks, watching for the train to come. The station clock showed the time to be five past three. The train from Dover should have arrived five minutes ago. Where was it?

"It's late," he turned around and said to Dean and Juliet. They looked as anxious as he felt.

He walked to the edge of the platform. A faint rumbling sound approached, and he gazed at the vibrating tracks leading to the distant area outside the station. The train engine with smoke shooting up its chimney came into view. The clacks of the locomotive's wheels grew louder and louder, as did his own heartbeat. He checked each rail car that passed him by, searching for the face of the girl he longed to see. And then, there she was, looking out of an open window.

"Tessa!" He ran after her car, pushing past everyone in his way. "Tessa!"

He didn't know how she could hear or see him with all the noise and people around, but she did. "Anthony!" He ran alongside the train, chasing after the voice he longed to hear, calling his own name. "Anthony!"

She looked as beautiful as ever. Exactly the way he remembered her.

"Anthony!"

No sweeter voice had ever called out to him. Wherever they were in this world, his heart would always follow when she called his name.

The train came to a stop with a loud hiss and a whistle. Tessa stepped off onto the platform. "Anthony!" She ran straight into his arms.

"Tessa!" He wrapped his arms around her and swung her off the ground. He never wanted to let her go again.

"You're squishing me." She laughed. "I can't breathe."

"I don't care." He kissed her face, her hair, her lips. "I'm not letting you out of my arms, ever." Neither of them could stop laughing.

"Tessa," Juliet said behind them.

Tessa stopped laughing. "Mother." The sight of her parents made her momentarily speechless. "Mother. Father."

"Tessa." Dean's voice shook as he called his daughter's name. Anthony let her go and she ran up to them.

"I'm back," Tessa said, her face filled with emotions. "I'm back. I'm in London again."

"Welcome home." Dean gave her a big hug.

"You've grown so much." Juliet, too, embraced her.

"I missed you," Tessa said.

"We missed you too," Dean said, stroking her head.

With gratitude and relief, Anthony watched Tessa reunite with her family. How close he had come to losing her. How fortunate they were to have escaped from the claws of death and could now be with each other again.

Noticing Anthony standing beside them, Juliet took his hand and pulled him closer to invite him to join them. Anthony put his arm around Tessa. He wanted to hold her and reassure himself that she was really here. She leaned her head against his shoulder. No words could describe how happy he felt. Everything was now as it should be.

CHAPTER THIRTY-FOUR

In the rose garden in the Graham's backyard, Tessa separated the cut roses, while Anthony helped her wrap them into small bouquets for her mother's patients. As she laid the last rose on the ground, she noticed he had stopped. Anthony was lost in his thoughts again. Every so often, a haunted expression would flash across his face. She wondered what he was remembering this time. What had he seen in the last two years, and how long would these memories continue to haunt him? She thought of the boy he used to be back in Chicago, the one who exuded optimism and joy. He still carried that positive energy, but now that energy was marred by a shadow of pain. The war had left its mark on all of them. Their wounds might heal, but the scars would always be there.

She reached out and touched him gently on the face. Her gesture brought light and spirit back to his eyes and he smiled.

Yes. She thought to herself. In the days to come, she must do everything she could to brighten his life, just as he would brighten hers. After all that he had been through, he deserved to be happy again.

"I've been thinking," he said, "when we have our first child..."

"Our first child!" She drew back her hand. Dear Lord! She had barely settled back into civilian life.

"Well, yeah. We're going to have children, aren't we?"

She felt herself blushing at the thought. Unable to deny it, but too proud and embarrassed to say yes, she looked away from him. Still, she couldn't hide her smile.

"When we have our first child, we'll name him Jesse. Jesse Garland Ardley. What do you think?"

Jesse...

The pain of losing him still hurt so much.

"How do you know it'll be a boy? What if it's a girl?"

"We can still name her Jessie, with an 'ie'."

Tessa thought of Jesse and his propensity to flirt. She tried to imagine Jesse's reaction if he knew they were naming a girl after him. No. That would not do. She chuckled to herself. It had to be a boy to live up to Jesse's tomcat reputation. Tessa looked at Anthony again. His expression was straight and sincere as always. Obviously, Anthony hadn't thought of the ramifications of naming his son after a master deceiver.

"What's so funny?" he asked.

Tessa shook her head. Changing to a more serious tone, she asked, "What do you want to do after we return to Chicago?"

"First thing, I'll go back to school and finish my degree."

"And then?"

"And then, I'll start working for Father. I used to wonder if I should strike out on my own. I always felt I was held back by the way everything was laid out for my future. No risks, no surprises." He stared at the roses. "I think I've had enough risks and surprises for a while. Some predictability and stability would be good." He took her hand. "If I work for Father, maybe I can use our family's resources to do something good.

Maybe I can help create more jobs for the returning veterans and help the war widows and their children."

Tessa was glad he thought this way. It is so good to hear him speak of the future with such hope.

"Before the war," he said, "I worried I wouldn't be able to prove myself if everything were given to me. I was afraid the Ardley name would be the only thing that would define me, and I would never find out who I really am. I'm not afraid anymore. I'm not worried about who I am either. The important thing is what I'll do with what I have."

"I'm sure you'll do a lot of good things, whatever choices you make."

"What about you?" he asked. "What do you want to do?"

She knew her own answer too. "I want to paint. I'd like to go back to what I started. I want to see if I can become truly good at it."

"I love your paintings," he said, excited. "I'll back you. We can open an art gallery to show your work."

"No, not so fast," she said. He was already racing ahead of himself. "We'll have to see if what I paint will be any good. Besides, this is something I want to do for myself, not because I want to impress anyone."

He held her hand up to his heart. "We'll have good days ahead of us. Everything is going to be great." A warm breeze blew past them, and he leaned over and kissed her.

From inside the house, Juliet stood looking out the window at Tessa and Anthony in the rose garden while soft music played from the radio. A very long time ago, she and Anthony Browning had tended the rose garden together in Chicago. She had so many sweet memories of the place where she had grown up. Looking at Tessa and her young husband now brought her back in time. Anthony reminded her of everything in America that she had left behind. Through him, she could see glimpses of everything she missed from her past.

She had thought that part of her life had perished, but it hadn't. What was once lost, her daughter and son-in-law had brought back to life.

"How much longer are you going to stand there and watch them?" Dean came up behind her and put his arms around her.

"I can't help it." She stared out the window again. "I'm so happy seeing them like this."

He followed her eyes and looked outside. Tessa and Anthony in the garden surrounded by blooming roses were a beautiful sight to behold. They looked so happy. No one could know the hardships they had gone through. Dean hadn't said this to his son-in-law, but he was beyond pleased to see his daughter married to someone who was so devoted and in love with her. He only wished he could have walked his daughter down the aisle on her wedding day.

The radio music suddenly stopped and a woman's voice came on. "We are interrupting the program to bring you a news flash."

Dean and Juliet looked at each other and held their breaths. A male BBC reporter began to announce, "This is London calling. Here is a news flash. The German radio has just announced that Hitler is dead. I'll repeat that. The German radio has just announced that Hitler is dead."

Overjoyed, they hugged each other.

"We have to tell Tessa and Anthony," Juliet said and ran outside.

From the garden, Tessa watched her mother come running out of the house.

"Tessa! Anthony!" Juliet called out to them. Dean came out the front door behind her.

"What is it, Mother?"

"Hitler's dead. The news reporter just announced it on the radio. Hitler's dead."

"He's gone?" Anthony dropped the bouquet of flowers from his hands.

"It is true," Dean said. "Hitler's dead. The war's ended."

Anthony took Tessa into his arms. He felt the entire weight of the world had been lifted off him. "It's over." He heard Tessa say again and again. "It's over."

The victorious rings of Big Ben roared as Tessa and Anthony walked hand-in-hand down the London streets. In every corner, hordes of people had filled the city to celebrate VE Day. Victory in Europe. Thousands had gathered in front of the House of Commons, waiting to hear Prime Minister Churchill speak. At the base of Nelson's Column in Trafalgar Square, a large sign reading "Victory Over Germany 1945" proclaimed the good news to everyone near and far.

The crowds on the streets hushed as the voice of the Prime Minister came over the loudspeaker.

Yesterday morning at 2:41 a.m. at General Eisenhower's headquarters, General Jodl, the representative of the German High Command, and Grand Admiral Doenitz, the designated head of the German State, signed the act of unconditional surrender of all German land, sea, and air forces in Europe to the Allied Expeditionary Force, and simultaneously to the Soviet High Command...

Today, this agreement will be ratified and confirmed at Berlin...

Hostilities will end officially at one minute after midnight tonight, but in the interests of saving lives, the "Cease fire" began yesterday to be sounded all along the front, and our dear Channel Islands are also to be freed to-day...

The German war is therefore at an end...

Long live the cause of freedom. God save the King.

Cheers erupted and continued as the Prime Minister led the members of the House outside. Sounds of whistles and applause followed them as they marched in a procession to a victory thanksgiving service.

Joining the masses outside Buckingham Palace, Tessa and Anthony waited. People around them were breaking out into spontaneous celebratory dances. Intoxicated from hours of drinking that had begun the night before, they sang in drunken excitement, and fell and tripped over each other.

"Have you ever seen anything like this in London?" Anthony asked Tessa.

"No," she said. "I've never seen this many people out on the streets, ever."

The royal family made their appearance on the palace balcony. King George and Queen Elizabeth, flanked by the two princesses, waved to the crowd. Their people cheered, waving the Union Jack and holding up their fingers in the shape of a "V" in a sign of victory. When the royal family retreated back inside, the crowd began to chant, "We want the King. We want the King."

The royal family returned to the balcony, this time with Prime Minister Churchill.

"The war's over, Tessa," Anthony said. "It's really over. We can begin our lives again."

Yes. It was really over, and Anthony was still here, still alive.

Tessa was thankful for that more than anything. "Let's go find Father and Mother."

They pushed through the crowds to head to the West End, where members of Dean's theater troupe were gathering for a celebratory dinner. The entire city was jam packed with people, and they could hardly move through the crowds. An American military jeep passed by. Noting Anthony's uniform, a soldier leaned out of the vehicle and asked, "Captain, wanna ride?"

"You bet," Anthony said. He climbed into the jeep and pulled Tessa up by hand. She got on and fell right on top of him. "Ah!" She laughed. "I'm sorry."

"I'm not sorry." He pulled her into his arms and kissed her like never before. He wanted her to remember this day, to remember this kiss, for all their days ahead.

REMEMBRANCE

Part Eleven

CHAPTER THIRTY-FIVE

THE SHIP DOCKED at the port of Manhattan at half past six. After days of being confined inside a vessel and tossed around by the ocean, Tessa could not wait to step onto stable ground again.

The last time she had stepped onto American soil, all she wanted was to leave. She had wanted to go back to London so badly. How could she have known that five years later, she would want nothing except to return and call this country home?

Soon, Anthony would be discharged. When he returned, they would all reunite and be together. The two of them, his parents, her parents, everyone.

Her parents had wanted to come to America with her. They had decided it was time to rekindle old ties. And it was time. They had been away from their family in Chicago for far too long. The war was over and the seas were safe again. Uncle William, Uncle Leon, and Aunt Anna. They were eagerly waiting for her and her parents to arrive.

Despite everyone's anticipation for a big reunion, Tessa had chosen to come back alone. She had decided to travel separately from her parents to America. She had something unresolved that she wanted to do. This was a trip she had to make by herself.

The Brooklyn Bridge came into view as the ship approached land. While the ship docked, she kept her eyes on the awe-inspiring sight. This famous bridge was one of the places that Jesse had wanted her to see.

We're here, Jesse. The summer wind blew past her on the deck as if answering her. *We're going to go to every place where you wanted to take me.*

Tessa disembarked the ship and found her way into the streets. While she marveled at the worldly feel of the city, the cold, unyielding environment made her feel a bit sad. Everyone seemed to have someone more important to see, or someplace more important be. No one stopped for even a moment to give anyone else a second thought. Such was the place where Jesse had had to make his way in the world.

She walked to the edge of the sidewalk and hailed a taxi. During the ride, she looked out the window. So many cars zooming down the streets, crisscrossing the lanes while they honked and cut each other off. Pedestrians dodged between moving vehicles, trying to get to the other side of the road. New York was definitely a place for daredevils.

Jesse always took chances too. Risks never fazed him.

The taxi arrived at a hotel in the Greenwich Village neighborhood where Jesse used to live. Tessa didn't know his address. There was no way for her to get inside even if she did know. That was all right. What mattered was that she was here.

She wondered what happened to his home and the things he left behind. What had Jesse left behind, besides her own memories of him?

She freshened up at her hotel room, then headed out again. Following the directions given by the concierge, she walked to the subway station. Soon, the streetlights came on. Night had fallen.

Night. The hallmark of New York.

Next stop, Times Square.

Tessa went into the subway entrance down the steps to the platform of the underground train. It might only be her imagination, but the New York subway trains sounded much noisier than the London Tube or the Chicago Alley L. They carried loads of passengers, all hastening about and pushing their way through. The scene got even more bewildering when she arrived at the mid-Manhattan stop. The station was a shady underworld unto itself. Crowds of people came toward her or passed her, their faces guarded with no show of emotion. The only ones who appeared friendly were men and women whose eyes betrayed ulterior motives. Their affable pretense neither sincere nor genuine. As she walked toward the exit, a sleazy looking man brushed past her and mumbled to her words that she would rather not repeat. How was Jesse able to live in such a place without it polluting his soul?

She followed the signs upstairs onto the street and came upon a spectacular scene beyond her wildest imagination. All around, everywhere, there were the lights. Gigantic billboards with lights shining in varying shades illuminated this famous landmark from every direction.

Dazzling. Absolutely dazzling. Just like Jesse. He carried an aura so bright, it lit up every shaded corner. It overcame the darkness of the night. In a world full of deceit and malice, he remained pure at heart, untainted by the rottenness of the world around him.

Standing in the midst of the blinding lights, Tessa could no longer control herself. Tears flooded her eyes and she began to sob. Passersby gave her odd and curious looks, but she could not stop. She cried for the loss of one whose future was so full of promise, none of which would now be fulfilled. She cried for a life that shone so brightly, but was brutally cut short.

How much had to be lost for the sake of war? She stood in the middle of Times Square and cried.

Will you miss me?

Yes. Jesse. I miss you. Always.

Tessa began the next day at the Fulton Fish Market. It was only mid-morning, but the day's activities were well under way. All of today's catch for sale was laid out on display. Whiffs of the salt and iron smell of fresh fish infused the air as she passed by each stall. Shrimp, prawns, crabs, oysters, and other shellfish filled the buckets and push carts like treasure troves from the bottom of the sea.

You'll never see such an amazing variety of seafood in one place. How animated Jesse had looked when he told her all about this market.

He was gone now. But here, life went on. Workers wheeled carts of seafood to trucks for transport to other places. Barrels upon barrels of fish were lined up on the streets, waiting to be taken to restaurants and other markets. The city hadn't stopped for Jesse. The city didn't remember him.

With a solemn heart, Tessa turned away from the seafood stalls and walked on.

From the marketplace, she went to the edge of the piers. Ships were entering the port, and smaller boats were sailing about. The water and everything on it was so calm. Nothing like how things were back in Anzio.

When was the last time Jesse had come here? Did he stand at this same spot where she was standing now? If he did, what was he thinking about when he gazed out to the sea?

Noon came, and the market's trading activities for the day were coming to an end. Tessa continued on to the Lower East

Side, through the Jewish neighborhood on to Chinatown, then to Little Italy. Just as Jesse described, each area could be distinguished by the way the people dressed and the different ethnic foods they sold. She made her way further uptown. By the time she reached Washington Square Park, it was already past two o'clock.

She stopped by a deli and bought a sandwich, then sat down on the steps of the large fountain behind the park's famous arch to eat. A shabbily dressed man in his fifties came to the bottom of the fountain about twenty feet in front of her. He laid his violin case on the ground and took out his instrument. At first, she ignored him. Not offended, he placed the violin between his chin and shoulder, and winked at her while he tested the tuning. He then glided the bow across the violin strings and began to play a song with tunes of gypsy music. The entire time, he smiled at her through his gray stubble, begging for her approval. Finally, she gave in and smiled back. His cheerful tunes soon drew a crowd.

I live in a neighborhood called Greenwich Village. A lot of artists live there. Washington Square Park is two blocks away from my place. Folksingers and street musicians perform there. Sometimes I go sit in the park and listen to them.

More and more people gathered around the fountain. Tessa peered at each of their faces. She knew it was impossible, yet she kept hoping she might see Jesse among them. She knew it wasn't real, but she could nonetheless feel his presence here with her.

The man finished playing his song, and the street audience applauded. Some dropped pennies and nickels into his violin case. He bowed and began to play another song. The next piece of music seized Tessa's attention from its first wailing note.

Tango Jalousie.

She stared at the gypsy man. How did he know?

But he didn't know. He wasn't even looking at her.

Coincidence. It was only a coincidence.

But this music. She closed her eyes and let the music take her back to the night when she and Jesse had danced together. At that moment, she realized, he was with her. He would always be with her. When the years had gone by, and the war had faded from everyone's thoughts, she would be the one to keep remembrance of him. As long as she held on to his memory, he would not be forgotten.

On the third day, Tessa took extra time to get ready, making sure that she looked the best she could, just as if she had been on a real date with someone. Today was her last day in New York. She had saved for last the place where Jesse had most wanted to take her. The Empire State Building.

Before entering, she stood on the sidewalk and looked up at the building's stunning exterior walls. A stretch of white cloud spread over the pinnacle of the skyscraper like the wings of an angel.

Are you ready, Jesse? We're heading up. She drew a deep breath, her heart brimming with excitement she could barely contain.

She thought she had come early, but other visitors who had come before her already formed a long line for the elevator to the observation deck. Summer tourists, school students, veterans passing through New York. On this beautiful summer day, all were eager to see the view of the city from this architectural wonder.

A rush of elation swelled inside her as the elevator ascended to the 102nd floor. She stepped out, unsure of what she would see. This was the highest she had ever been in a building. She circled around the observatory terrace, taking in the sweeping view. The scenery was amazing. Here, she could see the Statue of Liberty, Times Square, Central Park, the

Chrysler Building, the Manhattan Bridge, and the East River. Everything was as incredible as Jesse had described.

It's spectacular, Jesse.

She stopped at a spot where she could see Washington Square Park, far downtown, and took her angel amulet out from her pocket. Holding it tightly against her heart, she gazed up into the sky. Wind blew all around her, and her scarf fluttered in the air.

The sky was so close. She could almost reach out and find him.

Can you feel it, Jesse? The gusty wind continued to blow. *Can you feel it? We're soaring!*

She looked at the clouds and imagined herself riding the winds into the heavens, where she could see that Jesse was all right, and finally at peace.

CHAPTER THIRTY-SIX

BACK IN HER room in the Ardleys' house in Chicago, Tessa opened the windows to let in the sunlight. The Ardleys had filled the outdoor swimming pool again for the summer. Any day now, Anthony would be back. And then, everything would return to the way it once was.

No. She touched the rose pendant around her neck and thought of all that had happened since the day she first wore it. Some things would never be the same again.

A knock on the door interrupted her thoughts. "Tessa?" It was her mother. "Are you ready? All your friends are here."

"Coming." Tessa came out of her room. While she was in New York, her parents had arrived in Chicago for a visit to America that was long overdue. Today, the Ardleys had organized a welcome-home party for her, and invited all her old friends. She took her mother by the arm. "I can't wait for you to meet everybody."

"Likewise," Juliet said. "Your father and I will miss you when we leave, but I'm glad to know you are well settled here with friends and people who care about you."

Downstairs, they followed the guests' chatter and laughter to the parlor.

"Ruby!" Tessa saw her old best friend at once.

"Tessa." Ruby turned around from the sofa and stood up. She looked more mature and feminine than Tessa remembered. Her green dress looked smart and stylish on her. Ruby must have designed it herself.

"Long time no see." Henry came up to her. Tessa almost couldn't recognize him. He had grown taller. His body had filled out, and his clothes no longer hung on his body like an oversized garment bag. His bushy hair, now trimmed short, no longer covered his head like an unruly mop. He looked every bit a young gentleman.

"Henry." She squeezed his arm, then turned her eyes to the rest of the room. "Where's your brother?"

"Right here," Jack said from behind Henry. Except for his limp and his cane, he looked happy and well.

Nadine and Laurent were there too. "We're so glad you're home." Nadine held up a bottle of champagne. "Look what we brought you. Laurent picked this out especially for you."

"Nadine!" Tessa gave her a hug. "You shouldn't have."

"Of course we should. You're home. We have to celebrate."

Tessa accepted the gift. "Thank you."

"Tessa," Jack said, "there's somebody I want you to meet." A pretty young woman with dark brown hair and a shy smile came forward next to him. "My wife, Lucy."

"You're married?" Tessa put down the bottle of champagne. "Congratulations!" She held out her hand to Lucy, and noticed Lucy's waistline. Doubly surprised, she looked at Jack. Jack nodded with a huge smile.

"You're going to be a father!" Tessa said, thrilled. "Jack! I'm so happy for you."

"Lucy's Mr. Mason's daughter," Jack said. Mr. Mason was the head property manager at one of the Ardley's residential properties in Lincoln Park, where Anthony had helped Jack get a job when he had returned from the war. "I'll have to thank Anthony when he comes back. I wouldn't have gotten my job working for Mr. Mason if it weren't for him, and without that job, I would've never met Lucy."

"This is wonderful." Tessa took both Jack and Lucy by the hand. "You're still working for Mr. Mason as the assistant property manager then?"

"He is," Lucy said, "but he's taking night classes now too." Her eyes were beaming with pride. "He's getting his college degree."

Jack tapped his limp leg with his cane. "Some good came out of this after all. The GI Bill. I can go to college for free because of my service. I've always been good with machines and tools. I thought I'd give mechanical engineering a try." He glanced at Henry. "I never thought I would go to college."

Henry shrunk away. "He's trying to get me to enlist."

"The war's over," Jack said. "You won't even have to fight. All you have to do is enlist, and you can go to college too after you serve your time."

Not convinced, Henry rolled his eyes and made a face.

The parlor door opened. "Would you all please come into the dining room?" Sophia asked. "Lunch is ready."

Everyone cheered at the mention of food. As they followed Sophia to the dining room, Ruby pulled Tessa to her side, "Tyler's coming to Chicago."

"He is?" Tessa asked. "You've stayed in touch with him?"

"He's been writing me since he returned from that awful Nazi ordeal you all went through. You're so brave, Tessa. All of you. I don't know what I would've done if I were in your place."

Tessa thought of the Blade, Mathias, and his grandfather. "We did what we had to. We survived." She didn't know how she could ever explain to Ruby or anyone else at home what it was like in Anzio, in the Ardennes, or to be captured. She couldn't see how people at home could ever fully understand. "When's Tyler coming?"

"Next week. I can't wait to meet him in person. He's so sweet. He sends me the funniest drawings. Thanks so much for introducing us."

In the dining room, William, Dean, and the Caldwells were already waiting. Tessa took a seat by her father, while her mother sat down with Uncle Leon and Aunt Anna. Uncle Leon had not left her mother alone since her parents' return to America. He and her mother had not seen each other in years. Uncle Leon was thrilled to see her again and have her reunited with the family. Even her father, who ordinarily did not enjoy being around a lot of people, looked pleased to be surrounded by family and good friends. In any case, Alexander wasn't leaving him be. Now an overachieving teenager with a passion for the classics and literature, Alexander had been peppering her father with questions about Shakespeare.

William took his seat at the head of the table. "We have a full house."

Tessa looked around the table. Almost a full house. Only one person was missing. She turned her hand. Her golden wedding ring glistened under the dining room chandelier.

———

At the Separation Office at Camp Grant, the staff officer recited to Anthony a series of GI benefits. This would be his last duty with the military. Once his exit interview ended, he would be a civilian again.

While the officer filled out the last of the necessary forms and paperwork, Anthony thought of the first day he had arrived here for processing as a recruit. This was the place where his military journey had started. Somehow, he made it through. Fate was releasing him back to the world where he belonged. Others were not so lucky. He slid his hand into his pocket to check and make sure the lucky seven dice were there.

The staff officer handed Anthony his discharge papers. "Sure you don't want to sign up for another term, Captain? You have a stellar record. You'll do well if you stay on. You can build a great career."

Anthony didn't answer his question. "Thank you." He took the discharge papers, picked up his bag, and walked out. He could not wait another minute to get onto the bus to go home. The barracks could no longer bind him. At last, he was free. He could go anywhere he wanted.

The bus dropped him off in downtown Chicago, where he found himself standing before the familiar sight of the Wrigley Building, the Tribune Tower, and the Michigan Avenue Bridge. He was back in civilization. Men, women, and children passed him by. Shops of all kinds lined the streets. Clothing stores, shoes stores, department stores. How he had taken these luxuries and conveniences for granted.

Passing by the Civic Theater, he noticed the large poster for the current production of *The Glass Menagerie.* On his way back to Chicago, he had read the review of the play's premier performance published in an old copy of the *Chicago Tribune.* He had wanted to take Tessa to see this after reading Claudia Cassidy's enthusiastic endorsement of the play. Thinking of how delighted Tessa would be, he decided to make a quick stop and buy a pair of tickets.

While waiting to make his purchase at the ticket booth, he noticed the newspaper which the man standing in line before him was carrying. The headline, "Atomic Bomb Story! How the Deadly Weapon Was Developed," seemed to be shouting at him. Four years ago, Professor Vinci had tried to recruit Anthony to join the scientific team that was developing the atomic bomb. Back then, he had declined the professor's offer.

He didn't want to be a part of something with such an unmeasurable power to destroy. And he was correct in his estimation of what the weapon could do. The professor had succeeded. The atomic bomb was as ghastly as he had promised. It had destroyed the Japanese cities of Hiroshima and Nagasaki, leaving millions of people behind on the trail of death.

Knowing what he knew now, he wondered what difference his choice had made. While at war, he had taken the lives of countless people. Some were even killed under his direct command. Regardless of what he had wanted, the war left him no choice but to play a role in the most destructive event men had brought into this world. Today, he could no longer be that innocent boy who saw right and wrong the way he did before he went off to war.

"May I help you?" the cashier at the ticket booth asked Anthony. The man in front of him had finished his purchase.

"Yes," Anthony said. "Two tickets for *The Glass Menagerie* please."

The cashier proceeded to assist him. The man who had purchased tickets before him smiled at Anthony and walked away. The headline of his newspaper still seemed to be shouting out to Anthony, wanting to be seen. Anthony lowered his eyes.

For all its horror, the war did not destroy everything.

Tessa.

He had to get back to her. She was the one thing that was still right in his world.

He went out to the street and hailed a taxi. On his way home, he thought of the girl he loved. As long as she was by his side, there would always be something worthwhile to live for, no matter how ugly this world became. Together with her, he would rebuild their lives. For as long as there was love, there would be hope.

The taxi dropped him off at the entrance of the familiar driveway in front of his home. In the August summer heat, the roses in the garden were in full bloom.

He walked toward the house. With each step, his heart quickened. Before he was halfway there, the front door opened. Tessa, standing in the doorway, was the most beautiful sight he had ever seen.

She ran out toward him. He dropped his bag and took her into his arms.

The soldier had come home.

EPILOGUE

May 1946.

IN THE STUDY of her new house, Tessa lifted the lid of the oval-shaped music box on top of the desk. She ran her fingers lightly over the scalloped edges. The instrument was beautifully designed with a mother-of-pearl inlay of tiny diamond-shaped patterns. Its smooth midnight black surface reminded her of the color of ravens.

Raven-dark hair. One night, more than two and a half years ago, her guardian angel with raven dark hair came into her life and demanded that she take notice of him. He had been with her ever since.

She placed the figurines of a man in a tuxedo dancing with a woman in a red ball gown on the base of the music box and watched the figurines twirl and rotate to the tinkles of *Tango Jalousie*. With this music box, she and her guardian angel could always dance together.

My last tango will always be yours.

She took the mementos she had kept from the war out of

the music box's jewelry compartment. An angel amulet, a pair of lucky seven dice, and a dog tag bearing Jesse's name. Holding the three items in her hand, she turned toward the door. Sometimes, she felt as though Jesse was standing at the door, watching her like he used to back in Anzio.

She put the amulet, the dice, and the figurines back into the jewelry compartment and put the music box away. She then opened a little tin box on the desk and placed Jesse's dog tag inside before she took it with her and left the room. As she walked past the door, she could still feel his presence. She could almost see him leaning against the doorway, smiling at her. He remained forever young, forever handsome. His smile remained ever so radiant. She reached out, but he was not there. All she could grasp was air.

She drew her hand back and went outside. The new house was nowhere near as big as the Ardleys' mansion, but she and Anthony had looked forward to moving here. This was their own home, where they would begin their new life and create new memories.

There was one thing she had insisted on: having Mr. Miller put in a rose garden for their new home, and Anthony agreed.

She came to the front yard where the gardener was busy at work. "Good afternoon, Mr. Miller. How is the rose garden coming along?"

"Wonderful. It's coming along very well. I brought several new specimens to plant on this patch here. And take a look at these." He pointed to a spot where the flowers were blooming directly under the sun. "These are turning into beautiful blossoms."

"They are beautiful." Tessa knelt down by that spot and dug a hole with a small shovel Miller had left on the ground. She placed the little tin box into the hole, covered it, and patted the soil. Satisfied, she gazed up into the sky. Somewhere, out there, she knew Jesse was watching over them.

The sound of Anthony's car came in from the driveway. Tessa stood up and called out to him. "Anthony!"

He parked the car and walked toward the garden with a shopping bag. "The flowers look beautiful, Mr. Miller."

"Thank you. I'm glad you like it," Miller said as he planted more seedlings in the flower beds.

"Look what I got," Anthony said to Tessa. He opened the shopping bag to show her the plaque inside. "I picked it up from the garden supply store just now. Does it look okay?"

She examined the plaque and the words engraved on its surface, *In memory of Jesse Garland, 1920–1944*. Even though time had passed, it still hurt. Jesse, so young, and gone too soon.

She knelt down again and placed the plaque on the soil on top of the spot where she had buried the tin box. Only the touch of Anthony's hand on her shoulder could give her solace for all that was lost. She smiled at Anthony.

"Come on. Let's go inside." He took her hand. Together, they walked back into their house. She wanted to wash the dirt off her hands, but he wouldn't let her go. "I've got something for you." He took a velvet jewelry box out of his pocket and opened it. Inside, there was a rose pendant, gold, with a diamond in the center. "Happy birthday."

"Anthony!"

"Do you like it?"

"It's gorgeous."

He caressed her lightly on the neck. "Let me put it on you."

She turned around and brushed her hair to one side. He unclasped the necklace of the pink rose pendant she was wearing and replaced it with the new gold one. "What do you think?"

She touched her new pendant. Gold. Everlasting. For all eternity.

Smiling, she turned around. He embraced her and kissed

her, passionately the way he knew she liked. She put her own arms around him and looked him in the eyes. "You're forever etched in my heart."

Eternal Flame

A Rose of Anzio spinoff story

Want more of **Rose of Anzio** stories? Check out **Eternal Flame**, a love story about Edmond Ferris, the young soldier who appeared in *Rose of Anzio Book 4 - Remembrance,* when he time travels forward to 1989.

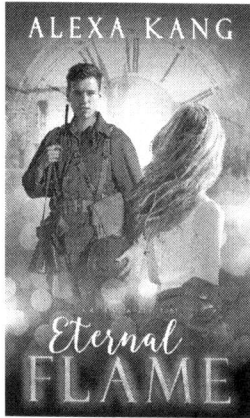

"Last night, I loved you a lifetime and more."

What readers are saying **Eternal Flame**:

- "A love story like no other."
- "One of the best time travel books I've read."
- "Be prepare to stay awake reading past your bedtime."
- "Thought-Provoking Romance."
- "Thoughtful, intense, and very well written."

Eternal Flame Book Description

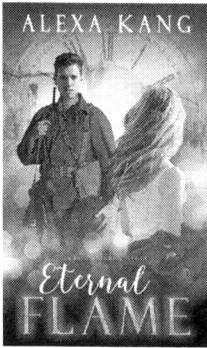

What's an ordinary girl to do when a time-traveling WWII soldier crashes into her room?

Sixteen-year-old Julia's world is already a mess. Her quarterback boyfriend just left her and broke her heart. Her high school counselor wants to know why her grades are taking a tumble, but all she wants is to hide. And what if she can't get into a good college? Would her parents understand?

But her world is about to get even more complicated when she woke up one morning and found a soldier from 1944 in her bed.

Eighteen-year-old Edmond thought he was dreaming when he fell asleep in his own room in Chicago. What grunt wouldn't dream of leaving the miserable battlefield in France, go home to America, and have a good night sleep in his own bed.

But when he woke up, he finds a strange girl lying beside him. He was home all right—in 1989! To his nightmare, the girl drives a Japanese car and listens to Milli Vanilli, a German band.

Is their encounter an error in time or a will of fate?

Get your copy on Amazon today.

Enjoyed reading my stories?

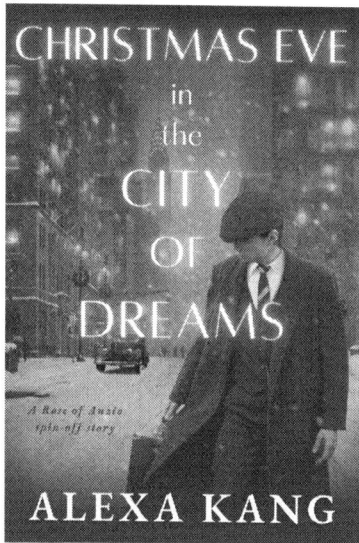

Subscribe to my Substack, and you will receive:

- A free copy of ***Christmas Eve in the City of Dreams***, a story about Jesse Garland before he went to war
- Fascinating articles on things related to WWII
- Behind the scene tidbits about my books
- Discussions on topics of interest to fiction readers
- News on my book releases
- More free stories.

https://alexakang.substack.com/

ABOUT THE AUTHOR

Alexa Kang is a WWII and 20th century historical fiction author. Her works include the novel series, *Rose of Anzio*, a love story saga that begins in 1940 Chicago and continues on to the historic Battle of Anzio in Italy. Her second series, *Shanghai Story*, chronicles the events in Shanghai leading up to WWII and the history of Jews and Jewish refugees in China. Her other works include the WWII/1980s time-travel love story *Eternal Flame* (a tribute to John Hughes), as well as short stories in the fiction anthologies *Pearl Harbor and More: Stories of December 1942*, *Christmas in Love*, and the USA Today Bestseller *The Darkest Hour*. Her latest work, the *Nisei War Series*, is a collection of novels exploring the different facets of Japanese-American experience during WWII.

Get in Touch!
I would love to hear from you.
alexa@alexakang.com

Sign up for my Mailing List on my website at:
www.alexakang.com

amazon.com/Alexa-Kang/e/B01AXTLTS4

facebook.com/roseofanzio

goodreads.com/alexa_kang

bookbub.com/profile/alexa-kang

Printed in Great Britain
by Amazon

50903694R00229